DEADLOCK

DEADLOCK

CHERRIE

LYNN

Entangled Publishing, LLC
2614 South Timberline Road
Suite 109
Fort Collins, CO 80525
Visit our website at www.entangledpublishing.com.

Amara is an imprint of Entangled Publishing, LLC.

Edited by Liz Pelletier
Cover design by Liz Pelletier
Cover images by iStock/FGorgun
iStock/D-Keine
Getty Images/ TaManKunG
Getty Images/a-r-t-i-s-t
Interior design by Heather Howland

Print ISBN 978-1-64063-535-7
ebook ISBN 978-1-64063-536-4

Manufactured in the United States of America

First Edition July 2019

AMARA

ALSO BY CHERRIE LYNN

For Brandon, as always. You handle my doubts and meltdowns like a champ and never fail to offer cupcakes. You're the best!

CHAPTER ONE

I'm going to kill my sister.

Lindsey Morris gritted her teeth into a smile for the photo her jolly aunt Martha snapped, the silent threat in her head becoming more of an inevitable truth with each passing moment. God knows, it wasn't unlike her twin sister, Lena, to flake out on her, but their parents' fortieth anniversary party was something the two of them had been planning for *months*. All for Lena to leave Lindsey holding the bag. Again.

Relieved from picture duty at last, she left her parents and hustled in her towering heels across the banquet hall to check on the champagne, dodging cousins and uncles and aunts. She hadn't seen some of them in years. If a certain sister hadn't left her running this entire show, she might have had time to stop and catch up with each of them.

All of it had come together nicely, though. Her parents were beaming in front of a life-size poster of one of their wedding pictures, forty years having done nothing to dim their happiness and love for each other. Lindsey snapped a picture of her own before slipping out the door into an echoing hallway to dial Lena. As expected, her sister's voicemail greeting chirped in her ear.

"Hello?" A long pause ensued, during which Lindsey's blood pressure spiked. "Gotcha! Sorry, you don't get to talk to me right now. If you want to talk to me later, better make it good."

Lindsey waited for the tone. "I don't want to talk to you. I want to *strangle* you. Dammit, Lena, *where are you*?"

Hours passed before she could get away to the blissful solitude of her apartment, where she hoped a glass of wine and a *Simpsons* marathon might make her feel a little better. But even Bart and Homer's animated antics weren't enough. Her anger had burned away to sad ashes, and she couldn't get her parents' disappointed faces out of her mind. It would serve Lena right if none of them ever spoke to her again, as drastic as it sounded, but something about Lena made one eager to trust her and believe her when she made the promises she never kept. And the anger Lindsey felt when that inevitably happened could just as easily be turned on herself for enabling her twin, for never enforcing any consequences when Lena flaked out.

But how many times had she tried? How many times had it worked?

Then her glass was empty, and she poured another, sitting alone on her couch and staring at the way the light from the TV played hypnotically through the crimson depths as she swirled the liquid in her glass. Everything she was doing to make herself feel better was having the opposite effect. The fact she had no one to vent her frustrations to made it worse. Bad-mouthing her sister to their parents wasn't an option, especially today—they were probably on the plane for their anniversary trip to Cabo San Lucas.

Lucky them.

"I need a vacation, too," Lindsey told her wineglass.

It was the only one there to listen. Then, sighing, she set it down on her coffee table and picked up her phone, shooting ramrod straight when she saw that she had somehow missed a text from Lena twenty minutes ago. She'd probably been in the kitchen scavenging.

> *Sorry. Ran into some trouble. Give Mom and Dad my love. I need a favor. Go to this address and ask him for help. Please. It will all become clear.*

An address followed, which Lindsey's eyes scanned without seeing. Her brain had shorted out on the word "favor."

"Are you freaking kidding me?" she asked her phone, gripping it with a force that threatened to shatter it.

Lena in trouble was nothing new. Ever since high school, on through college, and even after, she'd been getting herself or someone else into shit she couldn't always talk her way out of. Thinking Lindsey would simply forget about tonight and rush in to help her was simply par for the course, but Jesus, it had to stop sometime, didn't it?

One thing was for sure. No *way* was she going to that address, wherever it was. To some strange place to ask someone she didn't know for—what, even? Who was she supposed to be looking for? She wasn't about to let Lena make her look like an idiot on top of everything.

No one else could get her out of her warm cocoon on the couch to face the biting cold. She didn't know what she might find at her sister's apartment; she didn't care, but she was going all the same. Lena probably wouldn't be there, but maybe it wouldn't be too difficult to nose around and find out where she was. Then she would go find her, even if she had to hop on a plane to do it.

There were some things she desperately needed to say to Lena's face, and it was well past time.

She rushed through her apartment, throwing on a coat and shoving her feet into boots, her pulse pounding in her ears. No one else on earth could push her buttons like this. Lindsey hadn't trusted Lena since college, her twin's antics during that particular time of their lives having been the final straw.

Yes, she was her sister. Yes, Lindsey still loved her as such. Gossip sessions, shopping trips, friendship…those areas had always come easily. But real *trust*? That ship had sailed years ago, when Lena had pulled what was probably her cruelest stunt of all—at least that Lindsey knew of. The skeletons that could lurk hidden in Lena's closet were enough to give her cold chills. The two of them had the same face, and Lena probably had enough enemies that Lindsey should look over her own shoulder when she walked down the street.

In the back of the Uber she called because wine and rage and driving didn't mix, she white-knuckled her purse straps all the way to her sister's apartment, going over everything she wanted to say in her mind in case Lena was there. Confrontation ordinarily tied her tongue up in knots, and no doubt it would this time.

She had to have her words straight in her head or they would slip right out. But niggling in the back of her mind was the fact that their parents would never get over an irreparable rift between them, no matter the cause. It was enough for her to zero in on a few of the epithets she wished to hurl at Lena's perpetually smug face. But not many.

If Lena was off having a grand adventure with plans to show up next week thinking all was well—she added the epithets back in.

Long ago, Lena had given Lindsey a key to her apartment so she could water her plants while she was away. The plants had died anyway—Lena didn't even take care of them herself after she got home from wherever she'd been. But Lindsey had hung on to the key, and it had come in handy more than once. She stalked directly to her sister's door, lifted her fist to beat on it, thought better of it—she might not even answer—and fit the key into the lock.

The sight that greeted her as she flipped the nearby light switch caused her heart to stutter and her breath to catch, momentarily choking her.

Her sister's apartment was trashed.

CHAPTER TWO

Only one bulb remained in the overhead light, but it was enough to illuminate the chaos around her. Lindsey brought a shaking hand to her mouth as her mind tried to make sense of the destruction, of Lena's overturned furniture, slashed couch cushions, scattered knickknacks, broken picture frames. Terror froze her thoughts in its icy clutches, and she surged blindly forward. "Lena? *Lena.* Are you here?"

Only silence greeted her, terrible and absolute, broken by the crunch of glass under her feet.

She bent down to lift the remnants of a picture frame that had once held a photo of the two of them. Lindsey owned the exact same frame and photograph.

Summer Memories, the frame read, along with a cute beach scene in one corner: a chair in the sand, a bucket, an umbrella. But the picture was gone. Lindsey cast a glance around the immediate area and didn't see it. The fine hairs at the nape of her neck prickled. Whoever had come here, whoever had done this—would they be looking for her next?

Don't touch anything. Call the police. Her mind shouted instructions at her, but numb panic kept her rooted in the middle of the destruction.

There was a chance Lena might have collapsed, or been hurt, or—*Don't even think it.* The picture frame clattered to the floor. Lindsey charged through the apartment, flipping on lights, calling her sister's name—nothing but silence pulsed around her.

Think, think. Lena's mattress was askew in the bedroom. All the drawers had been rummaged through. Her clothes hung half off the hangers, and a jumble of sequins and silks and lace littered the closet floor. But the designer purses were all here. So was all her jewelry, even the most expensive pieces. Someone had been looking for something specific, and this wasn't a robbery.

Lena's not here.

She didn't know whether to be relieved or worried.

What if whoever did this kidnapped her? Ugh. Or she could be partying out of town, the victim of an unfortunate break-in. But why send the weird text with the address?

There was nothing she could do here on her own. Time to call the police.

She lifted her cell phone in shaking hands and had dialed the nine when the sound of footsteps reached her from the living room, and, all enmity forgotten, Lindsey sprinted from the bedroom on reflex, expecting to see her twin in the doorframe, surveying the destruction with the same shocked confusion Lindsey felt.

Then they would figure this out together, and all would be well. Despite all her machinations and flaky behavior, things always had a way of working out in Lena's favor, and nothing could be wrong with her indestructible twin, not really.

But it wasn't Lena standing in the living room. Lindsey's feet stumbled to a halt as she took in the dark-haired man she didn't recognize. The front door stood wide open—damn, she hadn't closed it behind her, had she? This guy had walked right in. All the blood in her veins froze at once.

"Who are you?" she demanded as his gaze jerked up toward her. For a split second, something like shock crossed his features before understanding settled in.

"You must be Lindsey," he said. That he came to that conclusion so quickly unsettled her a bit.

"Who are *you*?" she asked again.

His eyes were steady on hers when he said, "Your sister is in trouble."

That was such a familiar statement that Lindsey might have scoffed, but the disarray around her was evidence enough that Lena had reached a whole new level of trouble. And he still hadn't answered her question. His jaw tightened beneath its coating of dark stubble. Sickness yawned in Lindsey's stomach, spreading its way up into her chest, and warning bells were going off in her mind.

"What kind of trouble?" she asked, hearing the tremor in her voice.

The man drew a breath and cast a sweeping glance around. Nothing about him was menacing, even if his presence made her want to run. His gaze alighted on a picture of Lena with their parents, its frame knocked sideways on the wall, and something softened around his eyes. "I don't want to talk here," he said. "Someone could be listening."

"Who?"

"Follow me." Ignoring her question and without waiting for her reply, he turned and exited the apartment. Lindsey crossed her arms and rubbed her chilled flesh. All she wanted to do was slam the door behind him and finish her call, but if he might have information, maybe she needed to listen. On unsteady legs, she trailed after him into the hallway, closing the door behind her. He led her to an alcove near the elevator, where silence stretched all around them. It was almost as if everyone else in the building, the entire world, had disappeared.

"When was the last time you talked to her?" he asked, and she shuffled through her memories, fighting to maintain control of her emotions. She thought of the message sitting on her phone right now, sent only an hour ago, if that long. But something made her not want to divulge that information to this man.

"Thursday," she said and hoped the deception didn't show on her face. That was only the last time she had seen her face-to-face.

She's fine. I just heard from her.

What if Lena hadn't sent the message? What if someone else had her phone?

"Thursday," he muttered gruffly to himself, and she could see the calculations going on behind his eyes. Today was Saturday. Whatever conclusion he came to, he didn't let her in on it. Lifting his gaze back to hers, he asked, "Early? Late?"

Lindsey's brows drew together. "Late Thursday. And then I tried to call her Friday night and all day today but couldn't get her." As he began to look more concerned and more contemplative, she had to try to hang on to some shred of optimism, on to everything she knew about Lena and how she operated.

"Look, she's probably only skipped town for the

weekend. Right? If I know Lena—and I promise you I do—she's in Vegas or New York right now. She didn't want to help me with my parents' party, and she'll show up around Wednesday acting like everything is normal, wondering why everyone is pissed at her. That's how she is." She gestured toward the apartment. "This? It could be a random break-in. It happens."

He was shaking his head even as she spoke. "You don't know her like you think you do."

Really? She'd shared a womb with the woman. She considered herself the leading expert on all things Lena, ahead of even their parents. "Who *are* you? Don't ignore me this time."

"Call me Griffin."

"She has never mentioned you. Not once," she informed him icily. "I need to get back in there. Call the police or—"

He stepped in her path as she attempted to go around him, but refrained from touching her. Good thing, because she was ready to start screaming.

"No police. Not yet. Not until we know what we're dealing with."

She swept another cautious glance over him. If anything nefarious was indeed going on, how did she know he wasn't in on it and this wasn't some setup or trap? So many terrible things Lena could have gotten mixed up in, if she wasn't indeed partying it up somewhere.

He seemed to interpret her thoughts. "She wanted to be there for the party. She was looking forward to it. She wouldn't have missed it." He drew a deep breath. "I was supposed to go with her."

"Are you her boyfriend?"

He chuckled grimly. "I wouldn't go that far."

Lena had mentioned nothing about a man lately, boyfriend or otherwise, and she was usually loose-lipped about even her most casual sexual conquests. Lindsey's wariness factor notched up a bit. He was Lena's type, though. She liked them dark and intense. Lindsey usually preferred cute and nerdy.

"And you just happened to show up here at the same time as me? Checking up on her?" What if Lena had texted him, too? Her mind was so crammed full of suspicion and possibilities that she couldn't see a clear path. She shook her head as he opened his mouth to speak. "I don't know what to think. But I'm family, and you're not, and this whole thing is making me uncomfortable. You should leave."

"Just don't go to the police yet. All right?"

He turned to go, leaving her with five million questions zinging through her brain, but she couldn't settle on one to ask, and she wanted him gone anyway. He creeped her out. No police? When there was obvious trouble? He had to be shady. When someone says don't call the police, that's when you should.

The question that chilled her to the bone was this: How shady was Lena?

"Jesus," Lindsey muttered to herself after the elevator doors closed on Griffin's brooding expression.

Lindsey didn't want to think her twin was capable of getting caught up in any criminal activities, but she wasn't sure. What secrets would an investigation uncover?

She didn't know what to do. She hated the fact that protecting Lena and making excuses for her had become second nature. She hated thinking her sister might be a victim…but she almost hated thinking she might be corrupt even more.

"Okay," she muttered to herself, letting herself back into the apartment and trying not to let the horror of finding it this way engulf her again.

If Lindsey had seen that text and written back, *Sure, sis, whatever you need, I am your willing servant*, and not gone straight to Lena's apartment, she would never have known about this.

The safest bet right now was to leave everything untouched. In case… Well, she didn't want to think about possible outcomes that might involve the place becoming a real crime scene if Lena wasn't found. Everything could be cleaned up later. After she came back. Safe.

I'll even help you. Like always. Jesus, Lena.

Lindsey surveyed the wreckage and sighed. All her sister's pretty things. Her pictures. Lindsey plucked her cell phone from her pocket and went to Lena's last message, the one asking for a favor. *Go to this address and ask him for help.* An address here in Denver. Well, at least she wasn't asking her to gallivant across the country.

Ask him for help? Who? And what help? *Thanks a lot, sis.* She shot a message back asking for specifics, but minutes ticked past and no response came. She hadn't really expected one. Something told her Lena withheld that information for a reason. That was never good.

Sighing, Lindsey let the back of her head meet the door behind her with a thud. She stood that way for a while, exhaustion seeping into her bones.

It was when she lifted her head that she noticed something odd. Across the room, Lena's PC sat intact. Burning at the top of the screen was the tiny light that signaled the webcam was on.

Icy fingertips slid down the back of her neck. *Someone could be listening*, the stranger had said.

And watching.

Lindsey hauled ass out of Lena's apartment without another glance.

CHAPTER THREE

Jace Adams realized the barest strip of sunlight peeked around his blackout curtains. Turning off 3TEETH's mind-scouring "Antiflux," he stared at the last remnants of code on his laptop and leaned back in his chair, then pushed his fingertips into his burning eyes. He'd been at it seven hours, countering every network security measure they'd thrown his way, and his brain felt like a fucking wad of cookie dough. These Libra fuckers were pretty good, he had to give them that. Pretty good, but not great. He'd been foiling them for years now.

But he might be losing his touch if he was already wiped out. As he stood and stretched, his muscles pulled taut and protested the movements, joints creaking and popping. Yeah, losing his touch, and if he kept neglecting his gym time, he was gonna get out of shape, and that wouldn't do. His body needed to be as well-oiled a machine as his mind.

Bare chested, he strolled over to the window and lifted the edge of the curtain, wincing as the sunrise hit him dead in the face. Denver was waking up, dark buildings silhouetted against a sky blazing red and orange. And he was winding down, but maybe he still had the stamina for a run and a shower before he crashed. Clear his foggy head.

He quickly threw on sweats and sneaks and rode the elevator down the twenty-four floors from his penthouse. Hannah, who worked at SmarTech, got on at floor ten, and he greeted Jen, who worked at

Encorp, as he exited on the first. Both of them had been trying to hook up with him since they'd moved in. But he and the rest of the guys in the Nest who owned the building hadn't rented to them to get into their pants. They'd rented to them—and many others in the building who worked in the tech industry—because they needed to piggyback on their IPs.

But they didn't need to know that. So he beat a hasty exit into the cool Colorado morning.

The brisk air and the pumping blood quickly restored his clarity, and soon he was in an easy, familiar rhythm. So many times in life, running had been his only outlet—well, running and computers, though sometimes only one had been available to him. One had helped him escape; the other had helped him connect. Neither had been easy. Not in the foster homes. Maybe even less so in the Air Force.

But it was too beautiful a morning to dwell on it. The birds were frolicking, the traffic was cheerfully homicidal, and he had a long stretch of sleep ahead that would surely recharge all his batteries. Jace focused on the rap blaring through his earbuds, on his breathing, on the beat of his Nikes on the sidewalk. Despite the crispness outside, he was soon shining with sweat. He was about to turn a corner to head back around the block when a face in the crowd outside a coffee shop stopped him dead in his tracks, and he panted lightly as he squinted.

As soon as he'd glimpsed her, though, she was gone, swallowed up by the steady stream of pedestrians. Surely that had been a trick of the light…but even if it hadn't been, even if it was her, what the fuck did it matter? He damn sure didn't need his day ruined by being reminded of *her*.

Too late. He hadn't seen her in years, but he could re-create that face out of the mists of his memory as if he had talked to her yesterday.

He could say that woman had ruined his life; it damn sure felt like it at the time. But now, with the benefit of hindsight, that wasn't necessarily true. She'd only set him on a different path. A *vastly* different path, sometimes a shitty one—during the darker, scarier moments he definitely cursed her name for denying him the cushy lifestyle he'd always envisioned for himself. But he wouldn't be who he was today without her and what she'd done. He supposed in some twisted fucking way, he should thank her.

Nah. She'd fucked him over, plain and simple, regardless of the outcome. The memory of the betrayal scratched at a sore spot in his heart, and his run back to the high-rise was at a faster clip, the blood pounding in his ears more forcefully than it had before. Somewhere, Christmas music was playing.

Good luck going to sleep now, with visions of Lena Morris dancing in his fucking head.

The knock on the door was timid, but it roused him nonetheless. Due to circumstances stretching back as far as he could remember, he was a light sleeper. A pin drop outside the door might have him on his feet even before his eyes opened.

This time, he grumbled a curse as he hauled his dead ass out of bed and trudged to the door, banging his toe on a table leg in the process. So he almost snatched the door open without checking his video feed, prepared to unleash a tirade on the unsuspecting person, but it wasn't just anyone standing outside. The delicate features were unmistakable and seared into the most hellish depths of his memory, along with all the other laughing demons from his past.

It was *her*.

"Fuck me sideways," he growled at no one in particular, rubbing furiously at his messy hair. "Are you fucking *kidding* me?"

What did he even *do* with this? Suddenly, he knew. He snatched the door open, schooling his expression into the most impenetrable sheet of ice he could.

Lena's eyes flew open wide, and her jaw worked soundlessly for a few seconds, as if she had expected a friend to open the door and was instead being greeting by a hockey-masked killer wielding a machete. She even flew back a step, a hand fluttering to her throat. And she looked…different. Softer. Her hair was loose and lustrous, honey-blond, and her green eyes shone with an innocence he did not remember at all. Then again, it had been what, seven years? Eight? Maybe bitterness had twisted her image into something sinister in his head. Didn't matter. She was probably still a deceitful bitch.

"You— You're— *Jace?*" Her gaze swept down the length of his body, stuttering a little over his bare chest.

"At least do me the courtesy of remembering my fucking name," he snarled at her, and her eyes snapped back up so fast she might have sprained her eyeballs.

"I re-remember. I said it, didn't I?"

He scoffed. And waited. Whatever reason she had for showing up after all this time, it had to be good. He almost looked forward to it. Almost.

"Um, I don't really know where to start," she began haltingly, "but could you maybe…put a shirt on?"

"What for? This is my place. You're lucky I'm wearing pants."

"Whatever, I just need you to hear me out. I think you're mistaking me for—"

"I don't need to hear shit. What I really don't need to hear is that you've found Jesus or some shit like that and you're coming to ask my forgiveness for past sins. Because you can shove *sorry* straight up your ass."

She took another step back, her features stricken. "But I didn't—"

"Hang on." He slammed the door in her face and stood there for a moment, a thin haze of red covering his vision. The *balls* on this woman. There was a discarded T-shirt by his bed; he stalked to his room and shoved his arms into it, pulling it over his head and hardly believing this was reality.

MIT. Gone. Because of her. Years of dreaming. Years of work. Years of suffering. Flushed away, and he honestly didn't even know *why*. Maybe today he would learn. Maybe she would tell him why she'd done it. No matter how pissed off he was, he deserved the explanation, didn't he? But he didn't have to make it easy on her.

He carried a little blame in the situation, after all. One simple *no* from him all those years ago, and maybe he'd be living in a mansion somewhere right now, king of a software dynasty.

Yeah. Maybe.

But despite any wrongdoing he may have done for her, there was *nothing* filthier than a rat. And Lena Morris was the filthiest rat of all.

• • •

Lindsey knew those words had been meant for her sister, but nothing could stop the tears that pricked at the backs of her eyes. She gritted her teeth and willed them to go back to where they belonged.

She didn't even know why she was here, why in the hell Lena wanted her to find *Jace*, of all people. Back in college, Lena had ruined the guy's life right before Lindsey's eyes, and now she'd sent her to bear the repercussions? Was this all just a big joke?

Almost more astonishing was that Jace had… changed. Drastically. When he'd jerked the door open, she honestly hadn't known for a split second that it was him, and the recognition had hit her like a kick to the stomach. The funny, outrageous guy she remembered from college was gone, and in his place was this big, hard man with a drill sergeant's voice and a body that looked as if it had been chiseled from stone.

Her throat was still dry from that stuttering

exchange. She had to do better if he came back. She still hadn't heard from Lena, and she might be putting Jace in some kind of trouble just by showing up at his door. She had to warn him about that, *had* to. And give him even more reason to yell at her, probably, but it didn't matter.

Minutes ticked by, and she feared he wasn't coming back despite his admonition for her to wait. A door opened across the hall; she glanced back to see a guy with tattoos on the side of his shaved head exit an apartment. He looked at her curiously before moving on down the hallway toward the elevator. The guy didn't fit with the opulence of the penthouse floor of a high-rise. But then, thirty seconds in Jace's company, and she thought the same of him. What had he done with his life after Lena had gotten him kicked out of MIT?

She started as the door flew open, and the few minutes he'd left her waiting had done nothing to compose him. He still glowered at her, eyes like chips of dark ice, jaw a stony line. The only soft-looking things about him were his hair and his lips. He'd dressed and tamed the thick black hair that had been mouth-wateringly sleep-tousled earlier. When he jerked his head toward the interior of his apartment in invitation, though, she stood her ground. "I'm not coming in if you're going to be hostile. We can do this right here."

"If I'm hostile, I have damn good reason to be."

"Okay, then. All the more reason for me to stay out here."

"Listen, Lena, if you're—"

"*I'm not Lena.* Lena might be in trouble, and I

need your help." The words burst out of her.

He looked her up and down, a dark, burning gaze that made heat rise in her face. At least it had shut him up. For about five seconds. Before she could gather her thoughts to launch into the whole weird story, he took two steps toward her.

"What kind of shit are you trying to run on me now?"

"I'm not running anything—" She stepped back to make up for the space he had gained.

"Sure you are. You're good at games." She backed up even more until finally he was crowding her against the wall opposite his door. So close she could smell the mint on his breath, feel the coolness of it. A shiver worked down her spine. It stole all the words from her throat. "I was the ignorant jackass who fell for them, though, wasn't I? Threw my fucking life away for you. Put it all in your pretty hands. And what did you do? You *fucked* me."

Damn you, Lena. Lindsey stared in a torturous mix of awe, fear, and arousal as Jace Adams, the guy she'd had a raging crush on years ago, pressed the hard planes of his body against the soft curves of hers, then claimed her mouth in a blistering rush of mint and heat.

Fierce, dominating, draining, until the wall behind her was all that was holding her up, his tongue seeking and tasting and owning. Her knees collapsed. Her world tilted dizzily. His fingers bit into the flesh of her biceps to keep her in place, to hold her steady, while he laid her senses bare and assaulted them one by one. He kissed every thought out of her head. Weakly, she slid her arms up around his neck, ready to let him take her into his apartment, ready to be Lena for him and let him exact his revenge on her in whatever sordid ways he desired—

But he stepped back and left her half leaning against the wall, shaken and aching, her knees knocking into each other. Something hot and dangerous surged in his eyes, but just as soon as she'd seen it, it was gone. His face smoothed out, and then those eyes went cold, impassive, empty. Not even his rage was there anymore. A cruel scoff escaped him.

"All this time I wondered if it would've been worth it," he said. "I kinda held on to the fantasy that it would have been—it made me feel better when I was lying awake in my bunk at night." He shook his head and turned away. "What a dick punch to learn I threw it all away for *that.*"

Lindsey somehow snapped out of her funk, surged through the hurt, and chased after him several steps. "But *I'm not—*"

She barely avoided his door slamming in her face. Putting a hand against it, she leaned her forehead against the dark, shining wood panels. What was she supposed to do? She'd found him.

That's all Lena had asked, right?

He was a real asshole.

She kind of hoped whoever had Lena—if someone had her—got him, too. But not really. Lena had screwed this guy over big time. Hell, she'd turned him into a monster. Or something had, but she had the sneaking suspicion her sister had set him on that particular path.

It was no wonder he didn't remember Lindsey. She'd had a class with him at MIT before he'd gotten kicked out. But she'd been going through a bit of twin rebellion, chopping her hair off in a pixie cut and dyeing it black, while Lena had kept the long, natural blond they both sported now. She'd never spoken to Jace, only admired his looks and his skill and his wizardry from afar. He hadn't even known she existed. And then, suddenly, he wasn't in class one day, and the gossipmongers' gleeful whispers had flown.

She had never been so ashamed or embarrassed in her life to learn what had happened. Lena had happened. She'd gone to Jace and asked him to hack into the system and change her grade. He'd done it, and in fact, his intrusion had been so flawless, or so Lindsey had heard, that he never would have gotten caught. Until Lena rolled on him.

Lindsey had no idea why. She hadn't wanted to know—she'd been so fucking done with her sister that she hadn't spoken to her for almost a year afterward. She figured it was because she knew Lindsey liked him, and she wasn't above setting her sights on Lindsey's boyfriends to fuck, literally or metaphorically. Even preemptively. And someone capable of such an act, something so cruel and heartless, so senseless, wasn't someone Lindsey wanted in her life.

But their parents had begged and needled and schemed until the two of them gradually started speaking again and finally fell back into a semblance of sisterhood.

Now this.

Why? Bile rose in her throat.

She wanted to go home and leave her sister to her fate—maybe she even deserved it. She was a literal life-ruiner.

But she wouldn't. Something told her that whatever Jace Adams had become, he might be the only person who could help her. She had to make him understand. Frustration ate into her stomach. She wasn't the most articulate person on the best of days, but this man turned her into a quivering pile of mush. Maybe the only way she would be able to get her point across was to write it down.

Scrounging in her purse, she drew out a scrap of paper and a pen. Putting the paper against the wall, she scribbled.

Lindsey Morris. Meerkat

Blowing out a breath, she slipped the paper under his door.

She didn't bother adding a method of contact.

He would find her.

CHAPTER FOUR

It was late afternoon, and he should be asleep. He had a long night ahead. Instead, he was at his system, staring at all the information he'd gathered about the name she had slipped under his door.

Lindsey Morris. Meerkat. She was a decent coder, and he knew a script kiddie when he saw one.

So did she.

She could eradicate their asses.

Now he felt like a moron. He hadn't known Lena that well outside of frat parties and mutual friends, so who was he to say she didn't have an identical twin sister? It wasn't outside the realm of possibility. But after what she had done to him, even more believable was that Lena was a duplicitous piece of shit. Could he really be blamed for questioning it? Who knew what schemes a mind that demented could cook up?

So the girl he'd practically assaulted was *Lindsey* Morris, and he should have known it, but he also couldn't ignore the notion that Lena had probably put her up to whatever scheme they were trying to run. So far, though, she turned up clean.

He'd hacked into everything he could find about Lindsey. He read her emails. Her Facebook messages. Looked at her pictures. She'd known he would, or she wouldn't have given him the information. She wouldn't have given up her hacker name.

She was a software engineer at Denicorp. She'd

apparently gone to MIT as well, but she must have kept a lower profile than her sister, because she wasn't anyone he'd known. All her social media pictures were of the girl who'd knocked on his door this morning. And when it came to the resemblance between the sisters, he was fucking seeing double.

The odd thing was that Lena had no online presence. He'd checked up on her a couple of times in the past few years and hadn't been able to find anything beyond where she lived and some financial information. It was the same today. No social media accounts, no online footprint.

He could have had all the revenge he wanted right at his fingertips. A few keystrokes, and her identity, her bank accounts, her credit information— everything she was—would belong to him.

But he hadn't done it.

He'd sunk pretty low more times than he liked to think, but there was some shred of humanity that had kept him from ruining her life the way she had his. He liked to think he hadn't sunk quite *that* low yet. But if she didn't stop screwing with him, he might get there fast.

Even if everything Lindsey had said this morning was the absolute truth, and Lena was in trouble, why in the hell should he give a rat's furry little ass? She was going to have to do way better than that to mobilize his abilities. *Way* fucking better than that.

Then again, here he was, digging into everything he could find.

Lena hadn't been the best-looking girl he'd ever seen. It was the way she carried herself, the sultry-siren act down to an absolute science. The fit of her clothes that accentuated every luscious curve. The voracious heat in her eyes, the promise of her full lips. And damn if she hadn't turned out to be that siren, luring him to his doom, while he'd gone willingly, grinning like a gullible son of a bitch.

One drunken bet at a party, and he had brought her F in computer science to a B with scarcely a thought, enough to keep her scholarship but stopping short of an A because it might be overkill. She sucked at everything else, so an A in computer science might raise some eyebrows, and a quick survey of her records had shown him she'd only earned one A in her entire college career.

Which was in—surprisingly enough—abnormal psych. He'd even changed a few other random students' grades to take the heat off her in the event the intrusion was found. More fool him. It had never occurred to him in a million years that *she* would be the one to put the heat on *him*.

A knock on his door sounded at the same time a text popped up on his phone, jarring him from his thoughts. *Me*, it said, coming from Helix. He always announced himself, for some reason.

Come in, he texted back without getting up. Everyone in the team knew one another's entry codes. A second later, he heard the beep of the keys being pressed, and the door opened at his back. Jace glanced over his shoulder to see his hardware specialist walk up behind him, all-seeing blue eyes focused on the twenty-three-inch monitor in front of Jace…where a picture of the woman who called herself Lindsey Morris was clearly displayed, her smiling face between an older couple who, given the resemblance, could only be her parents.

"Cute girl," he commented, rubbing a hand over his bald head. "I thought the same when I saw her looking freaked out in front of your door this morning. And you hadn't even mentioned a lady in your life."

Jace grunted and shook his head, clearing the screen. "*That* is one lady I want out of my life, stat."

"I can make her microwave kill her," Helix commented happily.

Motherfucker probably wasn't kidding.

The one person Jace would trust with his life—and had on several missions—pulled up a chair and sat in it backward, folding his arms across the top and facing him like an interrogator. "All right. Who is she?"

"You've heard me talk about Lena Morris, right?"

"The soul-sucking harlot who got you kicked out of MIT and hurtled headfirst into our festering depths?"

"The very one."

"I might remember. Let me think."

Jace chuckled. "Fuck you, man. That woman who showed up at my door out of the blue this afternoon claims to be her identical twin. Said Lena is in trouble."

"And you would care because…?"

"I don't."

"Yet you've been creeping on her since she left."

Yes, he had. And when Jace glanced at his brother—best friend and team member didn't cut it—he found himself under a scrutiny that made him squirm. It saw everything, inside and out. It could also bring things to the surface better left submerged. "Lena Morris wrecked me."

"Maybe she rebuilt you."

"I rebuilt my goddamned self. And I told myself I had moved on. But I still found myself looking her up in the middle of the night sometimes. Wondering if she went on to have a good life when mine all went to shit."

"And?"

"I really don't know. She's a ghost."

Helix sat up straighter, his dark brows drawing together. "That's weird."

It kind of was. A young woman growing up in the internet age, the age of social media and selfies and mass hedonism…why no duckface shots of her clubbing with friends on Instagram, why no record of ridiculous dog-filter pics on Snapchat?

Lindsey was a different story. While her online life was nowhere near as wild as he would have figured Lena's was, she was there. She was a participant. From what he could ascertain, she was also single. Any pics of her with men were few and far between, so at least he wouldn't have the headache of some asshole trying to start trouble with him. Not that he would be too worried about it.

"So do you believe her? Is she really her twin?"

Jace thought about it long and hard. Helix had a way of making him cut through the bullshit. "Maybe. But it's like you said. If everything she told me earlier was the absolute truth, why the fuck would I even care?"

"What exactly did she say?"

Hell, what *had* she said? He'd been overcome

with so much angst at seeing her face outside his door, he could barely remember what color she'd been wearing.

Green, actually. She'd been wearing green. It had brought out her eyes.

Fuck.

"When you weren't barking at her, I mean," Helix added with a crooked grin that made him look more maniacal than he already did.

Jace supposed he could have listened a little more closely. "Just that Lena was in trouble."

"Well, I, for one, am intrigued, and I know you are, too. She must have some reason for coming to *you* when she could have gone to anyone else in the entire world, Jace. You might want to find out what that reason is, don't you think?"

"How dare you be reasonable," Jace grumbled.

Helix laughed. "It's one of my most endearing qualities."

"Hardly. But suppose she does have a reason. It can't be good."

"All the more reason to find out what it is." Helix's face hardened. Reasonable and jovial as he could be most times, no one wanted to see him when he wasn't. No one. "So we can deal with it," he finished coldly.

"This isn't your problem, man."

"Now *that* just pisses me off."

Sighing, Jace leaned back in his chair and wiped his face hard with both hands. "The all-for-one, one-for-all bullshit gets a little old sometimes, I have to admit."

"It does, right? Oh well. It's what we signed on for."

He hadn't signed on for a Lena Morris clone to show up here, that was for damn sure, stirring up the world he had managed to build for himself after she tore it all down around him. "The most horrifying thing of all of this is that there might actually be *two* of her out there in the world."

Helix burst out laughing. "All jokes aside, I say we get to the bottom of it. If only because it's gonna drive you nuts thinking about it, and you know it."

"If Lindsey is who she says she is, she's a good coder. Goes by Meerkat."

"Fucking hell, dude. You *know* sysadmins and coders don't mix."

Jace ignored that, true as it was. "Thing is, I doubt Lena could *turn on* a computer, much less write script."

"Meerkat, huh? Small, cute. Won't back down from a cobra. I like it."

He'd backed her down this morning, though, with that caveman routine he'd pulled and the blatant lie he'd told her afterward.

His response to her soft lips yielding to his demanding ones was probably the only reason he'd even bothered picking up the slip of paper he'd noticed on the floor just inside his door. Reading it and sprinting straight to his desk to sleuth on her, where he still sat now, digesting everything he'd learned.

Hadn't he known, really, deep down? She had the same face, but it couldn't be the same woman. That soft, trembling creature standing outside his door had lacked the loud, good-time confidence he remembered. She had felt good. Too good. And when he'd sent her away with those harsh words, he'd lied, but she couldn't ever know that.

"I don't know," he said, if only to fill the silence that had fallen between him and Helix. "I say we let it go. Whatever bed Lena's made, I'm sure she deserves to lie in it. We have more important things to concentrate on."

"Well, if you're sure, that's what we'll do. But I still think the smart move is to determine why she came to you. I can try to work on it, if you want to wash your hands of the whole thing." Just as Jace began to shake his head, Helix put in, "She *found* you, Jace. How?"

He tried to leave as little a presence online as Lena did. It was necessary in his line of work. Obviously, he hadn't succeeded. "I thought of that, too."

"If we've been compromised, we need to know. Maybe it's bigger than you. I say we bring the team in on this."

Jace didn't want to admit he was right. Pursuing this meant he wasn't free to forget about it, but hell, it was too late for that. The door had been opened, and his only choice was to revisit all the dark, festering things that still lingered inside him when it came to Lena Morris.

He shouldn't give a shit, but he did.

"If everyone agrees to let it go, will you listen?" Jace asked, cocking an eyebrow at Helix, who shrugged and stood, putting the chair back where he'd gotten it.

"Sure. I'll listen. But you know how we are. No one will let this go."

That's what he was afraid of.

CHAPTER FIVE

The Captain was having none of their bullshit today.

Snow had begun to kiss the windows of the conference room, a blustery cold having set in that was hindering the efforts of Christmas shoppers... not that Jace was among those. He didn't have anyone to buy for, except maybe the people sitting in this room, and none of them gave a shit, either. But he found himself zoning out while watching the white stuff fall outside.

It had been snowing in Cambridge the day the Captain had walked into the room at MIT where Jace sat, dejected and destroyed after learning of his dreams being flushed down the crapper, and made the offer that would change his life. For better or worse.

You have a set of skills that caught our attention, Mr. Adams. We'd like to put them to the test. Would you be interested?

Sure, what the fuck else did he have to do with his life? He thought he'd actually said something like that.

And found himself hacking the Pentagon a few weeks later in a bug-bounty program.

The Captain was a shrewd man, no-nonsense and stern. Cold, even, yet every one of them sitting here would put their life on the line for him. And had. The gray peppering his dark hair more heavily with each passing year did nothing to reduce the severity of his appearance. If anything, it somehow enhanced it, as if age was doing nothing but sharpening his edges.

He was the only father figure Jace had ever known. He didn't know how Cap had pulled this thankless job—leading their misfit ex-military group of ethical hackers—but he was damn glad to have him in control. *Ethical hackers*. There was a misnomer. But it was their job to outthink the criminals, to find and fix the weaknesses in government and sometimes corporate IT systems before worse people could find and exploit those weaknesses first.

To defeat your enemy, you must first know your enemy.

"Got anything you care to contribute, Jace?" The voice brought his head around. It was cool, always controlled, but commanded attention and respect. Jace racked his brain, trying to sort through the bits and pieces of conversation he'd picked up while he'd been staring out the window like an idiot.

"No, sir."

"Something on your mind?"

"No, sir," he said at the same time Helix piped up, "*Yes*, sir. Ask him to tell you about it."

Now all eyes were on him. The Captain folded his hands calmly in front of him and waited without a word.

"You have been oddly absent for this entire meeting," Drake pointed out. He was the malware specialist of the Nest, having created viruses that brought down financial institutions, governments, satellites, and cellular networks all over the world and beyond. And Jace didn't even want to know the things he'd done back when he wore a black hat.

Ignoring the remark, Jace turned instead to Sully, their resident cybersecurity engineer. "Has our network been compromised lately?"

She scoffed and ran a hand through her short, messy white hair. "Like you wouldn't have heard about it yet. Besides, anyone who can crack this wall deserves an engraved invitation to join."

"That's what I thought."

"What's this about?" the Captain asked.

"I had a visitor the other day," Jace said, leaning forward and staring at a neutral spot on the table. "I'm not sure how she found me. Everything seems to be sound, but she showed up, and she claimed to be the twin sister of the woman who got me kicked out of MIT. She's the mirror image of her, to the point that I thought it *was* her."

A collective silence fell across the room. Every one of them had heard his Lena sob story, and he didn't feel like recounting much of it now.

"And she's the reason you ended up here," Sully pointed out. Jace shrugged.

"Sure, if you want to look at it that way."

"What did she want?" Drake asked.

"All I got out of her was that her sister—Lena, the one who set me up—was in trouble. She was asking for my help."

"Does she know who you are?" *Who you are* in this context went far beyond name.

"Whether or not she's *made* me, I don't know."

"Don't you think you ought to find out?" Sully looked around at them all. "If someone can find one of us, they can find all of us. We need better security—*physical* security—in this building. I've been telling you and telling you."

"We'll address that," the Captain said. "Is that all that's concerning you, Jace?"

He considered his words for a long moment, then shook his head, glancing at Helix. Helix nodded, encouraging him to go on. "Not just the how but the why. Why me. To help *her*. I don't get it."

"Why didn't you ask?" Sully asked.

I was too busy kissing her brains out wouldn't be an acceptable response. "I guess it didn't occur to me," he said, letting his voice drip with enough acid to discourage further questioning on the matter. "I just didn't."

Sully, as unfazed by his tone as always, scoffed at him. "The next time strange women show up at your door, call me."

"Can I watch?" Helix asked, grinning lasciviously until the Captain put the kibosh on the subject. Yet again having none of their bullshit.

"She's also a competent coder," Jace continued once everyone had heeled to the Captain's command. "Goes by Meerkat."

"So you got that out of her but not her reasons for coming to you?"

"She wrote it on a note and stuck it under my door. I thought it was Lena fucking Morris standing in the hallway of my building. Forgive me for not being exactly rational."

"Some of the most high-stakes military operations in the history of the Air Force," Sully said, "and he's scared of a girl." She *tsk*ed at him but winked to take the sting off the words. He loved

Sully as much as anyone, and she loved getting under his skin. She was just so damned *good* at it, too. He scratched his nose with his middle finger in her general direction, and she laughed while the Captain sighed.

"Children," Helix called, holding up both hands.

"Thank you, Helix," the Captain said with a rare note of sarcasm. "What do you propose, Jace?"

From the time he was a kid, no one had listened to him. Not his parents who abandoned him. Not the foster parents who ignored him. Teachers hadn't known what to make of the troubled kid with brilliant computer skills. Professors had begun to somewhat understand him. But the Captain—he was the first person in Jace's life to *listen* to him, to value his opinion, and he did not take that lightly.

"*I* propose to forget about it. My distinguished colleague, however"—he indicated Helix—"does not agree and wanted to bring you all into the loop because of the vulnerabilities this incident might have exposed. Once those are addressed…" He fumbled with his words, trying to be respectful and failing miserably. "I really couldn't give less of a shit about Lena Morris. Or her sister."

Cap turned to Sully. "See if security has been compromised. Run a comprehensive check. Overturn every rock." She nodded, suddenly serious. Then Cap's piercing dark eyes turned to Jace.

"You do need to determine why this young lady approached you."

I was afraid of that, he thought. "Yes, sir."

"This could have been something she was instructed to do, if her sister is being held hostage.

We need to know why and by whom. It might not be anything that serious. Hopefully it isn't. But we can't know that."

"Makes sense." Even if he didn't like it one damn bit.

The meeting then turned to other Department of Defense cases, and the heat was off him, thank Christ. He hadn't liked sitting under the scrutiny of his team members while they no doubt picked apart every move he made or word he uttered. Like being naked under a spotlight. He breathed a sigh of relief when Cap dismissed them, but then he asked Jace to hang back.

Jace watched his team file out with sympathetic glances back at him. He wanted to tell every one of them to kiss his ass.

Cap got up and moved to the coffeepot, where he poured them both fresh mugs. Jace accepted his gratefully and downed it, scalding his throat in the process.

"Now. Tell me everything you wouldn't tell the others," Cap said, spearing him again with that assessing gaze.

"That's really all there is. I sent her on her way." He knew the man could smell a lie like a blood-hound. "I might have…kissed her."

A laugh from the Captain was a rare thing. "You might have?"

"I definitely did. The woman makes me crazy."

"That's obvious, Jace, but let me caution you against letting her get to you. We need you level-headed."

"You don't have to caution me. I'll get to the bottom

of this if you need me to, count on it."

"I believe you. But let's not seek revenge on this woman, either."

Jace met his gaze head-on. "Believe this, sir. If I wanted to do that, it would already be done."

Cap looked at him for a long time, then sipped his coffee. "Understood." He set the mug down and wiped at an invisible speck on the table. "You still have a lot of bitterness. But if I haven't said it enough already, your contributions to this team are invaluable. Frankly—selfishly—I'm glad you're here, whatever it took to get you here."

What it took was the singlehanded destruction of his future, but he supposed he could understand that viewpoint. It still made him grit his teeth.

"I didn't scrape you from the bottom of the barrel like some of my past recruits," Cap went on. "You had a bright future ahead, while some of the others had nothing, and you had that stolen. I understand the anger. You have to leave it behind, son. There's no place for it here."

Jace laced his fingers together and exhaled long and deep. "In the end I was facing what they all were, though, wasn't I? Jail time. That's why we're all here. We didn't want to do time. You saved us all. So, thank you. I guess I seem like an ungrateful asshole sometimes."

"The main reason I want you to look into this situation further…" Cap produced a nondescript manila folder from his high-security briefcase and slid it across the tabletop with the tips of his fingers. "…is this." Jace lifted his gaze from it and cocked an eyebrow at the older man before reaching forward and drawing the folder to himself. He flipped it open to find a picture of Lena staring up at him from—

CIA credentials?

What?

"The fuck?"

"Apparently, there is a missing CIA agent." Cap drew a long breath. "One special agent Lena Morris."

It was all Jace could do, considering their conversation a few minutes ago, not to explode from his chair and throw the table across the room. Instead he said, very calmly, "You're shitting me."

The Captain let that go without comment. "I didn't want to drop this information on you in the presence of the others. Let them do their jobs, but I want your special attention on this."

So everything Lindsey had said was true.

"It's quite possible, actually likely, that the sister who came to you has no idea her twin is CIA. Jace, I'm telling you this with utmost confidence that, if you have further contact with this woman, you won't blow any cover Special Agent Morris maintains."

"Of course I won't." His pulse felt ragged in his ears. Lena Morris. CIA. It explained so much. Yet…

"Do you have any questions?"

"Yeah. How did she pass the goddamn psych eval?" The Captain gave a long-suffering sigh, and he quickly added, "Any other intel I should be aware of?"

"I'm afraid this is all we have at the moment, which is precisely nothing. She was undercover and hasn't reported for days. That's all we know. I'm hoping you can change that soon."

"Yes, sir. So you were about to put this to the

team before I opened my big mouth about my visitor the other day?"

"I actually wasn't, not yet. I was waiting until we had more to go on." One corner of his mouth tilted up. "But then you opened your mouth."

Yeah. That had gotten him into trouble more times than he could count.

CHAPTER SIX

The email had no subject and no sender, but Lindsey didn't need either.

You have my attention, Meerkat. Come back and we'll talk.

She glanced up from her phone, sweeping a glance around at the bustling Christmas shoppers braving the cold and the snow. That creeping feeling of eyes on the back of her neck made her skin crawl beneath her scarf. The stores twinkled with festive lights and decorated trees, and everywhere was the sound of holly jolly music and laughter, but she couldn't shake the perpetual darkness she'd felt suffocating her in the few days since Lena's disappearance.

But was he *insane*? She wasn't going back there. Jace Adams had an anger management problem, and she wasn't about to knowingly put herself back in the position of being its target. They didn't have anything to talk about. She had no more information today than she had when she'd built up her courage to knock on what she thought was a stranger's door.

Well, she had at least a *little* more information now. She knew what his mouth tasted like. She knew the invasive insistence of his tongue, and she also knew the feverish dreams of having it elsewhere on her body. Any man who could kiss like that would surely be more than capable of giving a multitude of oral pleasures. Despite her anger at his asshole ways, she couldn't stop thinking about it.

The hottest kiss she'd ever had, and someone who hated her had given it to her.

He didn't hate her. He didn't know her. He hated Lena, and with good reason. She had to remember that.

Her dreams hadn't all been good. Dark, twisted nightmares had woken her more than once. With each one, she became more convinced something was terribly wrong and she was insane for not bringing the police in.

All of those dreams had involved the horrible things her twin could be enduring right now. But Lena was strong. She could hold her own. It was the only thought that gave Lindsey any comfort, that and the overly optimistic idea that Lena might show up at any moment, vibrant and happy and full of life. Ordinarily, Lindsey was livid upon Lena's jovial reappearances, but right now, she would give anything to see her that way again.

Leaving her house had become difficult. She was scared.

But the walls had begun to suffocate her, and like it or not, there weren't very many shopping opportunities left between now and the holidays. Her mother's chipper voice asked her over the phone every other day if she was getting her shopping done, always worried that she worked too much.

It wasn't unusual that she hadn't asked about Lena. They knew her ways as well as Lindsey, if not more so. The only comment she'd made was wondering if she was going to make it for Christmas dinner. Lindsey could only bring herself to reply, "I don't know. I hope so."

Tears burned the back of her eyes now as they had then. It hadn't been a lie, but she hadn't been forthcoming with the truth, either.

What was she going to do?

The jewelry case blurred in her vision, and a puzzled saleslady asked if she needed any help, but Lindsey shook her head and turned away, shoving her hands in her coat pockets and hunching her shoulders. She wasn't up for this today, wouldn't ever be up for this until Lena was back. She had to *do* something. If she did meet with Jace, she needed more to give him.

Early evening enshrouded her as she left the department store, burying her mouth into the warm fabric of her scarf against the cold, keeping her eyes downcast.

Lena didn't have any real friends. It had occurred to her many times over the past few years that she didn't know one single person to call for help when Lena pulled her disappearing acts.

How could that be so? When she left, who did she go with? What did she do? And how was it that she had always been so adept at dodging questions? Now she was gone, and Lindsey had no one to turn to.

Of course, she wasn't quite sure who Lena would turn to should their situations be reversed. She'd always liked it that way. She supposed her twin did, too.

There was one bar she knew Lena frequented, however. She talked about it sometimes, though going out for a night of drinking wasn't something Lindsey did, so she'd never joined her.

An outrageous idea occurred to her, one that was absolutely insane, really, and not something she was sure she could pull off—if she dared to try. But if she wanted to find out information about her sister, she had the best weapon imaginable in her arsenal.

She had Lena's face.

It's a long shot. She stared at herself in the mirror, but she was desperate.

Lindsey had stabbed herself in the eye no less than three times trying to get the perfectly winged liner her twin always wore. The big, loose, effortless curls Lena sported took a hell of a *lot* of effort. And the slinky sequined top showed way more skin than she was comfortable baring, one of many insanely skimpy items her sister had talked her into buying in anticipation of wild nights that had never come.

But if she showed up anywhere not looking like she was coming home from a nightclub on a Saturday night, anyone there who knew Lena would probably wonder what the hell was wrong with her.

It was disconcerting to look into a mirror and see not herself but someone else. She rubbed sweaty palms on skintight, destructed jeans.

You have to get yourself together. Lena never fidgets.

There was a grim set to her mouth that was also very unlike Lena, but no amount of makeup was going to hide that.

Well, she couldn't worry about it. All she planned to do was perch up on a barstool and observe, see if anyone seemed to recognize her or if they seemed overly surprised to see her. She also realized she was setting herself up for trouble—maybe she would see her sister again.

Then Mom and Dad will be dealing with losing both *daughters. Smart.*

Shaking her head, she grabbed her handbag and headed out.

It wasn't a long drive, but with the way the snow continuously drifted against her car's windshield, she began to think she would never feel warm again even with the heater going full blast. A chill had sunk into her bones, freezing her from the inside out. This had to turn up something. And then, maybe she would go to Jace, if he could behave himself.

Faces turned toward her as she entered the bar, but she detected little more than male appreciation or feminine dismissal behind any stares she received. It was fairly crowded and warm despite her chilled blood. She sidled around people standing at tables to find an empty spot at the bar, quickly learning how difficult it was to appear inconspicuous when you were scoping people out. The bartender ambled over and looked at her expectantly.

"Cape Cod," she ordered, citing one of Lena's go-to drinks. When it came, she only dared a couple of sips. Not that she never drank, but she didn't want to dull her senses. She might need them.

Then again, she might not.

Minutes ticked past.

Ball games and sports channels played on various TV screens.

The mood was happy and celebratory. Christmas was coming. All the while, Lindsey looked for anyone, anything suspicious, but no one seemed to be paying her much attention. Maybe Lena had no friends here after all. A man swayed up and offered to buy her another, but she turned it down. Thankfully, he moved on without fuss.

She began to despair, staring down into her drink's crimson depths. At the bottom of the glass, at its darkest, it looked like blood. A low voice spoke in her ear.

"Lindsey, what the *hell* are you doing?"

Startled, she whirled on her barstool, then reared back as she felt her own blood drain from her face. Griffin glared at her with his brows drawn together. She'd been sitting here for at least half an hour and had missed seeing him. She was a horrible detective, and this entire idea seemed ludicrous.

"Nothing," she said, grabbing her purse. The creepy, crawling feeling on the back of her neck, which she had been feeling for days, began to make sense, not that she liked knowing its source any better. Then again, if he wanted to remain unseen, why had he approached her? "I was about to leave. What are *you* doing here?"

"Maybe the same thing you are," he said, sounding dejected even as he cocked a meaningful brow at her attire.

"Have you been following me?"

"No. I just saw you."

She didn't believe that for a second. "Have you heard anything?" she asked, watching him closely.

He shook his head. "Have you?"

How much to tell this guy? Her gut insisted on *nothing*, but something told her he already knew far more than he would ever let on. He could be complicit. He could have been the one who trashed Lena's apartment, who'd stolen the picture of the two of them together. Hell, at this point, everyone was a suspect, every nondescript face she'd passed on the street, every person in this bar.

"No. And I really do need to be going now."

She slid off the stool and strode quickly away, looking for the exit, any escape. He fell into step beside her, matching her strides with much longer ones, and she realized she didn't want to leave with him beside her. She stopped and looked at him.

"Why don't I believe you?" he asked.

"I might ask you the same thing," she said. "Please stop following me."

"I'm not following you."

"You're following me *right now*."

"Dammit, I only want to find her. I have no motives beyond that. I'm not the bad guy."

"I'm supposed to believe that just because you say it? I'm suspicious of *everyone* right now."

His face fell. "You do know something. Listen, you need to get out of here. Let me buy you a cup of coffee somewhere else, and we'll talk about it. Public place, you don't have to worry."

Jace Adams's face flashed through her mind right then, hard-chiseled and disapproving, and despite spending less than five minutes in the man's presence, she wondered what he would think about all this. What advice he would give. If he would tell her to flee from this guy right now or take up his offer and see if she could get anything out of him.

She felt so in over her head. Face-to-face interaction wasn't her forte. Reading cues or body language or any of that stuff eluded her. She sucked at it. She never knew what to say or when to say it or when to not. Lena had told her time and time again she was too trusting, too naive. That was why her sister had been able to burn her so many times, she was sure.

How quickly that had changed, though. The best idea right now was to stay guarded.

"I'm sorry, but no. I don't have time."

"At least give me some way of reaching you if I need to."

"Tell you what, you give *me* some way of reaching *you*."

He cursed under his breath, slipping his hand inside his coat to draw out a pen. Lindsey fumbled through her purse and produced a receipt for him to write on. He scribbled a number and handed it over. "Don't hesitate to use that if you learn anything. *Anything*, Lindsey."

Before she could agree—or not—he walked away, leaving her in a sea of people but never having felt so lost or alone.

CHAPTER SEVEN

Jace hadn't named a time, but the other day she'd woken him, and that had been in the afternoon. It was eight thirty now, so it seemed as good a time as any.

Lindsey trembled inwardly as she knocked on his door. She hadn't even gone home to change out of her Lena costume. As soon as he answered, she launched into her prepared spiel, stumbling over the words. "I told my best friend exactly where I am and who you are. If you're going to be an angry brute, I'm leaving, and if I disappear, the police are going to know exactly where to come." It was a lie, of course. She had no one to tell.

He scoffed, then swung his door open wide. "You're perfectly safe. I promise."

Why she was willing to believe him and not Griffin, she wasn't sure, but she took a few tentative steps inside and let him shut out the world behind them. His apartment was spacious and sparse, utterly masculine in its minimalist design, dominated with chrome and glass, granite and glossy dark woods.

"Drink?" he asked, moving toward the kitchen area, which was full of stainless-steel appliances. Whatever Jace had gotten into after having his education dashed upon the rocks, it must pay well.

"No, thank you," she said.

He got himself a beer out of the fridge and twisted the cap off, then leaned against the island

and surveyed her casually from his safe distance before taking a pull from the bottle. "I'm sorry."

Lindsey cleared her throat and stared at her boots. Lena usually wore heels, but on that, she had to relent. She couldn't go breaking an ankle on the sidewalk.

"I still don't know what the fuck is going on, but you asked me to hear you out, and I want to do that."

"Before you decide again that I'm lying and throw me out?"

One corner of his mouth tugged upward in a smirk before he took another drink. "If it comes to that, I'll try to be more gentlemanly about it."

"I can't see you ever being a gentleman."

He put a hand to his chest in mock offense. "That wounds me. Okay, Lindsey Morris. Meerkat. Like I said, you have my attention. How long you keep it is on you."

"Are you always this arrogant?"

"Always. So begin."

No. No, she couldn't let him dominate this conversation, because something told her he would steer it to places she didn't want to go. Maybe she needed a beer for this after all. It was going to be a long night.

It didn't help matters that his T-shirt could scarcely contain his muscles, and the way his jeans hugged his hard thighs made her mouth water. Yeah, she normally liked cute and nerdy. Jace had been the one glaring exception, having always been a little more ripped than your average geek. Now, though, he was built like a god, and when it came to pure appreciation of the masculine form, she was a sucker for thighs. She'd seen his pumping and glistening with sweat while he was out on his run the other morning.

"Lena didn't show up for my parents' anniversary party that she was supposed to help me with. I didn't think anything of it at first, except to be pissed off because that's just how she is."

"Right," he said, but the scathing bitterness she'd witnessed from him the other day was absent, at least somewhat. Encouraged by that, she went on.

"Later that night, I got a text from her. I can show it to you, but all it said was that she ran into trouble. It said 'go to this address and ask him for help.' When I did that, Jace, *you* opened the door."

"She specifically told you to come to me."

"Yes."

He set his beer aside and gave a weary shake of his head. "Unfuckingbelievable."

"I completely agree, I promise. It makes no sense. But wait, let me back up. Before I came here, I went to her apartment. I thought even if she wasn't there, I might be able to find out where she'd gone, rather than knocking on some stranger's door.

"At the time, I had no idea that address would lead to you. But her apartment was completely trashed, and some strange guy showed up while I was there. He said he was supposed to be her date for my parents' party and he had reason to believe that something was wrong with Lena. He said she was in danger."

"Did you get his name?"

"He said to call him Griffin. He said it like that. So whether it's a first name or last or alias, I have no idea."

"Griffin," he muttered to himself, seeming to search through his inner filing system. She could practically see the synapses firing behind his eyes.

"Do you know anyone by that name?" she asked.

"It isn't ringing a bell yet. Did you tell him about the text from her?"

"No. I told him I hadn't heard from her in days."

"Why?"

"Just—something about him. I don't know him. I was suspicious." Speaking of suspicious, something about the way he was watching her made the floor seem to tilt under her feet. She now understood how it felt to be deemed untrustworthy upon first sight. She didn't like it. "What is it?"

"You don't know him, but you don't know me, either."

Lindsey went to lick her dry lips, only to find her tongue was dry, too. "She sent me to you."

"You don't know that it was her who sent that message, though, do you?"

"No," she admitted sadly. "I'm flying purely on instinct here. I don't know who to trust."

He was silent for a moment. She found his agreement in that silence—he didn't trust her, either. Then he said, "You're the spitting fucking image of her. I mean, it's uncanny."

"I know."

"Have you two ever switched places before?"

The way he asked it felt like an interrogation. She stared at him. "Until tonight? No. Never. Whether she's pretended to be me, who the hell knows. I wouldn't put anything past her."

Jace held up a hand when she would have said more. "Wait, until tonight? What the hell happened tonight?"

"I went to a bar I think she frequents. Thought I would see if anyone approached me or acted surprised to see me." When he crossed his arms and tilted his chin back somewhat, as if surveying her in a new, suspicious light, she rushed on, feeling she was in danger of losing him. "I'll explain in a minute. When I was at her apartment, as far as I could tell, nothing of value was taken. She has some expensive jewelry and purses—they were still there. One thing I did notice missing was a picture of her and me together."

"They might want both of you, then."

His bold statement of something she'd been trying to shove away from the forefront of her mind, and the offhanded, careless way he said it, made her rub at the sudden eruption of chill bumps on her arms.

"Then they could have taken me," she said through an involuntary flash of defiance. "I think someone might have been watching through her webcam. They probably knew I was there." She'd been keeping a Post-it note taped over her webcam at home ever since.

"What were you supposed to do with me once you found me?"

"Ask for help. That's all she said. I asked for clarification. I haven't heard from her since." Carefully, she watched his controlled reaction to that, the way his dark brows drew together minutely in concentration as he looked off at some neutral point.

Somehow, watching him think was as fascinating as his thigh muscles. "I didn't want to put you in danger, too, but I didn't know what else to do."

He picked up his bottle again and waved it in a dismissive gesture. "I'm not worried."

No, he wouldn't be, arrogant as he was. "So, what do you think? This is connected to you in some way or she wouldn't have asked me to come to you."

"Or whoever has her wouldn't have asked," he added, deepening her misery. She hated the thought that he *relished* the idea of Lena in danger.

"The glitch in this theory is that I'm not sure why anyone—especially Lena—would think I'd give two shits about her."

"I get that."

"So tell me one thing, Lindsey Morris. Why did she do it?"

Lindsey shook her head, not having to ask what he meant. "I don't know, Jace. I honestly don't. I didn't speak to her for…God, so long."

Jace frowned. "Why would you care?"

"I knew you at MIT. We had a class together. I don't guess you would remember me; I looked different then."

Now Lindsey found herself under that intense scrutiny, and she tried not to fidget under it while her heart rate kicked up and she thought of all the things he might find lacking. "I'm not sure how I could have missed you."

"I had much shorter, darker hair. I didn't talk much." She chuckled. "Still don't if I can help it."

"You do your talking in code," he said. "I was impressed."

Great, now she was blushing. His complimenting her skills was somehow better than his complimenting her looks.

He wiped both palms down his face. "All right. So, let me get this straight in my head. You were my classmate."

"Yes."

"But Lena didn't go to MIT. She went to UMass."

"Right."

"I met her at a party, but I find it hard to believe I wouldn't have noticed a carbon copy in my classroom."

"If you want, I can show you old pictures. I tried to look as different from her as I possibly could. That persisted for years, actually. I just needed to be my own person." It had been aggravating early on to be confused for her sister so much. Mainly because people had hated Lena. A lot. Lindsey had nearly been on the receiving end of more than a couple of butt-kickings that were intended for her sister.

"The twin sister of one of my classmates approaches me at a frat party—even though she doesn't go to our school—and talks around to betting me that I can't hack into UMass's grading system and change her grade. I do it, and she turns on me. All along you knew who I was and, apparently, what I could do. It smells rotten, Lindsey. It smells like some kind of setup."

Alarm flashed through her at his hardening expression, and she shook her head. "I swear to God, Jace. I'll swear on anything you want to put in front of me. I didn't know about all that until you were busted for it."

"You got that part wrong, sweetheart. I wasn't *busted*. I was ratted out. Your sister is goddamn lucky I didn't return the favor."

"Why didn't you, then?"

"You don't know how I struggled with that. I wanted to, trust me. I lost sleep over it. But in the end I didn't do it because that's not *who the fuck I am*. I wouldn't sink to her shit-scum level." He bit out every word, aiming them at her like daggers.

"I know you have every reason to hate her," Lindsey said softly. "But there isn't anything I can say that will lessen that. I can't speak for her; I can't apologize for her. Because to this day, I don't know if she's sorry or not. I don't know if she even thinks about it anymore."

"I think about it every day of my life," he said, just as softly but far more dangerously.

Somehow she knew that attempting to put a positive spin on what he'd suffered would be very ill-advised, so she reserved comment. "What did you do…afterward?"

"Military," he said, running a hand through his hair. "Funny thing is, little did I know I would have royally fucked myself if I had turned her in. They wanted my skills, and they wanted to know I could keep my mouth shut. So don't ask any more questions about that."

He'd made a comment about lying in a bunk at night, so the admission wasn't a surprise to her. Neither was his reluctance to divulge any further information.

"Anything else?" he asked once the silence had stretched thin between them.

"Yes. Tonight. This Griffin guy was at the bar while I was there, and he approached me. I didn't tell him anything I'd learned. He said he hadn't learned anything, either." She chewed her lip thoughtfully. "I haven't gone to the police. Griffin told me not to, and for some reason that seems best, until we know what we're dealing with."

"Worried about what sweet Lena might have been into?"

That he had picked up on that so fast unsettled her. "I don't know, Jace. I guess that's part of the reason why I'm here. First of all, that she asked me to come here, and second…well, I remember you, even if you don't remember me. And I know if anyone can help me find out what's going on, you can."

"If I decide to help you," he said coldly.

After all this, he might still decide not to help her? After all the questions? She'd thought he was intrigued, but he was only feeling her out. He might still shove her out and slam the door in her face again.

"Please, Jace," she said softly, trying to rein in her desperation. "I have no one else."

He sighed, setting his beer bottle on the island with a finality that told her either he'd decided or was simply tired of her whining. "All right. Tell me all about Lena. Everything. What she was like in high school. In college. What she did afterward. Email addresses, all of them that you know. Phone numbers. Any enemies she has. Any friends. Neighbors, even. I want her entire life fucking history."

Lindsey scoffed. "Oh God. Seriously?"

"Seriously." His expression brooked no argument. "If we're going to find her, then I need to unearth everything about her."

Crossing her arms, Lindsey looked away, taking a deep breath to even her pulse rate. Lena, for all her outgoing, charismatic behavior, had been such a private person. Lindsey had tried for years to get her on Facebook, *anything*, but she'd always laughed off her attempts and changed the subject.

"You aren't going to find anything on her."

"Doubting my abilities already? We aren't going to get very far."

"How do I know you aren't going to use anything you find to ruin her?"

"If I were going to do that, it would already be done."

There was no arrogance behind the statement, only pure confidence. If she didn't think Lena's very life might depend on his abilities, she might not have trusted him. Under the circumstances, she wasn't sure she had a choice. "All right. Fine. But I have to warn you, there's more I don't know than I do."

"That's true of every person you know. So shoot."

She cocked an eyebrow at him. He hadn't moved a muscle away from the kitchen. "You aren't going to write anything down?"

Grinning, he gestured casually toward his head. "Sure I am. But come on, take a seat if you want." Leading her into his living room, he indicated the navy blue couch while he headed to his desk against the back wall. As he dropped into his desk chair,

Lindsey sat, imagining the havoc he could create at that keyboard with only a few strokes of his fingers. Instead of turning to his computer, though, he only watched her, waiting for her to begin.

She tore her gaze away and stared at the glass coffee table in front of her. Even so, she felt those eyes on her, but she could breathe easier when she wasn't looking at him. Quietly, methodically, she began telling him the story of her twin sister's life. Everything she knew, anyway.

Carlton High School. Party girl. Undeniably smart, but more street smart. Good grades but *amazing* judge of character (except, it seemed, for her own). Always told Lindsey who to trust and who to not among her circle and was unfailingly dead-on in her assessments.

Like a natural-born human lie detector.

Problem was, a human lie detector knew how to lie. Orchestrator of much demise. Ruiner of many lives. UMass. The saga continued, as Jace already well knew, so Lindsey didn't expand much on the college years, mainly because she didn't know a whole lot beyond Lena getting him kicked out. Afterward, however, Lena had moved away and put her criminal justice degree to work. She became a police officer in Washington, D.C. At that point in her story, Jace perked up.

"That's where you'll start finding a trail," he said, and for the first time since beginning her story, Lindsey looked over at him.

"Enemies," she said softly.

"Maybe. Maybe not. But that's where I would start, anyway."

"Makes sense," she said. "She never talked much about it, but she seemed to enjoy it."

"It doesn't matter. I'll find every report she was involved in."

"You're going to hack into police records?"

He shook his head with mock sadness, cocky grin in full force. "Doubting my abilities."

"I just…" Leaning forward, Lindsey put her elbows on her knees and rubbed her temples. "It's not your abilities I doubt, trust me. But don't get yourself in trouble over—"

"That's doubt." He watched her for a moment, then leaned forward himself, gazing at her earnestly. "It's that you're still afraid of what I might find, isn't it?"

CHAPTER EIGHT

Jace watched her struggle with what to say, trying to figure this girl out, trying to determine if she knew more than she was telling. There was a lot of that going around.

Your sister is fucking CIA, Lindsey. Jesus Christ.

He had to hold himself back from wondering how in the hell she hadn't figured it out. Not everyone had his wary mind or his insight into this kind of shit, but she was obviously smart. Naive but smart.

"A little, maybe," she said in answer to his question, dropping her hands from her head and looking at him sadly.

"It's always hard to find out someone isn't who we think they are."

"Thing is, I know I shouldn't be surprised with whatever you find. Maybe she was crooked, maybe…"

Jace leaned back in his chair, the springs squawking loudly in the silence following her forlorn words. He rubbed his thighs with both hands, itching to hurl more obscenities about just how *crooked* Lena was. She knew. She didn't need him bitching about it anymore, no matter how much he wanted to. "More likely is that she pissed off the wrong people, you know. Maybe she did that by doing good. We can't know yet."

"Thanks," she said, sounding so glum he didn't have the heart to tell her how much he doubted his own words. "And thanks for helping me sort this out."

Guilt bit into him with surprising ferocity. He wasn't doing this for Lena or even for Lindsey, and he damn sure wasn't doing this because he was a fucking nice guy. She needed to get that straight in her head from the start. "Don't thank me yet."

"I'm so worried about her. My parents—we were later-in-life kids for them. They just celebrated their fortieth wedding anniversary. I haven't even told them about this, because this news would worry them so much."

Her delicate profile and downturned mouth were captivating, luring his eyes where they shouldn't be going. "I really don't get how two identical twin sisters could be so different." In fact, he was suspicious as hell about it. And he needed to remember that, too. She made it hard to do so. "I mean, you seem pretty genuine."

She looked at him incredulously. "I *seem* genuine?"

"Yeah, don't get offended. You seem that way, but so did she. Look, I'll check all this shit out as best I can. But I'm warning you, this had better not turn out to have some kind of blowback on me. It's not all ringing true."

"I'm just as much in the dark as you are about all of this. I didn't *ask* for this. I don't know why you were brought into it. I get that you probably don't fully trust me. Well, I don't trust you, either. You're right, Lena and I have always been different. How we dress, how we act—I don't exactly know where she came from. We look like the same person, but it ends there."

Granted, he hadn't often been around Lena, and

hell, it had been a decade ago. But somehow every moment he had spent with her had become committed to memory after what she'd done to him. With her soft eyes, her caring nature, Lindsey couldn't have been more opposite.

Or maybe she was just a damn good actress.

"I got her story," he said, "now tell me yours." He scrutinized her reaction, honing in on her body language.

She shrugged. "College. Work. And now this."

"How is it at Denicorp?"

If he expected outrage, he didn't get it, solidifying his earlier thought that she'd known he would creep on her. All he detected was a faint hardening around her pretty eyes. "Fine. I like it. I do some tech writing, too, if you must know."

"I do know. I read some of it."

"Then why ask me about my life, if you already know everything?"

"Because who we are online is not who we are offline."

"I don't think that's true in all cases. I think I'm pretty much the same."

"Really?"

She nodded. "Yes. Absolutely."

"Do you have a boyfriend?"

Now she shifted uncomfortably. "No. As you well know if you saw the 'single' status on my Facebook profile."

"Please. People change that status as often as they change clothes."

"Again," she said obstinately, "I don't. And I won't. Because I refuse to be like that. I'll be 'in a relationship' when I'm actually in a relationship. When you looked at all my emails and messages, did you see any from a man?"

"You got me there. No nude pictures from you at all. So disappointing."

"Speaking of things I would *never* do—" she said, glaring daggers at him while he laughed.

"I wouldn't, either. That stuff never goes away."

He couldn't be mistaking it—was she blushing? And then there was absolutely no denying it, as her cheeks began to blaze bright red before his very eyes.

Okay, tone it down, asshole.

He ran a hand through his hair and stood. "Are you sure I can't get you something to drink?"

"Water, please." While he went to get it for her, she said across the distance, "I do have a phone number for Griffin. He asked for mine, but I made him give me his instead."

"Awesome. Let's see it."

She pulled a crumpled receipt from her purse and handed it over while he passed her a glass of water. Her fingers were long and slender and unadorned. Her nails were short, bitten, and bare of any embellishment. He always liked to take note of people's hands. They said a lot about character.

Lena… She'd had velociraptor nails. He remembered that because he'd imagined them ripping his back apart as he cracked UMass like a fucking idiot with his first hard-on. Of course, he never had that chance, and now he was fucking glad of it.

Never again. A lesson hard learned.

As he took a seat at his keyboard with the phone number, he sensed Lindsey move up behind him, no doubt anxious as to what he would uncover. His fingers flew over the keys while her scent teased vaguely at the edge of his senses, something warm and soft and lightly floral. Despite the distraction, he had a trace on the guy's location within minutes. "He's at this bar. Is that where you were?"

Lindsey leaned closer, staring at the map on the screen. Her hair was so long it fell down his arm. That's where the scent was coming from. It filled his nostrils and intoxicated him. "Yes. I came straight here."

"Hmm. Then either he's still there or he powered down his phone there and hasn't turned it on since."

"Is there some reason why he would do that? How am I supposed to call him if I find out anything?"

"Maybe he doesn't quite trust you, either."

That made her straighten in a huff, but he found that he missed her nearness. "I haven't *done* anything for all this mistrust. Jesus."

He chuckled. "Get used to it. And it's never occurred to you that someone could be doing all this to get to *you*?"

"That's stupid, Jace. I mean, you really don't understand how stupid it is. Who am *I*?"

Yeah, he didn't quite believe it, either, he was just trying to cover all bases. Most likely, someone was doing this to get to *him*. And it might even be Lena herself, though why she would want to come back and destroy the pieces of him she'd left in her wake was beyond him. Lindsey had said it herself. Who was *he*? Why him, out of all the schmoes at MIT?

He turned his chair to face Lindsey directly, her troubled eyes following his movements as he crossed his arms. "Apparently we've accomplished jack shit today. I guess we wait for their next move."

"Whose?"

"Whoever's. Lena wanted you to find me. Well, you found me."

"Should I do anything? At home? I hate even sitting in front of my computer now, afraid of who might be watching me."

"Truthfully, Lindsey, I think you should carry on like everything is normal. Act like you don't give a shit. Do your work, Christmas shop, demolish the skiddies, Meerkat." His mouth tugged up in a grin despite himself, and she returned it shyly. "My associate appreciated your alias, by the way."

She shrugged. "I've always loved Timon from *The Lion King.*"

"Aw, how sweet."

"Don't be fooled."

"Ooh." He leaned forward, lacing his fingers together between his knees, staring her in the eyes. "And here you've spent all this time trying to convince me that you're the *good* sister, Lindsey."

He saw her efforts to maintain an aloof composure and her stark failure to do so as color crept up into her cheeks again and she glanced away from him, shifting on her feet. Her split-second ability to turn bright red was fascinating. Just how deep could that color run?

"Not always," she said, bringing him grudgingly back to the conversation.

"Name one bad thing you've done."

Her gaze dropped to the floor. "Lying to my mother."

"About Lena?"

Only then did she lift her eyes to his, the sadness like a weight there, and he thought he saw the beginnings of tears. "Yes."

Oh, shit, no. He couldn't have any crying females in his apartment. Standing, he took her gently by the shoulders, not letting her look away from him this time. "Know this," he said firmly, watching her lashes flutter as she blinked at him. "This is one of your better days. It's only going to get worse. Save your tears for that day. Save them all."

She'd been looking at him for reassurance, and he watched those hopes fall. That wasn't what she wanted to hear, but it was what she must understand if this went sour. And it would. Missing CIA agents? Shit.

She drew a deep breath, her body relaxed, and finally she nodded. "Okay. I'm okay."

"Good."

The sudden wash of guilt was surprising to him, but Christ, she didn't have anyone else to turn to. She was facing this all by herself, and who knew what might happen next? What if these assholes, whoever they were, struck out at her? Jace released her and ran a hand through his hair. He didn't need to get this involved.

While he struggled internally with what to do, Lindsey watched him with her big green eyes. Kind, curious, unassuming eyes. Nothing like Lena's sly, calculating snake eyes.

"What are you thinking?" she asked at last.

"Nothing for you to worry about yet. The first thing I want to do is go to your sister's apartment. Have a look around there."

Lindsey nodded eagerly. "I figured. Can we go now?"

"I'm sorry, but I can't tonight."

Her face fell. "If she's really in trouble and I'm not doing anything—"

"You're doing what you were told, and that's all we have." He sighed. "Look, I'm helping, okay? For now. I'll spend all night following the leads you've given me. Tomorrow, we'll take a look at her place first thing. Will that make you feel better?"

"I'd rather go tonight."

"I get that, and I would if I could, but I have a prior commitment."

He didn't, actually, but there *was* something he needed to do, and he had to make sure he had access to do it.

Steeling himself against her disappointment, he saw her to the door. Then, without her knowing, he saw her to her car and into her building. Purely for investigative purposes, of course.

He had the bad feeling that she hadn't been brought into this by accident. And he always trusted his gut. Well—usually. He'd seen what *not* trusting it had gotten him, at least.

He also feared she had no idea what she was in for.

Hell, for that matter, he didn't, either.

CHAPTER NINE

Jace showed up at Lindsey's apartment the next morning a full half hour earlier than he'd scheduled, leaving her panicked and having to dress while he patiently waited in her living room. She had to resist the urge to doll up, suddenly missing her sister intensely, since she had always been the siren.

In the end, frustrated, she settled on her usual practical winter garb of a sweater and jeans. Who the hell was she trying to impress, anyway? But his presence made her uncomfortably aware of how long it had been since a man was in her apartment.

The drive over to her twin's building was tense and mostly silent, and Lindsey watched the snowy city pass by outside Jace's window, speaking only to give him directions. He drove a new Dodge truck, so new the fumes from the carpet stung her eyes a little.

Once upon a time, years ago, she would have been thrilled to climb into a vehicle, any vehicle, with him. Maybe she still felt that way; she only wished the circumstances were different. She wished she could be anywhere else in the world at this moment, rather than right here, and for this reason. It was a terrible way to feel.

And the drive was entirely too short. A sense of dreadful déjà vu plagued her as she led him to Lena's apartment and then inside. He took immediate control, flipping on the lights, surveying the room's chaos with those calmly assessing eyes that seemed to miss no detail. She drew strength from that, somehow. His presence steadied her.

But being in this place, with her sister so close but so far away, sucked all the air out of her lungs.

"You good?" Jace asked, his gaze on her as he strode across the room to Lena's computer.

Lindsey forced herself to nod before slipping out of her coat and unwinding her scarf from around her neck. It was a leopard print, Lena's favorite pattern, and she'd given it to Lindsey as a gift some shared birthday long ago. Being a decidedly non-leopard-print-wearing person, Lindsey had buried it deep in a drawer. But now, wearing it made her feel closer to her twin.

Since she didn't need Jace giving her another talk about holding it together, she forced steel into her spine and tried to block out the upsetting images around her. Now wasn't the time for a breakdown. There was work to do.

"Someone was looking for something, don't you think?" she asked, attempting to take in the damage with fresh, non-panicking eyes.

"Maybe. Maybe they just wanted to get your attention when you showed up. Like they knew you would."

"That would seem to lead back to Griffin. He showed up when I was here."

Jace leaned over Lena's desk, disconnecting cables from the back of the system without comment.

"Are you taking that back to your place?" she asked.

"Yeah. You said you thought they were using her

webcam. I'll see what I can find."

If she'd been brave enough, *she* could have tried to find something.

While he was occupied, she wandered into Lena's bedroom, looking around to see if it appeared anyone had been here since she'd last left it. She saw nothing out of sorts—at least, nothing that hadn't already been out of sorts.

Lena's bed was in disarray, the comforter balled up at the foot, the sheets ripped back. Somehow, the sight of it was worse than anything else. Lena always made her bed. Ever since she was big enough to do it, she'd made her bed before school, and nothing had changed as the two of them aged. Lindsey had been the messy one.

She was in the middle of straightening the fitted sheet when Jace came into the room. "What are you doing?"

"I can't stand seeing her place this way," she said, voice shaking. "Maybe I can't put it all back together, but I can do this one thing. My sister couldn't stand an unmade bed. She would make mine if she came to visit me and found it messy."

He watched her for a few seconds, then moved to the other side and helped her straighten the comforter over the mattress.

"You don't have to do this," she told him, not daring to look up as he leaned over to swipe a wrinkle smooth.

"I know."

Lindsey found the decorative pillows on the floor and arranged them the way Lena had always liked. Then she set the bedside lamp upright again, and the room looked almost normal.

They walked back into the living room, where Jace lifted Lena's all-in-one unit and tucked it under his arm, glancing around. He seemed to read her thoughts: it wasn't right to leave it like this. "Don't worry about it. Help her put it in order when we get her back, Lindsey."

When we get her back. Such an optimistic idea. But it also drove home the fact that this was really happening. It all still seemed too surreal, like Lena should walk in the door right now.

Maybe if Jace could figure something out, that day would come soon.

He wasn't like most men she'd known. Though frankly, she hadn't known many, at least not intimately. Her guys had been mild-mannered, a little geeky, and safe. A shelter she could run to, rather than the storm that caught her out in the middle of nowhere.

While Jace had forced her to find her own strength instead of leeching off his. Though why she was comparing him to past boyfriends, she had no idea; it wasn't as if he would ever fall into that category. He was an address she'd been given, a name dredged up from the mists of the past.

But he insisted on taking her somewhere for dinner, to her utter confusion. While they sat mostly silent waiting for food, she tried to watch him over her cup of coffee without being too obvious about it. He wore jeans and a black sweater, and not a single person who came in the door was spared a full assessment by his sharp, dark eyes.

"Do you think we were followed or something?"

she asked at last, having to mentally prepare herself for those eyes being turned on her.

"Nothing is beyond the realm of possibility." He seemed to remember his own cup of cooling coffee and picked it up. His hands were big, graceful, capable of flying across a keyboard with blinding speed, as she'd seen, but also hard and calloused and no doubt capable of fucking someone up. They'd felt so strong holding her shoulders yesterday that she still felt them there. It took her a moment to steady her breathing.

He'd told her not to ask any questions about his military service. Okay. But she was dying to. "Will you at least tell me what branch you served in?" she asked, prepared for a brutal refusal.

"Air Force," he said with an unmistakable note of finality. But she couldn't stop herself.

"You saw combat?"

The way his eyes flickered up at her then, catching the light and flashing, he didn't even have to answer the question. They were full of festering darkness, hidden nightmares. "I did."

"Sorry. I'll shut up about it."

It's all Lena's fault. My God. Why is he here?

"Thank you for doing this. I know you don't have to or have any reason to."

"I have my reasons. I wouldn't be here if I didn't."

"Okay." The man seemed to have a firewall around his heart, but there had to be something in there she could find, something to connect with. "You got my story, but I never really got yours. Are you from Denver originally? Kind of weird that we all ended up in the same place, don't you think?"

"I live where I'm told. So originally, no, I'm not from here. I was bounced around Texas foster homes until I aged out of the system."

"Oh," she breathed. "I'm—"

"Save your sympathy."

Lindsey stammered for a moment. "I-I just mean… it's not an ideal life for a child."

"Neither was a fucking abusive, alcoholic father who used my head as his personal punching bag and a mother who didn't give a shit." He rubbed absently at a spot just outside his hairline over his right ear. Once he seemed to catch himself and dropped his hand, she noticed a faint scar where his fingertips had been.

When she'd been in his apartment earlier, she'd noticed nothing festive, no Christmas decorations, not a single thing that would indicate the spirit of the season, while all around them, even now, lights sparkled and carols played.

Lindsey would love to get caught up in it herself, but she had too much on her mind to partake in any Christmas joy. It was normally her favorite holiday, but she hadn't put her tree up yet, either, even though she'd told her mother another lie and said she had.

"Do you have any family you ever talk to?" she ventured, feeling intensely lonely all of a sudden.

"I have the only family I need," he said. Whatever that meant.

"That's good."

The waiter came and delivered their food—a burger for him and a tuna melt for her—and she took in his every move as he forcefully salted everything on his plate.

I can't stop looking at him.

The realization was the disturbing impetus she needed to tear her gaze away and pin it to her food. Even when he'd insisted that he feed her before she went home tonight, she'd struggled to find any shred of an appetite. It hadn't been there then, and it wasn't there now. Her anxiety had ratcheted up to levels that eclipsed everything else.

He didn't have any such qualms. Lindsey forced herself to nibble her sandwich, but he was done before she'd even managed to get through half of her food.

A group of adults and laughing kids came into the grill, bundled up in coats and scarves, and she smiled at their carefree merriment, almost wishing she could be one of them.

When she glanced at Jace, she found he was watching them, too.

And she realized she was a whiny brat. She *had* been one of them, once upon a time. Except for Lena's occasional shenanigans, she'd had a model childhood.

Abused, removed from his home, probably moved all over the state…and then horribly betrayed just when his life was looking up, had Jace *ever* known much happiness? No wonder he had no room for her tears. *Save your sympathy*, he'd said, but how could she?

"Do you have a girlfriend?" she asked, blurting the question before she could talk herself out of it. He'd mentioned a "prior commitment" last night, after all.

"Why?" he asked.

Lindsey shrugged. "You asked me about my love life yesterday. I can't return the favor?"

"Did you see my place?"

"Yeah."

"Did it *look* like I have a girlfriend?"

"No. It was supremely male. But that doesn't mean you don't have a girlfriend, just that she doesn't live with you."

"Supremely male." He chuckled, wiping his hands on a napkin. "No. No girlfriend. Even one who didn't live with me would probably try to liven up the place."

"I don't know. Maybe she's a goth chick or something."

"I did have a goth girlfriend once."

"Ah. What happened?"

"Well, we were only seventeen, so it's not like it was going to last."

"My parents started dating at sixteen. They just celebrated their fortieth wedding anniversary."

He lifted his beer bottle. "God bless 'em."

"They're pretty incredible."

"Poor you for getting stuck with Lena for a sister." He winced as soon as he said it, rubbing the back of his neck. "I guess I need to stop doing that, huh?"

"I get it. And you're absolutely right. Sometimes I've wished *so* hard for another sister or brother to share the Lena burden. But my mom had fertility issues, and apparently they were lucky to even get us."

She could practically see the disparaging comment about Lena being more a curse than a stroke of luck trying to make its way past his lips, but he held on to it somehow.

"I don't know what to do," she admitted, picking at the toasted crust of her sandwich. "I don't know whether to bring them into the loop or not. It'll kill them, and we don't even know yet who has her or why. Or even *if*."

"Better to keep them out of it as long as possible, at least in my opinion," he said.

"They'll be furious at me for doing that, though."

"I get it, but most likely it's for their own good."

Lindsey nodded and glanced around again, feeling eyes on her even though no one appeared to be looking.

Ever since Griffin and the webcam, she'd felt that cool phantom breath on the back of her neck, the skin there prickling as if waiting for the slice of the ax.

"I'm scared," she admitted. "I feel like anyone who walks in the door might... I don't know. Do something horrible to me. If it happened to my sister, why not me? I have my cell phone off right now, but it's scary to think someone could be tracking me as easily as you did Griffin. The thought of not having it on me is even scarier, though."

"Keep your phone." He crossed his forearms on the table and leaned closer. "Lindsey, I don't mean to alarm you, but depending on who we're dealing with, they're going to find you if they want. Giving you my location wasn't a fluke. For whatever reason, they wanted you to know it, too. They probably knew I'd get that computer eventually. They might have even planned on it."

She didn't like hearing that. She hated the mysterious *they*. But with each hour that ticked by, it seemed less likely Lena had up and disappeared on her own. She had to face that sooner or later.

"It doesn't make any sense," she fretted. "We're just supposed to wait until someone lets us know what to do?"

"That isn't my style."

She hadn't been in his company for very long, but she already hated it when suspicion filled his eyes. When he studied her a little too closely, wariness tightening his jaw and his delectable mouth. He didn't trust her, and she couldn't exactly say she blamed him, but it grated her nerves. She'd done nothing wrong, but how could she prove to him that she'd told him everything?

This shift in his demeanor seemed to happen every time she expressed her utter confusion about the whole thing. But there was no other way to feel about this.

"You asked about Lena's enemies. What about yours? You're involved in this, too."

"My enemies are my business."

"Dammit, Jace." Realizing she was getting loud, she lowered her voice and leaned forward herself. "I think they're my business, too. It's at least somewhat possible someone is holding my sister hostage. I can't even think too much about what she might be going through, and don't you *dare* say she would deserve whatever she gets or I'll—"

"I would never say that." His voice had chilled at least thirty degrees. Something about his expression told her he'd seen things no one would deserve, not even an archenemy.

"Okay, but I can't stand feeling this helpless while it doesn't seem to be bothering you at all."

"Because I never feel helpless."

"Never? Never once in your life?"

"I grew up with some of the roughest sons of bitches you could ever imagine. I could have curled up in a corner and felt sorry for myself, but I didn't. I learned from an early age how to help myself."

"You still feel sorry for yourself."

"What?" Now his voice was an arctic blast, so cold she sat back, but despite the trembling in her very bones, she pressed forward.

"You're still so bitter about what Lena did to you that you practically assaulted me in your hallway the first time I came to find you."

"If I wanted to assault you," he said, "you would know."

"That makes me feel so much better."

"I really don't give a fuck how you feel. We're not friends. We never will be. I don't know you; you don't know me. You're not going to gain any insights into my soul. It's not here for you to analyze. So don't think you're going to kick your way inside just because someone told you to knock on my door after all these years. No one else has ever cracked me open, sweetheart, and there's no reason to think you're fuckin' special."

He was right. They weren't friends, so the reasons for the pain that lanced through her heart would remain a mystery to her. Snatching up her purse, she rummaged through it for her wallet.

"Stop. I got it." He'd leaned to the side, digging

in his back pocket for his own wallet. But before he could draw it out, she'd thrown a couple of bills on the table and shot to her feet, jostling silverware and accidentally knocking a glass over in the process. Someone a couple of tables over snickered, probably thinking a date was going terribly wrong.

"You're an asshole," she informed Jace Adams, but as she was marching out, he only laughed.

CHAPTER TEN

She marched blindly toward the parking garage, her breath steaming in the wintry air. The restaurant was around the corner from Jace's building, so it wasn't a long walk, but it felt like five miles. Snow flurries flew around her face, tiny cold kisses on cheeks burning with anger, as her legs ate up the distance.

Footsteps pounded behind her, but she only sped up, even though it was futile to try and outrun him. Jace fell into step beside her. "It's not something I didn't already know," he said, and she figured he was referring to her calling him an asshole.

"Good. Now it's been reaffirmed for you."

"I'm sorry if I hurt your feelings."

"Just speaking truths, I guess." She pulled her coat tighter and quickened her steps. "Please leave. I'll let you know if I hear anything. It'd be great if you do the same. Until then I don't think there's any need for us to speak to each other."

"Why are you so mad?"

"I'm not."

"If calling me an asshole and stomping away from the table is you *not* mad, then…"

"When I get mad," she snapped, tossing his words back at him, "you'll know."

He laughed. Like this was all a game to him. For all she knew, he'd set all of this in motion. He was downright scary on a computer; he always had been. What if he was exacting his ultimate revenge on her sister for the years of hell she'd subjected him to and was taking Lindsey down for good measure? Far-fetched? Sure. But this whole fucking situation was far-fetched. Dear God, why hadn't it occurred to her before? What if she'd walked right into a trap, and he'd set it?

"Really," she said, "I want you to leave me alone."

"You shouldn't walk at night by yourself."

"I walk at night by myself all the time. I'm a big girl. Good night." She couldn't go much faster without breaking into a trot, though, but she pushed herself until sweat trickled down her back even in the frigid temperatures.

Jace didn't falter, matching her stride for stride, shoving his hands into the pockets of his black coat.

"What's the matter?" he asked. "You're pissed, I get that, but you look like you've seen a ghost."

"I'm fine. Just cold. And exhausted. I'm ready to get home to bed. So please, leave me alone."

"Lindsey." He put a hand on her then, stopping her, and her heart leaped into her throat.

"If you try to hurt me, I swear to God I'll start screaming," she ground out through chattering teeth. "And maybe you can take me down, but you'll have a hell of a time trying."

"Hey," he said, his dark brows drawing together. "Hey, now. I talk a lot of shit, you know? But I would never hurt you. In fact, if another motherfucker laid a hand on you right now, I'd rip it off."

"Why? We aren't *friends*."

"We don't have to be. I'd do that for a stranger."

Maybe he was right, and she needed to stop getting so offended about everything.

It was only that she remembered those feelings all those years ago—the flutter in her belly when she watched him in class. The way she'd thought of him in the darkest hours of the night when she touched herself.

It had been his name ricocheting through her head when she came, sometimes even during her rare college sexual encounters. No one had affected her like he had, all from simply sitting across the room from her.

And to stand in front of him now, all these years later, and think about those harsh words shooting from his lips, aimed at her like bullets…

But he couldn't know any of that. It shouldn't even matter, because he wasn't the same person. In many ways, neither was she.

Even though her mind had taken a dark detour, imagining that he might be behind all this, looking at his earnestness right now, his sincerity, she found she couldn't truly believe it.

Or maybe she didn't want to.

The falling snowflakes caught in his dark hair, glistening under the street lights as she stared up at him, and it was all Lindsey could do not to reach up and brush them out. God, was she going insane? Her brain was like a pendulum, swinging from one extreme to another.

From *he's going to hurt me* to *oh God, I want to kiss him.*

"So, um…if I need you, is there some way I can reach you?" she asked.

"Call me."

She'd expected something a little less overt than

that, but like he'd said: these people no doubt knew right where they were. Probably at this very moment. She felt that breath at the back of her neck again, freezing the sweat that had gathered there during her speed-walking attempt.

She pulled her cell phone from her purse and powered it on, then navigated to contacts and handed it over so he could list his information.

"You can disable the GPS in your phone," Jace said as he typed, "but regardless, you can still be tracked if someone has the know-how."

And they probably did. She also figured Jace had her number from his cyber snooping, so she didn't bother offering it.

"Any time," he said as he handed her device back. "All right? Night or day."

"Okay."

"Leave it on. Yeah, that does mean anyone can find you, but it also means *I* can find you. Leave it on, never power it down. Never let your battery run out. That way if I can't get a trace, then I know something's wrong."

She nodded.

"And let me walk you to your car."

Lindsey agreed to that, too, her exhaustion so heavy that she couldn't think around it any longer. If he or anyone else wanted to knock her in the head and drag her away to wherever her sister was, let them. She'd been dumb enough to stumble into the trap, right? She'd always thought she was pretty smart, but she didn't know which way was up anymore.

Jace opened her car door for her after she remote

started it, admonished her to be careful, then closed it after she got in. He even stood watching until she turned a corner and was no longer able to see him in her rearview mirrors.

Emptiness crowded around her. Heat blasted from her air vents, blowing her hair with its force, but she was still chilled inside. And would be until this was over.

CHAPTER ELEVEN

What a jackass he was. An asshole, like she had said. But Jace had to force himself to walk back to his apartment instead of following Lindsey home and camping out in his truck all night to make sure she was okay.

Getting emotionally involved would get his ass in the most trouble. Lena's computer was still in his truck, so he made a stop to get it while an image of Lindsey's amazingly astute green eyes lingered at the front of his brain. Yeah. Keeping her at a distance would probably turn out to be the hardest thing he'd ever done.

He wanted to be, well, *nicer* to her, but she had the wrong fucking guy if she wanted this shit sugar-coated.

He banged on Helix's door, ready to talk through everything he'd learned and come up with a plan of action, but there was no answer at his brother-in-arms's door.

The others were always an option, but Helix was usually the first one he went to. The two of them had seen things together that might send someone else screaming into madness, and there was nothing quite like that bond, that shared understanding.

But it looked like a brainstorming session would have to wait.

Which sucked, because now he would be stuck in his own head all night, rehashing everything she'd said, everything he'd said to her. The hurt, the briefest flash of absolute utter devastation in her expression at the restaurant when he'd slammed down his walls and severed her feelings in the process. It was for the best, and someday she would probably realize that, but that didn't help him feel like any less of a shit for saying those things to her.

He'd have to be more careful with her fragile heart in the future. Lena had been mean as a snake; she could take any shit anyone could dish out. Lindsey was obviously the total opposite. He could keep her at a distance without being a complete dick to her, he supposed, even if it was the easiest way.

He didn't want her to hate him so much that she wouldn't come to him if she got into trouble.

Sitting at his desk, he brought up her cell phone GPS and watched as she maneuvered through the streets. Someone, anyone else, might be watching her at this very moment, too, and his jaw muscles clenched.

Don't get emotionally involved.

He was already breaking his number-one rule, and he'd only spent a few hours with the woman.

But there was no telling what kind of dark-web shit these women had unwittingly been caught up in. It might very well be that someone wanted revenge against Lena even worse than Jace did—or it might be way, way worse than any of them had ever imagined.

Human trafficking immediately sprang to mind. Except that she would just be gone. No phone calls, no demands to find Jace or anyone else. Lindsey would never see her sister again, and he couldn't bring himself to think of what she might be enduring, no matter how much he hated her.

There was another alternative niggling at the back of his brain, but it was one he only wanted to extract and examine with Helix. So he could tell him how stupid he was being by even bringing it up.

Scrubbing his hands over his face, he glanced at the clock and then finished watching Lindsey's journey home. He stayed with her until it looked as if she entered her building on the other side of the city and then moved no more. She was home. He checked on Griffin—still no movement. Jace wasn't sure how the guy fit into anything. He might very well be who and what he claimed—a concerned friend. But very few people were who and/or what they claimed.

Which was why, earlier tonight while Lindsey had been dressing, he had installed a listener on her computer to see if there was anything she was keeping from him that he needed to know. It wasn't that he genuinely thought she was in on the whole thing anymore, though it might be good to keep her on her toes in that regard. But if she was compromised or being forced into doing something against her will, he needed to know. Shitty and intrusive, yeah. But utterly necessary.

Never mind that he was holding a secret about Lena that could shake the very foundations of everything Lindsey thought she knew about her twin. There was nothing to be done for it. He had to cover his ass, and as he'd told her—he wasn't her friend.

He'd planned on doing it through her email at

first, since it was still easily accessible to him, but then he had the golden opportunity to visit her apartment. Lindsey probably wouldn't have trusted anything he sent her himself. His plan had been to clone one of her work contacts and name his payload after a file they'd recently exchanged—something she would readily click on, which would allow him to exploit her system and give him access to record from her computer's mic.

No need for all that now. He sat back and tried to tamp down on the guilt over invading her privacy like this. He could let those feelings through if he didn't find anything. If he did...well, he would be glad not to be made into a fucking sucker again over a pretty girl asking for his help. Surely she wouldn't fault him over a little self-preservation, and if she did, that was her problem.

Never again. Never, ever fucking again, Lindsey. I'm sorry if you can't understand that.

He wasn't able to gain access until the next evening. And he began to see what a quiet life she led.

Since he'd seen her apartment, he could imagine her there amid the cozy and comfortable surroundings—nothing like the chic and modern decorations and furniture that had been strewn around Lena's place. He listened while she talked on the phone to someone who could have only been her mother, never mentioning Lena.

He sipped coffee, listening to her voice, her laughter, her efforts to sound normal, and wondered if only he could detect the faint tremor underneath her words. After she assured her mother more than once that she was fine, he decided that no, he wasn't.

Silence fell for a while after she ended her call. In the background, he could hear her TV and the unmistakable voice of Bart Simpson. He had to chuckle. In fact, she surprised him even further as time wore on and she flipped over to *South Park*, giggling at the most inappropriate jokes.

His need for knowledge about her activities became a fascination with *her*. What made her emit that musical laughter despite everything happening in her life. The sound of her typing—he imagined slender fingers flying over her keyboard with lightning speed.

When he heard her munching on something that sounded like potato chips, he thought of those pretty downturned lips he'd scarcely been able to look away from over dinner.

And later, of all things, she started playing *The Legend of Zelda*. He knew that old-school, original Overworld theme music anywhere. It had been one of the constants he had relied on during his years of foster-home living. Video games and computers. They had saved his fucking life, given him a connection to people and to the world outside.

But some of the memories that jaunty tune unearthed made his breath burn through his lungs and his heart lodge in his throat. It was so familiar to him it had practically become ingrained in his soul.

All at once, he jumped up and turned his whole fucking system off. There wasn't any time for shit like that. It was as if she had plugged into his head and downloaded information she shouldn't have any access to.

She couldn't have any way of knowing. There was no other explanation aside from her being a fan of the series, too. Which meant she was girlfriend material.

And there *damn* sure wasn't any time for thoughts like that.

He plugged up Lena's computer and set about finding out who had exploited her system and how. It didn't take him long.

Crafty bastards, that's who. But there was nothing he couldn't find if he worked at it long enough; this was his art. After hours of staring at the screen, he sat back, fingers steepled under his chin, one uncovered message on his screen, the letters standing ten feet tall and burning themselves into his mind.

    hi wraith

He knew his next move, at least, if Lena's captor didn't make one first. But he needed to talk to Helix, the idea in the back of his mind growing larger with each passing minute, no longer capable of being ignored.

But Helix had been MIA for a couple of days—nothing unusual, really, the man's sex life was the stuff of legends—so Jace was left to his own devices. All he learned during his intermittent snooping and listening in at Lindsey's apartment was that she was a homebody, a gamer, had few truly close friends—if any—and was a bit of a geek. She talked to herself sometimes. She hummed to herself a lot. She sang

Christmas carols in the shower—surely that was a seasonal thing. *Hopefully.*

Nothing sordid. Nothing suspicious. She talked to no one about Lena. She talked to no one about him. He began to feel like an even bigger asshole than he had already. So after day three, he stopped listening to her altogether, when that huge weight of guilt he'd been holding back finally crashed through to suffocate him.

She must be telling him the truth. Unless, of course, she'd fully expected him to do something like this.

"I don't know," Helix said a day later as the two of them went over everything Jace had learned during his stakeout. Where he'd been—or whomever he'd been with—had put a spring in his step. "Most people don't have the suspicious minds we do."

Yeah, he had a hard time remembering that sometimes. "You're probably right. I only spent a few hours with her, but she never came off as insincere. I can't see her having the guile to pull off something like this."

"But we've been wrong about that before," Helix pointed out, turning his chair in a lazy circle.

And that was the damn truth, too.

"Seems to me," he went on, "you need to spend more time with her. Get closer to her. Obviously you aren't finding anything out this way."

Jace grumbled an incoherent response.

"Do what I just said instead of growling at me."

"Fuck off."

"I'm thinking Sully might be on to something.

I've seen you run laughing into the face of death before. Right into it. Sometimes I never thought I would see you come out again. But here you are, avoiding this girl who apparently couldn't hurt a mouse."

Jace glared murderously at him, gunfire and explosions ringing in the spaces between his ears. "I'd hate to have to physically remove you from the premises."

Helix laughed. "I'd hate that, too."

"What do you expect me to do? Move into her fucking apartment?"

"Nothing that extreme, and you know it."

"Yeah, yeah. I know it wouldn't hurt to go check in on her. We didn't part on the very best of terms. But look at this."

He brought up a map, zooming in until the center of the screen rested on a rectangular, nondescript building on the outskirts of the city.

"What am I looking at?" Helix asked.

"I traced the IP of Lena's attackers to this place. But it's air-gapped, and I can't get in."

"Could be a proxy."

"I'm sure it is. But it's all we have to go on, unless we want to sit back and let these assholes come to us. If I can get in there, I can figure out our next move."

"Great! When are we going?"

Jace shook his head. "When am *I* going, you mean."

"That's what *you* meant," Helix said cheerfully, "but what *I* meant was when are we going?"

"Has it ever occurred to you that this has something to do with Rhys?"

Helix's expression froze, and he fell silent—which was remarkable for him. Jace watched his throat constrict as he swallowed.

"I'm sorry to bring it up," he quickly added, hating to have to drop that particular ax on his brother's jovial mood.

It had taken a long time for Helix to forgive himself for what had happened all those years ago. If he ever had at all.

"I just... It's me, man. It has to be me these fuckwads are targeting, no one else. She was told to come to *me*. It probably doesn't have anything to do with Lena or Lindsey. I'm not saying it's a sure thing, but who else would have this much of a grudge against me? Who else would know the perfect way to drag me in?"

"Then I'm damn sure going with you when—"

"No. I want you out."

"*Jace.*"

"Don't even ask again."

"Then why the fuck tell me at all?"

"Because I hoped you'd tell me I'm way off on this."

Helix cursed, rubbing the back of his neck, his agitation heartbreaking to see. "No, you aren't. It makes sense. But I don't get why you want me out. He wouldn't only target you. He would target all of us. We all have a stake in this if what you're saying is true."

"Because I'm the one who ruined him."

And almost killed him.

But no one knew about that, not even the Captain. He didn't necessarily want them to know now. It wasn't something he was proud of. But after what Rhys had done, what he'd used Helix to do, he'd deserved every blow Jace had given him.

And he'd given him plenty, at least three for every death their former brother had caused. "Look, I didn't want to think it myself. I want to keep all options open. It's just that this one is starting to make sense. He knew all about Lena and how I ended up here. And he knows my call sign." Jace brought up the message he'd uncovered and showed it to Helix, only for him to curse a blue streak.

He could sympathize. He felt like doing the same or saying "fuck it," jumping a plane, and running from past demons forever. But that was chickenshit and wasn't him.

Question was, how much did he tell Lindsey?

CHAPTER TWELVE

It wasn't long before the call she'd been dreading above all others came.

"Lindsey? I can't get ahold of Lena. Have you talked to her?"

Lindsey finished stirring sweetener into her cup of hot tea and closed her eyes as she set her spoon aside. "Um, no, I haven't, actually."

"That's odd," her mother said. "I know she tends to disappear, but she usually returns my calls eventually. When was the last time you talked to her?"

"I'm not really sure. It was before the party."

"Me too."

It was sad that her sister's disappearances were so sudden and so common that no one really thought anything of them, not even her own parents. If Lindsey had dropped off the face of the earth, there would have been a manhunt organized. Because she was always home. She had no life.

"I hope she's okay," her mother was saying.

"She's always griping about the cold. She's probably lying on a beach in Bali. You know Lena."

"True." But her mom didn't sound quite convinced this time.

She needed to see if Jace had found anything. What was taking so long? It had been five days since they'd visited Lena's apartment, and nothing. Patience wasn't her virtue. That was a trait she and her polar opposite twin actually shared.

Thank God, her mother didn't stay on the phone long, so Lindsey didn't have to perform too many mental acrobatics to deflect her questions. But guilt was like a gut punch. If her parents found out— *when* they found out—she had been keeping this from them, they would never forgive her.

As she carried her cup of tea into her living room, ready to pile up on the couch in her sweatpants and Netflix the day away, her doorbell rang.

Ugh. She was so not in the mood for company. But when she pressed the speaker button and said "Hello?" the warm male voice that answered nearly made her drop her cup.

"Hey, it's Jace. You got a minute?"

"Uh. Um, uh, yeah, sure. Come on up." Damn. She was in sweats, a hoodie, and a two-day-old topknot. For him, she had all the time in the world, but couldn't he swing by when she looked presentable?

Why did she care so much?

Gently, she set her cup down. And then she bolted around her coffee table in a dash to her bedroom. A glance in the mirror showed her how hopeless it all was—one look at her hair down made her pile it back up again. Then she only had time to brush her teeth before he was at her door.

He, of course, was perfection. She tried her damnedest not to notice, but all her efforts were futile. The cream sweater and brown leather jacket he wore accented his tan complexion, and those thigh-hugging dark jeans just wouldn't quit hugging those thighs.

"Did you find anything?" she asked by way of greeting, beckoning him inside. As he walked past, she inhaled the scent of leather and something subtly sweet that made her want to push him down and lick him all over.

"Maybe," he said after she closed the door. Her cooling tea still sat on a nearby accent table. She picked it up and walked toward the kitchen, at once dreading and anticipating what he might say.

"Can I get you anything?"

"No, I'm good."

"Sorry, I wasn't expecting anyone or I might've tried to look more presentable."

"You look fine."

Gee, that was reassuring. She wanted to pull her hood over her head, run into her bedroom, and jump under the covers. But she watched him closely as he slipped his jacket off, taking note of the grim set of his lips, the tension in his jawline.

He looked as if he were ready to leap out of his skin, and that couldn't bode well. Lindsey felt the beginnings of panic build in her chest. Mechanically, she tossed her tea down the sink, her stomach roiling, and rinsed out the cup.

"Jace? Tell me."

He took a seat on her couch, leaning his elbow against the arm and rubbing his brow. "I don't know where to start."

"Is my sister—"

"I don't know any more about her or her whereabouts than I did."

Lindsey, suddenly overheated, unzipped her hoodie and tossed it away, not giving a crap anymore how she looked or that underneath the jacket she was wearing an old T-shirt she'd had for years. "Okay." She dropped into the chair across from him, watching him over the coffee table between them. "Isn't no news good news?"

He looked at her then, seemingly for the first time since he'd come in, eyes taking in her sloppy hair, her makeup-less face. And then her T-shirt. "Are you wearing a *Zero Wing* shirt?" he asked, murdering her fantasy that he might have been staring at her boobs.

"Oh God. Yes." Blushing madly, she tugged the shirt hem outward so he could see the badly translated *All your base are belong to us* quote.

He laughed, and it was a thing of beauty. Not the cruel, biting laughter she had heard from him before but a genuine, robust laugh that brightened some of the darker places in her soul. "That's awesome," he said.

"I'm a bit of a retro gaming geek." She crossed her legs under her and gestured toward her entertainment center, where some of her consoles were on display and some were stored in the various cabinets. "It's readily apparent, huh? I have no life."

"Ah, but you do. Since you're a gamer, you have many."

"True, true. But, um…can we get back on the subject of my sister?"

"Sorry." He leaned forward, bracing his elbows on his knees, his posture more relaxed now. "I traced the IP of the people who were watching you from her webcam. I know where it's coming from, but I can't find any information about the address, and I can't get into their network because it's air-gapped."

Lindsey sat up straighter, fired with excitement. "Do you think that's where she is?"

"Not necessarily. In fact, not at all. I seriously doubt they would just give me her location like that."

"Well…maybe they're stupid?"

He chuckled, but this sound rang hollow, no humor to be found. "I doubt it."

"But we're going to check it out, right? I mean, leave no stone unturned."

"Of course," he said, raising an eyebrow at her, "but what's this *we*? 'Cause that ain't happening."

"Don't you dare think for a single minute that I'm not in this with you. She's my sister. I'm going to be there when we get her, Jace. How do you think she's going to feel if *you* bust in to rescue her? The one man who probably hates her more than anyone else on earth? It'll probably scare her to death."

"Aren't you the daredevil," he said. "I like it. But there is no fucking way I'm bringing you in on this. If I can get in that building and scope it out, crack into their network or security systems, I'll be able to figure out what's going on. There's no need for you to put yourself in danger, and I won't let you."

"You can't go by yourself. What if something happens? What if I never hear from you again? If these people can make you disappear like she has, I'll lose it, Jace." At his odd look, she added, "You're the only hope I have in this. Who would I go to then?"

"That isn't going to happen. You have my word."

"Oh, bullshit. What's your word worth if bullets start flying?"

"It wouldn't be the first time I've faced a bullet, Linz. It probably won't be the last."

She sat back, chewing on her bottom lip.

"Look, if it'll make you feel better, I can tell you who to get in touch with if you don't hear from me after a few days."

"That *won't* make me feel better."

"You'll be a liability, all right? I can't focus on my own safety if I have to be worrying about yours, too."

"But—" Her doorbell rang again, cutting off her protests. "Grand Central effing Station," she muttered, unfolding herself from her chair and stomping over to the speaker. "Hello?"

"Hey, sunshine. Got a minute?" It was her dad.

Lindsey drew a long, tortured breath. Wonderful. "Sure. Come on up."

Jace raised his eyebrows as she sat back down.

"That was my dad."

"Oh yeah? Is he a big guy? Should I be worried?" That cocky grin showed he wasn't worried at all, but the implication made Lindsey jump to her feet again.

"*Shit.* What will he think? You're here, and I look like I just tumbled out of bed."

The grin widened maddeningly. "I can answer the door shirtless, if you want."

"Dammit, Jace." Lindsey looked around in a panic but then forced a few calming breaths through her lungs and put her palms out to mimic pushing her worries down to a tolerable level. "Okay. Who are you, and what are you doing here?"

"Quit worrying about it. If you answer the door with a bloodred face, you're only going to arouse more suspicion. Act normal. I'm a friend. Nothing more."

Right. He was totally correct, but the little pang that went through her chest hurt regardless. "Oh, so *now* we're friends?"

"Or not. It's up to you."

Before she could bite back at him, she was opening the door for her dad, trying to look normal…most likely failing miserably.

"Merry Christmas!" He held up a little wrapped present that would fit into the palm of her hand, his blue eyes twinkling.

"Dad! You shouldn't have." She stepped back so he could enter, getting on her tiptoes to kiss his scruffy cheek, which was still cool from the chill outside. "We always open presents on Christmas Eve."

"I know, but I wanted this one to sit under your tree and torture you for the next week." His perceptive gaze landed on Jace over her shoulder. "Oh. I'm sorry, I didn't realize you had company."

"Um, Dad, this is my friend Jace. He just stopped by a little bit ago. Jace, this is my dad, Edward."

Jace stepped forward with his hand offered, cool as ice. "Pleased to meet you, sir. I'll get out of your way so you can visit."

"Oh no, that isn't necessary at all," her dad said, his sudden eagerness as he pumped Jace's hand bringing Lindsey's head around to him incredulously. God, even her dad realized how dry her dating pool had been lately. "In fact, I was going to ask Lindsey if she wanted to ride home with me and have dinner tonight. You should come, too, Jace; you'd be more than welcome."

"Mom didn't say anything about dinner," Lindsey

protested helplessly, that panic swelling up in her throat again. "I just got off the phone with her."

"Do you *really* think Mom would mind? She'd be thrilled to have you. Both of you. Let's surprise her. It'll make her day."

Jace's dark eyes were laughing as he took in Lindsey's absolute sputtering confusion at the turn of events. "Dinner sounds great with me. I appreciate the invitation."

Lindsey stared at Jace as if he'd lost his mind, while he looked like the cat who'd eaten the canary. He might think this was funny as hell, but she hadn't brought a man to meet her parents since... Oh, it didn't even bear thinking about. This was a cruel thing to do to her, and he didn't even realize it.

"Fine," she relented. "We'll be there. I need to get ready. Is a couple of hours okay?"

"That's perfect. Nothing fancy, though."

"Okay. Thanks for the present. I'll put it right under the tree." She'd finally gotten around to putting it up a couple of days ago.

"No peeking," her dad said sternly. Then he said his goodbyes and was gone.

Trying to maintain her composure as best she could, Lindsey walked over to her little tree and placed her gift under it. Then she whirled on Jace, wishing she had something to throw at his head. "How dare you do that."

"What?" he asked innocently, surveying some pictures of her family on her wall. Of her and Lena, the same one that had gotten broken and stolen at Lena's apartment.

"Going to dinner at my parents'? Really?"

"Consider it investigatory," he said casually, not even looking at her.

"Investigatory? What for? They didn't kidnap their own daughter."

"Maybe not, but any little clue might lead to something. Does Lena still have a bedroom at your parents' house?"

"We both do, but you aren't going to find anything there. She hardly ever visits them."

"All the more reason for her to keep something there."

"I doubt it. But we'll do it anyway." She stalked toward her bedroom. "I have to take a shower. Wait out here." *Or please don't; I wouldn't object, even if I'm mad as hell at you.*

"Why are you snapping my head off? What's the big deal?"

Hadn't he seen it? Couldn't he tell? Did she really have to stand here and spell it out that her parents were getting on up there in age? They'd lost all hope in one twin daughter ever reproducing before they passed away—Lena flat-out refused to ever have a child—and now they were quickly losing hope in her. Her dad finding a man in her apartment was probably a cause for a damn celebration. He might be on the phone to her mother right now, who would be brimming with hope that her daughter had gotten spectacularly laid today.

But Jace wouldn't understand that at all. He would think she was insane; he didn't feel those pressures, no parents waiting on him to present them with a chubby-cheeked grandchild.

And Lindsey herself wasn't necessarily in any hurry to do that. But her parents were another story. They were always trying to set her up, get her out of her apartment, introducing her to their friends' sons and even grandsons. She'd walked into that trap more than once and had spent most of the time hiding in the bathroom or staring at her plate throughout painfully awkward dinners.

She just wasn't good at it. If Mr. Right didn't fall in her lap, she wasn't ever going to find him. Because she wasn't about to go out looking. Constant rejection and reminders of her social ineptitude were too emotionally taxing. Who needed it?

"You just don't get my parents. They'll be planning a wedding shower by the time we get there. I don't want to give them any ideas, but I know how they are." She sighed. "And they're going to embarrass me. I feel it."

He turned to look at her then. "What do you have to be embarrassed about around me?"

Everything. "There will be something. I promise."

"Afraid they'll break out the baby pictures? Be glad you have some. It should make you feel better knowing I'm not there as a date."

It should. But it didn't. Even as she was in her shower, shampooing her hair, she imagined opening her eyes to see him standing on the other side of her fogged-up shower door. As built as he was, he would have no trouble lifting her against the wall. As hot as he was, he would have no trouble getting between her thighs; she would gladly wrap them around him. A gasp escaped her lips at the mere thought of his cock sliding home, hard and forceful, pinning her against the wall.

It had been so long. It would hurt. She would want it to. His body would invade hers, hard and slick and unforgiving, driving her wild, forcing a cry from her with every thrust, obliterating the loneliness, the fear, until nothing existed but the two of them—

Shit. Lindsey yanked herself from the fantasy, one she might happily revisit tonight while she was under the sheets with her vibrator, but not right now while the man was two rooms away and about to be sitting next to her at dinner with her parents, of all things.

Get it together.

She had to convince him to let her in on the stakeout.

When she emerged half an hour later feeling somewhat presentable, he glanced up from the couch where he sat thumbing through his cell phone. "You look nice," he said.

Nice worked for her about as well as *fine*, but she supposed she shouldn't expect miracles from him. She wore jeans and tall boots with a long black sweater, leaving her hair in its natural waves.

"I need to go with you when you move on this building," she said in place of a response. "I mean it, Jace. What if I can see things that you won't? What if, for instance, Griffin is part of this whole thing, and I see him on the premises? You wouldn't know him if you saw him. I have information you need."

"Maybe you have a point there," he said. "If this guy approaches you again, though, snap a picture of him—if you can get away with it. We'll see if he's someone I recognize."

Enemies. The first time she'd asked him if he had any, he'd turned the question sharply aside, but that only proved to her it was an avenue worth investigating. If they were going to work together, he couldn't keep these kinds of things from her.

"Why do I get the feeling there's something you're not telling me?"

He unfolded from her couch, stretching to his full height. "Not sure."

God, he was frustrating. She put a hand to her forehead. "Are you sure this is the best idea? We can always cancel. It's not you, really, it's that I'm afraid I won't know what to say if they start asking too much about Lena. I'm afraid I'll break down and tell them everything."

"I always advise against bringing in too many people when there's trouble. But you know them best. Will it do any good to make them worry yet?"

"No," she said sadly. What he said was the best course of action. It was the idea of sitting with them under the weight of this knowledge, this danger, while they were completely oblivious.

"You'll be fine," he said casually, strolling toward her door. "Should we go now? Do we need to stop for a drink or something first, maybe get our stories straight?"

A drink sounded magnificent. "Maybe. Actually, yeah. Let's do that."

He chuckled as he shrugged back into his jacket. "Of course, alcohol acts as a truth serum for some, so you'd better watch out for that."

"I'll take it easy," she said as she slipped into her

own coat. Maybe at some point, she needed to get *him* good and wasted.

CHAPTER THIRTEEN

He was still amazed this woman could have an identical twin sister in the CIA. How could these two have turned out so different from each other? One of those mysteries of life he would ponder from now on. Maybe some of the pieces to this puzzle would start to come together tonight. He was actually looking forward to getting to know her parents.

And she was damned adorable.

They'd made a quick stop for one drink before heading over to her parents' house. Jace watched her as she surveyed the bar around them and wished, completely out of nowhere, that there weren't any walls between them. They'd been erected by him and were necessary, but it would be nice if they could dispense with them just for a night. Have a real conversation. But there was so much he couldn't divulge, and everything he said seemed to rub her the wrong way.

"So, Lindsey. Why is it I don't remember you from MIT?"

"What, do you want to see my transcript?" she asked warily, and there it was again. He sighed.

"No, that's not what I meant at all. Maybe I just want to get to know you a little better."

He'd already seen her transcript, anyway. Impressive.

"Why?"

Blunt, wasn't she? He thought carefully about his answer. "Any girl who wears a *Zero Wing* shirt is worth knowing."

"Oh, please. That's like the dorkiest thing I own."

Dorky, maybe. But it had made him want to strip it off her and see what was underneath it.

"I already told you," she said in answer to his question. "I kept to myself in college. I focused on my work. I didn't party or even date much. I'm still that way." She screwed her face up in a rueful expression. "That's sexy, isn't it?"

"What if I told you that was incredibly sexy?"

She'd been fiddling with her drink coaster, but she fumbled and dropped it as soon as he said the words. "I'd tell you that you have odd ideas of sexy."

"Sexy is relative. Beauty is in the eye of the beholder and all that. Fuck what anyone else thinks, right? You should have approached me. You're the kind of girl I would've loved to hang out with back then."

She blinked at him. "Really?"

"Well, you know. I was a pretty happy-go-lucky guy. I mean, here I was, a kid a step away from living on the streets, and somehow I managed to land one of the most prestigious universities in the world. It was a dream come true, and I was so glad to be there, I walked around feeling like I had hit the jackpot."

"I bet," she said, a note of sadness entering her voice. "You must have worked your ass off to get there, and—"

He waved the words off. He didn't want to rehash all of that tonight. "No use going over it again. What's done is done. Point is, I was a stupid kid walking around on cloud nine with no fucking clue what was coming my way. Anyone could have screwed me over. I try to be more perceptive these days."

"I know you don't want to talk about it, really," she said, still fiddling with that coaster, her eyes on it instead of his face. "But…I might have mentioned to Lena that I had a thing for you. I have no idea why she would target you that way. She did have a habit of flirting with my boyfriends. I mean, not that you were or anything."

It was dim, but the color rising in her cheeks was plain to see.

"There weren't many for her to go after. But you…" Trailing off, she lifted her eyes to him again. "Maybe she thought she would move in first. And then maybe something went wrong and for whatever reason she wanted you out of the picture. I don't know. I honestly don't. But there it is."

"You had a thing for me, huh?"

"Oh God." She dropped her face into her hands, propping her elbows on the table. "All that I just said, and that's what you focus on?"

Not only was that his focus, but he'd barely heard anything else she said. "Why didn't you ever talk to me, then?"

"Because I was dorky and shy and awkward, and there was simply no way in hell I could've walked up to you and started a conversation. I can barely do things like that now."

Hell. And he'd acted like such a fucking asshole to her pretty much since she had knocked on his door. "I'm sorry, Lindsey."

Surprise registered across her face. "For what? You couldn't have known. You don't even remember me, and I don't blame you."

"No, I'm sorry for how I've acted since you came to me. I'm sorry I don't remember you. I'm—fuck, I'm just sorry for everything. You don't deserve any of this that's happening to you."

She waved a hand as if it were no big deal, but he knew better. "It's okay."

"It's not. I wish there were some way I could make it up to you."

"Help me get my sister, Jace. And let me help. That's all."

He would do his damnedest.

Lindsey's father beamed as he answered their knock at the door, and her mother threw her arms around Jace's neck as if he were a long-lost relative. He had long enough to see Lindsey's stricken expression, but she had nothing to be embarrassed about. As she gave her mother a hug of her own, he let his gaze tangle with hers and sent her a wink.

The table had already been set in the dining room, and it was all he could manage to not stop and gawk for a moment. Roast chicken, an abundance of veggies, mashed sweet potatoes, even lemon pie for dessert. How many times in his life would he have killed for a meal like this?

"I hope it's enough," Mrs. Morris fretted, standing behind her chair and surveying the spread critically.

Enough? He could have invited the whole team and fed them all.

"It looks great, Mom," Lindsey said. As she moved to the chair to Jace's left, he stepped over to pull it out for her. She blinked at him but didn't comment, letting him push it in as she sat. In the soft lighting—hell, anytime really—she was a stunner. He barely took his eyes from her as he pulled up his own chair, but she kept her gaze fastened to her plate.

He hadn't missed the approving glances her parents kept exchanging. Maybe it only meant he was playing right into Lindsey's biggest fears, but he enjoyed the fantasy of being the guy she was bringing home to meet her folks. Maybe a little too much.

"Well, dig in," her mom said brightly.

Her parents kept the conversation light, which was fortunate because Lindsey was wound so tightly next to him she was ready to launch into space. They talked about the weather. About Christmas. He noticed there was no mention of Lena whatsoever.

Just as Lindsey seemed to go off alert, her dad wiped his mouth with his napkin. "Where are you from, Jace?"

Lindsey went still. Jace set his fork down and gave his full attention to Mr. Morris's polite inquiry. The lies usually came easily, but for some reason, they didn't this time. These people were too nice to deceive, but he never risked the truth in these situations. His made-up past was far preferable over his real one. "Boulder, sir."

"How did you and Lindsey meet?" Mrs. Morris's eyes sparkled at him from across the table, as if she were preparing to hear the most romantic tale of her life.

They'd already gone over this on the way over, choosing the safest route. "We work together."

"At Denicorp?" her dad asked. "That's great. I have a joke for you."

"Oh God," Lindsey groaned under her breath, but her dad went on, heedless.

"A programmer's wife says, 'Honey, please go to the market and buy one bottle of milk. If they have eggs, bring six.' So the programmer comes home with six bottles of milk. When his wife asks, 'Why in the world did you buy six bottles of milk?' he says, 'Because they had eggs!'"

Jace had heard it before, but he laughed anyway because it always got him. Lindsey put her face in her hands. "He loves that lame joke."

Jace nudged her with his elbow. "How many programmers does it take to screw in a light bulb?"

"Spare me, please."

"None. It's a hardware problem." That one was Helix's favorite.

Mr. Morris cackled. Jace grinned at Lindsey, seeing her shoulders shake with laughter she tried her best to suppress. "Come on, you know that's killin' ya," he teased, and finally she lifted her face from her hands, reluctant amusement written all over it. She'd never looked more beautiful to him than at that moment. She wanted so much to laugh, *needed* to laugh, and didn't want to let herself. But he'd learned to grab moments of joy when he could.

"Eat your food," she said, prompting another round of mirth.

"Yes, ma'am."

He met every question after that with a carefully

cultivated lie, the same ones he had been telling for years when the situation called for it. Lindsey let him take the lead for the most part, sipping from her water glass and keeping her mouth resolutely closed. Easy for her, since he was the one under the gun here.

She was right about what she'd told him back at her apartment. Her parents were desperate to see her married off. He kept those expectations at bay as best he could, if solely to spare Lindsey from having to explain their "just friends" status over and over.

She had so much to offer. How was it no one had come along and snatched her up? He maintained a cynical view on such matters, ordinarily— the common denominator for someone with a graveyard of failed relationships in their wake was *them*. But Lindsey seemed like a genuinely good person. Maybe when it came to relationships, she had a little Lena in her after all. He kept waiting to see it emerge, but so far it hadn't.

The Morrises had a nice place, with a huge Christmas tree dominating the living room, almost as tall as the balcony of the second floor that overlooked the massive room. Underneath were piles of elegantly, brightly wrapped presents and gift bags.

He looked at them after they retired from the dining room and wondered how many were for Lena. If she would ever get to open them.

Lindsey helped her mother clean up while her father poured Jace a glass of scotch, which he took reluctantly. One wouldn't kill him, though he needed to stay sharp to keep up this charade.

When he spied the large family portrait over the fireplace—Mr. and Mrs. Morris seated in elegant chairs with both twin girls standing behind them— he studied it closely. And he found it was true: even though both of them were dressed conservatively and giving demure smiles for the photograph, he could tell Lindsey apart from her sister immediately. There was a sweetness in her expression that he suspected Lena simply did not possess in the entirety of her soul.

"Amazing resemblance between the two of them," he said anyway, gesturing to the picture with his glass.

"I'm so used to them that they look entirely different to me," Mr. Morris admitted. "In fact, it surprises me when people comment on it."

"I can see that," Jace said.

"It's a shame Lena hasn't been around much lately. You could have met her. Then you'd see how different they are."

Trust me, I already know. He shuddered at the thought of coming face-to-face with the woman again, taking a drink to hide his distaste.

"Do you have any brothers or sisters?"

"No, sir." It was easier than explaining he probably did, somewhere. He didn't keep in touch with his parents any longer, but they were still out there, and no doubt they'd procreated again at some point. Unfortunately. "And I actually haven't minded that fact, truth be known."

Mr. Morris chuckled. "I have three sisters, and believe me, there have been times when I would've completely understood where you're coming from."

Jace almost, for a moment, wished that this whole setup could be the real deal. A great girl, a good family, a gigantic Christmas tree with a metric fuckton of presents under it. Nothing like that had ever seemed to be in the cards for him, but that didn't mean he didn't think about it sometimes.

Helix and Sully and the other guys would blow a gasket if they knew. Sully viewed the idea of marriage and kids like most people did a root canal. And Jace would say that Helix's bed was like a revolving door, but he never brought his women to his own bed at the Nest. He always took his carnal delights elsewhere, which was a good thing.

But yeah. Getting out, making a break, leading as normal a life as possible. The thought held its charms at times.

"Yes, night and day, those two," Mr. Morris was going on, still staring fondly at his daughters' images. "Lena's the more free-spirited of the two. Can't keep that one in one place for too long. Half the time we don't know where she is or what she's up to, but I guess she likes it that way." He sipped from his glass. "Frankly, sometimes, I think that's probably for the best."

Sir, you have no idea.

"What are you two talking about?" Mrs. Morris asked cheerily, breezing in from the kitchen with Lindsey on her heels. The latter looked a little down, but she forced a smile for him, and he wondered what sort of conversation had transpired while the two ladies were cleaning up. She'd probably endured her mother going on and on about what a respectful gentleman caller she'd brought home to them—

when he was anything but. He'd have to make this up to her somehow, he decided.

"How different the girls are," Mr. Morris said.

"And thank goodness for that. I'm not sure we could handle two of either of them." Lindsey's mom laughed as she sat on the couch beside her husband, which left Lindsey to perch on the loveseat next to Jace, frowning in confusion.

"What would be wrong with having two of me?" she asked.

Cuteness overload, Jace thought as her mother said, "Oh, Lindsey, for all of Lena's wildness, it's you we worry about the most. She can take care of herself."

"And I can't?"

"Well…" her dad said, probably sensing the impending conflict. "I'm sure that's not what she means, sunshine. But sometimes I think if we didn't make you get out, you'd hole up in that apartment of yours and never be seen again."

"I do go out. Just because I don't tell you guys every time I do doesn't mean I'm sitting alone dying of spinsterhood. And this didn't get incredibly embarrassing just now, thanks."

Her mom and dad laughed while Jace put his nose in his drink and let them carry on. The situation seemed better off without his input. But as the evening wore on, she relaxed a little, even sitting back next to him as if she didn't want to take his head off for subjecting her to this whole thing.

Eventually, what he figured was her worst nightmare came to pass, and her mother dragged out old photo albums. She was as cute as a baby as she was now. He also laughed to see there were several photos of Lena torturing her in some way when they were children. Lena always seemed to have a big wicked smile on her face, while Lindsey was caught in the middle of an epic-looking wail.

After a time, though, Lindsey quit smiling as she looked down at the pictures, reality obviously intruding on her thoughts. The one her parents had no idea about. He didn't think she would hold it together for much longer. After a few seconds, he managed to get her attention when she glanced up at him, and he tipped his chin toward the upstairs area.

"There's probably a lot more old pictures and stuff in our bedrooms," she said, maintaining eye contact with him. "Let's go see what we can find. I'll give you the grand tour."

He stood with her, not missing the hopeful smiles her parents exchanged.

It almost made him glad he didn't have anyone to meddle in his affairs. Almost.

"You two didn't share a room, huh?" he asked as she opened a door at the end of an upstairs hallway.

"Hell no. Not since we were tiny. I hated sharing a room with her as much as she did. If not more so. Do you really think you're going to find anything here? Seems a long shot."

It was. He'd just needed an opportunity to do a little recon on Lindsey and her folks, and this had seemed like a good one. "You'd be surprised how often long shots hit the target."

"Right. Well, there's her old laptop—no telling how long it's been sitting there or even if it still works. I have no clue where to begin looking for anything else. Like I said, she hardly ever stays at home. Maybe at the holidays. Sometimes not even that."

Because she was out of the country so often, no doubt. Lena was obviously a master at maintaining such a level of secrecy, but he wondered how she accomplished it. It was easy for him. He had no close relatives endlessly sticking their noses in his business.

He sat at her laptop while Lindsey stood at the door, making sure her parents didn't come snooping while he was snooping. As he figured, her machine was clean, but that didn't lessen his frustration.

"I guess we're on," he said, shutting it down.

"Surveillance?"

He spun the little desk chair around to face her. "*Only* surveillance. All right? If you're insisting on going, Lindsey, I'm not risking anything more. We'll watch, but we won't interfere."

She actually looked excited, and for some reason that broke him down a little. Her expectations were too high. "When? Jace, we can't wait—"

"Tomorrow," he said, cutting her off. Dread churned in his gut as soon as he said it, but he confirmed it all the same. "Tomorrow, we'll go."

She nodded. "Okay."

"Now. Show me yours."

"Um...huh?"

"Your room," he said, grinning. "Show it to me."

"Checking on me, too?"

"Maybe." He stood and followed as she led him to the next door down, taking note that her hair was quite remarkable in this muted light, the paler individual strands catching what illumination there was and sparkling. The scent she left in her wake, that soft floral essence… He wished he weren't so ignorant about such things. Was it lilac? It fit her, somehow. Whatever it was, he liked to think that if he came across that particular flower at some point in the future, it would immediately remind him of her.

"I'm afraid you're going to be disappointed," she said as she opened the door in front of them and flipped on the light.

He was anything but. Lena's room had been sparse, but Lindsey's looked as if someone still lived here. No machines he could snoop through, but it had the personality that had been lacking in her twin's room. A whimsical canopy still hung over the bed. The drapes were airy, the bed piled with fluffy pillows. It was the room of someone who wanted beautiful things around her.

"This is the house you grew up in, right?" he asked, turning to look at her from the center of the room. She still stood near the door, for some reason looking as if she wanted to bolt.

"It is."

She really didn't know how lucky she was. Or maybe she did, but in his experience, most people who had grown up in a stable home didn't. They always had something to whine about. All he had ever wanted was parents who gave a fuck. At the same time, he wondered if he would've worked as hard trying to make something of himself.

"You know, you shouldn't be so hard on your

mom and dad for only wanting to see you happy," he told her.

That brought her gaze up to meet his. He could clearly see she wanted to argue but maybe thought better of it when she reflected on what she knew of his history. What little she knew. Drawing a breath, she gave a nod. "Maybe you're right."

"I am. They obviously love you very much."

"So…you…I mean, I have questions. But I don't know if I should ask them."

"You can ask." He shrugged. "I might even answer."

"You're from Texas?"

"Dallas, originally."

"How old were you when you were removed from your home?"

"Eleven."

"God. So young."

"Yeah. They voluntarily terminated their rights. Didn't try to get me back at all."

"I know you told me to save my sympathy, and I will. It's only that I find it so hard to believe they didn't see what a brilliant kid they had."

"I guess it's hard when you're high or drunk all the time. And I admit, I was difficult."

"Well, of *course* you were," she said as if it should be patently obvious, and he noticed it wasn't only her hair that collected the light beautifully but her green eyes, too. Those impossibly deep, understanding, green, green eyes.

Dude. Stop. Last time you got caught up in eyes like those, you lost your fucking soul.

They had been staring from a completely different mind, though. A different personality, a different set of intentions.

"Did you ever come close to being adopted?"

"No, not really. People looking to adopt want cute babies and toddlers. Impressionable kids they can make their own. Hardly anyone wants a troubled little shit. I'm sure people who would are out there, and I'm sure many of them have good intentions, but I was never interested. I learned to make my own way. I liked it like that."

"I would imagine, given your particular skill set… I mean, have you…?"

"Have I looked up my parents?"

"Yes."

"No. Not once. Never. I have no idea if they're dead or alive. I don't care." They hadn't even come to any visitations child services wanted to set up. They hadn't been interested in counseling or parenting classes. Some of his fucking caseworkers had been more motherly than his own mom. But the agency had a lot of turnover, and no one had stayed in his life for very long. "My mom and dad gave up on me, so I gave up on them."

"Wow," she said softly. She crossed her arms over her midsection, almost as if she were hugging herself, as if the very thought caused her to need comfort. He rubbed at the back of his neck, glancing around at the warmth and safety of her childhood bedroom.

"So, yeah. You have it good, all right? I wouldn't mind some meddlesome, matchmaking parents myself at this stage of life."

She chuckled. "Well, you might change your mind if you had them, but you *have* given me a new appreciation, I guess. Thank you."

"My pleasure, Lindsey."

She blushed. And speaking of pleasure near a blushing, beautiful Lindsey looking impossibly luminous with a bed ten steps away was a dangerous thing. He didn't give a damn they were in her parents' house. In fact, every new wall that sprang up between them only made him want to tear through them like the fucking Hulk. Every new reason why he shouldn't want her, even one as trivial as their current location, only made him want her more. It had always been so easy to turn himself off, to not feel anything he didn't want to. This time was different. And he didn't understand it, nor did he like it. At all.

He didn't have time for relationships, didn't want the entanglements and deceptions that often came with them in his line of work. This was a relationship kind of woman. She was made for candlelit dinners and midnight promises, and he didn't have any of that shit to give. She needed some button-down type from her job or something. That kind of guy would fit in with this life, her, and those nice people downstairs.

Lindsey cleared her throat, bringing him back from the sheer fuckery of his thought process right then. "Should we go back down?"

"Yeah. Sure." Taking one last look around, at everything he'd never had and never would, he followed her out.

CHAPTER FOURTEEN

"N-Tech," Jace said, staring at the nondescript, unimposing structure on the quiet, tree-lined street. "At least, that's what it was, a data storage facility, though everything I found said it was no longer in operation. Now I don't know what the hell it is; they want to keep it secure." It was just a boring building.

But Lindsey supposed that not all bad guys' lairs could be decrepit and sinister. It was only a couple of stories tall, rectangular and sitting at a quiet intersection.

The large street numbers above the door were the only signage: 1248. Jace and Lindsey sat in a car across the street that was as unremarkable as the building. She found that funny. It seemed even more suspicious.

Might as well be in a plain white van. It was broad daylight, and all they were doing for the time being was watching. Lindsey sipped her coffee, her eyes on the glass front doors. "I know what you said about the IP address," she said, "but I can't help but wonder if my sister is in there right now. It makes me want to storm the place."

"I know what you mean," Jace said. "There's always the possibility that it's the safest site to keep her because it's too obvious. It's happened before. Still, they shoot themselves in the foot by doing that."

And she discovered, as time crept past at a snail's

pace, that she sucked at this. She wasn't a person who could sit in one place for very long…at least not in a car, staring at one door because she feared she might miss something if she looked anywhere else. This was boring as hell. Jace had the patience of a saint.

"So your parents are nice," he said after silence stretched out for so long that she almost nodded off.

"Oh. Thanks. Yeah, they're not so bad."

"I guess you had to put up with a lot of nudge-nudge-wink-wink. Sorry about that. I didn't realize when I accepted the offer."

"So you saw, huh? You get it now?" She could feel the color rising in her cheeks as he chuckled.

"Oh yeah, I get it."

God, how frigging embarrassing. Poor single girl who couldn't get or keep a man. Thing was, as much as she'd like to make her parents' dreams of grand-children come true someday, it wasn't a need she felt on some primal level of her being. If someone came along, wonderful. Awesome. But if he didn't, then whatever. She wasn't out desperately seeking male companionship. And while she wanted to tell him all that, it would probably only ring hollow.

Yeah, sure. Like you wouldn't jump his bones right this minute if he offered.

Okay, so she would. That was beside the point. It wouldn't mean anything, only sex.

"Have they tried roping all your boyfriends in like that?"

"The couple I let them meet, yeah. Same thing."

"So tell me about the exes," he said casually, his eyes still on the front doors of the building. "What's your type?"

"Um…I don't think I have a type. I try to keep an open mind. I dated a police officer who my sister knew once. That didn't last very long. I dated a guy from work. But he quit and moved away and didn't have any interest in keeping up the relationship. Neither did I, frankly."

"That it?"

"What, you want my entire history?"

He glanced at her briefly, but his sunglasses shielded his eyes from her. "No, I only figured you had something more serious in there somewhere."

"I don't. I haven't had a relationship that lasted longer than three or four months."

"So. Is it them, or is it you?"

"It was never either of us," she said, her voice rising more than she'd meant it to. "I don't know, reasons have ranged from no chemistry to nothing in common to just no damn reason to keep going." She shrugged. "No excitement, I guess. And hey, why am I always under the gun? What about your exes? This I can't wait to hear."

"I lost my virginity when one of my foster sisters crawled into bed with me one night," he said conversationally. "Do you want to hear about that?"

"God no! I didn't ask anything about sex. Oh my God. That's horrible, Jace."

"Hey, I didn't find it so horrible. I was a horny sixteen-year-old. She was seventeen. It was pretty awesome."

"I don't want to hear about how awesome it was."

"Aw, why not?"

His cocky grin was not having the desired effect this time. Instead of setting her on fire, it was pissing her the hell off. Maybe because all she'd been thinking about was having awesome sex with him, and it made her a little jealous to think of all the women who had come before. *Pun intended*, her mind added, and she dropped her forehead into her palm with a chuckle.

"What's so funny?"

"Never mind. I'm over here making myself laugh."

"I can't be in on the joke?"

"Nope." How long was she going to have to sit in this car with him? He was awful. "You're a bad man, aren't you?"

"Damn right I am." It was said with no bravado whatsoever.

"If we got irrefutable evidence that she's in there right now, what would you do?"

"Me? You're the one talking about storming the place. What would *you* do? I want to hear this."

"I would get myself killed. You're the military man. So, tell me?"

"I'd get her, Linz. Never you mind how." That was said with even less bravado. It was a cold, hard fact.

"What are they waiting for?" she asked miserably, feeling the helpless rush that accompanied the question every time it flickered through her mind. "And do *they* really even exist?"

Jace sighed, running a hand through his hair. He left a little tuft sticking up, one she immediately wanted to smooth back down. "I haven't quite told you everything," he said. "I'm debating whether to tell you at all, because I'm not one hundred percent about it."

"What?" she asked, turning in her seat to face him.

"I'm not going into any more detail than I divulge right here in this car, Lindsey, and if it leaves this car…" He trailed off, and if he couldn't even finish that thought, she knew she didn't want to chase it down.

"Okay," she said quickly. "It won't leave this car."

"I'm part of a team. We'll leave it at that. This team has an ex-member who left under bad—under *extremely* bad circumstances. You asked about enemies once? I have one. This enemy knows about Lena. If he's the one who got her, then he's the one who was in her apartment, which means he would know about *you*. What he's doing, or what he's after, I can't even guess at right now. If I knew, I would tell you, I promise. I have no idea what he's waiting on, but whatever his reasons, they can't be good."

"Oh my God, Jace. You think he's only using my sister and me to get to you? I mean…okay, but *why*? Why bring us into it?"

"None of us on the team was squeaky clean to begin with. Hell, you know what I did. Some of the others have done way worse. Rhys—he was one who'd done way worse. Thing is, he didn't stop. And the last straw, the last thing he did—I beat him to within an inch of his life. If he has a beef with anyone, it's with me."

"What did he do?" she asked softly, fearing to know even as she asked.

He sighed and put both hands on the steering wheel, and she noticed how white his knuckles went as he gripped it. "He killed seven people by hacking into their pacemakers. Only one of them was a target. But the same way I changed several students' grades to protect Lena and myself, he took out innocent civilians to cover his tracks. My friend—my brother—who wrote the code had no idea he was going to do that."

Her hands went to her mouth in horror. "That's even possible?"

"Oh yeah. It's possible."

"Jesus Christ. And *this* is the guy behind this whole thing. Holy shit, Jace."

"Lindsey, I don't *know*. That's what I want to find out. That's why we're here. He's been off the map for a few years now. I figured he had skipped the country. I told him if I ever saw him again, I would finish the job I started."

"I can't believe this is happening," she whispered, staring out at the obscenely bright day. Up above, the sun was shining, the sky was blue, the ground was blanketed with beautiful new fallen snow from the night before. And there were fucking awful things happening in the world, right under their noses. "I don't know what to say. But we have to *hurry*. He could be hurting her."

"If it's any consolation, and don't take this the wrong way, but I don't see why he would think hurting her would be any kind of revenge on me. I'm no fan of hers, as he well knows."

"That makes sense, I guess."

"When I cleaned her computer, looking for the exploit that gave him access to her webcam, I uncovered a message. It was to me and used my call sign."

"Which he would also know."

"Exactly."

"You say you don't know it's him, but it sounds pretty certain."

"It's—I don't know. It seems obvious. But he's making it too obvious, you know? I would expect more cat-and-mouse from him."

"Maybe you're jaded. This seems pretty cat-and-mouse to me."

He looked over at her then, reaching over to take her hand in his. "I'm sorry. This has been stewing in the back of my mind. I debated telling you, like I said. At the end of the day, though, it's at least some insight as to why this is happening to you, and to her. If this is true, then it's all my fault, and I'm so sorry for that."

She stared down at their joined hands, absorbing the warmth and the strength of his, then placing her other over it to give it a squeeze. "It's not your fault. You couldn't have known."

"I can make you this promise: I'll get that son of a bitch. It's the only way I can pay the debt."

"Thank you. That's all I ask. And I promise, your secret is safe with me. I won't tell a soul, ever."

He didn't let go of her hand even after they fell silent for the better part of an hour. The sun kept the interior tolerably warm, but soon enough it went behind a cloud, and Lindsey's breath began to frost in the air. Jace cranked the car to run the heater, but only briefly.

Pacemakers, she thought, still chilled from that confession. Her father had a pacemaker for his bradycardia. If Lena could be a target, why couldn't he?

"My dad has a pacemaker, Jace. I'm scared."

He looked over at her, stroking her hand with

his thumb. "Shit, Lindsey. I didn't mean to scare you like that. I'm sure he'll be fine."

"How can you be sure, though? He struck out at Lena. If he's that evil, then he could be after me, my dad, any other members of my family, just for the hell of it. Now I feel like I need to warn them all somehow, but I can't."

"There isn't anything you can do. It isn't as if you can tell your dad to have his pacemaker removed. But maybe you shouldn't stay at your apartment anymore."

"I'll be okay." Even though she didn't feel like she would be—ever again. The phantom breath on the back of her neck—it followed her everywhere. But he thought she was pathetic enough, so she tried to inject some steely confidence into her voice. "Security is good at my place. Better than Lena's. I don't think there's any way someone could get me there. And I mostly telecommute, so I'm not going in and out all the time. Besides, I don't even know where I'd stay."

"We have extra room." He looked at her for a minute, then chuckled. "I can kind of see your parents' concern. Do you want to turn into the old cat lady?"

"I'm allergic to cats," she said smartly.

"All right, fine. You get my point."

"I like staying home, damn it. I'm not agoraphobic; I'm here with you. I go out when I need or want to freaking go out. I'm fine."

"All right," he drawled, a playful little smile teasing at his lips. He hadn't shaved this morning, and the dark scruff on his jaw boosted his virility into atmospheric levels. She'd love to feel it chafing her in places she shouldn't be thinking about.

Not while on a stakeout where I may need to save my sister.

Jace lifted his camera and snapped a photo of someone entering—he'd parked at an angle that assured them a good view of the faces of anyone going in. There hadn't been anyone she'd recognized.

More time ticked past. Her stomach rumbled, and she shifted in her seat, hoping he hadn't heard. But he had. "Maybe we should take a break."

"Whatever you think. I'm good."

"Are you sure?"

It had become a vendetta. If they left this spot, they would miss something. "You said you have a team. Why isn't your team helping out on this?"

"We tend to deal with our own problems until they become too big to handle on our own."

"Could this one be becoming too big? If this is someone who betrayed your team?"

Jace scratched disconsolately at his jaw. "It could very well be. I wanted concrete proof before I went to them with this. The guy I'm closest to—Helix— I've already fucked him up by even mentioning it. He's the one who wrote the code."

"Jace, maybe it's time. Things seem concrete to me. I'd be willing to gamble on this being the guy, whether you think it seems legit or not. Even if it isn't him... don't they have the right to know? To help?"

She didn't have to know him well to see his stubbornness. "It's all on me," he said quietly, gazing out his window. "I'm the reason there's trouble."

"Will they see it that way?"

"No. They won't. But I do."

"You're being unreasonable. You're not putting the needs of the team ahead of your own personal issues. I don't even know them, but even I see that."

"Astute, aren't you?"

"Well, I try to be."

"Let's go grab some lunch," he said, cranking the engine in a burst of motion that almost startled her. Had she pissed him off?

"Are we coming back?"

"You're determined, aren't you?"

"This is our only lead! If this doesn't pan out, what then? I can't stand the thought of sitting around and waiting anymore. Aren't you still wanting to get inside?"

"You're working your way around to something," he accused, pushing his sunglasses to the top of his head and then putting the car in gear.

"Maybe. But—" She grabbed his arm. "*Stop!*"

"What?" He whipped his head around, and she pointed at the dark-haired man striding to the front doors. "That's Griffin! Jace. That's *him*." Jace lifted his camera and snapped a picture, and then was quiet for so long she nearly smacked him. "What *is* it? Do you know him? Is that Rhys?" How horrifying to think the enemy had been tracking her down.

Griffin pulled open the door and walked in, disappearing from their sight.

"No," Jace said then, sounding forlorn. "Never seen him before in my life."

CHAPTER FIFTEEN

"**O**h, we're going in, dude," Helix said. "No doubt about it now. There's no way you're keeping us from it."

Jace nodded, accepting his fate—or all their fates. After their discovery today, he'd assembled the team and explained the situation. Everyone had sat in stunned silence through most of it. Everyone except Helix, who already knew his suspicions. The only thing Jace had left out was Lena's CIA connection. Only once he'd gotten assent from every one of them had he brought Lindsey in, introducing them all.

"I can't believe you didn't bring us in on this the second you had a suspicion," Sully said, shaking her head. "Not cool, Jace. This affects all of us. You put us in danger by having to be little glory boy all the time."

"What the fuck did you say?" he snapped, not in the mood for any of her shit today.

"You heard me. You always have to be *the man*, rushing in before anyone else. And in the meantime, we had no idea about any of this. You think Rhys planted the code that led you to this place, and you went without telling us, knowing full well if he's behind it, he could have picked us off like sitting ducks any time he wanted."

"News flash, Sully, Rhys can pick your ass off whether you know he's there or not. Today, tomorrow, hell, thirty minutes from now. Instead, he's playing with us."

"At least I would've had the *chance* to—"

Lindsey sat quietly at his side, her head down. She'd remained all but silent the whole time they'd been hashing this out. He tuned out Sully's ranting and focused on her, hoping she was okay.

None of this should be her burden, none of this was her fault in any way whatsoever, but the slope of her shoulders told him that she felt otherwise. "Are you okay?" he asked for her ears only, leaning in a little closer. Dumb question, but he would get her out of here if she wanted to go.

She nodded. Instinctively, he put an arm around her, catching the notice of the others, who exchanged glances. He didn't give a shit. Let them think what they wanted. Lindsey leaned into him, only a little, and he found that she fit perfectly there.

And she could stay there as long as she damn well wanted to.

"Sorry you're going through all this," Drake said to her now. "It's a shitty deal all around."

"It is," she agreed softly. "Thank you."

"We got your back," Helix said.

"Absolutely," Sully put in, though she was still giving Jace a death look. "We would've had it all along. You don't have to go through any of this by yourself."

"She isn't," Jace snapped.

Lindsey looked up at them all through her lashes. "I am, though. I appreciate everyone, I do. But this is the most isolated and helpless I've ever felt."

Jace gave her shoulder a squeeze. She wouldn't want to hear it right now, but he knew that feeling all too well and had for most of his life. Until the Air Force, until the Nest, until this team. "It won't last forever," he assured her.

"We're a family," Sully said. "Like all families, sometimes we fight, sometimes we dislike one another for a while. But like all families, we take care of one another; we'd fight and die for one another. As of now, that includes you, too. If Jace says you're good people, that's enough for us."

"Until you fuck us over, at least," Helix muttered.

"Hey," Jace snapped at him.

"*Hey*, I'm just saying. Rhys wouldn't argue with me, would he?"

"Can we use that name as little as possible?" Drake asked. "Asking for a friend."

"Better get used to it," Sully told him. "I have a feeling you're going to be hearing it a lot. Somehow I always knew that fucknut was gonna show his face again."

"Who is this Griffin guy, though?" Helix said. "We need to figure out how he fits into everything."

"Okay. What do we know?"

"He claims to be my sister's friend, maybe more," Lindsey said. "He showed up literally minutes after I found her apartment trashed."

"It's at least possible that he's telling the truth and he's being set up," Jace told her. "Let's keep that in mind."

"I know. You're right."

"What else?"

"He gave me a number and apparently turned his phone off, which is weird."

"He wanted your number first, though, and you

made him give you his. Which to me says he didn't want to look suspicious by refusing, but he didn't want us to track him."

"Yet they allowed you to trace an IP to a place he apparently goes."

"Maybe he's a catspaw."

"We're chasing our tails here," Helix said. "We can sit and theorize all fucking day long—we excel at it. But we aren't going to know anything until we get off our asses, get out there, and gather some intel, my friends."

"When do we go back?" Lindsey asked, perking up for the first time since the meeting started.

"Hold on there, buttercup," Sully said. "Nothing I said earlier meant that you're now eligible to put yourself in danger."

"She's right, Linz. That's the deal I made with you, remember? Only surveillance. I can't let you in on this. We can't risk them getting you, too." The mere thought made him want to tear down a wall or two.

"I have to help somehow. Tell me what I can do."

"You can stay and be safe." Jace removed his arm from her shoulders and faced her fully. "I know you want to be there when we find her, but even with what we've learned, there are no guarantees where she is. Let us go in and see what we can find out. You know I'll keep you in the loop."

"I want to get a look at their security footage," Sully said. She always did. "We can feed it to the Nest and have ourselves a little viewing party."

"Let me write that code," Lindsey said eagerly, her entire expression brightening. He could plainly see how much it would mean to her, but the others were already shaking their heads, and so was he.

Sully was the one who spoke for them all. "No way."

"I can at least feel like I'm contributing somehow."

"No offense, but we don't know you. All we've got is Jace's word that you're good people, but how long has *he* known you? I may trust him with my life, but that doesn't extend to you, and, frankly, it probably never will."

A lesser person might have been intimidated. Sully's tone brooked no argument, and she aimed her words with wounding precision. But instead of shrinking under that steely tone, Lindsey seemed to puff up with indignation at every word. "Frankly, I'm not concerned with earning your trust or anyone else's in this room. My one objective is Lena. She's the only reason I sought any of you out. What good have I done her if I don't help?"

Sully's lips curled in a particularly dangerous, feline smile. Lindsey's mere offer to write code had aroused more suspicion in his crew than confidence. One fuckup—intentional or otherwise—could leave them vulnerable. "You wanna do good, sis? Let the grown-ups handle this."

As the two stared each other down, Lindsey fuming in the face of Sully's casual mocking, Jace might have been content to see how the feud played out, but discord at this point in the game wouldn't help anyone. "I've seen what she can do," he said, looking around at them all. "She showed me."

"She hasn't shown *us*, though, has she."

"Then let her," he fired back at Sully.

"All right. I wanna see her hack the motherfucking FBI."

Eyebrows went up all around the room, but they nearly flew off their foreheads when Lindsey fired back, "Give me a motherfucking challenge, at least."

"Oh!" Helix bellowed, clapping. "Shots fired. It's about to get lit."

Jace rubbed his hand hard down his face. How the hell had it come to this?

"Talk is cheap," Sully said, but she sounded a little less confident than she had a moment ago. "I want hard, cold proof. Bounce off a minimum of six satellites. Show me an internal memo from Deputy Director Briggs. Then maybe you can play our reindeer games."

"Briggs? What a dickhead. I'd rather know what kind of porn he watches. Gimme some dirt." Drake rubbed his hands together in glee. He was all about unearthing what lurked in the darkest black soil of the human heart—most of which could be found online.

Sully rolled her eyes. "Dude, you're such a pervert."

"I accept your little challenge, such as it is." Lindsey got to her feet and looked at Jace. "May I?"

This could all fall spectacularly to shit within the next few minutes, but the gauntlet had been thrown. If Lindsey didn't prove herself here and now, none of them would ever accept her. Sighing with resignation, he waved an arm in the direction of his desk. "You may."

She sat in his chair and rolled her neck on her shoulders, cracked her knuckles…all her rituals. He had them, too, and while he wanted to move to her side and watch, he gave her all the breathing room she needed. Several pairs of assessing eyes watched her back, the rhythmic clatter of her limber fingers across the keyboard almost musical.

Even her posture seemed straighter, more self-assured. This was where Lindsey was at home. All traces of the helplessness she'd spoken of earlier were wiped away. Fascinating to watch. Jace could scarcely take his eyes off her even as the others shifted to other interests. Helix fired up Jace's PS4. All the while, Lindsey worked. He watched her out of the corner of his eye, even when Drake roped him into playing *Black Ops 4*.

He knew cracking an FBI server wasn't hard. Neither was removing all traces one had been there. Remaining undetected, *that* was the tricky part. Their bots ran constantly, sniffing for shifting IPs.

Jace was rooting for her, but deep down he didn't have a lot of faith. He knew how *he* would crack Briggs. But if she—

All heads turned as Lindsey stood up from his computer and stretched. Sully glanced over and back at the game, snickering. "Done already, huh? You might as well come over and let us kick your ass here, too."

"First-person shooters? Meh."

"Yeah, you look like an RPG girl."

"Oof," Helix said, then cursed as his shooter got taken out.

"Do you like playing as the wizard or the mage?" Sully asked sweetly, batting her eyelashes in Lindsey's direction. She ignored her.

"Got any beer, Jace?"

That was the last thing he'd expected to hear. "Yeah, I should. In the fridge."

He barely managed to contain his curiosity as she strolled casually into the kitchen, even whistling to herself, ignoring Sully's continued barbs. Had she fucking done it or not? She damn sure hadn't produced the requested memo. What was the holdup?

"Lindsey. Yo. You look pretty pleased with yourself," Helix pointed out, surely speaking for all of them as Lindsey came back in from the kitchen. "For someone who's not showing us shit."

"Patience is a virtue," she said and handed Jace a beer of his own.

"Thanks," he told her uncertainly, a little scared of her right now. This was a side of her he'd never seen before.

"My ass, patience is a virtue," Sully muttered to herself.

"What'd you say?" Helix asked. "Your ass is a virtue?"

Sully turned a little on her side and gave said ass a smack. Everyone laughed. Lindsey settled next to Jace on the couch, watching the antics play out onscreen in contemplative silence, sipping her beer. Every so often, she checked her phone.

He had the distinct impression that some shit was about to jump off, but when or where, he could only guess—but it was approximately an hour and a half later, in his apartment in Denver, Colorado.

Lindsey's phone chimed with a notification. Jace glanced over as she got up from the couch and took her seat at his desk again. This time, silence followed her, and then the others, curiosity finally getting the best of them.

"All right," Sully said. "What the hell have you been doing?"

Jace's printer spat out a sheet of paper. Lindsey snatched it, then slapped it down on the desk for them all to see. "There's your memo. Are you sure that's all you needed? I'll be happy to take all his files, if that's not good enough for you." All her earlier nonchalance was gone without a trace. Pure savagery burned in her eyes now.

Sully grabbed the paper, with Jace reading over her shoulder. She'd done it. She'd fucking *done it*.

And Sully knew when she was beat. "How'd you do it? Explain."

"I didn't go through the FBI servers. I went through his home network. One layer of security, compared to several at the FBI. Then I attacked from his router, which was already whitelisted and wouldn't draw any suspicion. While I was setting up my proxies—six satellites, as requested—it was no problem to whip up a Trojan I could drop on his router and log his keystrokes to get his passwords, but I also realize that two simultaneous logins is a wonderful way to get caught. So, I waited for him to logout and go to bed. And now that he has, I have full access to his laptop, his account at the FBI, you name it. I can jump to their servers now and show you anyone's emails that you want."

Drake opened his mouth, shut it again. Sully simply stared at the paper in her hand. Jace rubbed the back of his neck and exchanged a glance with Helix, who was the first one to finally comment.

"Daaaamn," he drawled.

Lindsey stood up, facing Sully almost nose to nose. "I prefer to be the mage," she informed her, then glanced over at Drake. "By the way, Briggs likes MILF porn." She grabbed her beer, chugged the rest of it like a frat boy at a kegger, and slammed the bottle on the desk.

While they all stared at her in slack-jawed awe, Drake's gaze drifted over to Jace. "Dude. I am so erect right now," he muttered.

Jace knew the fucking feeling. He'd gone from six to midnight himself.

But if he knew anything about Sully, even when she was down, she was never out. She folded the page and tossed it in the trash. "So, you can write code. You're not one of us. I still say no."

Lindsey's mouth pinched as if she were biting down on words. It was Helix who spoke up. "Sully, put your ego aside for once."

"My *ego*?"

"She beat you. She fucking owned it."

The argument raged on between them, but Jace listened in silence. He should be more suspicious than anyone in this room. But then he examined his gut and looked at Lindsey's work here tonight. Obviously she could handle herself. There was no one more motivated in finding Lena than her own twin sister.

He broke into the fighting with one ringing command. "Let her do it."

"Don't just let her do it," Drake put in quickly, as if he had been waiting for a chance to jump in with his ideas. "Let her be the one to break in and install it. If these are Rhys's people, then one of us can be made on the spot."

Jace had to draw the line there. "It doesn't matter who they are. She's Lena's spitting fucking image. They know her, too. She can't be seen."

But Lindsey's face had brightened from the moment Drake had begun speaking. "Let me do it, Jace, please. I'll wear a wig or something."

"It's too dangerous."

Sully had fallen into an unaccustomed silence after being overruled earlier, stepping back with her arms crossed. But now she spoke up, irony dripping from her words, and she threw Jace's own back at him. "Let her do it. Let's not half ass this, Jace. You want her in so bad, she's in. Put her in the line of fire with the rest of us."

He only glared back at her as she gave him a sarcastically sweet smile. Why did she have to be such a pain in his ass?

"We'll get a couple of guys to head over there and see if they can get the lay of the land," Drake suggested. They employed some scouts for just that purpose. When it came time to get their hands dirty, though, they rarely trusted anyone else to get the job done.

Lindsey was asking for that trust, and he wanted to give it to her, to lessen that helpless feeling she kept describing. Because he knew it so well, had lived with it for so long, and he knew how precious a feeling it was to know someone believed in you. It was even more powerful and motivating than those three little words some people spent their entire lives chasing.

"I'll go home and start working," Lindsey said eagerly, snapping him out of his thoughts.

He had to drive her, since he'd picked her up in their unmarked car earlier. She seemed lighter, somehow, as if having an active part in their mission had given her new hope.

"I like them," she told him once they were navigating the streets. The sky over Denver was like a lead blanket now, no sign of the sunny morning that had greeted them. More snow. The meteorologists were predicting a big winter storm in time for Christmas. "Even if Sully hates me."

He smiled over at her. "Trust me, Sully liked you at least a little, or there would have been no talking her into this."

"Do you have the final say on these things?"

"Honestly, no. If she had kept protesting, I would've had to listen, Lindsey. And she knows that. She relented."

"You guys seem to really trust one another."

"We do." More than that. They were family.

"Thank you for giving me this opportunity."

"It's a big help, really. Frees us up for other things. But Lindsey, I wish you wouldn't insist on going."

"I need to do this." She was quiet for a moment, watching the city pass by. "Lena's always been the strong one. The one charging in, like what Sully said about you. Now it's my turn."

"Don't feel like you have to—"

"I *need* to do this," she repeated. "Even if something bad happens. I know the risks, Jace. It's not for me, it's for her."

"Getting yourself hurt isn't going to help her. Aren't you scared?"

"Of course. Haven't you ever been?"

His methods of facing fear and death had been to laugh in the fuckers' faces. After a moment, he said so.

"Well, there you go. Maybe I'll laugh in their faces, too. It might be a weak, sniveling laugh." She gave him a wry look. "Knowing Lena like I do, and getting to know you, I can't help but think you two should kiss and make up and get married or something. You're a lot alike."

He barked with laughter. "Fat fucking chance of that. Kill me now."

"I'm only saying. I think she was born without the fear gene. If you two didn't have all that crap hanging between you, you'd probably get along great."

"You really think that's what I want in a partner?"

Lindsey cocked her head at him. "Don't people tend to gravitate to those who are more like them?"

"Not necessarily. I don't need a woman to jump out of a plane or some shit like that before I'll give her a second look. I think your sister probably needs someone she can completely control. That ain't me."

"So…you're the one who needs control in the relationship?"

"I didn't say that. Since when does not wanting to be controlled equate to being controlling?"

"Never, but I still think you're wrong about Lena. She does like men who can challenge her."

"Well, for all I care, she's welcome to them."

"I'm only trying to get a rise out of you. And you

always take the bait."

"I do, don't I? Still trying to drive home your point that I'm bitter?"

Her smile was small and secretive and turned him the fuck on against his better judgment. "Maybe."

CHAPTER SIXTEEN

She worked late into the night, after moving the picture of Lena and herself next to her laptop so she could look into her sister's eyes as she did all she knew to save her life. Lena's smile was a tad on the bland side in the picture. But she always had that wistful distance in her expression, as if she constantly wished she were somewhere else, doing something much more exciting. The family had accepted long ago that was the reason for her frequent disappearing acts. Living life on her terms.

Well, she was getting a little more excitement than she'd bargained for now, wasn't she?

At three a.m., Lindsey pressed her fingertips into her dry, aching eyes. Done. She set her laptop aside on the bed and reached to turn off her lamp. Almost before her head hit the pillow, she was asleep, but the nightmares came soon after.

In one, she was fighting an unseen attacker, and she woke up panting and sweating. It took her half an hour to fall back asleep after being jolted awake from the panic, only to fall into a worse dream, one that had no images she could recall. A blank, black wall of dread and isolation and loss, where somehow she knew everyone she loved was gone.

For her, it was hell, and that one brought her awake gasping.

Dammit, she had to keep it together. She went to the kitchen for a drink of water, then strolled to her window to look out over the streets below. Flurries danced past her window, some tiny, some fat flakes that hit the warmer glass and immediately melted.

Lindsey watched the silent, hypnotic show outside, remembering snowy Christmases past when all of them were together, laughing, building snowmen, opening presents, drinking cider.

What would happen this year? When her parents didn't hear from Lena at the holiday, they would know something was wrong.

Was her sister even out there? Alive? She had to be. Some innate twin-sense would surely be thrumming in Lindsey's soul if the unthinkable had happened. Once, when they were seventeen, Lindsey had awakened in a panic one night for no discernable reason. Two hours later, her parents had gotten a call that Lena's then-boyfriend had driven off a snowy road and crashed, sending them both to the hospital. Thank God, they'd been okay, but she'd never forgotten that.

Hell, she'd been running on so much adrenaline and blind panic lately that she couldn't take comfort in that. She couldn't piece together any sense of her sister's well-being among all the noise in her mind. Besides, the eerie connection had only happened that one time.

She couldn't keep imagining the worst. Those were the thoughts Jace would tell her not to let in.

Lindsey went back to bed, but those doubts simply wouldn't stop. She tossed and turned the rest of the night, and when a cold, gray day finally greeted her, she felt as if she hadn't slept in years.

"I know you've vowed a dozen times you're only friends, but are you *sure* that—"

"Mom. Yes. God, please. Stop asking me about him." Lindsey wanted to crawl under the table, certain her face was blazing bright red at her mother's inquisition. But it was the first time they'd talked since the dinner. When her mother invited her out to lunch today, Lindsey knew what the topic of conversation would be. So far she'd managed to steer it in a couple of different directions, but it always came back to Jace.

She dragged her fork through her salad and checked her watch, hoping her mother wouldn't notice how little of an appetite she had. In a couple of hours, she would be meeting him, and every bite she took set her stomach to roiling.

Watching the snow in the silent predawn hours had put her in an odd mood, longing for simpler days long past. Just now she noted how the lines had deepened on her mother's dear, lovely face, and worry for both her parents chilled her blood.

I have to keep them safe. Whatever it takes.

Lena had been targeted—why not the rest of them? She found her blood could run a few degrees colder, and every eye in the restaurant seemed to focus on her. Her imagination, of course, but...she wondered if she would ever be free of feeling as if she were being watched. It was like that webcam light still glowed in her mind. Even in her sleep.

"Your dad really liked him, too. Imagine that," her mother said innocently.

"Mom, at this point, Dad would probably like a gang member."

"You know, you've never gone for brawn before. I was surprised."

"Stop trying to trap me. I'm not *going* for him."

Her mom shook her head almost sadly. "Honey, you're blind if you don't go for that."

Lindsey's jaw dropped. Of the very few men she'd brought around her parents, this was a first. "*Mom*."

"What? It was all I could do not to squeeze his muscles. I even told your dad that after you two left."

"You did not!"

"I did so. Just because I've been married forty years doesn't mean I don't know hot when I see it. So I have to ask again, and you've been avoiding the issue, but I want an answer. What's the problem?"

She didn't have Jace's stone-faced skill of crafting a background out of thin air. Or at least, she never had before. But she'd never tried it. "He isn't interested…like that."

"That's utter nonsense. He hung on every word you said at dinner."

He's a good actor. Lindsey frowned down at her barely touched salad. "I didn't notice that."

"Well, that figures, since you hardly looked at *him*, but the man barely took his eyes off you all night. Now, the untrained eye would think you're the one not interested, but I know you better than that. You get bashful when you like someone. Lindsey, I simply don't think you should pass this up. If no one has made a move yet, maybe you should try."

"You only met him once. I swear, I am *never* bringing a man around you and Dad again."

"Dad said he was at your apartment rather early for—"

"I am *not* sleeping with him, and I would *not* talk to you about it if I were."

Her mom laughed. "If you refuse to talk to me about it, then how do I know you're really not sleeping with him?"

Lindsey dropped her forehead into her palm. "Stop, just...stop. This is so gross."

"Why? Because I want to see my daughter happy? The one daughter who seems capable of it?"

That snapped her head back up. "What do you mean?"

Mom sighed and absently smoothed the napkin in her lap. "I've given up on Lena. Every time I have high hopes for her...she seems to delight in letting them crash. Sometimes I think her lifestyle must make her happy, so I try to be at peace with that. But if I know her as well as I hope I do—as well as I know you—I worry that's not the case. Why does she have to escape so often? Why does she run, and where does she go?"

"I wish I knew," Lindsey said softly. *Now more than ever.*

"But you—you're my stable child. You would make a warm, loving home for a happy family. So when a man stares at you like he sees how precious you are, and you're blushing and fidgeting and doing all the things you do when you're attracted to someone, I have to ask. Yet again. What's the problem? Why just friends?"

It was a most inopportune time to remember the kiss at Jace's front door. The angry, savage burn of his mouth on hers.

Precious? Hardly.

Pure hatred had raged in his eyes. It wasn't there anymore, thank God. Her mom hadn't seen the way he'd been with her then or heard all the rude things he'd said the night they went to Lena's apartment.

Jace had only been acting for her parents' benefit, putting on the mask of a man they wouldn't mind their daughter bringing home. And why did that hurt so much?

"I don't know what to tell you, Mom. It isn't going to happen."

"Why? I mean, my God, Lindsey, is he married? Entering the priesthood? Leaving the country for good? What is it?" She reached across the table to take Lindsey's hand. "I wish you would talk to me. I must have the most private daughters in the world."

Squeezing her mom's hand, Lindsey's heart broke for her mom, and a little for herself, too. She had been taking up Lena's slack for so damn long—was she now becoming just as bad in her own way? "I'm sorry. I don't mean to make you worry about me, but please don't." She drew a deep breath. "About Jace…you're right, I like him. No, he's not married or moving or celibate that I know of. I don't think he's interested, but who knows? Maybe I'll take your advice and make a move.

"But until then, I don't want to be pressured about it. If and when it's right, I'll know."

Her mom gave a little smile, a little nod, and sat back in her chair. "He does have great shoulders, doesn't he? I've always had a thing for shoulders."

"*Mom*. At this point I'm starting to think I need

to worry about *you* moving in on him."

At that, her mother laughed. "Nah. He only had eyes for you, my dear."

Lindsey wished she would stop saying that. The ache gnawed its way a little deeper every time.

CHAPTER SEVENTEEN

"Are you nervous?" Jace asked her on the tense ride to the former N-Tech.

"Yes," she admitted.

"That's not a bad thing," he said. "Keeps you on your toes."

She didn't tell him she hadn't slept a wink the night before, the fear and nightmares a constant companion. She'd always loved living alone, but lately, it seemed to have lost its charm. And as weird as her mood had been before, her mother had made it darker.

Can't imagine why.

"There's a night security guard at the front desk," he said, flipping his turn signal. "All Sully wants at this point is for you to get to his system and install your code. Keeping him occupied is her job. She's very good at it."

Now that the time had come and they were really doing this, Lindsey was struggling to hide her nerves. Jace was wary enough about getting her involved. She didn't need to give him a reason to abort the mission. "I'm surprised she doesn't want to do this part herself."

He shook his head. "I'm sure she would, but she also loves being the diversion. Playing with people's heads is her thing."

She wished that made her feel better. Her sister would probably love this, too—she was made for it. Lindsey slipped a finger under the brunette wig she wore and rubbed at her scalp. "This thing itches," she complained.

"It looks good on you," he said. "Don't mess it up."

"Do you have a thing for brunettes?" she teased.

Jace glanced at her with his devastating grin in full effect. "Could be. Think you'll have less fun?"

"Oh, is *this* fun?"

"It can be." His expression sobered as he saw something she didn't want him to see. "This is what you asked for."

"I know I did. And I'm doing it." If he saw how her hands were shaking, it might be all over.

"You're right, but if you want to back out, now's the time, Lindsey. Say the word before it's too late."

She shook her head. "I'm not backing out. Never."

For the briefest moment, his expression faltered with a resignation that frightened her. He didn't want her doing this, but that was one of the reasons she had to. Didn't he see that?

"When you feel weak," he said, "think about Lena and how she's counting on you, and maybe she doesn't even know it. Think about how proud she'll be when she learned the part you played in saving her. Think about how proud of yourself you'll be. And how proud I'll be."

"Really?"

"Damn straight. I think you're an amazing person, Lindsey Morris. In my life, I haven't known many of them."

She couldn't say the compliment chased her nerves away, but with those words, a sudden surge of confidence thrummed through her. *I have to be Lena.* How incredible it would feel to saunter into that place and do what needed to be done without even sweating over it. *I can do that. I will.* She had the skills. And now they might save her sister's life.

The car pulled to the curb, even farther back than they'd sat while staking it out the day before. Clouds blocked any light from the moon. Only more snow, glowing a ghastly orange in the overhead street lights. She was bundled in two sweaters, a coat, scarf, and gloves. Usually she handled the cold well, but today it had seeped into her bones, chilling her to the marrow.

Lindsey hadn't been let in on every part of the plan. She wasn't one of the team. Jace stared down at his cell phone, utterly silent, and they hadn't sat in the idling car for thirty seconds when he stepped lightly on the gas, paused when they were nearest to the glass front doors, and said simply, "Go."

Everything had been impeccably timed, she realized, right down to their arrival. Wow. But she didn't have time to marvel. She bailed out of the car and did exactly as she'd been instructed. Head down, hood up over her wig, her legs ate up the distance, and she was inside.

Nothing remarkable greeted her. After the dimness of outside, it was glaringly bright. Sparsely decorated. The air smelled sterile, like window cleaner and Lysol. A large U-shaped desk sat at the far end opposite the doors, hallways branching off to the right and left. Lindsey made for the single terminal on the desk, her heartbeat raging in her ears.

Even though she felt like the only person in the world in this too-bright, too-clean room, she knew she wasn't. An entire team was close by, ready to bust in and get her out if she got into trouble. She knew the signal if she needed to make a break for the front door. All she had to do was install her code. It shouldn't take even two minutes.

The monitor showed security footage around the premises on four screens. The guard checked on whatever suspicious activity Sully had set up, his flashlight sweeping around. Other than that, all was quiet.

But even her breath sounded too loud. She plugged her flash drive into the USB port, and even that tiny sound seemed to echo. Her .*exe* file popped up; she ran it, keeping one eye on that window that showed her the guard's whereabouts.

The progress bar crept across the screen at a snail's pace—God, how old was this computer? It shouldn't be taking this long. Lindsey glanced over her shoulder down one hallway, then craned her neck around the monitor to see down the other. She expected Griffin to jump out at any moment, whoever the hell he was. She looked back at her screen.

Error installing program.

"What?" she whispered out loud. Had she done something wrong? "Oh, you piece of shit."

All the pride Jace talked about everyone feeling for her efforts fell to ashes. As good as it would feel to succeed, she would be doubly disappointed to fail. She couldn't leave here without doing what she came to do.

The blinding white walls seemed to pulse and push in on her. She took a calming breath and did the simplest thing she could think of. She unplugged the tower and plugged it back in. It took fucking forever to reboot, and she almost voiced her frustrations out loud to no one.

No way anyone who could hack Lena's webcam would have this dinosaur at the front freaking desk.

As soon as it came back up, she pulled up the security software and froze. She could no longer see the guard. "Okay," she whispered, uttering a prayer to the technology gods as she ran her program again. With each second that passed, her entire being focused on that progress bar, her heart rate went up a notch. She chewed at a fingernail. She shoved her hood back, suddenly sweltering. *Come on, come on.*

The bar passed the point where it had errored out earlier, and wild, breathless hope blossomed in her chest. *Come on!* And suddenly it raced across the screen to the end point, and her most primitive of fixes had miraculously worked.

`Program Installed Successfully.`

Lindsey exhaled a long breath, with thanks and eternal gratefulness to the gods of technology. Grabbing her flash drive, she sprang from the chair, sending it in circles on its pedestal, and bolted for the front door.

And she might have made it. Whether he came around the corner and saw the spinning chair or caught the barest glimpse of her wig just before she went out, a booming voice belted out behind her, "*HEY!*"

Shit oh shit oh shit…

Rough hands grabbed her as soon as she hit the frigid night air, but when Jace's and Helix's faces swam out of the shadows, she managed to catch her scream before it escaped. "This way," Jace hissed, taking her in the direction of where the car was parked. Their feet crunched over the snow, slowing them, and the muscles in her thighs burned as she pushed them to their limits. Behind them, she heard the front doors burst open again and more shouting from the agitated security guard.

Helix intercepted him. "Hey, my man, you got a light?"

"What the fuck are you doing out here?"

"Strollin'."

"Did you see a woman run past?"

"Nah, man."

"You stay right here."

"Whatever you say, chief."

Their conversation faded as Jace forced her to keep running forever through the damnable snow. He was supposed to pick her up at the front. What the hell had happened? She'd taken too long, that's what.

She struggled to keep up with his pace, cursing herself for not having any kind of gym membership. Who would've thought it would ever come to this? One day you sit at a desk until your ass goes numb, and the next you're staking out buildings, running from security in a mad panic. Her heart pounded; her lungs burned. Jace pushed her harder, faster, and suddenly the car swung into view, sitting in an empty lot…thirty feet away, twenty, ten, five—

When he snatched open the back door instead of the front and shoved her inside, she didn't even have time to ask what he was doing. He dove in after her, slammed the door shut, ripped off her wig, and kissed her furiously.

Oh God. Stunned, she fell backward under him, something shaking loose inside her as she plunged her hands into his hair. Her heart began pounding for an entirely different reason, lust trumping adrenaline.

His mouth was hot, so hot, and his tongue dove past her lips, tasting, exploring. The weight of him pressed her uncomfortably into the door handle behind her, but the pain barely registered amid the firestorm assaulting her senses. Her hands roamed his shoulders, taking in the measure of him, the firmness of his muscles, while her lips savored the softness of his mouth, his tongue, the delicious burn of him, the way he didn't let her come up for air—

A sharp banging on the window broke the spell. "Hey! Hello! Hey, you can't be here! What the hell are you doing?" the muffled voice raged from the other side of the glass.

Jace lifted his head from her, giving her a crooked grin that he dropped a split second before turning to look into the blinding light of the guard's flashlight through the window. He struggled to a sitting position, untangling their limbs. Lindsey tried to bring her mind and heart back down from the stratosphere.

Jesus Christ, he can kiss.

She already knew that, of course, but it had been a stark reminder.

Jace opened the door and climbed out, maintaining a sheepish facade with the irate security guard while Lindsey straightened her clothes and tried not to stagger as she got out behind him.

"Are you all right, lady?" the guard demanded, looking her up and down from under a thick set of black eyebrows. He had an even thicker mustache and a fleshy, wrinkled face, ruddy from chasing them...or from whatever he'd been drinking beforehand. She could smell alcohol. It was probably why he hadn't been able to catch them.

"Fine," she said, trying to force all the assurance she could muster into the word because she could only imagine how she must look...red-faced and shaking and freaked the fuck out. Her lips still tingled from the pressure of Jace's, and she licked them to collect what remained of the taste of him. God, it was good. Like all at once having everything you wanted but thought you'd never get. Her knees still quaked.

"I suppose you were too busy to see if a woman just ran past here," the guard said, dripping with contempt.

"You know, I might've heard some footsteps—"

Out on the street, a car peeled rubber, the guard cursing as Jace tried to maintain a straight face. That would be Sully. Lindsey caught a glimpse of her platinum hair as she sped by. "There she goes, I bet," she said.

"This woman had black hair. The fuck is going on here tonight?"

"Sorry, sir, we didn't mean to give you a bad night. I know we shouldn't be here, it was just off the beaten path a bit and we got a little carried away. You know how it is, right?" Jace's conspiratorial manner wasn't having the desired effect. The guard's darkening expression said that no, he didn't know how it was.

"Take it somewhere else, son. There are a dozen hotels around here."

"Yes, sir. I will, sir." Jace was obviously trying not to laugh. Lindsey began to bite down on a smile herself, now that her blood was cooling.

"I ought to drag your asses inside and call the police," the guard bristled when he saw he wasn't getting the worry he obviously thought he deserved. "You got any ID on you?"

Jace opened his mouth to reply, and something in Lindsey snapped. She didn't know what, probably wouldn't ever know. Maybe it was empowerment of what she had just accomplished, or the kiss, but words burst from her in a tone she couldn't recall ever hearing from her own lips.

"You aren't *dragging* us anywhere," she said, hardly noticing when Jace looked down at her with his eyebrows in his hairline, "and I'm certain your superiors would like to get a whiff of that Wild Turkey you've been swigging on the job. I would let us go if I were you." The pause before she added on, "Sir," was filled with cold challenge while she stared at him. The guard's mouth worked soundlessly for a moment before he finally found his words again.

"Get the hell out of here," he snapped, then stalked away.

As soon as he was gone, her bravado deflated, and she couldn't scramble into the passenger seat fast enough. "Oh my God," she panted over and over. Jace slammed his own door and turned incredulous dark eyes on her.

"Where did *that* come from?"

"I don't know," she said, and the feel of his mouth on hers came flooding back as she looked at him. She raised her palms to her cheeks, feeling the fever in them. "I don't think I've ever spoken to another person like that before in my life. Well, except maybe you."

He laughed. "Glad I'm not alone in the club anymore, then. Hey. Good for you."

"What about what you did just now? Where did *that* come from?"

He tore his gaze away and cranked the car. "I had to think fast. I had to improvise."

That was all it had been. But still—he had awakened her. And shaken her to her throbbing, needy core.

"So did I," she said as he pulled away from the curb.

CHAPTER EIGHTEEN

"She did it," Sully said, and Jace breathed a sigh of profound relief. It had taken a huge leap of faith to let Lindsey take this on, but he'd wanted to see her work her magic, and she'd come through. The security feed was on Sully's screen. "Now we'll see who comes and goes through this bitch. And maybe you can exploit the connection and get into their servers."

He'd already planned on doing that. "On it," he said. "Thanks, Sull."

Jace left her apartment and crossed over to his own, where Lindsey waited nervously at his kitchen table, chewing her nails. "It worked," he told her, delighting in the huge, relieved smile that spread across her face.

"Thank God. After that hiccup during the install, I was worried."

"I'm sure it was nothing. Sully will watch the feeds and go through old footage. She'll make notes of everyone who comes in and show them to us. I'll snoop around their servers and see if I can find out how N-Tech fits into this."

She nodded. "Any theories on that yet?"

"Not especially. There must be at least some connection, since you saw Griffin there."

"Have you tracked his phone lately?"

"No," he said. "It didn't move for so long, I haven't bothered."

"Maybe you should try again."

"I can do that. Are you hungry? Thirsty? I know it's late."

"I could do with a gigantic glass of wine right now. One of those entire bottles with a top shaped like a glass? I need that."

He laughed. "Better not. The last thing you need is a hangover. Who knows when we'll have a big day ahead, depending on what we find."

"True. Darn."

"But one glass won't hurt, Lindsey."

"Even truer."

"I'm not much of a wine drinker. So I'll go out and get that, and you stay here and relax. What do you like?"

"Shiraz," she said. "Cheap is fine."

"Great. We'll toast your success." He expected her to beam at him, or blush, as she often did when he complimented her. Instead, she gave him a wan smile and looked down at her hands in her lap. He frowned. "Are you okay?"

"Sure. I'm fine."

She must be tired. He assured himself of it as he went out in the cold, snowy December night. He didn't mind the cold so much. It was the assault of Christmas lights and music that made him grit his teeth and wish Christmas would fucking get here and gone already.

He hated this holiday, something he didn't admit very often, even to himself. He didn't have many memories of his home life before getting kicked into the foster care system, but he did remember holidays being an excuse for his dad to get shitfaced. Afterward, when school resumed after New Year's, all the kids showed up in their new clothes with glowing tales of all the toys they'd gotten from Santa, and Jace had often wondered what he'd done that was so bad, because Santa never came to his house. It hadn't taken him long to figure out that Santa was a crock of shit. He'd even told a few of the kids that, making fun of them for believing in fairy tales, starting fights, adopting his dad's bullying ways.

A few of the foster homes had provided nice Christmases. Ill-fitting clothes he never would have chosen for himself, toys that he was too old for. It was one fateful Christmas morning, however, that he unwrapped his very first computer. Nothing fancy—cheap, not very powerful, but it had provided him a lifeline. And now that he was an adult, he knew he could make the holiday season what he wanted, make it his own...but he preferred to ignore it altogether. Seemed safer that way.

But the lights and carols and decorations persisted nevertheless.

So did Lindsey's melancholy mood when he returned with her bottle of Shiraz—one that was a little more expensive than she had suggested was acceptable. She deserved it.

Since he wasn't a wine drinker, he had no glasses, so they had to make do with tumblers. Unfortunate, because he would love to see her hand wrapped delicately around a fragile wineglass...and maybe even imagine that hand wrapped somewhere else.

That kiss in the backseat had been fucking with his head ever since it happened. For a moment, he'd forgotten he was pretending. Fuck it—he *hadn't* been pretending. The second his mouth had touched hers, it had been real. It had been like drinking fire. And when the guard had rapped on their window, it had taken everything within him to pull away from her.

What did that mean?

It didn't matter, because it couldn't mean anything. Lust, chemistry, sure… He wanted to sleep with her, but he'd be out of his mind not to want that. Beyond sex, though, there could be nothing for them. Too much was at stake, and involvements made him vulnerable.

"What should we drink to?" he asked her, setting down the bottle and picking up his glass.

"Success," she suggested.

"A job well done." He clinked his glass with hers.

The wine was deeply, seductively purple, and he got a very particular thrill watching it ease toward Lindsey's pink lips as she took her first sip. He'd been at those lips himself only a few hours ago, and as she drank, he couldn't take his eyes off her. Once she lowered her glass, she made a throaty sound of pleasure that he figured gave him a good indication of how she sounded when she came.

He'd like to hear that sound in his ear.

"God, that's good."

He'd like to hear her say that in his ear, too.

"Glad you like it."

"You chose well." Then, to his surprise, she quaffed the entire glass.

"I see you did need that."

"Yeah. I needed some liquid courage."

"Courage?"

"To say what I want to say next."

Oh shit. He wasn't sure he was going to like this, but he gave a chuckle to try to hide that fact. "Do I need to sit down?"

Lindsey's green eyes, always a little shy but assessing, met him with a directness he wasn't sure he'd ever seen there before. Until tonight.

"I need you to stop using me."

CHAPTER NINETEEN

Somehow, she'd suspected he was going to play dumb. As he blinked at her, she realized she'd been absolutely right.

"Using you… Huh?"

Lindsey blew out a breath, grabbed the wine bottle, and poured herself another glass, damn his earlier warnings. She needed to get this out. A pleasant warmth was already spreading in her chest, spurring her on. "Don't pretend you don't know. Your caveman routine the first time I showed up at your door. Putting on a show in front of my parents. Kissing me in front of that security guard. Why are you doing those things?"

"It's just a way to get us out of sticky situations, Linz. It always works, doesn't it?"

"But what do you think it does to *me*?"

He frowned at her. Did he honestly not know? Or was he still playing dumb? Because she knew he wasn't. Was she such a closed book, or was he just that dense when it came to matters of the heart?

"I didn't think it did anything to you," he said slowly.

"I'm not a doll you can throw around and do whatever you want with. I have feelings."

"Yeah? Everyone does."

She chewed her bottom lip before blurting, "Sometimes I think you don't."

"And you'd be wrong. I'm not a fucking cyborg."

"I know you don't have any feelings for me. You

made that painfully clear the first time you kissed me, telling me how awful it was. But—but you can't keep—"

"Oh, Jesus Christ," he groaned, the first real reaction she'd seen from him since she began speaking. He ran a hand through his hair, leaving that one tuft sticking up.

"Lindsey, I hope you don't consider anything I said that day as truth. I was pissed. I was so pissed I was seeing red. That's not an excuse, but if you think I don't look for reasons to kiss you every day, then that's something else you're wrong about. A couple of times I've gotten lucky, and that reason comes along. Most days, I think of all the reasons I *shouldn't* kiss you…and if we keep talking about this, I'm going to forget them."

"You want to kiss me?" she asked, the sense of wonder and astonishment shutting down all of her own inner doubts and rationalizations.

He stared at her lips, eyes dark, heated, and then drained his glass as she had a few moments ago. Watching his strong throat muscles work as he swallowed sent the warmth in her chest skittering all over her body. God, what he would feel like against her…

Jace slammed the glass down as if he'd just finished a whiskey shot. "Yes, but you shouldn't let me," he said, not looking at her. "Because if you do, I won't want to stop."

Oh God. Her pulse pounded in her ears, inner wrists, and between her thighs. His hand still gripped his glass as if he wasn't quite sure where his fingers might go if he released it. How would those hands stroke her body? Rough and insistent, gentle and unhurried?

She wanted it all. "What if I don't want you to stop?"

"When so much is wrong—are you sure about that?" He came around the kitchen island, still respecting the distance between them, but she had the distinct impression of a lean black panther stalking its prey, watching, waiting for the chance to pounce.

"It might not ever be right. I'll take any good I can get."

His warmth invaded her personal space as she looked up at him, her eyes barely on a level with his chin. She was prepared to stand on tiptoes and strain her neck to reach him, but in one move, his arms encircled her and he lifted her against him as easily as if she were weightless. Once she was on his level, he slanted his mouth over hers while she brought her legs around his waist.

All his kisses before had been demanding. They took. This one gave. It gave so much. Warmth and comfort. Passion and intensity. This showed just how fake the others had been, despite his protests.

Even though dreaming of him beside her, over her, in her, kept her up nights—it was almost too much. Almost. They made the journey to his bedroom with her wrapped around him.

He was hard between her legs—even through his denim and hers. Her nipples stiffened against his chest, the proof of his need igniting her own. Her hands tore his T-shirt upward as his mouth worked feverishly against hers, tongue sweeping in and out in a naughty rhythm. At last she crashed against his mattress, and he helped her pull his shirt the rest of the way off, baring that gorgeous chest.

But then it was her turn, and her breath caught as his fingers went to work on the buttons of her shirt. She was torn between the desire to rip them off and the need to hide. As he pushed her shirt off her shoulders, then drew her bra straps down, she trembled violently.

"Jace," she whispered, barely able to stand the burn of his gaze on her flesh. Gently, he tugged down one of her bra cups, baring her nipple. She closed her eyes as he lowered his head and took it in his mouth. "Oh God."

"How the fuck could you think I don't want you," he murmured against her skin. "I want you so much it hurts, Lindsey." His tongue painted a wet trail around the aching little peak, and she groaned, writhing under him. He coaxed her upward so that he could divest her of her bra completely, leaving her bare from the waist up.

"It's been a long time for me," she stammered as he tossed it across the bed, because it seemed important somehow. She didn't necessarily want his gentleness, not yet. But her oversensitive body might combust under him. She might not live through it. And she had another reason for telling him, too.

"That's okay," he said, bracing himself on his arms above her again. "I'll do whatever you need me to do, however you need it."

"But…I have this sort of latex allergy. I can't use regular condoms. And I don't have any of the kind I can use. I never thought…"

"Polyurethane?"

"Yes."

"I don't have any, but I'll make the fastest trip to the drugstore you've ever seen."

But she didn't *want* him to, so she slid her arms around his neck and tightened her legs around him, drawing him down. "I don't want you to leave me."

"Then what do you want, Lindsey?"

"I just want you. If that's okay. I promise I'm healthy."

"Are you on birth control?"

"Yes."

"I'm clean. The last thing I would ever do is hurt you."

He was here, and he was hers. She could hardly believe it, but damn him, he hadn't made any of this easy on her. She had to return the favor somehow, and the heat and solidity of him did things to her, went to her head, made her want to reconnect with the sexuality she'd let lie dormant for too long. "Hmm," she said, pulling him in for a kiss, letting it linger just long enough that she felt a shudder work through him. "So you say."

"Promise," he murmured against her lips.

She let him kiss her again, at least for a time, but then pulled away. "I don't know," she teased, resisting his efforts to reclaim her with a dark little smile. "On second thought, you might have to talk me into this."

"Oh yeah? What will it take?"

She gave a meaningful glance down the length of his body. "Let's see what I'll be getting out of the deal."

Never taking his eyes from hers, he rose up on his knees, giving her a fabulous opportunity to peruse his chiseled physique. Lindsey struggled not to bite her lip as she looked her fill, but then those big, deft hands dropped to his jeans, and she gave in to the urge. The anticipation was too much. He practically tore at his fly while her heart pounded so hard she thought he might see her breasts quiver with each beat. *God, is this happening?*

Every movement full of grace, he stripped his jeans down his powerful legs and then off, tossing them aside. His thighs made her mouth water. She couldn't wait to sink her nails into that firm muscle. Speaking of firm…

Black boxer briefs stretched tight over his erection, the tip of which reached his waistband. Thick. Hard. Long. It was really no wonder he had no shame. When he hooked a thumb into them and pushed them down, revealing with staggering confidence what was underneath, the breath left her body in a rush. He was sculpture brought to searing, uncompromising life, and her hands ached to get on him. Her tongue flicked across her lips, a gesture that drew his eyes to her mouth.

His hands moved to her jeans, and all thought failed her, the world a blaze of sensation. Unbuttoning, unzipping, the slide of denim down her thighs, her calves, off her feet. Only her panties barred her from his sight. Her little game seemed futile now. If he didn't take her soon, she would die.

Jace took her hands and pinned them back on the mattress. With him hovering over her like this, his cock brushed her clit through the cotton of her underwear, her hips lifting off the bed to rock against him until he groaned. She knew he could feel how wet he'd made her.

"Are you convinced yet?" he asked, voice a rasp.

"I'm not sure. You might have to investigate further." Who the hell was she right now? Who did he make her when he touched her like this?

He shifted back, his hand now where his cock had just been, fingers gently exploring her over her underwear. Lindsey's head fell back. She spread her knees wider. Her chest heaved; her body clenched on aching emptiness. When his fingers dipped underneath the waistband, she bit her lip and writhed up to meet them.

"Look at me," he said, and she did, her eyes narrowing in pure bliss as his finger slid into her, slowly thrusting into her wetness. So good. Once she accepted one easily, he slid in another, the stretch burning deliciously. "I'm going to lick you there," he said, so matter-of-factly.

The words came from somewhere. "Do a good job. Then maybe I'll decide."

"Dammit." His chuckle was pure evil as he pulled her panties down her legs and off. Then his big hands were parting her thighs, and he was looking down at her, and oh God, when was the last time she'd shaved? She couldn't be bothered to figure it out. Nothing mattered here except for him. And his fingers snugging back into her pussy, and his lips lowering over her clit, and then she was gone, lost in pleasure that left her shaking as he licked, and licked, and licked.

He laced his fingers over the flat of her stomach,

holding her captive to his exploration, not rushing, in no hurry to shoot her to the stars just yet. But she was in a hurry to get there. The scruff on his jaw chafed her inner thighs, and she rocked against him as best she could, but he didn't give her any control. His clever tongue worked miracles across her flesh, teasing her clit with the barest tip until she was moaning and writhing and desperate.

"Do you want to come?" he murmured.

"God yes!" *Make it all go away.*

"In my mouth or wrapped around me?"

"Can't I have both?"

"You can. You will. But I can't give you both at once."

How could she choose? But she wanted him close, she wanted to hold him, she wanted to look into his eyes. "I want you in me."

Slowly, too slowly, he crawled up the length of her body, pausing to kiss trails up her quivering belly, between her aching breasts, and to gently suck each nipple in turn. "You're fucking beautiful, Lindsey."

And then he was over her, braced on his powerful arms as her own feverish hands collected the feel of him, the strength of his muscles, hoping to borrow some of it for tonight, for the days ahead. His cock nestled between her legs, smooth and thick, and he slid it slowly, deliberately over her clit. She lifted her hips to take it, but he wouldn't be rushed.

"And so, you've decided?" he murmured, raining little kisses across her forehead. "I must've done a good job."

Her need would no longer allow for games. It

raged on unchecked. The ache low in her belly had become an inferno. His lips slid over hers, teasing them open for the invasion of his tongue, showing her a rhythm she began to crave between her legs.

Yes, yes, do it, please do it, make me whole…

"You're so wet, and I'm not even inside you yet," he groaned, still sliding against her. "You're going to feel so fucking good."

So was he, she knew it—he was going to be better than anything she'd ever known in her entire life, if he would only *hurry up*. "I'm so ready for you," she whispered back, linking her fingers behind his neck. "I've wanted this for so long."

In the midst of the passion darkening his eyes, something softened. "Let's not keep you waiting any longer, then." And he kissed her as he slid one arm under her leg and lifted it, opening her wider, giving him more control as he slipped the head of his cock lower and pushed.

It wasn't easy. It took effort. She whimpered, stretching to accommodate him, her forehead pressed against his as their breathing shuddered together, as he pushed and stopped. "Oh fuck, Lindsey. I don't want to hurt you."

"You can't, I promise." Two hot tears squeezed from her closed eyes, but not from pain. It wasn't her first time, but it was. It was her first time to feel *this*. He was all her love and fear and pain and rage, everything she ran from, coalescing into one place, taking her over all at once. "Just kiss me?"

He did, and as he moved forward inside her, inch by slow, delectable inch, her body adjusted and accepted. He broke out in a sweat, and so did she, loving him for being so patient, for considering her needs. "Thank you," she said against his lips, the words simply tumbling out without her permission. She ran her hands through his soft hair, loving the warmth of it, inhaling the scent of them together as he slowly began withdrawing.

The sound he made was the only response she needed. Knowing she was affecting him as much as he was her, that she was giving as much as she took. He pulled out of her, leaving her empty, seeming to pause to collect himself before taking her again. And again. Each thrust easier but no faster. She was panting with need by then, her nails digging into his shoulders, his biceps, and then his back as she tried to draw him closer.

"Faster," she whispered, the long, thick, slow slide of him curling her toes.

"Fuck, baby, I won't last." But he gave her what she wanted nonetheless, the warmth of his breath tickling her ear as he picked up his pace, making chills skitter down her spine. And despite his words, he did last, he lasted until she was panting raggedly, hanging on to him for dear life as the delicious friction they created swelled to a conflagration.

"Oh God."

"So good. So fucking good," he said, the words fading into a groan as she clenched on him, her body craving each thrust, pulling him deep. "I only thought I knew."

Those were the sweetest words he could have said right then, because she understood how he felt. The magic they created came from a place she never could have imagined existed in her mundane life.

It felt secret and special, something she was never meant to have. The tears kept coming, one after another, and for once she didn't mind them. He kissed them all away as he made her body feel as if it were full of starlight.

Then that magic became something seething and needy and desperate, and her excitement built to a peak that was sharp and merciless, screaming for release before it destroyed her. His thrusts became even faster, rolling and erratic, his breath rasping in her ear. "I'm gonna come, sweetheart. Are you with me?"

"I'm with you," she whimpered. She couldn't wait to feel him, to hear him, to watch him. The slick fire their bodies created had become like an electric current inside her, building, building. "Yes, Jace, yes…"

It all exploded at once, and the world fractured around her. From some great distance, she heard him and felt him and saw him like she wanted. But she was tumbled under the force of the pleasure he unleashed in her, and her heart struggled to keep beating, her lungs locked up in her chest. Her thoughts shut down like a plug had been pulled on her brain, but somehow she kept living.

And then, slowly, she came back to herself and back to Jace, who was collapsed over her and shaking. "Fuck," he cursed into her ear. "Jesus Christ."

She didn't have a voice yet. Her limbs were locked around his shoulders and hips, holding him deep inside her, and all she could think was that it was a good thing she was on birth control, because she wouldn't have let him pull out if he'd needed to. He was as deep inside her as he could go. She loved it, loved feeling him all over her.

"Are you okay?" he whispered into her ear, and she could only nod as he began to kiss the wetness on her cheeks. "Are you sure?"

"I'm sure." Her voice sounded as if she hadn't spoken for years.

"Talk to me, Lindsey."

"I can't right now. I'm not back yet."

He chuckled. "Where are you?"

"I don't know, but I love it here. It's a good place."

"That's good. Maybe you can visit again some-time soon."

"I'd like to."

His fingers gently caught her chin and made her look at him. "I'm there with you."

Then it was the only place she ever wanted to be. Their safe place, here in each other's arms. She managed to move her heavy limbs and capture his face between her palms, bringing him down for a kiss.

"You're so fucking sweet," he whispered against her lips.

It wasn't exactly what she wanted to hear—it seemed to be the story of her life, that no matter how wild or wanton she tried to be with a man, she was always *sweet* or *fun*. But somehow, coming from him, it wasn't so bad. He made sweet sound positively sinful, like a confection to be devoured at will. She could definitely handle that.

He held her for a long time and, when their

light kisses and caresses began to progress into heavy kisses and caresses, made love to her again. This time, he didn't make her beg. He was rough, driving her to a quick, violent orgasm that left her exhausted and panting.

She fell asleep only to dream of him, and then had to wake him at three a.m. to reach the completion she hadn't achieved in her dream. By then she was sore, but it didn't matter. Her need eclipsed all else, and she rode him, their lips centimeters apart, their breath mingling in the scant distance. He let her hold down his wrists even though he could have broken her grip with a mere twitch, and the power of feeling he was a slave to her pleasure was heady and intoxicating.

She couldn't get enough of this man. She never would.

And that was so dangerous.

CHAPTER TWENTY

He woke to the sun streaming through his windows and Lindsey curled into his side, her expression soft in sleep. Ordinarily, he wasn't a guy to linger in bed all day, especially with a woman. But nothing sounded more desirable to him right now than to spend the day right here with her, sleeping in between bouts of sex, laughing, drinking coffee, watching TV, more sex. All day. There was nowhere else on earth he would rather be.

He turned toward her, drawing her into his arms, and she snuggled there as if even in sleep, she wanted to be close. Her soft, floral-scented hair tickled his nose as he breathed her in.

Jace knew he should get up, shower, make her breakfast, something…but he couldn't bring himself to leave the warmth of her body to face the cold day. She murmured something, and he gently pushed her hair back to see her delicate face in profile. "Hmm?"

"Hurt all over," she repeated, wriggling even closer to him.

"Well, we got quite a workout last night."

Her answering chuckle was throaty and a tad on the naughty side, which he loved. "We did, didn't we? I woke up a couple of times thinking maybe I dreamed the whole thing, but I would look over and you were there."

He kissed her forehead. "I'm here. Do you need anything? Coffee, food, Advil? Me?"

"I need all of those things. We might need to

switch the order a bit, though."

"Am I still last?"

Lindsey lifted her head, a silky tumble of hair covering one eye, her lips still swollen and pouty from last night's kisses and sleep. "No. You're first."

He slipped under the covers and pushed her knees apart, putting his head between her legs and softly licking her until her body writhed and her hands plunged under the blankets to grip his hair. Her cries were so sweet, high, and musical, enough to incite any man into a fury of dominant lust, but he held her open and made her submit only to his gentleness until she was panting, then latched on to her and sucked until her hips came off the bed, offering herself up so he could feast on her as she came. At last, she dropped limply back to the mattress.

"I can't take much more of this," she said, giggling as he emerged from under the covers and kissed her. He liked knowing that she could taste herself, taste the two of them combined.

"Really? Oh baby, I thought we were just getting started."

"You'll kill me before it's over."

"Never. But now you've had me, so what do you need next?"

"Coffee," she decided. "But first, isn't it my turn?" Her hand closed around his cock, which was still hard from her flavor, her softness, her cries. "Oh yeah. It's definitely my turn."

"I wasn't going to ask, but…"

She pushed him back, and he went willingly, giving her free run of his body. And she explored every inch with her hands and her lips, teasing and enticing before finally going where he most ached for her, slipping his dick into the wet little cavern of her mouth. She sucked him down until he touched the back of her throat and, fuck, sucked him down a little bit more.

Her delicate hand wrapped around him where her mouth couldn't reach, enclosing him in heat and softness, the grip only tight enough to be maddening as her lips slid up and down, so sweet, and her hair slid like silk through his fingers. Pleasure so intense it was an exquisite pain. After last night, how did he even have anything left to give her? Somehow, she got it from him, holding her mouth on him and taking it all as he came, cussing a blue streak that made her laugh around him—which only shot him higher.

"Fuck, Lindsey," he groaned once he'd managed to come down again. "If we keep this up…"

"We'll never get out of bed? Sounds good to me." She crawled up and settled onto his shoulder while he wrapped his arm tight around her.

"What about coffee? Food? Advil?"

"I can do without it if I have you."

Uneasiness slithered through him, and he began to wonder if he'd just made a colossal fuckup. Sex was all fine and good until feelings got involved. He definitely had them, but he'd grown adept at shutting his feelings off like the flick of a switch long ago. He could survive. Lindsey, however…

Jace could resist his own feelings easily, yeah, but he was afraid he wouldn't be able to resist hers. "Come on. I'm not going to let you lie here famished. We had a long night." He grinned, kissing the top of her head. "Let's get up."

He let her have the shower first, and while he would have liked nothing more than to join her—and she offered—he let her have it so he could put the coffee on and start breakfast for her. Imagining her wet and slick and soapy in the steam as he made omelets almost got the best of him. Another couple of minutes and he might have said "fuck it" and broke into a run for her, but then he heard the water shut off.

It was snowing outside. He stood at the window, sipping from his cup and watching the white city below as Lindsey came up behind him, wrapping her arms around his waist and placing a kiss on his shoulder. "Food's on the table," he told her. "I poured your coffee, but I don't know how you take it."

"Do you have creamer?"

"In the fridge."

Her arms dropped, and he turned to watch her go. She was wearing one of his shirts, which was adorably large on her, hanging well past mid-thigh. The last thing he wanted to do was hurt her. He wanted to see where this might go, he really did. But things were so hectic in his life that subjecting her to it seemed to be the main way he *could* hurt her. Look what had already happened.

"Lindsey."

"Jace," she said almost as soon as the word had left his lips. "Don't, okay? I already know what's coming. I do. But can you save it? Can I enjoy this for a little while longer?"

She opened his fridge and surveyed the interior, then reached for the creamer. He only watched, his heart heavy in his chest. The effort it cost her to act normal was painfully apparent. To act like she didn't already know what he needed to say. When she pulled out the bottle, he saw how it trembled in her hand. "Sure," he said at last. "Yeah."

"I don't understand the mental shift that happens once the sun comes up," she said sadly, walking over to the table and fixing her coffee. "But whatever. I get it. Let's move on."

"If things were different—"

"No," she said sharply and pointed at him with her spoon. "Do me the courtesy of *not* telling me how close we are to having it all, *if only*. It's a tired song, and I've heard it sung before. At least be straight with me."

"I'm being as straight with you as I know how."

"And do you have to stand there *shirtless* while you tell me we would never work? Jesus, talk about cruel."

She was something else. He wasn't quite sure what yet. Shaking his head, he went into his bedroom and threw on a shirt. Hadn't he known from the start this was a huge mistake? But he'd gone and done it anyway. Story of his fucking life. Maybe the bigger mistake was trying to do damage control so soon after fucking her all night. She was right, and he should have let it rest.

At least for a day or two.

But if she gave him another day or two, he would happily spend those fucking her as well. Best to rip off the Band-Aid fast.

When he walked out of the bedroom, she was sitting at his kitchen table, staring off into a distance only she could see while her omelet grew cold. He ambled up beside her, then took a knee and put his palm on her back, rubbing small circles. Her head dropped, her mouth drooping.

"Last night was incredible for me," he began tentatively. "I think it was for you, too. Who knows what the future holds, Lindsey, for either of us. Once this is over, we can see. But right now, we both need to keep a clear head. Anyone can come along and use you against me. I can't have that vulnerability right now."

"I'm already a vulnerability for you," she said. "I was from the moment I first knocked on your door."

She had him there. If anyone tried to hurt her now, he might risk his own neck and those of everyone he'd ever known to protect her. It was a thought that terrified him, a weakness he couldn't afford to have.

"If I were smart," he told her, "I would send you far away. From me, from all of this."

"No." She shook her head furiously. "I would never go."

"You would if I said the word. You wouldn't have the choice."

She glared daggers at him. "Don't. You. Dare."

Sighing, he ran a hand over his head and got to his feet. "Eat, Lindsey."

She picked up her fork and went through the motions, but he'd already shattered the mood to hell and gone. Maybe it was for the best, maybe not. It wouldn't be the first time he'd been a dumbass. He doubted it would be the last.

All at once, his door flew open and Sully burst in, and if he'd had a gun on him he might have aimed and fired without a second thought. Her eyes were wild and furious as she took in the both of them, pure disgust brimming in her expression. "We've been fucking found, Jace." She stabbed a finger in Lindsey's direction, punctuating each syllable. "Her code had a traceback that led them *right. Fucking. To. Us.* You obviously just fucked the enemy."

Then again, maybe he'd been a dumbass for the last time in his life.

CHAPTER TWENTY-ONE

"I don't know what she's talking about, I swear to God. You have to believe me."

He'd shoved Sully back out the door almost as fast as his teammate had burst in, exhorting her to let him handle this. Lindsey's face had been awash with numb horror as soon as he had made it back to the kitchen, but he hadn't let that move him. He'd placed her on his couch, sat across from her on the coffee table, and said little as he stared her down, watching her every expression as she asked him to believe her.

He wanted to. Oh fucking hell, how he wanted to believe her. She was extremely convincing, but then he'd wondered at the very start if she was little more than a fabulous actress.

"Why would I do this? Why would I compromise my sister, put her in danger?"

"I don't know," he said coldly, though it shredded his heart to speak to her in that tone. "Why don't you tell me?"

"You can't believe I would do this on purpose. Maybe I made a mistake, or someone manipulated the code once I was done with it. Maybe someone hacked into my computer and did that, Jace. They want to turn you against me, or to hurt you. After last night, how could you possibly think—"

"That because you fucked me you would never betray me? That's a riot. Tell me another one."

"I didn't do this."

"All this time, I've wondered how it's possible that you and Lena could share the same DNA. It's all becoming clearer now, isn't it? You're exactly like her. To the marrow of your bones, you are your sister's clone. Actually, I take that back. You might be a little worse than she is. At least she didn't spout a bunch of bullshit about how much she cared about me before she tore my world apart with her bare hands. Maybe it's *you* who taught her."

"Jace!"

"Maybe the two of you cooked that up all those years ago. 'Hey, that unsuspecting son of a bitch looks like an easy mark. Let's fuck him up, why don't we?'"

"*You cannot believe that.*"

He leaned closer to her, bracing his elbows on his knees. "You don't get to tell me what I can't believe. I couldn't believe it when she—or you, or both of you—did that to me. I came to believe it pretty fucking fast, though, when I was facing jail time. *Jail time*, Lindsey. They would have locked me up for it. The Air Force saved my ass, but you know what? There were days of my service when I wondered if maybe I wouldn't rather be sitting in a cell somewhere with three hots and a cot, instead of bullets flying past my motherfucking head."

"I'm sorry," she said miserably, shaking her head. He had to give her credit: she never looked away from his eyes, which he'd been told in the past housed pure evil when he was angry. "I'm so, so sorry."

"Will your sorry give me back my fucking life?"

"No, but I didn't *do* anything—"

"Will sorry help when Rhys kills us all? Wipes out my team? Tortures them? *Will sorry help then?*"

"Jace, I don't have any reason to do this. And you know that, if you would take a single *minute* and think about it…" Her voice trailed away, her hands going to her mouth as emotion choked off her words.

She was getting better at holding it back, though. No sooner had those words failed than she drew a deep breath, wiped her dry, bloodshot eyes, and stared at him with a fierce determination that made him think the twins had truly swapped out somehow.

"You know what? Fuck you. Fuck you if you don't believe last night was real for me. Fuck you if you think I'm capable of that sort of betrayal. I don't have to sit here and listen to this, because I haven't done anything. So unless you have a badge I don't know about, unless you're capable of arresting me or detaining me, *fuck you*, I'm going home."

She shot to her feet, shoving him backward in the process, and stomped toward his bedroom, ripping his shirt she was wearing open so that buttons flew everywhere. It slid from her arms and made a sad heap on the floor, leaving her stark naked, that delectable ass swaying with every step. There was no seduction whatsoever in the movement, only pure feminine outrage, but damn if he didn't think it was the sexiest thing he had ever seen as she disappeared into his room.

He got up and followed her, feeling like a dog on a leash. When he entered, she was yanking her clothes from the floor. "Lindsey."

"Did I not express my *fuck you* loudly enough? Do you need to hear it again? Fuck! You!" She fought her way into her sweater before realizing she hadn't put her bra on first, then snatched her arms out and performed some intricate bra acrobatics to get it on without taking the sweater off her head. "Here's a tip for you, Jace—here's how you can know I'm telling you the truth about something—I get fucking pissed off. Upset at first, yeah, but when it goes on and on? I give no fucks anymore. I don't give a shit about any one of you, either, only my sister. I only came here in the first place because of her. And I'll get her back all by myself if I have to."

"You're out of your mind if you think that," he said flatly. "You're being irrational."

"I suppose rational is actually believing I could be involved in some intricate plot to take you down?"

"You understand I have to be on guard for all possibilities. Maybe you aren't involved in a plot. Maybe they made you a deal. Betray us and you get her back?"

"Oh, sure. I was lying in wait for *someone else* to suggest something that I could manipulate to my best interests. You have to know how stupid that sounds."

"Explain the traceback, then."

"I tried to! But you won't listen to anything I say, so I'm at a loss. I have no motive to hurt you."

"I don't know who to trust anymore," he said, the admission lifting her gaze to meet his. Sighing, he sat on his bed, the bed still unmade and unkempt from their feverish lovemaking all night. If he put his nose to her pillow, he bet he could still smell her there. She would haunt him long after she left.

"I don't know what to tell you." Lindsey jerked her jeans up her hips and fastened them.

"I woke up this morning, and all I wanted to do was stay in bed with you all day."

"Good thing we didn't," she remarked snidely. "That would have been even more embarrassing when Sully busted in your door. So what's your point?"

"It's funny how shit can change from one minute to the next, I guess."

"How insightful." She wound her scarf around her neck. "And now I'm leaving."

He raised his eyes to meet hers. "You're not going anywhere."

CHAPTER TWENTY-TWO

Lindsey felt her nostrils flare as she glared back at him. The nerve. "I'd like to see you make me stay."

"You leave here, and you put yourself and every one of us in danger. That's something I can't allow."

"I think we're all in danger whether I leave or not," she pointed out. He had to see that.

At least he'd calmed somewhat from his barking-drill-sergeant routine, which had only been to try to break her down...and it had worked. She was mad as hell, but not so much that she couldn't see he had a team to protect.

Still, having her word questioned was unfamiliar territory for her, and she *hated* it. She'd always been the good twin. It was Lena who was the liar. The Jace who had cornered her moments ago was the same one who'd answered her very first knock at his door, and she had never wanted to see that version of him again.

He looked her in the eyes for a long time, then let his gaze travel down the length of her body. Despite herself, it gave her a shiver.

"I'll do my best to make your stay as pleasant as possible," he said.

She crossed her arms, rolling her eyes. "How? Because I know you don't think you can screw me into submission every hour or so."

"Can you think of a better way?"

No, not really. Damn you. "If I stay, you have to

keep Sully away from me. She looked at me like she wanted to rip my head off. And like she could."

"She could. That's why I got rid of her." He shoved a hand back through his hair and sighed heavily. Just like that, all the fight seemed to have drained out of him, too.

"Please tell me at least part of you believes me," she said softly. "Please."

His dark eyes flickered back and forth between hers searchingly. Whatever he was looking for, she hoped he found it. "Part of me believes you," he said, and she closed her eyes in relief, but that only blocked out his face, and she couldn't have that. She opened them again.

"Thank you."

"Don't test me, though, Lindsey. Stay here with me. Do what I say. Don't give me any more reason to doubt you."

"I can try to do that. Until everything is sorted, anyway."

"I can't have you going near my computers, either. They're key-logged. If you touch them, I'll know."

Well, she had ways around that. But she only allowed herself to stare at him and give him a doe-eyed nod. "I have to be able to stay in contact with my parents, though."

"You can do that, but I want to hear every conversation you have."

"Jace—"

"No exceptions. You want this to be over with, this is how we get it fucking over with. You stay close, you do right, you listen to me."

She had to bite down on a retort berating him for the parts of him that still didn't believe her. Hell, she wouldn't believe her, either, if what Sully said was true. And here was Sully, a member of his team for who knew how many years…and Lindsey, a girl who showed up on his figurative doorstep one day with an unbelievable tale of identical twin kidnapping. Who was he going to trust? She didn't have to be Einstein to figure that one out.

"I'll stay close, and I'll try to be good," she said coyly.

Some of the tension around his eyes smoothed out. Nodding, he got to his feet. The irrational part of her needed him to come over to her and—do what? Do *something*. Anything. Hug her. Tell her it would be all right, that they would sort this mess out. But he didn't. He walked to the door, and only her voice stopped him.

"Can we at least go get some more of my clothes?"

"Yeah." His voice was glum. "We can do that." He left her standing there, feeling like a criminal in the same room where he'd made her feel like a queen.

He wasn't the only one. Everyone stared at her with cold, accusing eyes, and since the table they were sitting at in the large conference room Jace had led her to was round, there was no escaping every baleful glare. They cut into her like razor blades. She'd never handled confrontation well. She'd never been able to stand making mistakes or believing that someone was angry at her.

These people were fucking pissed off.

Worse, today their superior sat among them. They called him the Captain, and while he had an almost grandfatherly look about him, darkness lurked beneath his surface. She sank under the weight of that stare in particular. *Keep your head down. Shut up.* That proved difficult when every instinct screamed at her to defend herself.

"It might be a moot point," Sully said sourly after a slight lull in the arguing. "We've been compromised. Her people could hit us at any time."

"They're *not*—" Lindsey caught herself and fell silent. Anything she said was useless, anyway. None of them believed she wasn't complicit in this. She tried to tell herself that she only cared what Jace thought. And he, while not happy, was at least not being openly hostile toward her. Let all the others say what they would.

As she watched him scrub a hand over his face, her heart wailed in pain, and she wished she could just fly off the freaking planet. This wasn't supposed to be happening. They were supposed to still be celebrating her success. Instead, she had opened them all up to attack. And she didn't understand how.

"All right," Jace said, "enough. It's done. I don't give a shit how we got here. We need our next move, and we need it fast."

"Five minutes alone with this one and I could get the truth," Sully said, her cold expression leveled right at Jace. "Stop thinking with your dick and wake up to reality here."

"*Sully!*" he all but roared in a monstrous voice that made Lindsey jump. It had the desired effect.

Sully sat back and fiddled with a long black fingernail. Lindsey found herself irrationally wondering how she typed with those things. It was better than dwelling on the fact that this woman wanted to torture her.

"I say we go in and get those fuckers," Helix said. "We know where they are. What are we waiting for?"

"If anyone's going, I am," Jace said, and as the protests began anew, he lifted a silencing hand. After his outburst a few seconds ago, no one was going to disobey. "I got us into this," he told them all. "We're in this situation because of my dumbass decisions. So I'll get us out."

"No one's doing anything rash," the Captain said with long-suffering patience. "It will be a team effort. You like to forget, but I'm in command here. You'll get your assignments."

Everyone fell silent at that, but they looked relieved. Lindsey chewed her bottom lip, wondering what those assignments would be—certainly, she wouldn't be privy. She was surprised she was here at all.

My dumbass decisions, Jace had said. Her mind was stuck on that, replaying it over and over. He was talking about her.

"Don't blame yourself for this," Drake said to Jace. "You couldn't have known."

"No. It's entirely my fault. I'm not only talking about agreeing to get involved. It goes back much further than that."

Oh, she thought.

"What are you talking about, Jace?" the Captain asked sharply.

Watching Jace squirm under that inquisitive stare was heartbreaking. "I did something. To Rhys. I'm not proud of it."

Helix sat back and covered his eyes with one hand, rubbing hard at his forehead. Drake and Sully looked confused. The Captain sat as still as an ice sculpture, but he said nothing, prompting with only his silence.

"I beat that son of a bitch until I thought he might be dead," he confessed, dropping each word like stones in a still pond. There was a thunderous rage written across his face that said if he got the chance, he would do it again. And worse. "If he has a vendetta against anyone at this table, it's me. I'm the mark. He only brought in people who have history with *me.*"

"Nothing he didn't deserve," Helix put in, finally dropping his hand to the table.

"Definitely," Sully agreed after a moment.

"Funny you should say that," Helix fired back at her. "You were the one fucking him."

The news didn't seem to shock anyone at the table, but, suddenly under the gun, Sully seemed to blanch beneath her tattoos. "I ceased *all* contact with that bastard after what he did. You guys *know* that."

"Are we sure?"

"We can't start turning on one another," Drake said helplessly as accusations began to fly anew. He seemed to be the peacemaker among the group, Lindsey had noticed, though he was often drowned out.

"Funny that *you* were the one who discovered her

traceback, isn't it?" Helix had come half out of his chair, leaning over the table to get in Sully's face.

"This is exactly what he would want, you realize," the Captain said solemnly, no louder than Drake had been, but Helix put his ass back in his chair and shut his mouth. Sully put her elbows on the table and shoved both hands through her hair, shaking, trying to compose herself.

Lindsey felt sorry for her, despite any threats of torture. It had to be hard to find out a man you'd been intimate with was a murderer.

"All of you turning on each other, not trusting each other, is exactly how he would tear you apart."

Could it be? Lindsey wondered, watching Sully closely. Maybe the traceback had been Rhys's attack on his former girlfriend's vulnerabilities?

"I want you to compose yourselves. Jace, thank you for this information. While I think it's pertinent, I still don't think you're the catalyst here. As I said, you'll all get your assignments. Thank you."

One by one, everyone got up and filed out of the room, avoiding Lindsey's eyes as if merely the sight of her could give them the plague or something. Everyone except Jace and the Captain.

"I trust you won't mind being our guest until all this is sorted?" the latter asked her, not unkindly, and with a sideways glance at Jace.

Guest. A euphemism if she'd ever heard one, but much prettier than *captive*. "No, sir," she assured him. "I won't mind."

"We'll find your sister, Ms. Morris."

That brought her gaze up. *He believes me*, she thought, holding on to that. *But why?* She would never have gathered the courage to ask, and he got up and left them alone then anyway.

She almost wished he had stayed. Jace made her think of a lion pacing its cage, all its lethal grace restrained by nothing but the bars surrounding it. Only there were no bars between them.

"What are you thinking?" she asked him at last, when silence became insufferable.

"I don't know." *Or he's not saying.*

"I know what you're thinking."

"Oh yeah? Care to clue me in?"

"You're wishing you'd slammed that door in my face the first time we met, and left it shut, and ignored my note, and never thought of me again."

He was silent for a long time. With each second that ticked by without his denying her claims, she felt another piece of her heart break off. But at long last, he reached over, took her hand, and said, "No. Despite everything, I don't wish that at all. I couldn't have forgotten you if I tried."

"And there's still that part of you that believes me?"

"It's there, but if that part of me ends up getting one of us killed—"

"Look, I can't even begin to guess what the future holds, but if anything happens, the only blame that can be laid at my feet is that I came to you in the first place. That's it. I don't know what else I can do to prove it to you. I've said all I can say, done all I can do. So…if you want to lock me right here in this room until my sister dies or I die or we get blown up or whatever it is you expect to happen, my conscience is clear except for that one thing: that I came to you for help. I hope *you're* able to live with that."

He'd stared at her unnervingly the entire time she'd spoken, as if absorbing every word and the body language behind it. "I already live with a lot, Lindsey. You have to see how this looks from my perspective. These people are my family. The only family I have. Tell me you don't believe Sully is *lying* about the traceback?"

"I see from your perspective, but you're making no attempt to see from mine. All I'm saying is that someone else did this. They had to, because I didn't. *I did not.* It's really as simple as that."

"What exactly went wrong while you were loading it?"

"It crashed," she said thoughtfully. "It errored out. I panicked and rebooted. Then it installed. The system was a dinosaur; I blamed it on that."

His fingertips rubbed absently at his sensual lips, and she realized how much she loved watching him think.

"Jace, Lena knew where you were somehow. *She* told me to come here. Do you honestly think the people who have her don't? You said it before, they know everything about us. Seems to me all this is just some trick to make you not trust me. I don't know why, but…maybe that's all it is?"

"Maybe," he said, morose. "We've been here long enough. It's probably time to move again."

"Again?"

"Again. Just a question of getting it done before we're compromised."

Did that mean he'd disappear from her life? Like a puff of smoke?

The pain of it bit so deep she gritted her teeth, not trusting herself to speak for a moment. Not wanting him to see how it hurt. "Did you move after this guy—Rhys—after he was booted out?"

"Yes."

"Wow," she said softly, rubbing at a smudge on the glossy tabletop. She only made the smudge bigger. Much like everything in her life right now, the more she tried to fix it, the worse it got. She would get her sister back—she had to. But she would lose him in the process. "It is my fault, then, isn't it? I compromised you when I showed up here the very first time. But I didn't know. I promise. I was scared. I didn't know what I was walking into. I guess I still don't."

He was always so avid when she spoke of these things. It rankled a little. It meant he was seeking out some hole in her story. Some chink in her armor. Sighing, she crossed her arms on the table and put her head down, unable to bear the sight of his mistrust at that moment.

The worst part of everything, perhaps, was that he sounded so beaten. When his people had left the room, they seemed to have taken his strength with them. She didn't want to be the cause of any rift in this family of his.

She lifted her head and looked at him. "I just find it so funny that Lena is the manipulative one, and I never have been, and everyone is treating me like… like I figure people treat her. You're looking at me like you would her if she walked in right now."

He watched her, and for some reason, she thought of the time he helped her make Lena's bed because she was an emotional wreck. The same man looked at her now with such wariness, such mistrust despite his claim of wanting to believe her, and she didn't know how to make that go away.

"Not hardly," he said at last, his tone a shade lighter than it had been before. "That would be abject horror. It would be like Satan walking into the room to take the rest of all I hold dear."

She had to chuckle. Even he cracked a smile.

"Lindsey, everything I know about you says that you wouldn't betray me like that. My gut tells me. And I usually follow my gut, but I've been wrong before. That's all." And people had died, she knew. His beautiful dark eyes stared at some distance filled with memories only he could see, and her heart wept for him. She would take that burden from him if she could.

I'm falling for him.

It was so simple in its enormousness. *I've already fallen for him.*

She closed her eyes, fighting that knowledge before it could take root in her mind, in her heart.

Her feelings didn't matter. Because even when everything worked out and Lena was back where she belonged, Jace would be gone.

To him, Lindsey was a vulnerability. Now it was even worse—she was a human Trojan horse. He had let her in of his own volition, even welcomed her, and she had possibly destroyed them all. He wouldn't let her infect them again once he cleaned her out.

CHAPTER TWENTY-THREE

Jace felt her presence like warmth against his back as he worked. She was curled in the corner of his couch, staring at nothing, obviously bored out of her mind, since he wouldn't let her touch any devices. But she suffered without complaint, so quiet that it made him ache for her. Something seemed different about her since the meeting. Before, she'd been supremely pissed off. Now, she seemed infinitely sad.

He tried to focus on his monitor. On his work.

He didn't have much to say, either.

Couldn't she see that he didn't *want* to doubt her, dammit? But his team pulled him in one direction, and she tugged him in another. His loyalty told him to go. She couldn't ask him to toss away years on a whim, not when there was evidence of her duplicity.

Lena would've known where to find Jace—she was fucking CIA. Lindsey didn't realize that, though, so she seemed genuinely confused about why her traceback was a big deal. She'd said as much in the conference room, and he couldn't explain without blowing her sister's cover.

Sully had nailed it when she'd told him to stop thinking with his dick. He had to do his job, keep his mouth shut, and then he had to send this girl on her way. Far, far away from him. Too much history, too much heartache, and even looking at her today, at the mirror image of Lena's face, brought all his history back like a sucker punch.

He was already too hotheaded. He didn't need Lindsey making him irrational on top of it. After what he'd confessed today, he had to play it cool for the immediate future or Cap was likely to boot his ass as fast as he had Rhys.

There were plenty of empty apartments on this floor, and she could have any one of them, but then he wouldn't be able to keep an eye on her. The only thing worse than feeling her tantalizing presence behind him would be not feeling her at all.

"Motherfucker," he grumbled, letting his weight fall back in his chair, rubbing his eyes hard with the heels of both hands.

"What is it?" Lindsey asked, alarm flashing through her voice. He glanced back at her and saw she was ramrod straight, staring at him with her big, beautiful green eyes.

You. Everything. "Nothing," he told her.

"Oh." Her posture relaxed. "You scared me. I thought maybe you found something bad."

It was bad. It was all bad. "We're going to both go nuts sitting here like this, aren't we?"

"Yes. What do you suggest?"

He wanted to take her away until it was all over. He wanted to drink margaritas on a beach where it was hot and humid; he wanted to lick the salt from her sun-warmed skin. Wanted to lay her back across white sand while the surf washed around their feet and make love to her until she asked him to stop from sheer ecstatic exhaustion.

"What is it?" she prompted timidly, and he guessed he'd been staring at her like a psycho, imagining doing all those things.

"I wish I could've met you some other way," he told her. "I wish things were different."

"They aren't, though. They never will be." He knew then, as she said it, this was the source of this profound sadness that had come over her. She'd been feeling it, too.

He propelled himself out of his chair. "We at least need some kind of distraction, don't you think?"

"Like what?"

"Well. It just so happens…"

Her gaze followed him as he made his way over to the entertainment center, where any girl who owned a *Zero Wing* shirt and was a *Legend of Zelda* fan would appreciate his gaming setup. *If indeed she is a fan of those*, something lurking in the darkest corner of his mind whispered. All the old doubts from when he'd listened in on her for those three days came back to swamp him.

He had all the old consoles, though some were shoved in the back of a closet—a retro-gamer might get on his ass about that, but he was willing to take the chance. "I have *Breath of the Wild*," he told her, "or I have the original *Zelda* stashed somewhere, if you'd rather play that."

"Oh my God, seriously?"

"Sure." She looked practically giddy. Seemed convincing enough. "Funny how we like a lot of the same things, isn't it?"

A melancholy smile crossed her face, but he watched as it fell and consternation clouded her features. "How did you know I like *The Legend of Zelda*?"

He let her work that out on her own.

"Seriously. We never talked about that, did we? You came to my apartment once, but I don't have anything on my walls or... Okay, I'm sure of it. We have never, not once, discussed *Zelda*. I would have remembered. It's my favorite series of all time. But, I mean, that's not something you just pull out of thin air about someone."

She would get to it.

"I left you alone while I got ready that day. You were early. What did you do?"

"I listened through your mic. I heard you playing it. Pretty clever, knowing I would do that." It shredded him to say it. But he had to. He had to keep her away. Even if he had to break her heart to do it, and he knew her well enough by now to know that it would.

"Knowing you would— *What?* You bugged my fucking apartment?" She uncoiled herself slowly from his couch, and he also knew by now that Lindsey didn't only turn red when she blushed. She turned red when she was working herself into a towering rage.

"Come on. You knew I would."

"You knew how freaked out I was about Lena's captors possibly seeing me through her webcam at her apartment, and you *did* that to me?"

He shrugged. "I had to know what you were up to when I wasn't around. Who you might talk to. I have to say the *Zero Wing* and *Zelda* stuff was pretty clever. Things I like, things that might endear you to me."

"Believe it or not, you aren't the only person in the fucking universe who's heard of or loves *Zelda*. I've played every game in the series. I've been playing it since I could hold a controller."

She was on her feet now, glaring, and if looks could kill, he'd have a knife right between his eyes. "And you think—you *honestly* think I pretended to like these things to get you to…what, to *like* me? That's the stupidest thing I've ever heard. You said you believed me—"

"I said I wanted to. I said part of me does. There's still a much bigger part that thinks there might be more at play here than you're letting on, yeah. That I have to still be open to the possibility that you're even worse than your sister."

Her mouth worked soundlessly for a moment. He expected a verbal lashing to burst forth, and he would deserve it, but instead she said, "Test me."

"What?"

"*Test* me. Ask me anything about *Zelda*. If I can't answer, I'll let you tie me up and gag me for the duration of my stay here. I'll admit to whatever you want me to admit to. Let Sully torture me, hell, I don't even care. But if I can answer your questions, you have to believe me. About everything. There's no way Rhys or whoever he is could program thirty years' worth of gaming knowledge into my head. I think even you would agree with that."

He crossed his arms, tilting his head and studying her. Damn. The challenge in her eyes was enough to back down even him. And maybe he'd talked himself into a corner. "All right. In the original, where is the entrance to Level Nine?"

"Spectacle Rock," she snapped back. "Unless you're talking about the Second Quest, in which it is in the farthest northwestern corner of Hyrule."

Jace frowned. "Where is the Hammer found in *The Adventure of Link*?"

"Death Mountain. God, Jace, challenge me at least."

He shifted on his feet and brought a hand to his mouth, racking his brain. She was good. This was backfiring on him horribly. "What does the Cane of Somaria do?"

"It creates blocks you can push onto switches to activate them. Hum the 'Serenade of Water.'"

Any other time, he would have been able to, but the tune was nowhere to be found in his head. He gaped at her for a second, but before he could reply, she'd done it for him. "You call yourself a *Zelda* fan? What about the 'Bolero of Fire'? The 'Inverted Song of Time'? Let me do both of those for you." She did. "What are the names of the two Composer Brothers in *Majora's Mask*?"

"Flat and Sharp," he said eagerly, then caught himself. When the hell had this been turned back around on him?

"Let me tell you something, Jace Adams. I am a bigger *Legend of Zelda* nerd than you'll ever be. I've been to see *Symphony of the Goddesses* twice, and I bawled my eyes out both times. I've played every game through *multiple* times. In fact, the biggest insult you've given me isn't to mistrust me, it isn't that you invaded my privacy, it's that you questioned my *Zelda* fandom."

Jesus Christ, on top of everything, he'd been out-geeked. She'd determined which was worse of all the blows he'd dealt her, but he wasn't sure he could distinguish right now. "All right, Linz, I'm sorry. I believe you…about that."

She pointed a finger at him, stabbing it to punctuate each word. "No! No. That wasn't the deal. And you know what? I take back my terms. You don't get to apologize to me. That's a luxury, and it's beyond your reach as of *this very moment*.

"I don't think I've ever come this close to actively hating a human being in my life. Maybe you deserved everything you got all those years ago. Maybe Lena knew exactly what she was doing when she destroyed you, and for the first time, I think I'm glad she did it. If I ever see her"—she caught her breath in a sob—"*when* I see her, I'm going to give her a high five on a job well done!"

He deserved that. It was still hard to stand here and listen to it, her normally sweet-toned voice shrieking at him in fury, when what he wanted to do was take her in his arms and do something, *anything*, to calm her, make her see his side. Maybe it wasn't even the right side, maybe everything he believed was wrong, but it was all he had to go on. Nevertheless, he attempted, walking nearer to her while she crossed her arms and refused to look at him.

"All right, I won't apologize. You're right. I don't even deserve to try. That still doesn't change our situation." He paused, still several feet from her. "I concede you're a bigger *Zelda* nerd than me."

A chuckle. There was no humor to be found in it, and she still wouldn't look at him. Jace shoved both hands through his hair, knowing there was no way to dig himself out of this mess. Not with her, not with his team. He was right in the middle of this tug-of-war, and it was tearing him apart inside.

He knew which way he wanted to go. But he also knew which way he *needed* to go.

"For what it's worth, I didn't want to do that to you. I felt like I needed to. For our safety. Surely you can understand that. Not forgive it but understand it."

"No. Maybe someday I will. Right now? I feel violated. By you. By someone I had begun to feel incredibly safe with."

"You knew I would check up on you, or you wouldn't have given me your alias."

"Pardon me for not considering that you might go *that* far. All I can think about is what you might've heard, what *personal* things you might know about me now that I have absolutely no clue about."

"You like *South Park* and *The Simpsons*. You seem to lead a quiet life. That's about the extent of it."

"And knowing that, do you really consider me duplicitous enough to be involved in some scheme to bring you down?"

"If you'd seen some of the things I have—"

"But I haven't, see. That quiet life you mentioned is exactly what I have and what I like. It's all I know. I'm not putting on some kind of performance for you. I wouldn't even know where to begin. Lena got all the master-manipulator, adrenaline-junkie genes, and she's welcome to them. I don't ever want to go through something like this again."

He steeled himself against her emotions. It was all he could do. A lie, it all had to be some elaborate lie. Because in some twisted way, if she weren't playing him, it would be even worse than if she were…because he would have treated her this way when she didn't deserve it.

Betrayal he could handle. Turning from her and walking away when she looked at him so pleadingly, while her eyes, her very being begged him to believe her…living with that would be a hell like none he had ever experienced. And he'd known a fuckload of hell.

But he did it. Tore his gaze from hers, turned, and left her standing alone.

He didn't know what else to do, but it would be something he would regret for the rest of his life.

CHAPTER TWENTY-FOUR

Jace walked away, leaving her with a helpless, growing void in her heart. When his bedroom door closed behind him, it felt like being cut off from her only lifeline. For a moment there, she'd thought they could lapse into an easy camaraderie, at the very least. It would hurt, but it would be better than hostility. And then he'd taken that hope and murdered it before her very eyes.

Lindsey wasn't stupid, though. She knew why he'd done it. It was something that would upset her terribly, and he knew it, and he'd *wanted* her to know about it.

She didn't know whether to hate him or thank him for trying to make their impending dissolution of partnership easier for her to bear. He'd done it for her, really. He'd tried to make her hate him. But that's where he'd been wrong; it wasn't easier. If anything, it was harder.

She could understand why he'd done it all. Hated it but could understand it. After all, she was the virus. No one else. And when you were infected, you had to clean out the system or it was ruined forever.

Well, Lindsey could return the favor. She would clean herself out. She would self-destruct, if that's what it took.

To hell with all this planning. To hell with all their "assignments." Whatever N-Tech might be, it was involved in this somehow. Griffin had shown up there—the same man who'd come to Lena's apartment. To hell with caution and everything else. Maybe she could walk in that building *right now* and find her sister, and if not, she could find a clue.

She was tired of waiting on Jace Adams. Maybe their plan was to strike within the next few hours and she would jeopardize that by acting first, but she couldn't know that, because no one would talk to her. Well, maybe they would talk to her if she took the entire mission on her shoulders. Maybe they would believe her then. Even if she never had the benefit of that knowledge because she'd gotten herself killed trying to clear her own name.

Jace would be sorry then, wouldn't he?

Never in her life had she been faced with a situation where she was being called an outright liar while there was absolutely no way she could think of to convince the accusing party otherwise—until Jace Adams.

Lena would know what to do. Hell, Lena would *laugh*, and find a way out, and make the bastards rue the day they ever crossed her, looking fabulous the entire time. The image made Lindsey smile.

Somewhere out there, whomever had abducted Lena probably wished they'd made a very different choice. They'd picked the wrong one the day they picked her.

Because she was out there. Lindsey could see through her superficial doubts now. Despite their differences, their disagreements, if her twin were dead, Lindsey would *know*. Through that genetic connection that transcended all understanding, she would sense the void on the other end if her sister were truly gone.

Right now she needed that connection. She needed to think like her. Act like her. She needed to scheme. She needed a plan.

And what was Lena's main weapon in her scheming arsenal?

Sex. Seduction. The promise of it, in a look or a throaty laugh or a touch, even when she had no intention of acting on it.

Lindsey had blown that all to hell and gone because she'd given Jace the power to make her knees quake, and he knew it. She'd put all her cards on the table with him. It was too late for games, and this one she would lose anyway.

She didn't think her heart could take having him one more time before she left.

The walls around her began to close in. She dropped to the couch and put her head in her hands, deep breathing, not panicking yet but not far from it, either. Four walls had never felt like a prison to her. On the contrary, they'd always represented a sanctuary. A haven from the rest of the world. But now...

She had to get out of here. Had to. It was as much for self-preservation as for her sister at this point. And she didn't know how long he would hole up in his bedroom. Maybe five minutes. Maybe five hours.

She crossed the room and knocked on his door, swiveling her head to watch snow drift down in the gray dusk beyond his living room windows as she wondered if he would even answer. Would it ever stop snowing? Maybe she could simply walk out of the apartment if he didn't—

"Come in."

He was lying on his bed, staring at the ceiling with his hands laced behind his head and his ankles crossed. Lindsey's eyes couldn't help but wander to the swells of his flexed biceps, but then he looked over at her, and she managed to meet his gaze. His dark brows drew together. "Are you all right?"

She'd been through so much emotional turmoil, she must look a haggard mess, especially with the shock of that text message lingering on her face. Maybe one day, in some distant future she didn't dare try to imagine too clearly, she wouldn't be such a mess all the time. First, she had to survive.

And Jace was waiting for her answer, if he even cared. "As well as I can be," she told him.

"Do you need something?"

"Yes." His gaze followed her as she crossed the room and stood beside his bed. He didn't move. She didn't think he even breathed. She let her own perusal roam his body, let her intentions be known.

"Lindsey," he said, his voice husky with barely suppressed need. "You shouldn't be with me right now. I think we both need to cool off."

Her in his bedroom again was probably the very thing he'd been trying to avoid with that stunt just now. Well, she found that throwing a monkey wrench in his carefully laid plans was kind of fun. "Are you not going to let me sleep with you tonight?" she asked, keeping her voice small and hurt. "I don't want to be alone right now. Don't make me be alone."

It was the truth, even though she was doing the very thing he'd been accusing her of: deceiving him.

She let her bottom lip tremble and saw his carefully cultivated ice mask begin to shift, begin to crack.

It happened first in his eyes, in the softening there. And then, sighing, he opened his arms to her, and she went, absorbing the heat from his body into the cold places of her soul as he held her close to him. She would need this, she knew, for what lay ahead. His strength infused into her.

Her lips found the sensitive area beneath his jaw, and she kissed him there, feeling him tense, hearing his breath hitch. "Lindsey." Her hand trailed down the length of his torso, feeling his abs twitch under her touch, and then filling her palm with the bulk of his erection through his jeans.

"Jesus," he groaned, tilting his head back even as he tried to catch her wrist, to stop her explorations. Lindsey let her tongue flicker against his skin and performed a deft move with her fingers, and his grip relaxed, defeated. "This is the last fucking thing we should do," he murmured, sounded beaten and distressed and miserable and turned on. Well, then he felt like she did. Her heart beat throughout her body but nowhere so strongly as between her legs. She needed him there.

"Just once more," she whispered against his ear, the spice of his aftershave intoxicating her. "All these years, I remembered you and how much I wanted you then. I still do."

He went down snarling, but he went down nevertheless, his control snapping as he grasped her head in both hands and kissed the life from her, his lips searing all thought from her head. The pain and the sweetness brought tears to her eyes, how the two could intermingle, how her heart could break even as it sang. "Stop me, dammit," he rasped against her mouth, even between ravenous mouthfuls of her.

"Can't you stop yourself?" she asked innocently, then let her tongue duel sinuously with his.

"No. Only for you, only if you tell me. Fuck, Linz, can't get enough of how you taste."

He tasted like darkness and sin and honey. She tore helplessly at his clothes, needing his flesh beneath her hands. He helped, and then worked at her own, until both of them were naked and twined together.

Deceiving him wasn't right; this was where she felt like she belonged from now on. This felt like *home*, here, pressed against him. How could fate be so cruel as to give it to her and then snatch it away? She'd held them at bay for as long as she could, but tears filled her eyes when he entered her, the beauty of him shattering her as he held her gaze.

"Don't cry," he murmured. "I can't stand it. I want to tear the fucking walls down." He kissed her, and it should've made her feel better, but it didn't. To cover her weakness, she shoved him over onto his back again and straddled him, feeling him deeper and harder than he had been. How was it possible? His hands grasped her hips, setting her into rhythm. A sinful, sultry rhythm, a slow burn that would incinerate her before it was done.

She'd never really liked being on top. Until now. Having all this man beneath her instead of over her gave her an exhilarating rush of power, and she could always use one of those. "Yes," she whispered, letting her head fall back. "Oh God, yes."

Jace's big hands moved up and cupped her breasts, his thumbs stroking over her nipples as she rode him. His calluses rasped her tender flesh, making her bite her lip. He was so deep, so big, and her body knew its own needs even before her brain did. All she had to do was coast on this bliss, her hips undulating on his. He touched every inch inside of her.

And when finally he jerked her down into his arms and filled her up with him, groaning into her ear as his release throbbed inside, she tumbled over the edge with him, biting down on his shoulder to stifle her cries.

Minutes or an eternity later, he pushed her hair back from her face and lifted her chin to look at her. "Lindsey."

She laid a finger against his lips. He was still inside her, softened somewhat, but there was still life in him yet. She replaced her finger with her lips, light brushes across his mouth until he opened and let her in. "What are you doing to me?" he murmured after her tongue dipped teasingly over his, and she felt him harden inside her. *Knocking you out, dear*, she thought, smiling a little as she kept kissing him.

"Just this."

"Thought you were mad at me." His voice was dark, sex-roughened, and it reawakened all the places momentarily sated by her recent orgasm. God save her from all this sexiness, or she might not be able to leave. And leave she must.

"I can be mad and still want it, can't I?" She gave a tentative stroke of her hips, watching his eyes lose their focus with pleasure.

"Is being pissed typically an aphrodisiac for you?" His fingers curled around the back of her neck.

"Well, Jace, no one has ever made me as angry as you can. I guess I'm just now learning this about myself."

"Glad I could assist. I guess." He chuckled, letting his fingers slide through her hair.

"You guess?"

"I like that you want me. Don't like pissing you off."

"Why?" she asked.

"Hurts you," was all he replied as he began meeting the thrust of her hips with his own.

Then why did he do it? At that moment, she almost didn't care. She only wished she could stay here and love this man. If not for the rest of her life, then at least for a while.

CHAPTER TWENTY-FIVE

Somehow, before he opened his eyes, Jace knew she was gone, like the emptiness in the bed next to him had infiltrated his soul even through his sleep. Before he saw the rumpled sheets where her warm body had lain, he knew that Lindsey wasn't only gone from his bed but gone from his apartment, maybe even his life.

He erupted from under the covers stark naked, his feet hitting the floor at a run even though he already knew what he would find. No Lindsey in the bathroom. No Lindsey in the living room. No Lindsey in the kitchen. She had fucked him until he couldn't move anymore, and she'd split as soon as he'd passed out. He would be impressed if he weren't so fucking pissed off.

"Fuck!"

It was a long shot, but he grabbed up his jeans lying on the floor and shoved his legs into them, then slammed his way out into the hallway and pounded on doors. Everyone came sleepily, instantly awake when they heard the dilemma. Sully, of course, had a few choice words for his stupidity, but that was to be expected, and he deserved every one of them.

What a fucking number this girl had done on him. Somehow, that was the worst thing of all. Once again, he'd let himself be lured in by a pretty face. The irony was that it was the exact same face that had lured him in before, making him even doubly stupid.

Fool me twice, shame on me.

After all this was over, maybe the best thing he could do for all of them was leave. He would tell the Captain his judgment had suffered to the point he was a danger to all of them. He'd allowed his own life to be FUBAR, but he didn't have to subject the Nest to the same fate. It had lifted him up, saved him, and now he had most likely destroyed it.

There was no word for the raw, primal rage that slithered through his veins. It wasn't a towering thing—it was dark, and serpentine, something that had crawled up from the depths of hell. The only other time he could recall knowing its sinister lust for revenge was sitting in front of the dean's desk at MIT, learning of Lena's betrayal. He was ready to fucking unleash it on someone. Anyone. Rhys. Lindsey. Lena. All of them.

And God help them when he did.

Of course, most likely she had turned her phone off, but he woke up his computer to run a trace anyway. And frowned. A long note was typed out in a text program on the screen.

Jace—

Yet again, I'm going to say something you don't believe. I know what this looks like to you. Trust me, the last thing I want is to give you another reason not to trust me. But it's something I have to do. For me, for my sister.

I'm going to get her. I don't know what I'm walking into, but don't you dare follow me. Like you'll listen, but anyway.

Not a single thing I've told you has been a lie. If I die today, I will feel better knowing that you believe that, because maybe the only good thing that can come from something happening to me is that you'll know I never betrayed you. Lena did, and I don't know why, and I can't apologize for her. All I can do is assure you that I'm not my sister. I'm not out to get you. I wanted you from the moment I first laid eyes on you in class all those years ago, and I still do. Whatever else comes my way, I got to have you, however brief a time it was. I'll hold on to that through what's to come.

Someone has used me against you after you agreed to help me, and I can't live with it. I'm the virus they used to infiltrate your system, and you will never know how sorry I am about that. If I can make it right, I will.

Lindsey

He clicked off the letter, a knot swelling in his throat, and realized his system had been jacked by some kind of malware. She'd fucking set malware on him so he couldn't trace her. Jace wasn't too stunned to be a little impressed. Meerkat had struck.

But if everything she said in this letter was true, he didn't doubt Meerkat was about to go and get herself killed.

He also had to consider that nothing in this letter was true.

It didn't matter. A vision of her beseeching green eyes flashed in front of him, and all at once, he wondered how, even for a moment, he could have looked into them and not believed every word she was telling him. If he hadn't spent so much time holding back, wondering at her loyalties, checking up on her, letting Lena's phantom hang over him, they might have been able to get through this together. And now he'd made her feel as if going it alone was the better option.

But he had to keep his head on straight.

He searched through his registry to learn the source of her program, hoping to kill it so he could track her. *Damn, damn, damn.* She'd compromised the entire network, and he'd triggered it. He expected the outrage to explode from his teammates any minute now once they realized what had happened.

"Lindsey," he muttered, staring at the mess she'd left onscreen. "Oh no, baby. No, no, no, what are you *doing*?"

Giving up, he charged from his apartment. If nothing else, maybe he could find physical clues.

He took the stairs instead of the elevator, leaping down almost entire flights, nearly breaking his neck more than once. He ran through the lobby, dodging alarmed tenants all bundled up against the cold, many of them with arms laden with colorful gift bags. If there were such a thing as Christmas miracles, he thought, he needed one now. Maybe he would even start to believe again.

Her car was still in the parking garage. He stopped dead in his tracks when he saw it, and then surged forward all at once, reaching it at a full run. If it was here, then where the hell was *she*?

He cupped his hands around the passenger-side window, peering inside as best he could in the garage's muted light. Nothing looked out of sorts in there.

Running around to the driver's side, he moved so fast he almost tripped over the purse lying on the ground. He wasn't an expert of ladies' crap, hardly noticed them, but that taupe leather bag looked like something Lindsey would carry. Jace snatched it up and unceremoniously dumped everything out in his desperation. Keys, wallet. A wad of receipts and some lipsticks.

Sure enough, a quick survey of her ID showed Lindsey's sweet face, and his devilish fury from earlier only intensified at the thought of someone hurting her. Of someone somewhere hurting her *right fucking now* while he couldn't get his head together over her disappearance.

He was shoving everything back inside when he noticed the dark spots on the ground. They could have been oil spots to the untrained eye, but he knew they weren't. Dotting the ground next to Lindsey's driver's side door were drops of blood.

By the time he made it back to the apartment, her bag dangling from his hand, the others were gathered in his living room with grim faces. He took one look at his screen and saw that someone had pulled up the note.

"Fuck all y'all," he spat.

"Jace, come on, dude," Helix said, putting both palms out as if trying to calm a rabid tiger. "You know we had to question everything—"

"Oh my God, you guys are *dense*," Sully exploded. "This is all still part of her plan, Jace! Jesus Christ, she just wants you to follow her so that they can *take you out*. Don't you see that?"

"Sully," he said lowly, dangerously, closing his eyes. "Don't."

She threw her hands up. "Fine. If you're going to rush in and get yourself killed, then I am, too. We are not letting you do this alone."

"And that," Drake said, "is one thing we *all* agree on."

"Then that's too fucking bad."

"I'm calling Cap, then," Sully said. "You're out of control."

"Call him. See if I give a shit. She's only out there right now because she couldn't stand us not believing her." He threw her handbag down on the floor for all of them to see. "There. Her car is still out there. This was lying beside it. There was blood. She did try to leave, but before she got very far, someone took her. And I'm tired of sitting on my ass."

"Jace," Helix said, his eyes filled with the words he probably couldn't say. "I'm sorry. But this is a trap. Even if they did take her, they're doing it to lure you in. You *know* this."

They'd been through so much together, Helix had to know this wasn't going to cause a divide between them. He'd given Lindsey the benefit of the doubt more than any of the others. Even if he hadn't, Jace couldn't fault him for it when he hadn't fully trusted her, either. If anything happened to her, he would regret it for the rest of his life.

I swear on my life I'll make it up to you, he promised, wishing more than anything that she could hear him and that she knew there was no stone on this earth he would leave unturned to find her.

"You're right," he told them all. "It's a trap. But try and stop me from going."

CHAPTER TWENTY-SIX

"Lindsey? *Lindsey.*"

The voice wouldn't go away and let her sleep. It sounded like her own, and still she couldn't make it stop. It hammered inside her skull like the beat of her heart, and...*oh,* everything hurt. Every single cell in her body throbbed, fire racing along her nerve endings. Darkness sought to pull her back under, and she went gratefully.

Images flashed through her mind. Memories. Snow, endless snow. Rapid steps behind her. The sensations, something choking her, blinding pain. In her head, then everywhere. Cold seeping into her bones. More pain. Her face pressed against freezing concrete. Being lifted, moved, which only drove the pain deeper. Voices. No faces. Hoods. Maybe even masks.

The voice in her head wouldn't let her go. "Please wake up. Please be okay." Someone was patting her cheeks. Rubbing her face gently. Putting something cool and wet on her lips, which in contrast felt bone-dry. Even licking them did nothing to replenish the moisture. Lindsey tried to open her eyes, found even that tiny effort cost her too much, and let them fall closed again.

"Linz, if you can hear me, say something. Please."

She grunted. It was all she could muster. The other voice muttered, "Thank God," sounding extremely relieved. Darkness teased at the edges of Lindsey's mind again, beckoning her back into its warm void.

Minutes passed, or hours, or days…she didn't know, didn't understand anything except that every muscle screamed when she tried to move. Someone tried to give her water, but she choked on it and brought it back up. Then the other person—was it one or many?—began banging on something and screaming, each sound like an ice pick chipping incessantly at her brain.

"*Let me out of here, you motherfuckers! If you let my sister die I swear—*"

It was the voice that sounded so much like the one she heard in her own ears every day of her life. *My sister*, Lindsey thought. Oh God, Lena was dying. They'd been too late, and someone had hurt her. She groaned, crying, and the screaming stopped, except in her own mind. *Lena Lena Lena—*

Gentle hands cradled her head but didn't lift it. "Lindsey? Lindsey, baby, open your eyes and look at me, okay? It's me. It's Lena. You have to wake up. *You have to*."

All at once, her thought processes came online. She gasped in a desperate breath, forcing her eyes open as far as she could—which wasn't very—and looked into the mirror of her twin sister's face. "Lena?"

"It's me, I'm here, you're okay, I promise you're going to be okay, I'll get you out of here."

Lindsey sobbed. It was Lena's desperate assurances that spoke to the severity of her injuries. She didn't have to hear the fear in her sister's voice; she could feel the agony, the *wrongness* in her body. As if her heart fought for every beat and each breath made her lungs scream. *If you let my sister die…*

"Am I dying?" It felt like it.

"Hey, I said you're going to be okay, right?" She fussed with something, there was a rustle of fabric, and Lindsey felt a coarse blanket being tucked around her as tightly as Lena could without causing any undue agony. Still, every touch jarred through her like an electric current.

Bone shards grinding on nerve endings. Horrific, disjointed flashes came back to her then, the slam of a boot against her arm, her leg, her stomach. How everything had gone white and she'd thought she was dying then. How she'd cried for Jace, but he hadn't been able to hear her. Because she'd run from him. Because she'd thought she was so smart.

Somehow, that hurt worse than anything else she'd endured, any physical pain anyone could inflict on her. She'd been safe with him, and she'd run.

As soon as Lena had her tucked in, she was back at the door, banging on it and screaming. "Bring her some more water, you son of a bitch!"

"How long?" Lindsey croaked from the bed. "How long have I been out?"

"They threw you in here last night, and I've been going batshit ever since."

"Have you been here this whole time?"

"No, they move me. They always put a hood on my head; sometimes they even put sedatives in my food and knock me out. For all I fucking know, we could be in a different country."

"Have you figured out who has us?"

"No."

"You don't have *any* idea why this has happened?"

Lena was silent for a long time, then resumed her demand for water. But after what she'd said about their captors lacing her food, Lindsey wasn't sure she wanted anything they might bring.

"You didn't answer me," she said softly.

"I don't know."

"You're lying to me. God, Lena, of all places, don't lie to me here."

"I promise you I'll explain everything I do know when we get out of here. But this place isn't for the truth, either."

Lindsey focused on keeping her lungs working for the next few seconds. Then she tried to move her right leg and nearly blacked out. The room spun around her, weakness and nausea forcing her to close her eyes, but that only made it all worse, so she wrenched them open again. Her throat muscles tightened. "I'm going to be sick. I can't move."

Lena's steps shuffled quickly to her side. "Come on, I'll help you. Turn your head, it's okay."

Somehow she got Lindsey on her side, trying to soothe her as she grunted from the agony of what was most likely a broken arm, and to the edge of the cot just in time so that she didn't lie on her back and risk choking while she was sick. Lena stroked her forehead and cursed the whole time. "I swear I'm going to kill every goddamn one of these motherfuckers."

Lindsey listened to her rant as she caught her breath, wishing more than anything for a sip of water. "At least we're together," she said, looking at Lena through streaming eyes. *We came into the world together; it only makes sense we go out that way.*

Lena squeezed Lindsey's hand, looking earnestly into her eyes. "Don't you dare start saying goodbye to me. I told you, we're going to be fine. They haven't let me starve or die yet, and I don't think they'll let you, either. I've been as good as I can for them, but they're about to learn that they've fucked with the wrong one today."

She'd always talked a tough game; it was the former cop in her. But Lindsey wasn't convinced. "You're only going to get yourself hurt like me. Or killed."

"Yeah, well, I'll take some of them out with me."

"I know who they are," she said softly.

"How?"

"So much has happened since you disappeared. But I found him. I found Jace."

Lena went utterly and completely still, and for a second, Lindsey thought she was going to deny sending that text. But then she said, "You did?"

"It's a long story, but all this has something to do with an enemy of his. You must know something about it, or else why would you tell me to contact him? Lena, what's going on?"

"Not now."

The evasion only made Lindsey's anger rise. "Why did you do that to him?"

"Hey, what did I say, huh? Not here, not now. We have to figure out how we're gonna get out of this. There's no way you can run."

Likely she was never going to get the answers she wanted. "I doubt I can even stand up." Fresh tears squeezed from her eyes. "If feels like they broke every bone in my body."

"I do think you have a broken arm and leg. You might have a cracked rib or two and a concussion. I have *got* to get you out of here and to the hospital, if I have to fight through the fuckers to do it."

"Don't leave me, not when I've only just found you."

Lena squeezed her hand again, one of the few places on her body that felt as if someone could touch it without making her scream. "I won't if I can help it. But if I can break out and go get help, I have to take that chance."

Lindsey managed a weak smile. "If you could break out, you would've already done it, and you know it. You're just trying to make me feel better."

"I didn't have the incentive they've given me. I've been a good little captive, sat in my room, eaten my meals, watched TV when they let me."

"That's it?"

"That's it. But now I'm pissed. What the hell have you ever done to anyone to deserve this?" Seeing tears in Lena's eyes was a rare sight to behold, and nothing could shake Lindsey's faith in their survival more than seeing her fearless sister *afraid*. But Lena was scared for her. God, what hope did they have if Lena thought it was hopeless?

Maybe for once, she needed Lindsey to be the strong one. "We can do this," she said, swallowing against the dryness in her throat. Water, she needed water like she needed her next breath. She would lie here and die if she didn't get it soon. "If you can see a way out, Lena, I'll do whatever I can. I'll drag myself with my one good arm."

"I'll *carry* your ass if I have to." Lena's expression

softened. "Like when we were kids. Remember when we were up at the cabin that one summer with Mom and Dad, and we were hiking in the woods by ourselves where we weren't supposed to be, and you twisted your ankle and couldn't put any weight on it?" Somehow, through their tears, both of them found laughter.

"And you couldn't pick me up," Lindsey said, "so you kind of dragged me behind you, and when I kept complaining about rocks and roots, you started gathering all these sticks together thinking you were going to build me some kind of stretcher?"

"I knew everyone would marvel at my ingenuity. How old were we? Nine? Ten?"

"Something like that. You started to figure out you didn't have anything to tie the sticks together with. Finally you dragged me to my feet and made me walk when all I wanted to do was whine that I couldn't and you needed to go get Mom. You didn't want to get in trouble. But you carried most of my weight."

Lena drew a breath. "I'll carry it again, if I can't drag this fucking cot out of here. For now I want you to lie here and rest as best you can. Before we can do anything, I have to get them to bring you water."

Lindsey nodded, closing her eyes, thankful for the blessed darkness. The room wasn't bright, but any light at all was torment.

"Try not to fall asleep again," Lena said. "I'm going to check on you every few minutes."

"Okay." Sleep was all she wanted. An escape from the pain until help came for them. If it came. *Please, Jace, please find us.*

CHAPTER TWENTY-SEVEN

With no windows, she had no way to mark the hours. Was it day, was it night? Lena thought they were in a basement room. That's how she passed the time: speculating. Maybe they were here, maybe they were there. There was definitely more than one person in this operation, Lena said. Lindsey could agree; she didn't remember much from the beating she'd taken except that the blows had seemed to come from all sides and at the same time. If their places had been reversed, Lena probably would have found Lindsey a long time ago.

She tried again to get her sister to tell her why she'd sent her to Jace. And again, her twin turned her questions aside.

"I'm going to keep asking you until you tell me," Lindsey told her.

"Shh. Think, Linz. They *listen*," Lena hissed softly. She gestured toward the ceiling, then shot the finger in that general direction.

Lindsey turned her eyes, since it hurt too much to lift her head. Mounted high up in the shadowy corner of the room was a camera, a tiny white light burning. She couldn't believe she hadn't noticed it before, but most of the time her eyes were shut against debilitating pain.

Jace would be able to disable it in seconds. God, she wished he were here. To think, she had planned to run in here and save the day. But she hadn't expected this. Why hurt her so badly when Lena seemed fine…?

She was taking his punishment.

Of course. She should have realized it before. *I beat him within an inch of his life.* Jace's words about Rhys. But instead of Rhys doling out his revenge on Jace, he'd turned it on her. As someone he suspected Jace cared about? Well, he was most likely wrong.

It was hopeless. She wanted to believe Jace would come, that he *would* care. And that he wouldn't get himself hurt or worse. But maybe she could remove herself from this equation as much as possible.

"Lena?"

"Yeah?"

"I'm going to die here."

"No. You're not. Stop talking, Lindsey."

"He hates me."

"Who?"

"Jace. He hates me."

"The hell are you talking about?"

"I was falling for him, but he doesn't trust me at all. He thinks I'm a liar. He thinks you and I are both horrible people. He's the only one I know who could help us, and he won't come, he doesn't care…" It wasn't hard to bring up racking sobs. They were always near the surface. All the while, the little light burned on the camera.

"Lindsey, anyone who could hate you is a fucking jackass, and I'll tell him straight to his face right before I spit in it." *Dammit, Lena, go along.*

"I wish I'd never met him. He's the worst thing that's ever happened to me."

"When we get out of here and you recover, I'm

taking you on a trip. We deserve a nice vacation after this. I'm going to find you a man who's worthy of you."

She didn't think she wanted any other man for the rest of her life. She'd already found the one, no matter how infuriating he was, and she couldn't have him. Anyone else would pale in comparison.

Lindsey didn't want to believe it, but she thought she was developing a fever. The matter of *when* they got out was shifting more to *if.* Her thoughts seemed to be getting muddier, not clearer. Everything felt hot and sick; her pulse felt thin and rapid where it throbbed in her wounds.

"Come feel my head," she told Lena, who jumped up from where she'd slumped in one corner. Her sister's palm felt cool on her sweaty forehead.

"God. You're burning up."

She coughed and sobbed, raw agony spearing her broken rib. But the spasm went on, heedless of her injuries, and a coppery taste filled her mouth. She lifted her good arm and touched her lips. Her fingertips came away spotted with bright red blood. Panic stole what breath she could catch.

"Jesus," Lena whispered. "I am *not* going to let you lie here and suffer."

Die, you mean? Lindsey thought. *You might not have a choice.* This time, Lena turned her fury to whomever was watching their video feed, screaming at the camera. "She's bleeding internally, do you hear me? She has a fever. She needs a fucking hospital!

"Keep me but let her go. She didn't do anything to you! I swear to God if you let anything happen to her, there's nowhere on this earth you can run to hide from me. We will smoke your asses out and destroy every one of you."

We? Lindsey barely had time to puzzle over it. The door to their small room jerked open while Lena was still doling out threats to annihilate entire families of the perpetrators. She couldn't get a good look at whoever it was, only being vaguely aware of a dark figure. But Lena rushed him.

There had been a lot of hardships lately, but Lindsey didn't think there had been anything harder than listening to her twin scuffle with who knew how many baddies while being unable to help. Lindsey had never been in a fight in her life, but dammit, she could do *something*. If only she could move.

"Lena, stop!" she cried. If Lindsey's salvation was contingent on their good behavior, her sister had just blown it all to hell. Yelling sent her into another coughing spasm, which sent new waves of agony through her. By the time she managed to unclench her eyes and slide them open, Lena was over her again, smoothing her hair back, trying to soothe her. Tears leaked from her eyes.

"Here. They brought water. I tried to get past the fuckers, but I couldn't."

Lindsey drank gratefully as Lena lifted the glass and directed a straw to her mouth. It was cold and wonderful, soothing her raw throat, and she felt it go all the way down her dry esophagus and to her stomach. But Lena would only let her have small sips at a time.

"I have to tell you something," she said at last, her voice as unsteady as Lindsey had ever heard it.

She licked her dry lips to spread the new moisture and tried to bring her twin's face into focus. "Something I should have told you a long time ago, because I know I can trust you. You, more than anyone else."

"What?" Lindsey whispered.

"This is all my fault. You're here because of me, and I... You deserve the truth."

"Then tell me, for God's sake. Tell me why I'm here."

"You have to understand this is nothing Mom and Dad can ever know. They would never understand, and I know how they would worry. I can't ever tell them, and you can't, either."

"Do you really think I'm going to get out of here to tell them anything?" The thought of her dear, sweet parents possibly losing *both* their daughters at once shredded her heart. Lena closed her eyes, and Lindsey wondered if she was thinking the same thing.

"I'm CIA, Lindsey," she whispered.

At first, she wanted to laugh at the absurdity. Even in mortal danger, Lena had jokes. But the sound that came out was closer to a sob. Because the biggest missing puzzle piece that had ever existed in Lindsey's mind clicked suddenly, enormously into place. "You?"

"Don't even question. It's the truest thing I've ever said to you."

The disappearances. The unreliability. The secrets. Everything, *everything*. "Oh my God, Lena," she said, her voice tiny and sick. She thought she might throw up again.

"I sent you to Jace. I did. I knew where he was, I knew his connections, and this syndicate, these *fuckers* who have us… I was undercover, investigating them. The Libra Cooperative. They've had their hands in almost every cyberterrorism plot of the last six years, drugs, human trafficking, you name it. And Rhys is one of their newer recruits. I was connecting all the dots when I was made. They traced a code you wrote back to me."

Lindsey choked on her words for a moment. "*What?*"

"Come on. You know you always did my computer homework for me."

"Stop being so fucking glib about this, Lena. All this time I was wondering how you or I could factor in to all of this, and—"

"Shut up and I'll explain. Remember that night about three months ago, you and I were hanging out at my place, and I got you talking about salami slicing? Penny shaving, stuff like that? I told you I'd seen it in *Office Space* and wondered how it would work."

One of the few times Lena had taken an interest in Lindsey's prowess at the keyboard. She'd been so excited. Now she knew without even hearing the rest of the story that Lena had been serving her own purposes. Typical.

"You sat down at my computer, and within just a few minutes you'd started whipping up a code that would round up pennies and waterfall the excess into a separate bank account."

"You used my fucking code?"

"*Shhh.* I *didn't* use your fucking code, Lindsey. At least, not that one." She could only stare as

Lena sighed and went on. "The one I asked about afterward. The one that would reverse it all. Hell, I don't even remember what you called it. But I used that one. And they want their money back. What they didn't know was that you wrote that code, not me."

All along. All along, they'd had the wrong sister for what they needed but probably figured a CIA agent was as valuable a hostage as they could get. And now they had them both. There would be time later to add this to the long list of things she wanted to strangle Lena over. She needed the rest of the story. "Then what happened?"

"That's pretty much it. They grabbed me. Rhys had connected dots of his own and figured out who I was. That I was the one who was basically responsible for Jace landing in the Nest. He has his vendetta against Jace, but this is bigger than Rhys, so much bigger. I always remembered how you liked Jace and how mad at me you were back then, and I thought if I could get you two working together somehow, he'd keep you safe. These guys, they would go after my entire family. They already have my partner in their pocket."

"Griffin," Lindsey said softly, and Lena, who had been staring blankly at the wall, looked at her with wide eyes. She kept her voice barely above a whisper.

"Yes," she said. "But how did you know that?"

"I met him at your apartment the night you sent me that text. Have you seen your apartment?"

"Yes. That's when I *sent* that text. When I saw they'd taken our picture and I knew you might be a target next. But they got me soon after."

"What about Mom and Dad? You're leaving them unprotected like this? *Lena*—"

"I know, I *know*, and I wanted to get them into some kind of protection, but there wasn't time, and you know they won't go, Lindsey. *You know it.* Dad's had all these heart problems, and this might finish him. I was hoping these bastards would keep the focus on us and leave them out of it. But I don't know."

"They could wipe out our entire family."

"I know."

Lindsey wondered if ignorance had been easier. "Were you sleeping with your partner?"

Lena blinked at her. "Why would you ask me that?"

A question for a question. "Because he kind of insinuated it. You said he's dirty, but I think he cares about you."

"Oh, Jesus. Forget about it, and him. I don't have all the evidence I need on him, either, but when I do, I'll have to expose his ass, too." If she knew her twin—and, well, after this confession, Lindsey truly had to wonder—then she thought she saw a crack in Lena's tough exterior. She still hadn't answered the question. But she didn't have to.

The fact she was remaining silent on the matter said all that Lindsey needed to know. She was tired of thinking, anyway. The room was getting fuzzy, pleasantly so. Her eyes drifted closed.

"Lindsey?"

"Hmmmmm?" she asked, and a giggle bubbled up from somewhere.

"Jesus Christ. Those bastards."

What? This was the best she'd felt since…well, since all those orgasms Jace had given her, maybe.

Lena kept talking, speaking nonsensical words, something about drugs—but Lindsey couldn't be bothered to make sense of it anymore. She gave in gratefully to the numbness, to the darkness.

Her nightmares were vivid. Someone was standing over her, watching her. A dark figure blocking out the relentless overhead light burning beyond her closed eyelids, preventing true darkness. Awareness came back in fragments, but with awareness came pain. She fought it, struggling to remain where it was warm and black, where she drifted in an emotionless void. The darkness wouldn't let her stay. When her broken leg twitched, she came awake with a cry and saw her nightmare of being endlessly watched wasn't a dream at all.

Also, she realized that she was no longer lying down.

Someone had trussed up her injuries to the best of their abilities, and she sat in a chair, the unforgiving plastic cold on her back and behind. Since it hadn't warmed to her body heat, she must not have been here long. Being upright made her head swim, but she would prefer it to being flat on her back any day. In front of her, a glaring white blur slowly shrank into a rectangle, finally focusing into a laptop screen as her eyes adjusted. The room around her, while dim, was vast and echoing, emptiness pressing in around her like shadows.

She also sensed she wasn't alone even before the dark figure strolled casually into her line of sight, standing to the side of the table in front of her, where the laptop sat waiting.

He surveyed her distress from beneath a black hood, his face mostly hidden in its shadow from the few ceiling lights above him. She wondered vaguely if he'd cruelly kicked her injured leg to wake her up.

"We wanted to keep you together," he said conversationally, "but I'm afraid I'll have to deprive you of your sister's company for now. She's a volatile one, isn't she? Nothing at all like you."

It wasn't a voice she recognized. Was this Rhys? "Who are you?" she asked, looking around wildly, though she nearly blacked out again from sheer dizziness. Lena was nowhere to be seen. God, how much time had passed? Where was she now? "Please don't take her from me. I need her with me. If you're going to let me die in here, then at least leave her with me."

He only gazed down at her impassively.

She managed to find the shred of anger that still burned somewhere in her soul. "And if you're doing this to get to Jace, you know, you've wasted your time. He doesn't care."

"So you've said." He placed a hand against her forehead, and it was all she could do not to recoil. He left it there a moment and drew away. "You don't have much time, Ms. Morris. I suggest you proceed."

Lindsey blinked at the system in front of her. "What?"

"We want our money back."

Arguing or playing dumb at this point seemed futile. They knew. Lena probably hadn't wanted them to know, probably wanted to protect Lindsey with her dying breath. But it hadn't worked out that way. "I'm surprised you don't have people who can do this," she said.

"You're a talented coder," he said. "More so than I think you give yourself credit for. My people tried to redesign the code and back out of it, but this is why you're here."

"I'm touched."

"You have twelve hours. We have quite a few incentives at our disposal to ensure that you work promptly to return everything that was stolen from us."

Stolen from them. That was rich, when the money was stolen in the first place. "What happens in twelve hours?"

"I'm sure I don't have to describe that to you at this point."

"Pretend I'm stupid."

He crossed him arms, and what she could see of the grim slash of his mouth tightened. "We could always bring Agent Morris back into the room, as you requested. But I assure you, you won't like what we do to her."

A chill worked its way down her aching spine. She closed her eyes. "What if I can't type? My hands—"

"You have one good one."

"I'm too hurt to sit here and—"

"Twelve hours. You've had adequate rest. We'll bring you water and food and medication to replenish your strength, and my apologies for your discomfort. My associate was overly enthusiastic."

"*Enthusiastic?* I could be dying right here in this chair."

"Your vitals are satisfactory, except for that fever, which we'll try to bring down." He began walking away, everything about his steps casual and assured. "Twelve hours. Your time has begun." With one sweeping gesture, he indicated the white, nondescript analog clock on the wall to her left. It was six thirty-four exactly. Whether that was a.m. or p.m., she had no idea.

Lindsey stared blankly at the screen in front of her, flexing her left fingers, trying to get some feeling back into them. Twelve hours to write a code that would rip off people all over the country, even if it was such infinitesimal amounts that they didn't realize it.

How the hell had it come to this?

CHAPTER TWENTY-EIGHT

*D*on't *get emotionally involved*. How many times had he heard it? Too many to count. Jace scrubbed both hands through his hair, elbows on his desk, deep breathing. No one liked feeling helpless, but he hated it just a little more than the average person. For hours, he'd been poring over the information they had—which was far too little—looking for something, anything, that might trigger a plan for what to do next.

Lindsey had been taken. His gut told him that, that it was her blood on the concrete in the parking garage, and she was somewhere, suffering, in pain, scared, *right fucking now*.

He could proceed with this and remain cautious at the same time. Trap or no, Rhys was a threat that needed to be annihilated. Hell, he should have done it when he'd had the chance.

His email *dinged* him, as it had been doing for the past fifteen minutes or so. He didn't much care because anyone he needed to hear from right now had barely left his apartment over these dark hours. They were going over everything, too, looking for something he'd missed, trying to come up with a plan of attack.

"Jace. You good?" Helix asked, apparently noticing his whipped-dog posture. Eyes sore and burning, Jace lifted his head and swiveled his chair around to face them all.

"Good as I can be."

"We think the best course is paying the N-Tech building a little visit," Drake said. "It's our one and only lead at this point."

Thinking of that place made him think of her, but then, she couldn't have been erased from his thoughts with a fucking lobotomy at this point. How she'd melted against him when he'd kissed her.

To his team, he gave a grim nod. Nothing else to do. *Ding* went his email again.

"The fuck," he muttered. No one ever emailed him this much. He didn't have that many contacts—

Whirling back around to his keyboard almost before his conscious mind could catch up, he pulled up his email. Anything that out of the ordinary couldn't be a simple coincidence. When he saw the messages were from his bank, he frowned and sat back as he clicked through them.

"Dude, don't keep us in suspense. What is it?" Helix asked.

"I'm getting deposits every few minutes. They're only pennies. I'm damn sure not doing it." After a moment, he felt the others crowd in behind him, and as they watched, another notification popped up.

"Who has your bank account info?" Sully asked.

"No one I know of, obviously." *Or maybe anyone who has messed around on my computer, put malware on it, or knows how to code like Lindsey.* "She's talking to me," he said, mostly to himself. Then, louder, "She's fucking *talking* to me."

"Trace those!" Helix surged forward as if he meant to take over and do it himself in his excitement, but Jace knocked his hands away.

"Out, all of you out. Now."

"But—"

"I'll call you if I need you, but I have a lot of damn work to do." He watched as more and more pennies began falling into his account, waiting for Sully to caution him that it was a trap. She might have been thinking it, but if so, she maintained her silence.

"Let me help you on this, man," Helix said, the screen reflecting in his dark eyes. "This will take you hours."

"I know where you are if I need you," Jace said stubbornly. This was his problem. He'd brought Lindsey in. He'd unearthed the skeletons. He'd opened them all up to potential betrayal and danger. He would be the one to figure it out.

No matter what it took.

. . .

Lindsey was so hot, she thought even her eyeballs were sweating. Trying to move as few muscles as possible, she lifted the glass of cold water they'd left her, hand trembling as she brought it to her lips. Her eyes ached, but she knew she wasn't dehydrated, if only because of the steady stream of tears that leaked from them.

These things were fun to talk about in theory. But knowing she was sitting here taking money from actual people, even to save her and her sister's lives, opened an ache in her chest. She had done this, but if she could, she would do her best to make sure it was all returned.

"Sixty-five more minutes, Ms. Morris," that hateful

voice said from behind her. He hadn't left the room, whoever he was, but thankfully he hadn't watched over her shoulder this whole time, either. "We haven't yet been fully compensated. Is there some reason it's taking so long?"

She injected all the strength she could into her voice. "I'm sure you realize the government monitors the movement of large amounts of money since 9/11," she said. "I'm trickling the money through multiple accounts so it's harder to trace. It's taking longer, but it's safer."

Which was mostly bullshit. And the only account she was worried about was Jace's. The program she'd put on his computer had allowed her in to get the info she needed to access his bank accounts. Now she could only hope that he got frequent notifications, so he could see something abnormal was going on. And that he'd be smart enough to trace it back to her.

If he would even bother or care. It was the only thing she knew to do.

Her body was one big, throbbing raw nerve. They'd given her something, thankfully, and at least she didn't want to scream in agony with every movement, but it only took the edge off. She still needed a hospital. Her left eye was nearly swollen shut, and as she'd worked she'd feared the right might close, too, leaving her blind and unable to finish. Somehow, she'd managed.

A door opening and slamming across the cavernous room jerked her from her thoughts. The shuffling of feet and Lena's cursing injected new fury into her heart, shocking it awake like a defibrillator. A similarly garbed man to the first one was half dragging, half carrying her sister in and having a hell of a time with it, even given Lena's bound hands and feet.

Lindsey would have surged up from her chair. Moving her broken leg made her decide otherwise. "What are you doing?" she cried. "I've done everything you asked." Because she didn't think it was as simple as *Good job, here's your sister, you're free to go.* These people didn't operate like that.

"We're still eight million shy. My calculations tell me that we won't reach our total amount owed in sixty-five—actually, sixty-three minutes."

"But you'll get it. It's just taking longer than I thought it would, which I explained to you."

"Tell me you didn't do what they wanted," Lena groaned, still wrestling her captor as he wrangled her closer.

"I had to," Lindsey said softly, only to her. "I'm sorry."

"They're going to kill us anyway." And Lena would rather die on her own terms, rather than let herself be manipulated into doing their dirty work before she went. Lindsey got that. But first, she'd rather try to live.

Maybe it had been hopeless from the start. Maybe all they could hope for now was a more merciful death. Lindsey looked at the man who had been in the room with her all this time, whose face was perpetually half in shadow, and wondered again if this was Rhys, wondered if he had authority here and if there were any vestiges of sympathy lurking in some dark corner of him that she could reach.

Lena's masked captor paused with her a few feet away. Lindsey looked deep into her sister's eyes, trying to read something there, hoping for some shared twin insight or plan—but saw nothing. She couldn't be *resigned* to this. That wasn't like her at all.

Lindsey wasn't bound in any way. She couldn't have gotten herself out of her chair, much less walk. After all these hours, even if she didn't have the fractured bones, her butt was asleep, and so were the backs of her legs. She would fall as soon as she stood. No chance to fight.

She was pondering the impossible odds when Lena turned a scathing look on the man beside her and said, "At least have the sac to show me your face, asshole."

He stared back at her, the deep black eye holes of his plain white mask sending a chill through Lindsey's blood. Just when she expected he wasn't going to make a move or comment, he lifted his hands and pushed the mask back, taking his hood with it.

Griffin, Lena's partner, the liar who'd shown so much concern over her and now held her in chains. Lindsey found her heart could break just a little more from the pain that filled her twin's eyes.

Not surprise. Her sister had known who held her before she challenged him, but Lindsey could tell her knowledge didn't make the revelation any easier.

"How could you do this to me?"

If she was putting her feelings out on the table, he was taking his away, his face as flat and expressionless as that mask had been. There was no remorse, no apology there that Lindsey could see.

"Well, then, fuck you," Lena said, spitting the words at him. "You're going to get yours. And when you do, I hope my face is the last thing you think of before you choke on your own blood."

Lindsey expelled a shuddering breath. She wanted to lash out at him, too, but the words she was reaching for weren't there. Her mind had shut down, a cold numbness suffusing her. Is that what it was like to know you were facing the end? She could hardly spare a thought for the people she was leaving behind. They didn't exist in this place, and she wanted to keep it that way. Jace and everything he'd made her feel; her parents and all the love they'd given her throughout her life—this was a dark place, and their light didn't belong here.

But she still had her sister. "Let us be together, at least," she asked the man who stood back in the shadows, quietly watching. She figured his word was law, whoever he was. "I can't go anywhere. Let me hold my sister."

"Take these fucking cuffs off me, Sharpe," Lena demanded, glaring back at the man who'd told Lindsey to call him Griffin. "Congratulations, you've won. I won't fight. But after everything we've been through and everything you've done, I don't deserve to die this way. You *know* it."

He glanced to his superior for guidance. Lindsey didn't see the gesture, but it must have been given, because Sharpe moved up behind Lena and began removing her handcuffs.

"Agent Morris, I trust you realize the consequences of any foolish actions on your part."

"Yeah, yeah," Lena muttered while Lindsey bit her lip and winced from forgetting it was split. Her sister stood docile while her cuffs were removed, but Lindsey feared the worst. If Lena knew they had nothing to lose at this point, what might she do? As soon as she was free, though, she only ran forward and dropped to Lindsey's side, gently wrapping her arms around her and dropping her head to her lap. Lindsey lowered her face as best she could into her sister's messy hair and breathed her in, wrapping her good arm around her.

Now she was ready to face whatever they might dish out.

"I'll revisit you when we are fully compensated. Ms. Morris, Agent Morris." The man said their names politely in farewell, and Lindsey heard his departing footsteps, but a glance upward showed Griffin—Sharpe—still with them. He retreated to a distant corner and sat in a chair she hadn't noticed before. She had no doubt he was fully armed, should either of them try anything.

She'd tried to take stock of her surroundings while she'd been working. It seemed they were being kept in a warehouse of some sort. But who knew where or how far from home? She had no idea how long she'd been out or how far she had been moved when they drugged her.

Lindsey turned her head back to the computer screen and watched the account numbers slowly rise. Fractions of pennies. Sand in their hourglass.

CHAPTER TWENTY-NINE

It was a trap they were setting. So, fair enough. Jace walked right the fuck into it, head up, guns ready to blaze. His team had always accused him of being too reckless. He couldn't very well not live up to the label when so much was at stake. He was alone, but they were still with him. Helix was in his earpiece right now, giving direction, taking commands.

The address where they were holding Lindsey traced back to the Libra Cooperative, so Rhys had apparently found a new home for his talents. But even as Jace stalked through their compound, SIG in hand, they wouldn't catch him on their security cameras. Helix was disabling them as he went. But that alone would bring guards running. Blindly into his bullets.

He'd been coding for almost ten hours straight, and he hadn't had sleep since Lindsey fucked him to exhaustion, so he was running on pure adrenaline. She couldn't have much time left. Cap was bringing on Lena's colleagues at the CIA, but he couldn't wait for them to get their asses in gear.

When he had finally zeroed in on the source of the deposits, in addition to the time it had taken him to trace them, the flight to Salt Lake City had been almost two hours, then yet another hour to get to the warehouse the money was originating from. He had no time for fucking delicacy here, no time for surgical precision. This could only be a full-on raid, and his one blazing hope was that Rhys wanted to make this personal. That the asshole wanted a showdown and would keep Lindsey alive until he got it. Jace would gladly grant his wish, and this time he'd finish what he'd started years ago.

Three bodies in his wake. Now four. Dark hallways. Doors. He swept every room he found, taking note of the stock of weapons and drugs. They were running guns and who knew what else.

Panic surged with every room he cleared with no sight of Lindsey, his heart tripping in his chest, but he fought back the bright sickness churning in his gut. If she wasn't here—Jesus Christ, he didn't know what he would do.

If he had just listened to her, she might not be in this situation, her blood might not have been on the ground in his parking garage. His team thought he had lost it, that he was on a suicide mission—he didn't care.

In the back of one of the cluttered ground-floor offices—one that looked to be mostly used for storage—he found a descending staircase behind what he'd initially assumed was a closet door. Dark, cold, and echoing. He swept his light around, his blood rushing in his ears. The stairs made a turn on a landing below. Beyond that he could see nothing.

He made his way down and down again, the darkness swallowing his light only a few yards in front of him. He didn't trust the silence. It meant something was waiting. He much preferred chaos— he'd rather see the threat screaming in his face, where it could be neutralized. He could only handle what he could see and hear.

Gun drawn, he followed the tunnel until it met

another flight of stairs. These went up. He took them two or three at a time, following twists and turns. "Helix, I don't know where the fuck I am," he muttered into his mouthpiece. This was some deep level of dark hell.

"Keep going until you do," his brother advised.

Thanks, asshole. He thought he was on ground level again when two guys jumped him in a hallway. One of them he knocked out within seconds. The other he slammed against the wall, the barrel of his gun pressing hard enough into the bastard's chin to leave a permanent impression. "Where is she."

Furious dark eyes bored into his. He didn't recognize the face. A flunky trying to be the hero of his own story. But he could plainly see the guy wasn't up to spilling any information. "It's your lucky day, man. I've left a trail of your buddies behind me, and one more won't make a fuck of a difference. I suggest you start talking if you want to make it out of here alive."

With his eyes alone, he indicated Jace's right, where the hallway ended in a doorway, and since he hadn't rushed Jace with a gun, he did him the courtesy of merely cracking his head against the wall instead of killing him. The guard crumpled to the floor at Jace's feet.

Libra was definitely expanding, if they had so many guys on hand.

That grim knowledge was with him as he surged through the indicated door into a vast, dim room with a ceiling so high and shadows so deep that anything could be lurking. But he only saw one thing, sitting in one pool of light in the far corner.

Lindsey.

Clearly, he could not always handle what he could see. Because even from this distance, he could see her beaten face, the blood caking her sweet mouth and her bright hair.

"No," she cried softly when her eyes found him.

Only then did he notice that someone was crouched beside her, a woman with her head in her lap. She turned to present an identical face, and after all this time, all these years, all this trouble, he tried not to fucking recoil, but it was difficult. Lena.

Lindsey looked only at him, but Lena's eyes immediately darted off to the side. "Look out!" she cried, and immediately a shot rang out. One of the women screamed—probably Lindsey. Jace felt a searing pain slice his right biceps, an impact that nearly turned him in a full circle. Luckily, he was left-handed and returned fire as soon as he got his feet back under him. Whether it was the pain or the weakness from the hit he'd taken, he missed. The man stalked forward, his gun leveled at Jace's head. As he was contemplating another shot, to his absolute horror, the guy swung his aim over to the ladies, the barrel glinting in the dim lights. The sound Lindsey made would forever haunt his nightmares. Lena merely stared back at her assailant with an icy defiance he could almost admire.

"You put that right back on me," Jace bit out, knowing he needed to get pressure on his wound. He was losing blood fast. It pumped down his arm in hot rivulets.

"I don't think I will." As the guy strolled closer, Jace recognized him. He'd seem him when he was watching N-Tech with Lindsey. This was Griffin. "Toss down your headset."

He did, severing his connection with the team, Helix still yelling in his ear.

"Now put down your piece. Nice and easy."

"Man, you know, I just really hate putting my gun down. Because you should know that if I get this shot off, you're dead. Only you. *Maybe* you can fire before the bullet enters your skull, but most likely you won't. You'll swing wide with the impact, and if the gun goes off because your finger twitches, well, the bullet will only hit the wall or the ceiling."

"Except you're wounded, and I just saw you miss."

"I won't miss this time, motherfucker."

"Stop." The voice came from behind them, cold, dead, familiar. He didn't have to turn his head; somehow, he knew without looking when a gun was pointed at him. The chill was always the same, icy and precise on the back of his neck.

"Turn around."

Lindsey whimpered in the distance. Jace met her eyes for a heartbeat before slowly stepping around to face the one who had spoken.

Rhys.

All Jace wanted was to charge across the room and beat the bastard to the brink of death again. No, beyond. This time, he would go beyond that brink. He wanted him to suffer; he wanted him to die with Jace's hands locked around his throat. Maybe, just before Rhys succumbed to unconsciousness, Jace would let him draw a breath or two, then do it all again. Torture him.

He steadied his galloping heart. "It's been a long time."

His old teammate had always had a sinister gleam in his eyes. Hell, they all did—it was practically a requirement. The years had done nothing but define Rhys's gleam until it was as lethal and merciless as a blade's edge. He stood dressed all in black, his gun leveled at Jace's head. He didn't speak, only stared, as if grappling with the *need* to pull that trigger.

Knowing when he was beat, Jace presented his palms in a brief surrender, then knelt to gently place his weapon on the concrete at his feet before stepping back several paces. In these situations, not having his gun was like not having his hand. But it freed him up to clasp his bleeding gunshot wound, trying to stanch the flow.

"Jace," he heard Lindsey whisper, "no."

"Do whatever you want with me, but let the twins go."

"Touching," Rhys said. In one fluid motion, he withdrew and re-holstered his weapon, but Jace knew the threat was still there. Rhys was no slouch with a piece. Still, he released the breath that had been held captive in his lungs. "You're too easy sometimes, Adams."

"Why?" he demanded. "Why Lindsey? What did she ever do to deserve this?"

Rhys gave an easy shrug, the effortless, disarming charm still about him. It was how he'd kept them all fooled for so long. "We needed her, but as far as her injuries, perhaps the more pertinent question is, what did *you* do to deserve this?"

It was all his fault. Every blow Lindsey had

taken—she was bruised and broken all over—was in retaliation for the ones he'd dealt out to Rhys that day all those years ago. He'd snapped, and he knew it...but the loss of innocent life weighing on his conscience had broken him. It had broken all of them. But he'd been the only one to let it fester to the point of temporary madness.

In Rhys's twisted mind, the best revenge was rendering him powerless—hurting Lindsey, someone he cared about, while he could do nothing to make it better. His eyes burned, and he would have given anything to hold her right then. Every hurt, all her pain, all his fault.

"I should kill you for this," he ground out.

"You should, but you won't." Rhys picked at an invisible speck on his black shirt. "One wrong move from you and she and everyone she loves will die."

"These women don't have anything to do with you and me," Jace said. "Leave them out and take me. Do what you want. Break my bones, torture me, do what you feel like you need to do. I'm here. But she goes free."

"That's tempting. You probably could never even *dream* of what I'd love to do to you. If I hadn't already known you would make that offer, I might even jump on it right now. But I dealt with the disappointment of knowing I'd never get that chance a long time ago, and, well, it's not as fun if you're offering. I know you, so stoic, you'd take every hit and ask for more even though I think I could come up with some ways to make you scream. So...sorry, Adams. My answer is no."

"Why?"

"You're far more valuable to Libra alive than dead. Trust me, I'd put a bullet in your head right now if you weren't. It's inconvenient. But the best way to keep you docile as a mouse is sitting right over there, don't you think? She isn't all that valuable to us, not anymore. She did her part. No, she's pretty expendable to everyone—except you."

Rhys's words were so offensive Jace might have ground his own teeth into dust trying to maintain control. Looking over at Lindsey's wounds, her soft, pretty face so bruised and bloody, her hair matted and streaked with dried blood, a shaking fury spread out from his chest, but he didn't have anywhere to direct it. Rhys would kill her. It would be nothing to him to do so. But she was *more* than a fucking pawn in his game.

She was everything to him.

The Griffin bastard still held a gun on her. Whether it would strike her or Lena, he couldn't quite tell. Maybe both of them. They would die in each other's arms, reunited at last.

"However," Rhys went on, crossing his arms, "what you're failing to realize is that three is better than one. Why would I release them and keep you when I have you all right here? Think of all the fun I'll miss out on."

"What do you want from me?"

"Jace, really? You have to ask? A man of your talents?"

"If you think I'm leaving the Nest to join up with these Libra fucksticks, you've lost your damn mind, Rhys."

"Imagine what we could be, what we could achieve.

We balance the scales. Corporations run the world, Jace. They make up over half of the richest economic entities on the planet, a planet that should be ours."

"And you're going to take it back. Jesus. Who put all this bullshit in your head?"

"Someone I really think you should meet."

"Not interested."

He saw the glance that Rhys exchanged with Griffin and went on full alert, snatching his gaze over to Lindsey and Lena. A *ding* came from somewhere. "Ah," Rhys said. "Paid in full. Thank you, Ms. Morris, for your assistance. Your services are no longer required."

CHAPTER THIRTY

She'd tasted fear these past few days, but none like this. None like having an unwavering gun pointed at her, so that the world contracted to that tiny black hole in the end of the barrel, where something waited to leap out and end her life. She wished she could be more like her sister, who stared that horror in the face unflinching, but she couldn't. She could only watch Jace, trying to draw strength from the mere fact that he was here, and pray.

"Your services are no longer required."

The cold tone of Rhys's voice left no doubts as to his meaning. He would kill her now and not think twice about it. But if the exchange would be that Jace would be under his thumb, she was willing to give her life to free him from that. Lena's hands tightened around Lindsey's good one, her grip cool and clammy.

Jace surged toward Griffin as the latter adjusted his aim. All Lindsey knew was that the bullet would hit her. She didn't know where. Would it be fast so that she didn't feel it? Slow to add more agony to her busted limbs and ribs? "Don't you fucking hurt her anymore," he bellowed at Griffin.

"Say the word, Jace, and maybe soon you can talk me into letting them go," Rhys said. "Dependent upon your good behavior, of course."

He looked over at her, and she literally saw him weakening before her very eyes. And he was bleeding so badly. "No!" Lindsey screamed at him.

Little else had been worse than compromising her integrity to code for these people.

It was the last thing on earth she wanted for Jace.

Someone of his abilities… He could wreak so much havoc she could hardly bear to think about it. He was a weapon, and in the wrong hands, he could be destructive.

She'd been useful, but he'd been the prize.

"If you knew shit about anything," Jace said to Rhys, "*she's* the one you'd be after to join your band of merry assholes. Not that I would want that for her, any more than I want it for me.

"But you're missing the mark on this one. Look at what she did here today. You'd had her beaten half to death. Look at her. She literally did this one-handed, with both eyes closed, or close enough. Got you your money and got me here. And she's the one you want to kill to get to me? I'm *shit* in comparison to her. You don't need me. Take me the fuck out; get your revenge. Do it now." He lifted both arms out to his side, even his injured one. His blood dripped on the floor.

Rhys narrowed his eyes in contemplation. She shook her head furiously, though it made her even dizzier than she already was. He was trying to buy her more time, but his words were so wrong they were offensive to her. "Lena, we have to stop this," she hissed in her sister's ear.

"Shh. Let him talk."

"Come on, Rhys," Jace said to his ex-teammate. "I'm not who you want."

Rhys jerked his gun from his holster and leveled it at Jace's head. "You got that right."

A gun went off. Lindsey screamed, pitching herself from the chair, Lena catching her before she could fall to the concrete floor. More gunshots rang out, utter confusion setting in as Lena covered her with her body, keeping Lindsey's head pushed down. She couldn't *see*, and she couldn't hear from the ringing in her ears and her head, so much sound creating what amounted to a screeching silence. She fought like hell to get up and get to Jace, who was surely lying dead on the floor, but her sister's weight and her own injuries kept her from moving. All she could hear over the cacophony was Lena yelling Sharpe's name.

Jace, Jace, oh Jace, no.

The hard concrete beneath her couldn't absorb her tears. She wanted to just lie here, make an ocean, and drown. She needed to see, needed to get to him, but she didn't want to. She couldn't see him dead. Griffin—Sharpe—whoever-he-was should have just pulled the trigger and put her down. It would be preferable to the pain that tore through her heart at the thought of Jace bleeding out on the ground.

Then another voice rang out. It sounded distant, as if the fight had moved outside the room.

"Get her out!" *Jace?* "Lena! Get Lindsey the fuck out!"

"Time to drag your broken ass outta here, little sister." Her twin's hands, identical to hers but far stronger, seized under her armpits and lifted. Lindsey barely felt the pain, such was her elation. That had been Jace's voice, and it was the most beautiful thing she'd ever heard in her life.

"What happened? I thought—"

"My partner came through. He shot Rhys, but some of his cronies busted in and got the bastard out."

"Jace?"

"I think he got hit again."

"Oh God!"

"Lindsey, *focus*. He can handle himself. You're my priority right now. Come on, sister, step. Help me out. You can do it."

With Lena's cheerleading, she managed to step with one leg and sort of drag the other, leaning heavily on her sister for support. It was excruciating. It was physically the hardest thing she had ever done. But Jace was somewhere out there, hurt and bleeding, too, and that gave her the strength to trudge forward.

Just as they were reaching the door, Lindsey panting with her exertions, they stopped with gasps as another group of armed men and women burst in, guns drawn. Lindsey finally, thoroughly prepared to die. Lena only gave the bunch a hard glare and bellowed, "It's about fucking time!"

Lindsey had her cavalry. It looked as if Lena's had finally arrived.

CHAPTER THIRTY-ONE

Lindsey stared down at the cast that enclosed her leg from thigh to ankle. Never in her life had she broken a bone before. Now she'd had several.

They'd named the bones for her, but she couldn't be bothered to recall which they were. They freaking hurt when cracked and shattered—that much she knew. Her leg and a rib had required surgery.

Almost as bad were the bruises that covered her almost head to toe, sickening shades of black and purple, and yellow as more superficial ones healed before the darker, deeper ones did. Her body was one gigantic blur of pain and soreness. But the drugs were pretty good. She had no complaints about those.

Her mom and dad kept a vigil by her bedside. The story she gave them was that she had been mugged and beaten and left. She hadn't seen her attackers well enough to give a description. Someone had come along and brought her to the hospital. Yes, that was odd—why hadn't they called an ambulance? The police? Who the hell knew. She told her lame story so many times she almost believed it herself. Almost.

And she waited for Jace.

He was okay. The first bullet had grazed his right arm. A second had taken him in the left calf. He was hobbling a little but, all in all, was in better shape than she was. Sharpe, Lena's partner, had saved his life. His had been the gunshot she'd heard, the one she'd been certain had taken Jace's head off—and to hear him tell the story, he'd pretty much thought the same for a split second. Turned out Sharpe wasn't quite as deep in Libra's pockets as he'd wanted Lena to believe, but Lena still wasn't sure whether to trust him.

Her hospital room door opened, and Lena walked in. Lindsey choked on her breath. She would have flung her covers back and run to her twin if she could. The two of them had spoken briefly on the phone, but this was the first time they'd seen each other since her people had whisked Lindsey away to a Salt Lake City hospital. She was now back in Denver.

Lena's face, so like her own, was drawn and grave. "How are they treating you?" she asked, her gaze roaming over the IV and steadily beeping monitor as she closed the door behind her and approached the bed, all business.

"They're slowly putting me back together."

"They tell me you'll be good as new."

Lindsey gave a humorless laugh. "I don't see how. I can't imagine ever feeling normal again."

"You will." The knowing in Lena's voice made Lindsey wonder if she'd ever spent time recovering in a hospital all alone while her family cursed her absence and irresponsibility. How wrong they had all been.

"Lena…" She dropped her voice to a whisper and cast a gaze around. It wasn't as if someone was hiding behind the visitors' chairs, but God, this paranoia wouldn't leave her. After everything they'd gone through, Rhys had gotten away. "You have to help Jace."

All Lena did was lift a finger to her own lips in a shushing gesture. *I'm not being paranoid, am I? There's danger all around us.* "It's going to be all right," her sister said in a normal tone. But what did that mean?

"Have you seen Mom and Dad?" She had just missed them leaving by twenty minutes or so.

"Yeah. Told them I was sorry about skipping out on their anniversary party. I won't be forgiven for that anytime soon."

"I'm sorry. I'm so sorry about everything."

Lena gave a shrug, the picture of nonchalance. The exact same way she'd brushed off their scolding for years now. How had she carried this burden for so long without snapping?

Lindsey reached for her hand, and Lena took it with a swiftness that spoke volumes from someone who had an aversion to displays of affection. "Thank you," she whispered. "For all you do for us."

Except for a moment of weakness during their recent stint in captivity, she didn't think she'd ever seen Lena's eyes well with tears. Not since they were little. "It feels good to hear someone say that," Lena replied softly. Then she let go and flipped her hair behind her shoulder. "And now, hospitals make me feel gross, so I need to go."

"Promise me we'll see each other more. As often as we can." If this experience had shown her anything, it was that they had to stick together.

"Oh, you know me, Linz," Lena said airily. She couldn't stand being pinned down.

"Yeah. I know."

"Tell you what. Despite that fact—I'll do my best."

"I guess that's all I can hope for, huh?"

"You're lucky to get that. But I love you, little sister. Never forget it."

"Hey. Only little because you beat me out by seventeen minutes. But I love you, too."

"By the way, I talked to Dad yesterday, too, and he was upset that he couldn't get into your apartment to bring you his present. You know, the one he said he stopped by to give you."

"He shouldn't worry about that. I'll get it in time."

Lena dug into the depths of her handbag. "It just so happens I took it upon myself to get it for you." She brought out the little brightly wrapped box, holding it up with the tips of her fingers. "How come you always get the tiny boxes? That's always the good stuff."

"Because I'm the good twin." Lindsey reached for it with her intact arm. "How did you get in?"

"I went to your super and pretended to be you. God, do you know how difficult that was for me? I can barely pull off that wide-eyed, dewy innocence of yours. Being nice to people is so hard. Now open that before I leave, so I can be jealous."

Laughter hurt Lindsey's ribs, oh hell, how it hurt, but in her soul, it felt good. She opened the little box, finding a beautiful gold picture locket with an old photo of her when she was no older than six or so, and Lena on the other side. The only difference in their faces was that Lindsey was missing a tooth on the right and Lena was missing one on the left.

It was so like her father to give her this, to be the peacemaker after he'd known Lindsey was so upset about the anniversary party. There was a message here, and she tried her damnedest not to burst into tears. Even Lena was struck silent, simply giving Lindsey's hand a farewell squeeze before shouldering her purse strap and walking toward the door.

She reached for the handle just as it opened… and came face-to-face with Jace.

Lindsey's eyes flew wide, and she couldn't grasp onto any one emotion. Elation to see him. Horror that she might have to crawl from her bed, broken bones and all, to get between them. Jace's face underwent so many expression changes in the span of two seconds that she had no idea what was about to come out of his mouth.

Lena, however, didn't miss a beat. "I bet you've spent all these years coming up with the perfect thing to say if you ever saw me again, Jace. But I have just one thing, so let me say it. I'm sorry." She smacked him on the shoulder as she breezed past him. "Take care of my sister."

He turned about three shades of red before his gaze alighted on Lindsey in her bed, and all animosity drained from his features. "Please don't hold her against me," she said, hoping to pull him back from whatever dark place that rage had flung him.

Somehow, it worked. "Much rather hold you against me." One corner of his mouth lifted in that wicked smirk she loved so much. She wanted to weep from seeing it again, she was so grateful, but she managed to hold it together.

"I'm afraid I won't be much good for that for a few weeks yet," she forced out.

His expression gentled even further. "I'll wait." He carried a beautiful bouquet of flowers in one hand. She smiled as he limped over and set the vase on her table, keeping his right arm close to his body. "I wasn't sure, but I thought you could use a little color," he said, then leaned over to give her a barely there kiss on the brow.

She closed her eyes, breathing him in deep, savoring everything she thought she'd lost. He was all the color in this world that she needed. "They're beautiful. Thank you."

"You're beautiful. How are you feeling?"

"Well." She glanced down at her casts. "You see how bad it looks?"

"Yeah."

"It feels that bad, too."

"I bet." He took the seat by her bed and wiped a hand down his face. She knew what was coming, knew the guilt he would carry from now on, knew there was nothing she could say to ease that burden for him. But she would try.

"Please don't," she pleaded. "If you're going to say something stupid like being with you is bad for my safety, just don't, Jace."

"The evidence is pretty overwhelming," he said bitterly, his dark eyes roaming over her broken body. She had so many questions, but they would have to keep. Despite his injuries, he looked good. Tired, perhaps. She took in every square inch of his skin she could see but found nothing suspect.

His beautiful, intense eyes returned her assessment almost desperately. Her breath staggered from the warring emotions roiling through her.

"But it's over," he said at last. "For now, anyway. It's all over, and it's Christmas. I'm going to put it aside for now."

Nothing was over. She bit her lip on her many questions, winced from the pain, and chuckled. "I thought you didn't like Christmas."

"Maybe I like someone who likes Christmas." Whatever her mother had been talking about, whatever she had seen at their dinner that night, Lindsey thought she might see it now in his eyes.

She stared at him, at the pure miracle of him. And she let him see her stare. Let him know how beautiful she thought he was. Somehow, her lip didn't hurt quite so bad from a smile. "Really? Would that be me?"

Leaning closer so that she could get an enticing whiff of his familiar scent, he curled his fingers gently around hers. She absorbed the warmth, the comfort. This was all she'd needed. "That would be you."

"I kind of like you, too," she whispered.

"Lindsey. I meant to tell you sooner. I bow to your superior *Zelda* fandom and all, but I'm disappointed that you forgot *the* absolute most basic tenet."

"Huh?"

"'It's dangerous to go alone,'" he quoted.

Oh God. She loved this man. She couldn't help it; tears fell from her eyes, even as she laughed. "I did forget that, didn't I?"

"Yeah, you did. 'Take this.'" And he kissed her. To hell with split lips; he tasted so good, so warm, she closed her eyes and drank him in—the best medicine she'd had since she'd been here.

"I shouldn't be doing this, but I can't help it," he murmured. "I want to take you away from all this once you heal up. How does that sound?"

"A beach," she said longingly, opening her eyes. "Sand between my toes, the sun on my shoulders, and a margarita in my hand. Yes. *Please.* I do love Christmas, but I've had enough of the cold." She would ignore how he said he shouldn't be doing this. For now. He *was*, and that was what mattered.

"Your wish is my command. But that means you have to heal as fast as you can."

"Well, I'd speed along the process if I could."

"You never know. Maybe that's all the motivation you need."

He was all the motivation she needed.

His phone chimed with an incoming text message, and he pulled it from his pocket to read it while she took in his every move, marveling how the most mundane of activities were so intriguing in someone you were head over heels for. "We have that to look forward to, but Christmas is now," he said, getting to his feet. "Just so happens I have a present for you."

"You do?"

He walked to the door and yanked it open, and suddenly Christmas exploded in her hospital room. Sully breezed in yelling "Ho ho ho!" carrying a little tree complete with decorations. Helix and Drake hauled armfuls of presents and snacks, both in Santa hats.

In her moment of sheer joy and excitement, Lindsey almost surged upright, but her body quickly reminded her of its condition, and she yelped.

Jace was at her side in a heartbeat. "Don't hurt yourself. We thought maybe flowers weren't quite enough color. So here you go, baby. Merry Christmas."

He whipped something from his coat pocket, and she spied the little red berries on the greenery before he even held the mistletoe above her head, leaning over to give her a gentle kiss on the lips. Shivers ran down the length of her body. Shivers didn't feel too great on broken bones, but she wouldn't have changed it for the world.

"Lindsey, if you want to throw us out and never speak to us again, we get it," Sully said, approaching her bed opposite Jace. "We deserve it. Me especially. I know they altered your code, and you…" She gestured the length of Lindsey's body. "You are a total badass to take that on yourself. I know you didn't do it to impress us, but I for one am impressed. I'm here for anything you might need—just say the word. Or tell me to fuck off. Either way, I'm at your service."

"Thank you," Lindsey said, surprised at the weight that lifted from her chest during the apology. She didn't know them well, but she liked them. She respected them. It had hurt to be the source of their mistrust. "That means a lot. It really does."

"So we don't have to fuck off?" Helix asked from where he'd dropped into a chair in the corner of the room.

"No." Lindsey laughed. "Well, maybe when I want time alone with this one."

Laughter and catcalls filled the room while Jace gave them the finger.

She needed that time more than anything else right then. To know he was okay, that *they* were okay. Would he even tell her if they weren't? She stared at him as he joked with his team, his strong profile, his piercing eyes, and wondered at the secrets he was keeping from her at this very moment. It wasn't over. It couldn't just…be over. Not after everything Rhys had done, what the Libra Cooperative might do next.

After a time, the others left them so she could rest. Jace stayed, stroking her hand as he held it between his. She didn't want to sleep, though. She wanted to lie here and look at him for as long as she could. "Am I safe here?" she asked softly.

"We're monitoring the hospital network," he returned just as softly. She lay here day after day, helplessly confined to this bed with the knowledge that Libra could break in, alter her meds, and assassinate her in a heartbeat. Jace and his team had already been one step ahead. "I don't want you to worry about anything except healing."

"Will you have to leave me?"

His eyebrows drew together, creating a perfect line between them. "Why would I leave you?"

She blew out a breath. "You talked about having to move the team, so I figured that meant far away. Somewhere I wouldn't know about."

"If I were smart, that's what I would do. But turns out I'm kind of a dumbass."

Lindsey smacked his hand lightly. "No, you aren't. You're probably the most intelligent person I know."

He lowered his chin to rest it on her bed rail, eyes tilted up to her. She'd never really noticed how long and thick his eyelashes were. She would gladly spend the rest of her life noticing these beautiful little details about him. "I'm not. I didn't trust you. Not a hundred percent. I wouldn't let myself."

"Well, my personal feelings aside, that only *proves* you're smart."

"If I had, maybe you wouldn't have run off and gotten yourself hurt."

"Or maybe they would have found their moment and taken me anyway. Please don't beat yourself up. I got beat up enough for both of us."

"Christ, Lindsey—"

"Shh." She lifted a finger to place against his lips. He promptly kissed it, then captured it and pressed her hand against his clean-shaven cheek.

"I would've taken every hit for you," he said. "And more. I should have been there to do it. I wish it had been me."

She shook her head. "I don't. Never. Not for a second. In fact, this—all of this—led me to you. And no matter how hard I try, I'm not sure I can regret any of it."

So gently it almost made her cry, he smoothed her hair back from her forehead. "I wish I could hold you," he murmured.

"There isn't much room in this bed, but we can try."

"No, I don't want to hurt you. Just rest. Get better. I have a lot of time to make up for."

The thought of that time made her supremely happy. "Oh yeah, I meant to tell you. Thanks for not choking my sister on sight," she said. "I still don't have many answers there, but I think I learned a lot about her throughout this." Of course, she couldn't tell him everything, even if she eventually learned it all. And she never for a second believed he would forgive Lena, nor expect him to. But it was important, somehow, that Lena's sacrifices not go completely unappreciated. If she had to champion her sister to everyone from now on, well, Lena deserved that much.

He looked at her oddly for a moment, and she thought he was about to ask her something but thought better of it. Then he lifted a shoulder in a nonchalant shrug that was almost the mirror image of Lena's. Lena's *act*. "No problem. I think I can refrain."

He knows.

It was that deep, primal intuition that had no reason or explanation behind it. As usual, she wasn't quite sure she could fully trust it. But that faint whisper in the core of her soul couldn't be ignored. The one that said he'd known and he'd kept it from her.

He would've had to, though, right? He couldn't go around crowing about her sister being CIA. Not even to Lena's own family.

But what else was he keeping from her?

No. *No, no, no.* Whatever secrets and knowledge he had were his to keep, just as hers were her own. As of this moment.

If Jace were privy to her inner turmoil right then, he didn't show it. Maybe she was becoming a good actor as well. Hell, she was surrounded by them, so why not? She gave him a smile and asked him for another kiss.

His lips were infinitely gentle on her cut, but she felt the barely restrained hunger behind the sweetness. It called to her own. Even her battered body awakened, just from that touch of his lips, that tiny teasing swipe of his tongue against hers. She sighed, and groaned, and wished for more.

"I want to kiss you everywhere you hurt," he murmured.

"That would be everywhere."

"That's what I have in mind."

Doubts and secrets…those were for tomorrow. Those were for some future far in the distance. What she had right now was him, whole, beside her. She would focus on that. It was all that mattered. All the worry, all the fear, all the anxiety, had led her straight to here, right where *he* was. She was injured and in pain, sure, but she would heal in time. Physically, anyway. Mentally, emotionally, she would have a long way to go, but she wasn't as afraid of that road to recovery as she probably should be. Because he would be at her side through it all.

Everything else could wait.

EPILOGUE

She crossed her legs and laced her fingers demurely in her lap, staring at the panel of suited men and women in front of her. Her boss, her boss's boss. And his boss after that. The bureaucracy always amused her, the intimidating appearances, the assessing looks. They always thought they could see something she was trying to hide. How cute.

She felt as if a spotlight were shining down on her, but that had never bothered her before. It didn't bother her now as she returned their gazes blandly, keeping her own schooled and neutral.

The deputy executive director cleared his voice. "One final question, Agent Morris, and I think we're done here," he said, his beady dark eyes boring into Lena the way they had the entire time she'd sat through this debriefing when he wasn't murmuring with his colleagues. "To your knowledge, does Jace Adams suspect, in any way whatsoever, the true part you played in having him expelled from MIT?"

Lena Morris shook her head confidently. "No, sir."

"Good. That's perfect." He closed the file folder that had been open on the highly glossed desk in front of him throughout the meeting and gave her a single nod along with his serpentine smile. "Then everything is going according to plan."

Turn the page to enjoy

Breathe Me In

A ROSS SIBLINGS SERIES NOVELLA

by *New York Times* bestselling author
Cherrie Lynn

To all those who wondered what happened in the back of the GTO.

CHAPTER ONE

Seth "Ghost" Warren scrubbed a hand over the top of his head, rubbing futilely at the remnants of his headache and thinking for the millionth time about how badly he didn't want to be at work right now. He'd really tied one on last night; the repercussions were still pounding at the insides of his skull—a stark reminder of why he didn't do that shit too often anymore. But sometimes good friends, good music and good times won out over good sense. Such had been the case last night in Dallas after the rock festival, but it had been worth it to blow off some steam...or so he tried to tell himself.

Thankfully, it was a smooth ride at Dermamania so far—more hanging out than actual work, and anything too big or intricate he might've tossed another artist's way, anyhow. Unless one of his regulars came through the door begging, he'd declared himself strictly backup.

He yawned and checked his cell phone, puzzling over the text messages he kept getting from some unfamiliar number with a Dallas area code. Obviously a girl, though he didn't recall any errant hookups. For that matter, he didn't even recall giving out his number. And while civility wasn't always one of his strong suits under the best of circumstances, it just seemed rude to text back *Who the fuck is this?* to someone he might've had a drunkenly meaningful conversation with.

Growing bored with trying to put the pieces

of last night's debauchery together, he yawned
again and glanced around, noticing that no one
was talking much. Ordinarily the place was alive
with banter, laughter, or at the very least, loud
music. It was practically *serene* now. The funky vibe
couldn't be his imagination. Brian, his best friend/
long-suffering boss, had been uncharacteristically
impervious to Ghost's incessant ribbing about
his new girlfriend, who was currently holed up
in Brian's office studying. Or hiding out from her
parents. Or something. In all the years he'd known
Brian—almost fourteen now—he'd never really
seen the dude so tense over a chick. Especially
when, by all appearances and the fact that the two
lovebirds had pulled a disappearing act all last night,
Brian had gotten laid.

Then again, Starla had said in a moment of
confidence earlier that Brian's new lady love might
be of the hymen-bearing variety. So maybe last
night hadn't gone so well, after all.

The only client in the tattoo parlor headed out
the door. Starla took that moment to walk out
back for a smoke, and Brian had stared at the same
empty spot on the counter for two whole minutes.
So Ghost pounced on his chance. "Dude, what's
your problem?"

Brian's head jerked up and his expression
smoothed out to something resembling his usual
carefree countenance, but Ghost cocked a wary
eyebrow. *No way, man. I know you better than that.*

"Nothing," Brian said.

"Bullshit." Ghost crossed his arms. Now that he
thought about it, Brian and the new girl—Candace,

wasn't it?—had both seemed kind of on edge when they'd walked in earlier tonight. "Out with it."

Brian waved a hand. "Just some shit with her family. To say that they look at me like a bug to squash would be an understatement."

"Do you really need that in your life?"

"Do I *need* it? No."

"I'm just saying."

"What?" Brian glanced back in the direction of his office and lowered his voice. "Give up on her because she's related to assholes?"

"You're hardly in the game at this point, you know."

"Oh, I'm in the game."

Shit, he'd done the deed. "Still, there's time to bail."

"I'm not bailing. She…" Brian raked a hand through his hair. "Fuck. Do you remember Jameson Andrews from school?"

"I never forget a douche. Didn't I kick his ass once?"

Brian's eyebrows drew together. "Did you?"

"It rings a bell."

"Well, if you did, that makes two of us. He's Candace's older brother. I just damn near cold-cocked him on her front steps. In front of her mother."

Ghost smoothed a hand over his goatee. "Not the most brilliant way to make a good impression."

"Neither is calling my girlfriend a whore right in front of my fucking face, which he did. His own little sister." Brian gave a grunt of frustration and pushed away from the counter. "I don't want to talk about it. I'm gonna get her and go home. You guys can lock up and go, if you want. It's dead tonight."

"I think Starla has an appointment later. I'll hang around with her."

"Cool."

As Brian trudged down the hallway to leave, Starla came back in, her boots scuffing against the floor. "I'm really bored," she announced, hopping up on the stool at the counter in front of the computer. "And my ears are still ringing from last night. Brian taking off?"

"Yeah. Said we could too if we want."

"Can't. Got Jason coming in at six-thirty." She twisted her pink-and-blonde hair up in a sloppy bun.

"I thought so. I told B I'd stick around with you."

Starla shrugged, propping her chin in her hand in front of the monitor and looking as if she was settling in for a while. "Doesn't matter."

No question about it, his female coworkers could hold their own, but there were a lot of creeps out there too. He didn't like the idea of leaving her here to work it by herself. Of course, she often joked she had more to worry about from Ghost himself, but it was all in fun. "I don't have anything else to do."

"In that case, you know what I'm thinking? One of us should make a sushi run."

There wasn't much doubt in his mind that *one of us* meant him, given the fact that she didn't look like she was moving for the next hour or so. And that was cool; he'd been going a little stir crazy. He dug through the drawer at his station for his car keys and gave them a twirl as he headed for the door. "Shrimp tempura?"

"God bless you. I'll pay you back."

"Whatever." Scoffing, he stepped out into the mild spring evening just in time to see Brian's truck pull out of the parking lot. Poor guy. Brian had been there for Ghost when the girl-related bullshit had gotten thick a few years back, and now Brian probably didn't deserve for his best bud's only advice to be "bail out while you can." But that was the only way to avoid the inevitable crap—stay out of it from the start. Fact.

His '69 GTO was the only girl he'd ever let himself need again. If she let him down, he'd just fix her and carry on. Such could never be said for the human variety of female.

The thought was a comfort. No more heavy drama. Just good times with girls who weren't looking for an attachment. He could do that. What he couldn't do was put up with any angst, not from the Brookes of this world, or the Rainas.

Talk about two extremes. He hadn't been able to make Brooke stay, and he couldn't make Raina go. The mystery chick from last night hadn't been the only one blowing up his phone all night—his most recent ex had been rearing her dreadlocked head lately too. Thank God Raina hadn't stopped by the parlor. She wasn't above accosting him at work, and she was dangerously close to having her ringtone changed to Slipknot's "People=Shit"—his usual method of warning when someone he didn't want to talk to called his phone.

As his GTO rumbled into the parking lot at the sushi bar, he was content with his life decisions. As he nudged the car into a parking space and saw who

else was headed into the establishment, he wanted
to throw them all right out the damned window.

Candace's friend...Macy. She had come into
Dermamania with Candace a couple weeks
back and made it extremely difficult for him to
concentrate on work. She was fucking beautiful.
Beautiful in that she'll-never-look-twice-at-a-thug-
like-me way, except that she had. Oh, yeah, he'd
caught her looking...more than twice. Half jokingly
he'd pestered Candace for Macy's phone number on
the way to Dallas yesterday, but as he'd imagined,
Candace was locked down tight on that information.
Oh well. Couldn't blame a guy for trying.

Now, he sat and helplessly watched Macy walk
across the parking lot in front of him. Her long dark
hair fell in big loose curls, and now that she was
wearing shorts he could see that her legs were lean,
tanned, and toned in a way that surprised him. Not
just a prim-and-proper princess type like her friend,
then. Oh, Jesus, all he could think about right then
was getting those legs clamped hard around his
hips...

Shaking his head to snap himself out of it, he
left the safety of his car...even if every instinct he
had screamed at him to jump back in and speed
off. Circle the block. Get the food later. If he went
in there after her, he was going to make an ass of
himself in one way or another.

But he didn't listen to that little voice that
incessantly tried to keep him out of deep shit—
he never did. Number one, because he was an
idiot. Number two, because he was a glutton for
punishment. And girls like her...damn, they got

him revved. The ones who had a deer-in-headlights look when they were around him were always far more interesting to him than the ones he *should* be messing around with…the ones like Raina who were pretty much made for him. Except that he wasn't completely fucking psycho yet, unlike her.

He caught up to Macy just as her delicate hand began to reach for the door handle and, reaching past her, pulled it open before she could. Startled hazel eyes met his and the faintest gasp left those delectable lips.

"Allow me," he said, giving her a lopsided grin.

"Oh…thanks." Without a smile, without further comment, and most importantly without the slightest flare of interest or recognition whatsoever, she went in ahead of him. Well…whatever.

Whatever, my ass. You're fucking wounded, dude.

What had he expected? Girls didn't want guys hounding them when they made a sushi run. She also hadn't seemed to be the most outgoing person in the world. Shrugging it off, he went to the counter and waited while she picked up the order she'd apparently called in ahead of time, her faint vanilla scent igniting his senses. Where did it come from? Her hair? The soft hollow of her neck? Or maybe on the inside of her wrist with its tracery of pale blue veins visible now as she handed her credit card over…

He was focusing way too much on her. But a moment later, as she turned to leave, he found himself focusing on her eyes again. Because they were looking up into his with a directness that made his breath hitch.

"The tattoo parlor. You work with Brian." She smiled then, knocking the breath out of him...but not for long.

"What? I don't know what you're talking about."

As confusion began to settle onto her features, he chuckled. "Yeah. I work with Brian. Just fuckin' with you."

"Oh." Cue awkward silence while he couldn't seem to form a coherent thought after watching her lips make that sound. He only snapped out of it when she began to edge away. "Well...good to see you—"

"We were talking about you yesterday."

That got her attention. She gave him a wary look, head tilted slightly away while her eyes stayed on his. "Who was talking about me?"

"Me and Candace. On the way to Dallas."

"What were you and Candace doing going to Dallas?"

"She left Brian. We ran away together for the night."

Laughing, she shook her head. "Is anything that comes out of your mouth the truth?"

"Occasionally. See, Candace and I did discuss you on the way to Dallas yesterday. That much is truth."

"She didn't tell me she was going to Dallas with you or anyone."

"Does she tell you everything about her life?"

"Yes, she does." Her chin tilted up with just the slightest bit of defiance. Oh damn, it turned him on.

"Ah."

"So what were you doing?"

"It wasn't anything dubious. We all went to a concert. Candace came along."

"And this was *yesterday*? She was supposed to be in her cousin's wedding yesterday."

"I guess it was dubious, then, because she was with us. Which means she obviously doesn't tell you *everything*."

Macy's brow furrowed. He wondered if he had struck a nerve. "No wonder she wouldn't answer my calls. Oh, God. Her parents are going to kill her. *I'm* going to kill her." She seemed to be talking to herself now.

"Whoa there. She's a big girl. She can make her own choices."

"Excuse me? I've known Candace since she was born. I know more about the choices she should make than you do, I think."

"Maybe an outside perspective would be beneficial to you then. Leave her alone. Let her and Brian get things worked out with her folks."

"You don't just 'get things worked out' with Candace's parents."

"Is it really any of your business, Macy? I mean, really, is it? After all, she didn't tell you what she was doing, did she? Which implies to me that she didn't want you to know."

"Trust me, I *know* why she didn't want me to know," she said bitterly.

He stepped back a moment. This girl was... *angry*. Over stupid bullshit like this. Like she had stake in Candace's life or something.

What a fucking control freak.

"Yeah," he said. "I think I do too."

She glared up at him as he stepped past her to place his and Starla's order, and he fully expected her to be gone by the time he was done. But when he turned around, she was still there. Now looking pitiful in the ashes of the annoyance that had gripped her just a minute ago.

He should walk away because the absolute last thing he needed was to get mixed up with all this drama, but despite Macy's abrasiveness there was something so vulnerable about her that he couldn't keep quiet. And again, he never listened to *that little voice*.

"Hey," he said, "you all right?"

She avoided his eyes. "I'm fine."

"Do you…" Oh, shit, what the hell was he thinking? But she looked like she'd just lost her fucking best friend, and he couldn't stand it. Maybe she needed another one. "…I don't know, want to finish this conversation later or something? I have to get back to work right now but—"

She waved a hand and headed toward the door. "No, that's all right."

"Macy. Wait a second." He caught her arm. She looked down at his hand and, unable to read her expression—was she affronted? Or did she want it there?—he erred on the side of caution and jerked it away. "Don't go all pissed off at me. I'll feel bad."

"I'm not pissed at you."

"Well…just hang out with me later, then. We don't even have to talk about this other crap. You just…you look like you could use some laughs, and if there's anything I'm good for, it's a laugh."

She chuckled at that.

"See? You're laughing already."

She just looked at him.

"Oh, come on. You want to, I can tell. You should go with that gut instinct. It usually doesn't steer you wrong."

Her eyes flashed up at him with just the slightest, most enticing twinkle of humor. "Maybe it's my gut instinct telling me not to."

"Then fuck gut instinct. Meet up with me anyway."

"Look, I'll think about it."

"*Think* about it?" He was probably way off base, but given her little Mona Lisa smile, he couldn't shake the feeling that she was fucking with him right back. So he rushed on. "Tell you what. I'll probably leave around eleven or so. If you want to hang out, just come by the parlor. If you don't, well, I'll never forgive you, but I'll have my answer without putting you on the spot. Deal?"

She gave a little toss of her head, flicking the long lazy curl that had been resting on her chest back behind her shoulder. "Okay. That's a deal."

As she left, sending him one last smile before the door shut behind her, he wanted to fall down on his knees in gratitude that he never listened to that little fucking voice.

CHAPTER TWO

Macy Rodgers chewed her thumbnail and stared at the time on her radio display. She sat in her Acadia in the Dermamania parking lot, the last place on God's green earth she needed to be.

She didn't even know this guy's name. Now that she had agreed to meet up with him—and she had, since she'd shown up—it was going to seem really awkward when she had to ask.

The time was 10:43. She was early, even. But she hadn't wanted to risk him leaving work ahead of time and thinking she'd blown him off. As indecisive as she'd pretended to be about this whole thing, she'd never had any intention of not showing. It didn't make sense, but from the time he'd invited her, she'd wanted to. She'd wanted to really, really bad.

Taking a shaky breath, she stared at the building until the lights shining through the windows began to blur in her vision. When they suddenly snapped off, she jumped, her heart lurching into her throat. If the lone black car in the parking lot was any indication, he was in there all by himself.

Maybe she should've gone in to meet him—

Too late. The side door opened, and she watched as he came out and locked it behind him.

So not her type. Seeing him now in the dim light from the overhead lamps, it struck her again. But what struck her more—and this had been true the very first time she saw him in Dermamania with

Candace—was his broad shoulders. That *mouth*. Though she couldn't see it from her angle right now, she could never forget it. Sitting in the waiting area of the parlor while Candace had gotten her first tattoo from Brian, Macy had stared at this guy's mouth and thought it could eat her alive. Something about him made her weak in the knees, despite the shaved head and tattoos and piercings and the crass way he spoke. She'd never really been attracted to any of those four things in her entire life.

But here she was.

Meeting him. Alone. At night. A wild, party-hungry tattoo artist. The very thing she'd been trying to warn her best friend away from.

Hell, her hypocrisy alone should've been reason enough for her to stay at home. How could Macy tell Candace to run from a guy like Brian when she was meeting his friend in the dead of night?

He turned and saw her, a grin breaking over his face, and it was too late for any second thoughts. If he looked good when he was brooding or concentrating, he looked twice as good when he smiled. Hot. Dangerous. Full of mischief. Those dark brows pulled low over equally dark eyes that crinkled at the corners. He trotted over to her and she rolled down her window.

"You came," he said simply, not losing that smile.

Yes, hopefully I will.

The thought came from nowhere, and every-where, and she hoped her physical response to it didn't show all over her face. A slow burn began in all the places that didn't need to burn. Not now. Not for him.

"I wi—I mean, I did. I'm here. Looks like I'm here." Shit! She took a breath, drew it deep down into her lungs and tried not to show the effort it cost her.

What the hell *was* it about him? The sexiest cowboy she'd ever met—and she'd met plenty—had never left her this tongue-tied.

Probably because she was in her element with guys like that. She was in her world. With him— whoever he was—she was out on Neptune. Starving for oxygen and a coherent thought where there was none to be found.

This had been a bad idea. She even opened her mouth to say so, but he was opening her car door. "Come on."

"Um, where?"

He shrugged those broad shoulders. "I don't know. Don't care. We can go for a ride if you like. Or we can go inside, or we can just sit out here and talk."

Going inside wasn't her favorite of the options; the tattoo parlor freaked her out. She decided right then, before this went any further, that she needed to bite the bullet. "I'm sorry, but…what is your name?"

The grin came back. "Call me Ghost."

"*Ghost*?"

"You don't like it?"

"Well…I guess I just expected a…real name?"

"How conventional." He jerked his head toward the black car parked a few spaces away. "You coming out? Or you wanna do something else?"

"Just a second." She took a moment to roll up

her window and grab her purse, then she slid out of her safe zone and stood with him in the night. For a moment, the only sound was the faint buzz of the streetlights overhead.

What would they even talk about? She scuffed her boot on the asphalt and shoved her hands into the pockets of her jeans. She'd changed clothes before coming here, opting for jeans and a long-sleeve sparkly tee with her cowboy boots. Something to remind her of who she was and, well, something not quite so revealing. "There's nothing much to do at this time of night on a Sunday, is there?"

He chuckled. "You must not go to the right places."

"Well…I'm not really in the mood for shenanigans."

"Shenanigans. I like that." He grabbed her hand. His was big and warm and she clasped it back without a second thought. "Let me introduce you to my pride and joy."

The car. Oh, yeah, she could see how it would be. A GTO, sleek and shiny black, practically glistened under the lights. "I love it. What year?"

"'69."

She shot him a glance only to see him biting down on a grin. "Let me guess. Your favorite number."

"*Macy!*" he said with mock offense.

"Come on. You were dying to say it."

"We practically just met, and you already think you know me so well." He popped open the passenger door and gestured inside with a sweep of his arm, that smile promising all sorts of wicked adventures. "Hop in. I'll show you what she can do."

"You'll get me back in one piece, right?"

"I can't promise that."

"That's comforting."

"Naw, you're in excellent hands, love." He nodded toward the car's shadowy interior. "Let me prove it."

The endearment made her weak in the knees. Too many more of those, and she might let him prove it beyond his wildest fantasies. Though a guy like him probably had fantasies she couldn't even fathom.

A final moment of decision, and then she was walking toward him, feeling as if she was leaving behind everything she'd ever known...and it was okay.

Five minutes later, as she white-knuckled her seat with one hand and tried to keep her hair attached to her head with the other since he'd dropped the top back, she was rethinking that. This was anything *but* okay.

"We're gonna die!" she screeched over the roaring wind and the hard-driving metal song blaring over the speakers.

Laughing, he dropped his head back and howled.

Crazy! He was absolutely crazy, but she'd known that, hadn't she? They had to be doing 90, and nothing existed between her and the dark, rushing landscape and the ribbon of divided highway except this hunk of metal and a lap belt. Her heart thudded in her throat, and she was two seconds from covering her eyes when at last he eased off the accelerator. She glanced over to see him smirking at her. "Yeah, sorry. I just get caught up. Runs like a scalded dog, doesn't she?"

Her dad said that all the time. Macy smoothed her hair down and caught her breath. "Yeah. Do you have a glove compartment full of moving violations?"

"Not currently."

After a somewhat mellow chorus, the song kicked back into overdrive. Thank the stars above that he didn't. She had a sneaking suspicion his driving habits matched the speed of whatever music was playing. "God! What is this song?"

"That's Avatar, dude! 'Smells Like a Freakshow.'"

"That doesn't help me any, but I guess I shouldn't have expected it to."

And he'd called her *dude*. She liked *love* better.

As soon as he steered back into the Dermamania parking lot and braked to a halt, she threw open the door and scrambled out.

"Hey!" he protested.

"Sorry, I'm just going to fall down and kiss the ground." Seriously, her knees were shaking. But as she turned around and looked at him practically lounging in the driver's seat of his hotter-than-hell car, she wondered if maybe she was only blaming their tremor on his driving habits when in reality it was something far, far more disturbing. The lingering adrenaline had to be the reason she could only think about crawling over him, straddling him there and—

"I told you I'd get you back in one piece. I keep my promises."

"You actually *didn't* promise that."

"Well… I said you were in good hands. I meant it."

It was too much. He was too sexy. She turned and fled toward her safe, secure Acadia, which she'd never pushed over the speed limit on any given highway.

"Macy!" The sound of him getting out and slamming his door reached her just as she settled into her own driver's seat. She didn't know what she was thinking—she didn't want to leave yet, but she didn't want this attraction either. Before she could make any sort of move whatsoever, he'd gotten in on the passenger side. "Hey, did I scare you that bad? Jesus. I'm sorry."

Yes, you scare me that bad. You. Just you.

"It's all right. It's…" She didn't want to explain. Speed, any sort of speed—it was another somewhat freaky thing for her ever since her horse-riding accident. But she didn't want to tell him about that. Usually it didn't affect her to this extreme. Usually very little affected her. Until now.

"So what are your *real* thoughts on Candace and Brian?" he asked, and she appreciated the turn of the conversation. Macy, striving for normalcy herself, grabbed a ponytail holder from her gearshift and tied her hair back since it was probably a mess.

"I don't know him. I know she likes him a lot."

"Yeah, he seems pretty serious about her too."

"They have a tough road ahead, you know. Especially if her family blames him for her skipping out on that wedding yesterday, which they will. I know them as well as I know her. I was supposed to go to the wedding myself, but we had a horse down at my parents' ranch and we couldn't make it."

"They can't blame him for that. He didn't put a gun to her head."

"I don't know what happened. I need to call her."

"I can promise you, he didn't kidnap her. Or even twist her arm. If I were you, I'd leave them alone right now. It's like they've been in a little cocoon since last night."

Macy chewed her thumbnail for a second. Poor Candace. "So what *exactly* happened last night?" she asked.

"All I know is she came with us, we all went to the concert, and the two of them went off together alone all night. I guess they got a hotel room. We stayed at a friend's."

Candace had spent the night with Brian. Macy sighed and let her head meet the back of her seat. Ever since Brian had come around, their friend Samantha had been joking with Candace about handing in her "V-card," and it looked like she'd done so. Well…good for her. Really. It was about time. The girl was twenty-three and for whatever reason—probably fear of her parents' disapproval or just their hassling her—she'd rarely dated. Macy had been waiting for the guy to come along that Candace would stand up for…she just hadn't expected it to be a guy like Brian Ross.

"So they went off. What did *you* get up to last night?" she asked on a whim. He chuckled and rubbed his eyes with his thumb and forefinger.

"Nothing. I'm a saint."

"Right."

His cell phone buzzed from his jeans pocket and

he dug it out, giving a frustrated growl. "Dammit, I don't know who this is."

"What is it?"

"I keep getting texts from this person. They obviously know me but I don't know them."

She made a move to pluck it from his hand, not really meaning to succeed, and laughed when he evaded her.

"Hey! These are my private affairs."

"How many private affairs do you have? Are they private to each other too?"

"Apparently they're private to me. Like I said, I don't know who the fuck this one is. Someone I talked to last night, I guess."

"While imbibing mass quantities, I take it?"

"Well... I didn't get laid last night. I do know that."

Wow. *This* was a suitable conversation for a... what was this? A semi-date? No. It was nothing. It was just two friends of friends getting to know each other.

"But it's a girl?"

"Yeah, I'm pretty sure it's a girl. If it's a guy I'm gonna be pissed."

"What's she saying?"

He thumbed his phone, scrolling back through messages, then began to read. "'Hey you, did you make it home?' 'Hello?' 'Not gonna talk to me now?' 'Okay, I'm worried now! lol' 'I really hope you're not dead in a fuckin' ditch somewhere, that would suck, lol' 'Wasn't that a good time last night? I hope we can hang out again next time you're here!' And this one just now: 'You DID say you'd call me.'" He shook his head with a little scoff. "Damn. I always get stuck with the crazy."

"Have you responded?"

"*Hell* no. Cause like I said, I always get stuck with the crazy."

"You must make quite an impression."

"Well...yeah." He said it as if it should be patently obvious, and she laughed.

"Hmm. Well, let's just fix this right now." This time when she tried, she succeeded in taking his phone from him, and he looked at her with a startled frown.

"The fuck are you doing?"

Macy grinned. She might try to avoid drama among her friends, but she didn't mind it among complete strangers. It could be fun, in fact. And...oh hell, just like with this entire night, she didn't know what had possessed her. She hit the Call button on the message and brought the phone to her ear.

"Oh my God. *You're* fucking crazy," Ghost said, but the admiration in his eyes was obvious.

"I have my moments—" She cut off abruptly as a feminine voice purred a hello, then forced steel into her own words. "Who is this, please?"

The voice on the other end of the connection rose several notes. "Who is *this*?"

"I asked you first. Is there some reason you've been texting my boyfriend all day?"

After sputtering a few seconds, the girl seemed to find her spunk again. "Your *boyfriend* said he didn't have a girlfriend last night, just so you know."

"That *is* good to know. Thank you for that. But that didn't mean he wanted you to try to get the job,

I'm sure, or he might have answered you by now. Don't you think so?"

Seething silence met her sugar-sweet question, then the connection went dead. She tossed the phone at him, and he barely managed to catch it as he stared at her in open admiration. "Problem solved, I think," she said with a wink.

"You're awesome. She didn't tell you who she was, though? It probably wouldn't have rung a bell with me anyway."

"She didn't. But if you need me again to help clean out the crazy, just let me know."

"I will. I definitely will. In fact I have an ex I'd love to see you go up against. But we won't get into all that. It just puts me in a bad mood."

"No exes. Okay." She didn't much like discussing hers, either, but she was enjoying the hell out of this. "What else is going on in your life? Anything I can help with right now?"

"Nah. No quick fixes." He gestured toward the darkened building in front of them. "Just whatever's going on in there. And I'm in a band…we're on a bit of a hiatus right now. My family is mostly in Oklahoma. My grandmother's not doing so well. I've been going up there whenever I get a chance, which isn't often enough lately."

"Oh? Do your parents live there too?"

"Both my parents are dead."

"*Oh*. Oh…God, I'm sorry." She leaned forward a little to get a better view of his face, since she could only see him in profile. "Really, I'm so sorry."

He'd busied himself tracing his thumb around the edges of his cell phone. "Car wreck when I was six. Nah, it's all right. It was so long ago, I barely remember them."

"Still, though. I can't imagine the pain being any less. Seems…seems it would hurt just as much to not have many memories of them." She thought of her own parents and couldn't even imagine.

He shrugged. "I guess I wouldn't know. I remember the wreck, though. I was in the car. I have no idea why it was only me with them—I have a brother and sister too, but it was only me. Probably because I was being a little shit and wouldn't stay with a babysitter or something."

God, what did you say to something like that? Did he even want to talk about it? She was at a total loss, so after a moment she said the first thing that came to mind—probably not wise, but it was all she had. "All that, and still you like to live close to the edge, huh?"

He looked at her then. "I do?"

"Well…compared to someone like me, yes, you do. At least…me the way I am now."

"So...you weren't always the way you are now? Interesting."

Now they were skirting the borders of *her* taboo. "I used to be different. Yeah."

"How so?"

"A little wilder, maybe? More...I don't know, invincible. Or at least feeling like I was."

"And now you're just a killjoy," he teased. She laughed and gave him a little shove. "Nah. Are you sure you've change that much? You did just call up a chick you've never even met to lie for me. Not everyone would do that."

"Oh, I've changed." She tried to keep the bitter note out of her voice, but it crept in regardless.

"Why?"

"I just…decided to." That was it. That was all he got. For now.

He didn't look convinced, and she hadn't expected him to, but hopefully he would drop it anyway. "I think we're both doing a lot of dancing around each other right now, Macy."

Starting with the fact that he hadn't given her his real name. She wasn't about to dredge up any deep, dark secrets from the basement of her soul when he hadn't even put that much on the table yet. No way. He was an intriguing guy; that much she knew. Maybe that was all he needed to remain to her. A cool guy with mystique. She didn't need to be the one delving behind those dark, enigmatic eyes.

No matter how much she wanted to.

He sat staring thoughtfully ahead, his elbow propped on the door and his hand near that enticing mouth. She wondered what he'd do if she drew it away and put her lips on his. Hard to believe this man who seemed to exude raw sex hadn't made one move to get into her pants yet. He hadn't even really put forth any innuendos.

Macy fought desperately against the little part of her that was disappointed. An achy, needy little part. God. It had been a while for her. Too long.

The million dollar question was, if he made a move, would she let him? Really?

It almost reminded her of high school…sitting in the car in the dark with a guy, will-he-or-won't-he scenarios running through her head, along with her imagined responses. Her gaze strayed to his hand, and she pictured it on her thigh, its weight, its warmth pressing through the denim.

When she realized pretty much all of her imagined responses were edging toward the *yes-yes-YES!* category—hell, they were nearing the *jump-his-bones-NOW* category—she knew it was time to go.

"You know, it's getting kind of late…I have work in the morning."

"Ah. Gotcha. Didn't mean to keep you out past your bedtime."

"It's okay. Except for the part where I feared for my life, I've had fun. It's good to…get to know you." Ugh. Awkward goodbyes. She hated those. "Since it seems our best friends are pretty much inseparable now and everything."

"Right. Hey, thanks for chasing off my newest stalker."

Macy laughed. "No problem." Funny thing was, she didn't *want* to leave, even knowing she had work tomorrow. He was someone she could imagine talking to all night long, and it had been a long time since she had that, too.

"Before I let you go, though, I need proof this actually happened." Leaning toward her, he held his cell phone out in front of them. "Smile pretty." She made a silly face. When he snapped the picture and turned it around to have a look, both of them laughed—he'd made a silly face too.

Telling her to hang on a sec, he got out, and she watched him walk around the front of the car. It was only as he pulled her driver's door open that she noticed the black SUV creep by out on the street.

Strange, because it looked vaguely familiar—it looked like Candace's brother's Navigator, with the white sticker on the back window. Jameson had a Baylor sticker in the same place. She wouldn't think anything of it, except that Jameson was as protective of Candace as her parents were, and they probably *all* had it out for Brian right now if what Ghost said was true.

For a second, she debated whether to call Ghost's attention to the vehicle. But for all she knew, that wasn't even James, and she was probably just being paranoid as usual. So she kept quiet.

Anyway, what was Ghost up to? He leaned comfortably against the side of her car and chatted another minute, but other than that, made no move whatsoever. Didn't touch her. Didn't kiss her. Didn't…throw himself into her hard and put his hand between her legs.

God, what was wrong with her?

She was horny, that's what, and it was jacking with her judgment big time.

"Well, have a good night, Macy," he finally said as the conversation began to languish back into awkward-silence territory.

She gave him a smile. His gaze strayed to her mouth. This was it. He was going to kiss her. "You too," she said, resisting the urge to sweep her tongue across her lips.

"We should do this again."

Her heart flipped over. "Oh?"

"Sure. Any objections?"

"No." The one syllable slipped out with no hesitation whatsoever.

"Give me your number." He tapped it into his phone as she recited it. "'Kay. I'll text you mine. And I promise to answer. I don't mind *you* stalking me, if you're so inclined."

"I'll keep that in mind." That heart-stopping grin appeared one more time, to top off a crazy, heart-stopping night and rattle her brain a final time. He straightened. Put his hand on her door, let that gaze drift down again. *Kiss me.*

"All right," he said. Paused. "Sleep tight."

And he shut her door.

What?

He walked away. She couldn't not watch him go, and as she did everything *but* sleep tight later in her empty bed, it was that hard body she imagined beside her, over her, inside her.

CHAPTER THREE

Damn. He couldn't believe that had just happened. Even as Ghost tried in vain to get to sleep hours later, she lingered in his mind. And he'd only spent a couple of hours with her, if that. He was tempted to text her, but she might begin to think he was the stalker. Nah, he would play this one cool.

If anyone knew what an idiot he could be over girls like her, it was him. That self-awareness had come to painful clarity a few years back, and he always tried to hold the pain close so he never forgot.

Macy's smile, though…Macy's fucking smile could make him forget pain even existed in the world. From the angry, vulnerable losing-her-grip girl in the sushi bar to the carefree girl who'd called a complete stranger and chewed her ass out, she was alluring. Beautiful. And he wanted to know more, not only about that body but that mind, that soul. Something was behind those hazel eyes, something that shadowed them. Her beauty had caught his attention, yeah…but the rest of her would keep it. For far too long.

He hadn't even considered making a move. She'd have shot him down at that point. No doubt in his mind. For another far more compelling thing, even if she hadn't, he probably would have embarrassed himself.

Beneath the covers, he was hard from the memory of all the impossible ideas that had run through his head. Those gorgeously shaped lips sighing and gently panting from his touch. How soft and smooth her skin would be—he could tell by looking. How fucking good she smelled. Even the thought of her tentatively accepting his touch and then pushing him away set his blood on fire. He loved good girls. Loved to keep them wanting, questioning themselves. Giving them something to think about all night.

But something told him Macy might not *quite* be all that good. He had no fears whatsoever that she held the virginal status of her best friend. Here and there he'd seen flashes of hunger in her eyes that told him she knew what it was all about. Maybe he'd get lucky and that hunger would turn to starvation. Maybe he'd be the one she came to.

Yeah, fat chance, buddy.

Fuck. There was no fighting it, and hell, why should he? He slid his hand down his belly, toward his aching dick. Even if it was only her beauty in his head and not his cock buried deep in her body, it was release, and he needed it. He had the feeling he would need it a lot in the days to come.

He woke in a fog to a ringing phone, emitting curses that would've had his nana smacking him in the mouth. Sunlight streamed through his windows at an angle he rarely saw.

"Dude, what the *fuck*?" he answered without even checking the display.

"Get your ass down here," Brian said. He

sounded out of breath. Ghost immediately shot up, the sheet still twisted around his torso and haphazardly through his legs.

"Where?"

"The studio. Someone fucking trashed it."

"What?"

"Just get here, man. I need you." The connection went dead.

Christ on a cracker. Who the hell would trash Dermamania, and why? And when? He and Macy had been there till almost one in the morning.

Obviously later than that, dumbass. His head still hadn't cleared as he dug around for the jeans he'd discarded the night before, having no time to scrounge through the laundry for a new pair. He wasn't exactly awesome at domestic organization.

When he screeched into the parking lot of his workplace minutes later, Candace and Brian were having it out right in front of everyone judging by their wild, agitated gestures. Brian didn't need this shit right now on top of everything.

Behind them, the sight of the tattoo parlor was like a punch to the gut. Dermamania, which he'd left in perfect condition last night around one a.m., now had shattered front windows and no doubt massive damage on the inside.

As Ghost climbed out of his car, feeling sick, Brian and his brother Evan left in Evan's truck. Candace wandered off with Starla, her face drawn and devastated. Ghost plucked his cell from his pocket and fired off a quick text to his best friend. *You all right?*

No. Jameson Andrews fucking filing charges on me now. Fucker did this, I know it. I need you to stay there until I get back.

No prob dude.

Ghost turned Brian's accusation over in his head. It was an amazing coincidence if the parlor got trashed from an unknown the same night Brian decked Andrews in the nose, but Ghost simply didn't think Jameson Andrews had the brass cajones to do something like this to a bunch of big, tattooed motherfuckers, especially one who had just whooped his ass. Maybe he was wrong. Maybe the little douchebag thought his name would protect him. If it turned out he'd done this, he'd better think again.

The officer on the scene wouldn't let him inside, but he could see the damage clearly from his vantage point. It looked like the bastard had taken a baseball bat to the place, seemingly as fast as possible. Destroyed the TVs, as much of the equipment as he could, and tore Brian's art off the walls. He'd even spray painted some of the walls. Ghost laced his fingers behind his head and tried to maintain control before he hit something.

"You work here?" the nearest cop asked him.

"Yeah." He blew out a breath and forced himself to relax. "Anything missing?"

"Doesn't appear to be, according to the owner."

The angry rampage of a spoiled little shit. "Brian did tell you he has an enemy, right?"

"He mentioned it. Anything you can tell us?"

"Only that I was here until around one o'clock last night and the place was fine when I left. I didn't see anything suspicious." As the officer quickly made a note, Ghost chewed over dropping Macy's name and decided against it. Probably a bad idea, but really, she hadn't seen anything he hadn't. Why drag her into all this?

He scoffed at the idea of her spending a couple of hours with him and then getting a visit from the cops about it. How freaking classic.

The officer asked a few more questions, took all of his information down and gave him a card with a number to call if he remembered anything else. Whatever. Ghost doubted they'd be putting in overtime down at the station to investigate; this town was so fucking conservative the citizens and surrounding businesses would probably be more than happy to see the parlor shut down permanently.

So much for his livelihood the next few weeks.

The curse he muttered got Janelle's attention, and his coworker wandered over from where she'd been looking in the busted windows. Her short, usually spiked blue hair was flat and demure this morning. "Sucks, doesn't it," she said glumly.

He agreed, and then remembered the scene with Brian and his girlfriend. "Why the hell was Candace giving Brian shit?"

"I tried not to eavesdrop, but I couldn't really help it. I gather it was about the possibility of her brother doing this."

"Well, if he did it, the sonofabitch oughta pay. If she doesn't think so then—"

"I don't think she's mad because Brian thinks he did it. She's upset that her family would strike out at him and thinks he'd be better off without her."

She might be onto something, if *this* was the result of their hooking up. But he didn't say that. He might say it to Brian later, though. It was affecting them all now, and maybe he was a jaded bastard, but Ghost couldn't imagine any relationship being worth all this.

Macy's amused hazel gaze floated through his mind and he felt a little bit guilty and resentful about being such a jaded bastard.

"Did I hear you say you were here late last night?" Janelle asked.

"Yeah."

"Doing what? That's not like you."

"I wasn't trashing the fucking place, if that's what you're—"

"Oh God, don't be a dick. I'm just saying it's weird for you not to cut out soon as closing time comes around."

Again, he doubted Macy would appreciate him getting the rumor mill working overtime. He shrugged. "Don't worry about it. I was here late. I didn't see anything. End of story."

"Fine." She ambled away, leaving him alone for the moment. In a few minutes, though, Connor and Tay showed up to curse and vow revenge along with him. Not long after that, Evan dropped Brian off. The guy looked like a caged animal that had been zapped with a cattle prod one too many times, and they pretty much let him brood on his own as he paced around and muttered under his breath.

Ghost wasn't a big enough idiot to ask him if he was all right. He knew the answer to that. But he did walk over and stand beside him once his pacing slowed and he finally stood staring into the busted-out maw of his business and the detritus within with his arms crossed.

"I can't believe this, man," Brian finally said. He was positively trembling with pent-up rage.

"I know."

"I'm sorry."

"For *what*?"

"Well, it's not just me now; that fucker has dragged you guys into this too."

"We're with you. We'll get it all back."

"Just so he can do it again?"

"I'm sure there will be ways to persuade him not to do that, know what I'm sayin'?"

Brian shook his head. "Where will it end? We kick his ass, the pussy sends us to jail. We get out, kick his ass again, he sends us back. That's how little piece-of-shit piss-ant cowards operate."

"Right. That's definitely what we're dealing with."

"And Candace, she thinks the answer is to give that motherfucker and her entire family exactly what they want." Ghost remained silent for so long that Brian finally looked over at him. "I guess you have something to say."

"Something you might hit me for."

"Then don't say it. Not now."

"All right." He sighed then, defeat settling in when he realized Brian was quite possibly more upset over Candace's reaction than the building.

"No really, man. I'm with you. I'm on your side. You know what you have with her and if she's worth it, then hang in."

"I kind of need her on board with that too, and right now she's not."

"If she loves you like that, she won't stay away for long."

Brian scoffed. "When did you turn into a fuckin' romantic?"

Last night? "Oh, piss off."

The problem with first love was that it usually led to first heartbreak. Macy sighed after listening to Candace blubber for ten minutes and finally pulled her in for a hug when her words dissolved into hiccupping sobs. They sat on Macy's couch, having settled in for an ice cream binge while trying to find something to lift Candace's spirits on TV. It didn't look promising.

Seriously. How many people really ended up with their first love? Well…her parents, if they were to be believed. But still. It was rare. And while Macy wished she could spare her best friend the pain, she supposed in the end it was a necessary evil. Now Candace could work on getting over Brian and moving on with her life, maybe to another guy her parents wouldn't want to lynch on sight.

Macy wasn't trying to be the bad guy. She simply believed there was someone out there that Candace could love without bringing down the entirety of the Andrews family's wrath on her head. But Candace didn't need to hear that now. So Macy kept her mouth shut and murmured soothing nonsense while Candace cried all over her.

A knock at the door sounded a minute later—probably Sam. "Come in!" Macy called. Candace didn't even bother raising her head.

The door opened and Sam breezed in, her expression dangerously full of purpose as she tossed her purse aside and took Macy's burden away from her, grabbing Candace in a hug.

"I'm so sorry," Samantha crooned, stroking Candace's blond hair like a mom soothing a toddler with a boo-boo. "It's going to be okay."

"No it isn't!" Candace wailed.

"Honey, talk to him. You can work this out."

Macy wanted to throttle Sam, but she chewed her bottom lip to keep from screaming.

Candace sat up and swiped her palms hard over her cheeks, really only succeeding in smearing her mascara almost to her ears. "It's no use. They won't leave us alone. At least not now. Maybe after some time passes...but oh my God, I already miss him so much. And the thought of him finding someone else... It's killing me."

"Then fight for him, sweetie."

"*No*," Macy blurted. Both girls looked at her in surprise, then dawning anger. "Candace, you're right," she explained quickly. "They will *never* leave you alone. You'd end up having to run away with the guy, and I know you don't want it to come to that. You don't want to turn your back on the people who've been there your entire life. You don't want to have to leave *us*."

"It's not fair!" Candace cried. "That's almost exactly what Michelle said. But why is it that I have to turn my back on *him* just to make all of you happy?"

It felt like talking to a damn teenager. "Did you think he was going to *marry* you? Come on, Candace. This was a fling for him. Don't let your emotions get so tied up in it. Better for it to end now and be done with."

"Macy, I slept with him," Candace said. Sam didn't comment, but she hadn't stopped glowering at Macy.

"I know, but—" *Damn, no, I only know that because Ghost insinuated it.* "I mean, I know you've built that up into a big deal in your head, but—"

"*He* made a bigger deal of it than I did. I wanted him the first night we hung out together, but *he* stopped, Macy. He wanted it to be right for me. You don't know what he says to me. You don't know how he looks at me. I might be new at all this, but I know how he makes me feel. You don't. You don't know shit about it, so shut up."

"I'm just trying to—"

"You can think whatever you want, but I'm not going to listen to you cheapen what we have. What are you, jealous or something? I don't get it. You've been on their side from the start, and I'm fucking sick of it, Macy."

Macy could only stare. Candace had never, ever, *ever* spoken to her that way before…had never looked at her that way before. Right before her eyes, her friend appeared years older. Not a girl fostering a painful crush. A woman suffering dire heartbreak.

With her own eyes stinging, Macy stood and went to do something...what, she didn't know. After a moment of staring aimlessly around her kitchen, she put on a pot of coffee.

Maybe she *was* jealous. Maybe she did want what Candace had. Ghost's smile drifted through her mind, and she almost smiled in response to it as she watched dark, fragrant liquid fill the carafe. But heartbreak unfolding in her own living room should be throwing up red flags all over the place. That certainly wasn't what she wanted.

At least if she decided to see Ghost again, she would know from the start what it was all about. She wouldn't be stupid enough to fall in love.

And she *was* trying to be a friend. She was trying to treat Candace like an adult—unlike Sam, who'd taken to rocking her now while she cried. This was life. Life was pain. It was heartache. She could attest to that. The ex she'd loved the most, her own first love, Jared...she'd pushed him away in her own anger and fear, and he was married with twin girls now. Did Candace think it hadn't hurt her to do that? But it had been necessary. She hadn't wanted to do it; she hadn't wanted to watch him walk out of her hospital room without a backward glance any more than Candace had wanted to let Brian go, but it had been the best thing for everyone involved at the time.

But she didn't know shit about it, right.

How *dare* she?

Deep breath. In, out. In. Out. It was the only way she could keep from slamming the coffee mugs she'd retrieved from the cabinet down on the counter hard enough to shatter them. Let Candace believe she was the only person in the world who'd ever been in love, who'd ever had to make the shitty decision, who'd ever been in pain. That was fine; she'd find out differently one day. Maybe.

She took the two cups into the living room; she'd made the coffee, but didn't want any for herself. "Don't think I've never been hurt before, Candace," she said softly, settling back into her original position on the couch and folding her legs under her.

"I know," Candace said, sitting back and wiping her eyes with the back of her knuckle. "I'm sorry I said all that."

"It's okay."

It wasn't yet, really, but it would be.

"So tell us exactly what happened," Sam prompted. "If you're up to it. I don't think I got the whole story when you called yesterday."

Candace leaned forward and picked up her mug, staring into it for a long time before speaking. "You didn't spike this, did you?" she asked Macy with a little smile.

Macy gave her a solemn wink. "I thought about it."

"I wouldn't blame you. God. The last thing I need is you pissed at me."

"Don't worry about it."

"Anyway." Candace tucked a few stray hairs behind her ear. "We went to Dallas to that concert. And we spent the night together—"

"Okay, I have to stop you there," Sam said. "How was it?"

"It was amazing. It was sweet and hot and scary and overwhelming and everything I'd hoped it would be."

"Good. Continue."

"We got back the next day, got into a fight with my mom and Jameson—Michelle was there, too, but she was cool about everything. Brian hit James. Then I guess James trashed Dermamania and filed charges on Brian for hitting him. I told Brian this would go on and on and maybe it would be best if we didn't see each other anymore. That's it."

Macy recalled the black SUV she'd seen cruise slowly by Dermamania and wondered if she could actually place the guy at the scene. She hadn't seen James around in a while; did he even drive the same car? Ugh. Drama, drama, drama. But it was probably no coincidence that Brian's parlor had gotten trashed the same night that he hit James.

It occurred to Macy that she'd even seen a dark SUV parked in a lot down the street when she'd left. Shit. Was this really happening?

Her friends' conversation went on, oblivious to Macy's feverish speculations.

"Brian wasn't receptive to that idea, I take it?" Sam asked.

"To say the least."

"Oh, Candace, you can't do this to him now!"

"What am I supposed to do, Sam?"

"Stand by your man, and all that."

"It's my standing by him that would get him into trouble. The best way I can stand by him is to let him go."

The three of them sat in silence for a moment.

Sam finally spoke. "Well then, I think you're being very brave. I don't know that I could have the strength to do it."

Candace picked a thread from her pink T-shirt with her free hand. "He doesn't understand. He doesn't realize…" As if sensing another impending deluge of tears, she took a deep breath and shook her head, leaving the thought unfinished as she sipped her coffee.

He didn't realize what she put up with from her parents. Macy knew, and Macy hated it for her. It really *wasn't* fair. But until Candace was on her feet and done with college, she was kind of stuck under their thumb, and nothing could be done about it. She could only try to make life as easy as possible on herself until things were different. Sylvia Andrews was like a bloodhound; even a clandestine affair wouldn't remain hidden from her for long.

Candace's cell phone buzzed to life in her purse, which sat on the counter. She cast a forlorn glance back at it without getting up. "That's him," she said.

"You don't want to at least talk to him?" Sam asked. "This is killing me too."

"It'll only make things worse." She set her cup down and went back to worrying the thread with nervous fingers. Macy watched her while the ringtone ended and promptly started up again.

"Talk to him," she said.

Candace lifted puffy, red-rimmed eyes to hers and chuckled without humor. "You mean you'd *allow* it?"

"Hell, no, I'd make you stand outside. Yes, dummy, I'll allow it. Go in my bedroom. Take as long as you need."

"I don't know—"

"*Go*," both girls insisted, and Candace was up and dashing for her phone almost before their voices died away. After she'd answered and then closed Macy's bedroom door for privacy, Sam sighed and rubbed her temples.

"Right?" Macy said, suddenly wishing she'd poured herself a cup of coffee. And added some liquor.

"You could be a little more supportive, you know," Sam said.

"As opposed to you, urging her to remain in her fantasy world?"

"I just want her to be happy."

"So do I, Samantha. Look at her. Does she look very happy right now? There's only more of this in her future with him."

"With all due respect, I mean, I know you've known her longer than me, and you're more familiar with her family than I am, but as close as you feel you are to the situation, it's still really not any of your business."

Macy seethed at hearing those words again— Ghost had said more or less the same thing. "If it's not mine, then it's not yours either. But I consider my best friend since practically *birth* to be my business. I'm sorry if that offends you—actually, no, I'm not. The girl is in *my* apartment bawling her eyes out over the guy." She plucked at the shoulder of her own shirt, which was still damp from Candace's tears. "She cried her 'business' out all over me."

"I don't want to fight with you. I just think you're wrong not to be more considerate right now. I don't think I've ever met a bigger pessimist than you."

Well, she had every right to be that way, and if Candace wanted coddling, she should know better than to come to Macy for it. But whatever. Her own cell phone bleeped then, and she was glad for the distraction. Until she saw who it was.

She hadn't put Ghost's name—or his nickname, since she didn't even know his real name—into her contacts list. The text was from "1969" and it contained only one word: *Tonight?*

Her heart jumped up in her throat, and she tried in vain to swallow it back down.

"What is it?" Sam asked. "You look like you've seen a ghost."

Macy barked a laugh before she could stop herself. How could she see him now? She'd just sent Candace into a tizzy—again. Her hypocrisy had to have *some* boundaries, after all.

"Nothing," she told Sam as she typed back, *Can't. Sorry.* Then her finger hovered over the Send button for far too long. When her bedroom door flew open and Candace emerged, she hit it almost by reflex.

"Well?" Sam asked.

Candace seemed a little more composed. Her features had lifted somewhat and her eyes were dry though still red. "We just talked. He was checking on me and asked how I thought I did on my exam—I probably flunked, I was so upset. But it was good to talk to him. We really didn't get into... all the other stuff yet."

"You look like you feel better," Macy said.

She gave a tiny shrug. "He has that effect on me."

"I think you shouldn't worry. It's all going to work out."

Maybe Sam's words were true. Candace certainly deserved to be with the one she loved—but didn't everyone? Macy rubbed a hand over her face, suddenly feeling bad about sending such an abrupt rejection. She shouldn't see him, no, but it wasn't Ghost's fault she was feeling a little angry at the world right now. Since Candace had perked up a bit, she and Sam began pawing through Macy's movie collection, and Macy escaped to her kitchen again.

Maybe some other time, she sent. *Candace here now. She isn't doing so great.*

Ah. Neither is B. U guys sittin round man bashing?

I don't man bash. There are at least as many crazy women as there are men.

LOL! Ain't that the fuckin truth.

She chuckled. He'd hinted that he had experience in that department. Before she could reply, he sent another message.

You're killing my fantasy tho. You guys all sittin round with rollers in your hair, green crap all over your faces talkin bout what slime we are. Sounds HOT.

Now I KNOW you're sick.

Was there ever any doubt?

"What are you laughing at, Mace?" Sam asked from the vicinity of the TV, where she was feeding something into the Blu-ray player.

"Huh? Nothing."

There was a lot of *nothing* coming out of her mouth, and if she wasn't careful, they were going to catch on that it was indeed *something*. But maybe since Sam thought Macy should butt out of everything—and Candace probably did too—they didn't have to be privy to her business either. Sounded fair to her.

Macy settled in with the girls and watched both *Kill Bill* movies—strong ass-kicking women for the win—but she didn't really see much of it. She and Ghost texted movie quotes and witticisms back and forth the entire time. As she stifled her laughter so as not to clue the girls in to what was going on, she began to fervently wish she hadn't turned him down. As he'd said, she could use a few more laughs in her life, especially tonight.

CHAPTER FOUR

"What are you doing, dude? You're grinning like a fucking idiot."

Ghost shoved his phone back in his pocket and went back to work, schooling his expression into grim determination as he reached under the counter with his broom. "Nothing."

"Who are you texting?" Brian asked. He stood across the room with a paint roller, liberally smeared with the stuff. Brian was a gifted artist but he'd probably never painted a *wall* in his life.

"No one."

"Bullshit."

They'd wasted no time in trying to get the parlor back in order. Ghost's suggestion to go grab Jameson Andrews by the scruff of his fucking scrawny-ass neck and drag him here to help had gone unheeded. Didn't matter. They would get back on their feet without any help from anyone…except Evan, Brian's assistant-DA brother, who'd shown up unexpectedly a couple hours ago. He was currently hauling out the chairs with ruined upholstery.

That bastard had done more damage than they had initially thought.

"Is it a girl?" Brian asked.

"Don't worry about it, man."

"Just seems odd, from someone who's been telling me to bail this whole time."

"Don't be a bitch. I'm talking to someone. I'm not at liberty yet to say who."

Brian opened his mouth to retort but Ghost's phone rang then. Not Macy's number, but his older sister's. He got along well with Steph, but they hadn't exactly been close since she moved to Oklahoma to get married, and she usually only called him if there was something going on with his grandmother. He propped his broom against the counter and answered.

"Hey, have you got a minute?" Steph asked, sounding uncharacteristically strained.

This didn't bode well. He moved down the hall for some privacy. "Yeah, what's going on?"

She paused before answering, and he felt his stomach tilt. Damn. "It's getting bad, Seth."

Deep breath. He'd been waiting on a call like this, preparing for it, dreading it surely, but that didn't make receiving it any easier. "All right."

"I'm starting to worry about leaving her by herself. I'd love for her to live with us, but we barely have enough room for ourselves."

If it were possible, his heart sank further. His nana had always cherished her independence, even with the onset of her illness. A nursing home was the last thing she'd want. Hoping Steph was blowing things out of proportion, he asked, "What happened?"

"I went over yesterday afternoon and found her in the backyard in her nightgown. She was so confused. If I hadn't gotten there when I did, I'm afraid she might have walked off and gotten lost. It scared the hell out of me. She's never done anything like that before. I've taken off work a few days to stay with her. We have a doctor's appointment in a couple weeks." Her voice cracked a little. "Beyond that, I don't know what to do."

He didn't know if the insinuation was that *he* wasn't doing enough. And yes, he always felt terrible that he was stuck here leaving Steph with the bulk of the work taking care of Nana, who'd been diagnosed with early stage Alzheimer's—which apparently wasn't so early anymore—but Steph had never shown much weakness about it. Now... she sounded tired. And scared. "Do you need me to come up there?"

"No, that's okay. We'll see what the doctor says and decide something then. I just wanted you to know what's going on."

"It'll be all right. Just let me know. And if you need me for anything, I'm there. Okay?" God knew her other asshole brother wouldn't be. Seth had a hard time thinking of Scott as *his* brother. He had a hard time thinking of Scott at all without wanting to find the fucker and break something over his head.

Something must have been written on his face when he walked back to the front. Brian took one look at him and went back to painting without continuing their previous conversation.

His nana was in bad shape, and he wanted to break something over that sad fact, too. She'd raised him, raised them all. Left her life in Oklahoma to come and take care of three orphaned grandkids. She didn't deserve this shit. But then, no one did. His parents hadn't deserved to die broken and bloody in a crash, either, but that hadn't stopped it from happening.

He could move up there for a little while. Take

the burden off Stephanie. What the fuck he'd do in Oklahoma, he didn't know, but there wasn't much holding him here except for his job. He'd never find another Dermamania or another boss like Brian.

His phone chimed with a text. Macy.

> *Hey, you still there? She's about to do the five-point-palm exploding heart technique! "There are consequences to breaking the heart of a murdering bastard."*

And girls like Macy would be in short supply anywhere he went. He damn near texted back that he could fall in love with someone like her...but he knew all too well there were consequences to that, too.

Phase Two of nurturing heartbreak for Candace, apparently, was retail therapy. A few days had passed since the fallout, but they weren't through the worst by a long shot and wouldn't be for longer than Macy cared to imagine. She followed Candace from store to store, not feeling it in the least. Browsing racks bored the ever-loving hell out of her, but she humored her friend, giving her opinion on this shirt and that...noticing all the while that Candace's tastes seemed to be getting edgier. Brian's influence? Or rebellion? Probably a little of both.

"That's not you at all," Macy commented on her friend's latest selection, which was very black and very…not Candace, who was usually all about pink and pastels. Bright and cheery.

"Good," Candace all but snapped. "I'm sick of me." She added it to the stack in her arms.

So much for cheery. Macy didn't want to fight, but she couldn't stop herself. "You've got to snap out of this, you know."

She expected a sharp retort, but Candace all but deflated. "I don't know how. I just…honestly, Macy, tell me how, and at this point I'll listen. I promise."

"The grief will take time. But as far as…changing things about yourself?" Macy indicated the dark pile of garments in her arms. "Come on, Candace. That's a little much. Don't do that."

"You did."

Macy had been reaching for a blingy T-shirt that caught her eye, but froze at her friend's words. "What?"

"You changed. After your accident. After Jared. I mean, you still dress the same, I'm not talking about that. But you stopped doing things you loved. You stopped doing the rodeo thing."

"That had more to do with the accident than Jared."

"Did it?"

"Yes, it did. You know that."

"I'm beginning to think I don't know much of anything."

"You're having experiences, you're stepping out of your comfort zone, you're learning things about yourself and life that you didn't know before. It hurts, but it's good for you. It makes you strong. Trust me, I've been through it." She sighed. "I'm still going through it. You're right, I did give up things I love. I miss them."

"Thanks for being here for me. I'm sorry if I've been a bitch. You know I love you, don't you?"

"I love you too. That's *why* I'm here."

That one little admission about giving things up had taken a lot out of her, but she was glad she'd made it and even gladder Candace had turned the conversation. The air between them cleared a little, the tension draining away now that they had a bit of an understanding. And then, as they were walking out the door with Candace's purchases—she'd only put two items away and kept three—she had to go and say…

"I wish you could find someone."

"Oh, stop wishing that on me," Macy laughed, striving for a light tone.

"Hasn't it been a while since you've even had a date?"

"Hmm. I guess."

Candace huffed in frustration. "Do you just…not care to be with anyone?"

Macy cut her a meaningful look. "Gee, I can't *wait* to be in your shoes."

"All right, touché. Is that really why you don't, though? You're afraid of getting hurt? It sucks but how will you ever find the one if you don't try?"

Why the hell was *she* under the gun all of a sudden? "Because I haven't found anyone who could even be a candidate to be the one. I'm not worried about it. I don't mind being by myself right now. I like not having to answer to anyone else, or worry about someone else's moods—don't ever think there isn't a male equivalent to PMS. I like eating what I want to eat when I want to eat it and going where I want to go when I want to go. When you're in a relationship that isn't always how it is. You have someone else's wants, feelings, and even their schedule to consider."

"I know you want a family though. You've said it."

"I do, very much. Someday. Nothing wrong with enjoying my singlehood while I have it, is there?"

"You know, I never worried much about finding someone either. I always had a crush on Brian, but even when I went to him to get my tattoo, I never once expected all this. It just happened." She shook her head. "I miss him so much. We didn't have enough time together."

Oh, God. It wasn't like he'd *died*. "Well, you know…*you* imposed this separation on the two of you, not him. If it's eating you up that bad, go back." It wasn't what she wanted to see happen, simply because avoiding more days like this in her best friend's future was high on her list of priorities, but in the end Candace was going to do what she wanted anyway.

"I think it's inevitable. The thought of not being with him makes me literally sick to my stomach. I sure can't imagine being with anyone else."

Macy nodded, lost in her own thoughts. Candace had said 'it just happened.' That's how things usually went—that person you insisted you weren't looking for and thought you didn't need ambushed you and turned your world upside down. She damn sure hadn't been looking for Ghost…

who hadn't repeated his invitation of a few days ago, she'd noticed. But he did still text her pretty often, so maybe she hadn't put him off pursuing her completely.

Pursuing her. It had been a long time since she hadn't been the pursuer. Since Jared, really. He'd been pretty relentless. But after that catastrophe, she'd put up walls, and very few men had been brave enough to try to scale them. She could shut them down with a single look. She'd *perfected* that look.

Not that she'd been celibate. She loved seeing something she wanted and going after it. As such, there had been a couple of forays into exclusivity that seemed promising at first but fizzled before the six-month mark. There had been a fling—hot and fleeting, the way she'd wanted it. But nothing that made her too eager to give the whole relationship thing another try.

Then why in the hell was she so interested now?

"Oh, God. There's Jameson. He's probably fuckin' spying on me."

Candace's words jerked Macy out of her reverie just as memories of Ghost's smile began to creep in. She looked in the direction of Candace's gaze…and froze. The black Navigator cruising by in the parking lot was the same one she remembered Jameson owning, and sure enough, as it passed them, the white Baylor University sticker across the back windshield identified it. Without a doubt, it was the same one Macy had seen drive by Dermamania the night she and Ghost hung out there. The night it had been vandalized.

She had to tell Candace. She *had* to…but God,

the last thing she wanted was to get caught up in all this. For one, she would have to explain what she was doing at Dermamania in the middle of the night. Candace would probably hate Macy for meeting Ghost behind her back when Macy had been telling her all along not to see Brian anymore. How could she defend herself? How could she even *try*?

When the hell had this become such a freaking cluster?

Maybe she could say nothing. Jameson was already the prime suspect…but there was nothing pinning him to the scene. Macy's mother was best friends with Candace's mother. How would it affect everyone's relationships if Macy was the voice who brought shame to the entire Andrews family? How would it affect Candace to know she'd been keeping this from her? Even though they'd cleared the air a bit, it would probably take very little to set Candace off again.

A hand waved in Macy's face and she jolted out of her funk. "Huh?"

"I said, are you all right? You're pale. You could've seen a ghost."

She had. That was the damn problem.

"I'm fine." Jameson's SUV crept on by and finally, mercifully disappeared from sight.

"We can go home, if you want. I've done enough damage for today, I think."

"Whenever you're ready."

As they headed for Macy's car, she tried to pretend everything was okay, but she couldn't. Everything crashed down on her as she slid into the driver's seat, and she had to sit and catch her breath while Candace got in on the passenger side. "Hey… Are you sure you're all right?"

Not now. She wasn't ready to tell her right now. Soon. She would do it soon.

Clearing her throat and releasing her iron grip on the steering wheel—which she hadn't even noticed until she let go—she gave her friend a reassuring smile. "I'm fine."

"Hello?" Macy's heart dropped for a moment when Ghost answered his phone. From the sleepy gruffness of his voice, it was obvious she'd woken him, though it was well after noon.

"Oh— Hey. I'm sorry. Thought you'd be up by now."

She heard rustling on the other end of the line—as if he was turning over, or maybe throwing back the covers to get up. Macy cringed as her inquiring mind wanted to know if he slept naked. Of course, along with that speculation came a variety of possible images. "That's okay," he said. "I should be."

"Working late again?" The parlor had only recently reopened.

"Yeah, but I usually stay up for a while after, too."

"I can let you go."

"Naw. I'm good. What's up with you?"

She chewed her bottom lip. What *was* she doing?

They'd settled into a texting pattern, but neither had actually called the other. There almost seemed to be an unspoken competition between them...who would break down and call the other first.

Obviously, she'd lost.

She'd dialed him on impulse—part from boredom and part from wondering if he could give her some advice and part from simply wanting to hear his voice again. "I don't know. I have a dilemma."

He chuckled. "Lay it on me."

"What would you do if there was something you needed to tell someone, but to do so could...really mess some things up for you? And possibly for a lot of other people who consider you their friend?"

"Hmm. You're throwing deep shit at me first thing in the...well, afternoon."

Macy laughed. "Yeah, I guess. Sorry."

"You sound down."

"I am, a little."

"So you call me." She could practically hear him grinning, and it was impossible not to answer with one of her own.

"Yeah, why is that?"

"Why do you call me when you need cheering up? Because I'm fucking funny."

"There is that. But you're not the one to go to when I have a moral dilemma, I see."

"You're probably right about that. I don't know, Macy. As far as your dilemma, I guess it would depend."

"On what?"

"Who's getting the shittier deal here?"

It was all pretty much equally shitty. A bad deal

any way you looked at it, and she told him so.

"Well," he said, "without knowing the details, if someone's being wronged in some way then you— or I imagine *I* would need to come clean about it."

He'd only affirmed what she already knew, of course. Jameson Andrews needed to pay for what he'd done. Bottom line. End of.

"I'm being...a real coward," she admitted, cramming a knuckle into one eye in frustration.

For a beat, he didn't seem to know how to respond to that. "Are you all right?"

"Yes." All at once, she straightened, infusing herself with the needed determination to do what had to be done. "I should let you get your day started."

"I don't go to work until two. If you need some-one to talk to, I'm here. Or maybe tell me what's going on."

He'd find out soon enough, once she "came clean." And he'd hate her for holding out this long, too, wondering what the hell was wrong with her for not doing the right thing from the start. Or for not calling his attention to Jameson's creeping the night he vandalized the parlor. The whole thing probably could have been prevented if she hadn't been so stupid.

Hell, sometimes she thought if she could lock herself in her apartment and not have to deal with *any*one, *ever*, that would be just fine with her.

But becoming a hermit wasn't feasible, so she hung up with Ghost and decided to call Candace. Right then.

Which was how she found herself at Dermamania

later that afternoon, spilling her guts to Brian in his office while Candace visibly tried to hold it together in his presence. The longing coming off her best friend was practically palpable, and before long, Macy left the room to take a deep breath and to give them the privacy they so obviously needed.

She'd done it. Candace wasn't mad at her as far as she could tell. In hindsight, Macy realized how silly she'd been to be worried. Candace had forgiven her for far worse, and she'd shown little more than amusement over hearing about Macy and Ghost's rendezvous. Brian was so happy to have proof of Jameson's involvement that she doubted he harbored any ill feelings toward her, either.

There was no doubt about it: the tough exterior Macy tried to show the world had cracked and unexpected emotion had swamped her during the entire exchange. Worry over her best friend, worry over doing the right thing, worry over this unwelcome yet undeniable desire for this guy who shouldn't even be on her radar… It had all come to a head and she'd made a blubbering fool of herself. But it wouldn't be the first time. Her mom would tell her it was good for her to get knocked down a few notches every now and then.

As she entered the front area where the machines buzzed alongside happily obscene chatter, Ghost smirked at her. He looked as if he hadn't shaved head or jaw in several days; the shadow of his hair lent a ruggedness to his appearance that kicked her pulse rate up.

As far as she knew, he had no idea what was going on or what she was doing here. Except for the missing art and TVs, there was no indication Dermamania had ever been trashed. Those guys had really busted their asses to get it up and running again. Amazing.

Since Ghost seemed fairly idle—with no client under his needle and surprisingly not an active participant in the ongoing banter—she ambled over to his station.

It felt good to not be secretive. To not have that weight on her shoulders.

"Hey, killjoy," he greeted, hoisting himself up on the counter and resting his elbows on his knees.

"Hey yourself," she flirted shamelessly back. Maybe it was only Macy's imagination, but conversations dropped all around them. The pink-and-blonde-haired girl—Starla?—in particular paused and stared with open interest.

He'd called her "killjoy" again, but she hoped he was teasing. They'd had some laughs. She wasn't *that* bad, was she? Wouldn't her lighter mood show all over her face?

If his expression was any reflection of hers, though, she must look happy as hell. His grin, as usual, was absolutely killer.

"Long time no see," he said.

"I know. Sorry about that."

He gave a slight nod, his gaze steady upon her face. Right away, she knew he was thinking of their conversation earlier that day. "You okay?"

"I'm great." *For the first time since I last saw you,* she added silently. "You?"

"Hanging in there."

She didn't know much about his life beyond

his being Brian's friend, his job here and the sad story about his parents. By all appearances, he was a carefree guy. But no one was without cares. It occurred to her then that she wanted to know his. All of them. He'd listened to her yammer about her "dilemma." Maybe she could return the favor.

"So…" she began when it became apparent he was content to sit and grin at her. But she couldn't think of anything else to say.

"Are they working things out?" he asked, nodding toward the back.

"Oh. I don't know."

A dark eyebrow raised. "Then what are you guys doing here?"

"She…um, I…" Macy cast a glance around. Oh, yeah. He was someone else she needed to come clean to, wasn't he? He'd been affected as well. But she couldn't, not here in front of everyone. "Can we talk about it later?"

"Well sure. Are you finally asking me out?"

"What?" she laughed.

"Talking about it later implies I'm going to *see* you later."

"We could talk on the phone," she pointed out.

"I might not answer."

"You said you would."

"But I won't if it means never seeing you."

Was he really saying this now? In front of all his friends? She heard a few chuckles from behind her. "You're something, aren't you?" she asked him.

"Girl, you have no idea," Starla muttered. Macy threw her a grin over her shoulder.

"I haven't figured out what yet," Ghost said. "I

don't think anyone has. Makes you curious, doesn't it?"

"Say no!" Starla said. "For the love of all that's holy, say no."

Candace and Brian took that moment to come in from the hallway, expressions bleak, tension between them that practically vibrated. Macy and Ghost shared a grim look and he gave her a slight nod. She was at her friend's side and out the door with her in a second, all flirting forgotten.

"Candace, what happened?" she asked as Candace threw open the door to her car and flung herself inside.

Shit.

Sighing, Macy got in and pulled Candace into her arms, letting her cry as long and hard as she needed. She didn't ask any more questions, didn't judge, didn't dole out unwanted advice. Her sweet friend was beyond it all, anyway. Sometimes crying it out was the only thing you could do. Macy had been there.

She swore she would never, *ever* let herself be there again.

CHAPTER FIVE

The text didn't come until later that night as Macy was settling into bed.

Feel like finishing our conversation?

Glancing at her clock and frowning at the late hour—it was almost midnight—she tried to ignore the sudden throb of her pulse. *Now?* she replied.

Ah, past your bedtime. Sorry.

I was still awake.

4get not every1 operates on my schedule

She smiled into the darkness of her room, realizing she heard his deep voice saying the words as she read them. It made her toes curl. And she was *dying* to finish their earlier conversation, but the thought of her best friend at home no doubt sobbing into her pillow gave her pause. *It's okay*, she tapped. *But I really shouldn't. I'm drained.*

Ur friend ok? he asked.

No. Yours?

No. Tho he looked like a man with a plan when he left today.

Hmm. If Brian had a plan to fix this whole awful mess, more power to him. The way he'd looked at Candace today, as if she were the only precious thing in his universe...it had almost brought tears to Macy's eyes. She didn't think anyone had ever looked at her that way. It had certainly done more to change Macy's thinking about this whole situation than all of Candace's crying and anger. She knew how emotional her friend could be. Now she'd seen the other side. Brian was in as much pain as Candace, if not more.

She'd always tolerated Candace's parents pretty well. After witnessing that devastation today, she'd decided they needed to be slapped. And so did Jameson—but thankfully Brian had taken care of that, and now that he had Macy's information, he was about to hit him and the Andrews family where it really hurt. Their money, their pride, their status in the community.

Macy kind of wished he could do it without dropping her name, but oh, well. She would expect the incredulous phone call from her mother any day now, since Sylvia Andrews was Jennifer Rodgers's good friend. Though how her mother tolerated that woman, she had no idea.

I wasn't sure about Brian at first, she admitted to Ghost, *but I'm starting to change my mind.*

He's a good one. Don't worry.

After a moment of intense debate with herself, she tapped back, *What about you? Are you a good one?*

He was a long time replying, and she wondered if she'd said something wrong...or if maybe he was just trying to formulate his reply. She was beginning to enjoy the idea that she'd flustered him when his message popped up.

I can be good. Or I can be as bad as you want me to be.

God, she bet he could. She closed her eyes and breathed slowly through her nostrils, realizing she'd been rubbing her thighs together to assuage the building ache between them.

She couldn't remember the last time she'd wanted to fuck a guy this bad without going ahead and doing it.

So do it, she told herself. Just freaking do it, and get it over with. Where was the harm? Candace herself had been pressuring her to find someone. *Where are you?* she texted.

About to leave work.

I can be there in twenty minutes.

Then I'll wait.

Twenty minutes. She threw her covers off and her feet hit the floor. She needed this. She'd been thrust into the middle of a scandal, she'd been a terrible friend, and while she was glad she'd fessed up, the guilt still weighed on her. A wild romp with Ghost wouldn't take that burden from her, but it would damn sure help her blow off steam. It was only sex, and she couldn't have picked a better no-strings kinda guy. That was for sure.

There was no need to fuss over how she dressed.

It was a warm night, so she went for accessible. A mini-skirt, wedge sandals, a loose top. Maybe it all seemed presumptuous on her part, but she didn't think she'd read his signals wrong. She left her hair straight and unstyled, anticipating whatever style she put in it would undoubtedly be demolished if the night went how she hoped.

Every time she thought about the night going like she hoped, though, every time she imagined being so close to him, invaded by him, her heart would lurch. She would have to pause to catch her breath, and the thought would cross her mind to dive back under the covers. Text him that she'd changed her mind, just so she could go on living in her safe little world.

Because she had no doubt her safe little world was about to be well and thoroughly rocked, and who knew if it would even be recognizable after he was done with her.

When Macy's SUV pulled into the parking lot fifteen minutes after her text had arrived, Ghost glanced up at the ice-bright stars and thanked whoever in the hell was up there pulling for him. He'd fully expected her to change her mind.

When she slid out of her car and he caught a glimpse of those flawless thighs under the hem of her skirt, he thought maybe whoever was up there was intent upon killing him.

But what a way to go.

He stood gaping beside his car as she shut her

door and strode toward him, her smile as bright as the moon. As she reached him, her faint vanilla scent drifted forward and teased his senses, so sweet he wanted to close his eyes and inhale. He managed to restrain himself. Just barely.

"Hey," she said, when he obviously couldn't divert his blood supply from his dick to his brain to form a coherent greeting.

"Damn," he managed to choke out. "You look..." *Fucking hot.* Seemed too juvenile. This woman was...divine, and she deserved more than some compliment a horny ninth grader might toss at her. Keep it simple, right? "You're beautiful, Macy."

"Thank you," she said, seeming genuinely flattered.

He shoved his hands in his jeans pockets, feeling like said horny ninth grader in the presence of the prom queen. Remembering the ultimate outcome the last time he'd felt this way.

It hadn't been pretty.

"I'm surprised you came," he said.

"Really? Why?"

Why? *Why?* Did she really expect him to answer that? Look at her. Any guy with a brain ought to be shaking in his boots over the prospect of being shot down by her. "You weren't too receptive the last time I asked," he said in place of that idiotic thought.

"Oh. I'm sorry about that. I wasn't making an excuse though, I really...I was going through some stuff. And then there was Candace...you know."

"Yeah."

"But I'm here." She smiled, though it was fleeting.

"Even if I probably shouldn't be."

"Why shouldn't you?"

"I haven't been very honest with you."

Of all the things that could've come out of her mouth right then, that was the last thing he'd expected to hear. Hell, neither of them had been all that up-front, had they? He damn sure hadn't, and it didn't take a genius to see she was hiding some pain herself.

Both of them guarding their hearts so closely. It was that mystery behind Macy's hazel eyes—right now glinting at him in the shadows—that had him so intrigued.

And he had to be on guard right now, too. He shrugged off her statement. "For that matter, neither have I. Maybe that's best, right?"

Her perfectly arched brows drew together. "You're not even curious?"

"Do you have a husband at home?"

"What? No way."

"Boyfriend?"

"No."

He ticked off on his fingers. "Have four kids? Some deadly communicable disease? Really a man?"

"Oh my God! No." She propped her hands on her hips. "Would it matter if I had kids?"

"Well, it would if you had four. Three's my limit."

"You are terrible."

"I don't try to hide it. Macy, look. Feel free not to share any deep, dark secrets with me if you don't want to." Then again, if she remained a mystery, he'd end up falling all over himself trying to solve it. Shit.

"Maybe I do want to share."

"Then you would've told me before."

She shook her head. "Not necessarily. Hey, will you just listen? You said you wanted to continue our earlier conversation, and this is the continuation. This is 'later'."

Sighing, he crossed his arms and leaned against his car, steeling himself for the worst. She looked at him uncertainly until he gave a circular gesture with his hand. Macy drew a breath, and managed to surprise him yet again.

"I saw Jameson Andrews drive by here that night you and I were here. I guess he waited until we left and trashed the shop. I didn't point it out to you and I didn't tell anyone, at least partly because the Andrews family and mine go way back. But also because I've been upsetting Candace a lot lately, and I thought she would never speak to me again. It was selfish and it was wrong, and if *you* never want to speak to me again, I'll understand." He just stared at her. "I'll be sad," she added, "but I'll understand."

Wow. No wonder she hadn't been able to tell him this in front of everyone. Ghost scrubbed a hand over his head, wanting to be at least a little upset that she'd actually considered sitting on this information. But she looked so glum. It was plainly obvious she was a good enough person that this had eaten at her until she cracked. Besides that, he hadn't asked her if she'd seen anything. He hadn't told the cops she was with him. Either one of those things might have made her decide to come forward sooner. "Is that why you and Candace stopped by today?" he asked. "You did tell Brian, right?"

"Yes. I did."

"So really, in the end there's no harm done. The bastard's been busted."

"He could've been busted sooner. I know you guys have been miserable all this time. And you've worked so hard and—"

"Well, yeah. But we would've worked hard whether we had the proof or not." What he couldn't believe was that Brian hadn't breathed a word of this. In fact, he hadn't heard from Brian since he lit out of the parlor soon after Candace and Macy left.

Oh, shit. Shit, shit, shit.

"Fuck," he spat, digging in his jeans pocket for his cell phone.

"What is it?" Macy went from zero to panicked, and once realization dawned across her face, she raised a hand to her forehead. "Do you think he's gone after James? Oh, God. That was something I didn't really consider. He'll kill him."

"Get in. We'll see if we can find him."

He fired off a text to Brian as soon as they'd jumped into his car. *Dude where u at?* Macy buckled in and stared worriedly ahead, chewing her thumbnail.

Fortunately, the answer came just as he pulled into the street, and he almost laughed at how both of them practically dove for his phone. He let her get it since he was driving. "He says he's at his brother's and asks why you want to know," she said.

Ghost blew out the breath he'd been holding. "Crisis averted, then. Just tell him I'll call him later."

She relaxed into the seat, typing the message. "Okay." Then she laughed as she handed his phone back. "What were we going to do, anyway?"

"Hell if I know. If he didn't answer, I was ready to go try to bail him out of jail or something."

"You don't think he'll do anything?"

"If he were at home in a drunken stupor, I might consider going to babysit him. But if he's at Evan's, then that guy will talk some sense into him. It'll be okay."

"I don't know Evan, but if what I've heard about him is true, I'm sure you're right."

"Brian probably went there just for that reason too. He damn sure didn't want *my* influence."

"Great. *You* aren't going to do anything to James, are you?"

He chewed over that one for a minute, long enough to make her sit up straight and open her mouth. Grinning, he cut her off. "No. Though it probably wouldn't be too good for his health to cross my path in the very near future. That's all I'm sayin'."

"Fair enough." She watched the darkened buildings slip by them outside. "So where are we going now that our mission has been aborted?"

"Where do you want to go?"

"Hmm. I can't think of anywhere in particular." She shifted her legs.

He shouldn't do it, his brain kept telling him not to do it, but that was like telling his lungs not to need oxygen. He glanced down at those smooth-skinned thighs, swallowing hard as he saw exactly how much skin was showing, how it positively gleamed in the passing streetlamps.

He wanted to touch her. Oh, fuck, how he wanted to. And he damn sure couldn't do it while they were driving around...at least, not the way he had in mind. His fingers ached to chart every inch of her.

"Let's just go back," she suggested. He could get onboard with that. A parked car allowed for many more opportunities than a moving one.

Dermamania was dark and deserted when they returned. The past few weeks he and his coworkers had been worried about a repeat attack, and they'd discussed taking turns staking out the place at night, relishing the idea of catching the asshole in the act. But no one had seemed too enthused about doing it. There was a security system now, anyway.

"Crazy thing, isn't it?" Macy asked after he'd parked and killed the engine. "Our friends causing all this trouble."

"It isn't like they *caused* it. I'm sure they didn't have any idea it would lead to all this."

"Do you think it's worth it? I'm not sure I do. I mean...I don't know." She finished on a dejected note.

He'd had similar thoughts while staring into the destruction that was once his lively place of business. It was up and running again, sure, but something about it was...off. Like their happy little bubble had burst and there was no blowing another one so round and so perfect no matter how hard they tried. "I guess it doesn't matter what we think, right?" he said at last. "Only they can decide."

"I predict this separation won't last long. *Candace* won't last long. She'll go back."

"And he'd take her in a heartbeat. He isn't the problem, you know. He's willing to work through it. I guess he's willing to throw everything away. His business, us... everything, if he has to."

"Wow."

"Right." He thumbed the grips on his steering wheel, thinking of Brooke. How he'd wanted to scour the fucking earth to find her after she left him, no matter what she'd done. "I guess it's worth it, then."

"It seems pretty selfish to me."

Macy's voice had hardened, and when he looked over at her, he saw her mouth had, too. Usually those lips were generous and seemed to be hiding a smile like a precious secret; now they were tight and forbidding. "What's wrong with being a little selfish sometimes?" he asked. "In the end, we're the only ones looking out for ourselves. No one else is gonna do it."

She stared at him for a moment, a light "Hmm" escaping her throat. "I guess you're right about that."

Jesus. She was perfection from her sleek, shiny hair to the white-tipped fingernails she lifted pensively to her lips. To those killer legs. And everything he couldn't see...he was damn sure it was perfection too.

He was feeling selfish as hell right now. He hoped she was too. This was a *moment*, her gaze remaining steady on his, and he feared if he looked away, if he even fucking moved, he would break the spell and the moment would be gone forever. The moment she was thinking of kissing him.

But he wouldn't kiss this girl. Not now. She would fucking own him then. Next time, next time... if she came back, if she wanted him again...he would kiss her then—

He was about to put that vow to the test. In one fluid motion, Macy leaned closer, caught his cheek in her hand, and moved in.

Never once, not *once* that she could remember since she started kissing guys at age twelve, had Macy ever been rejected when she was the aggressor.

Not once.

But before she could lose herself in the insanity of putting her needy lips on Ghost's, he trapped her face between his palms, let his gaze sear darkly into hers for a heart-stopping moment, and—

He didn't push her away, which she'd expected in that one half-second of panicked mortification. Oh, no, he didn't. He tilted her head to the side and branded the side of her neck with his mouth, sucking the air from her lungs. Warm breath, firm lips, the gentle scrape of teeth... She'd always been a little ticklish there but not now, not with desire coursing a hot path through her veins. She only wanted to get him closer.

Why hadn't he let her kiss him? She'd been stealing glances at those lips all night. She'd dreamed of them. Now there was nothing she wanted more than to taste them. Drink him up.

Well, almost nothing.

His hand skated down her arm. Hers ventured up his hard chest, finding his neck and holding him to her. Breath teased her ear; he nuzzled into her hair and inhaled. Groaned.

She managed to get both her hands on him then, caressing each side of his jaw with her thumbs. Pushing back, she went in for another try. He had to let her. He *had* to.

Determined hands clamped hard around her wrists, halting her. "What's up with this?" he asked, the gruffness of his voice sending shivers through her entire lower body. His eyes glinted in the dimness. "Coming on to me just to shoot me down?"

"No, I…"

"No? You wanna fuck me?"

It was said with no wonder, no incredulousness, but with a rough edge of challenge.

Because that's what this was all about, and she'd known it. He wasn't up for anything less. Had he been anyone else, she might've been insulted. Not now, not when she'd known what she was getting into when she came here.

He was putting her to the test now, speaking so bluntly, moving closer and letting his mouth tease along her jawline, barely touching as he breathed on her skin.

"Yes." The word just slipped out. Absolutely no uncertainty behind it. In fact, that little word might've been bouncing around the inside of her head ever since she first laid eyes on him. Yes. Oh, hell yes.

A grin flashed across his face as he leaned back from her. "I don't think we have room up here. Climb in the back."

Macy glanced back between the front seats into the shadowed, *small* backseat area. "We wouldn't have room back there either. It looks…cramped."

"It'll be fine. Go."

"But we could—"

"Come on. Live a little dangerously."

"*Climb* back there? I'm in a skirt."

The tip of his finger trailed along her upper thigh, raising gooseflesh. She felt that touch all the way up her spine. "And in about sixty seconds I'm about to be all up under it, or so you tell me."

Jesus. "That doesn't mean *all* modesty automatically goes out the window."

"It doesn't?"

"No."

"You're not a lights-out, under-the-covers kind of girl, are you? You're too beautiful for that."

Despite herself, a warm thrill coursed through her with the compliment, mixing with all the other warm thrills he gave her. "No. I'm just not… an ass-in-your-face-before-we've-even-kissed kind of girl." She cocked a meaningful eyebrow at him.

He smacked his leg as if he'd just suffered a profound disappointment. "Dammit! I thought I'd finally found one."

Laughing, she gave his arm a shove. "Remarks like that won't get you laid, in this car or otherwise."

"Get your sexy ass back there, killjoy."

Go, go! her mind screamed at her, even as she probably would have sat and carried on the practically giddy banter until sunrise. Her pulse throbbed, her entire body burned…she wanted him, but nerves kept her planted to her spot.

Then he popped open the door. "Well, if you want me…I'm back here."

She watched in amusement as he got out and pushed the seat up so he could get in the back, then pulled the door closed. He settled back as if he was getting comfortable, resting his hands on his knees and glancing around. "I've never been in the backseat of my own car before. Interesting."

"Oh, so we'd be christening it?" she asked.

"I guess so. I will think of you from now on every time I get in."

It was time to put up or shut up. Taking a deep breath to bolster her courage, she let herself out as he had done, then slid into the back beside him and closed the door. It was even smaller back here than it had looked.

Ghost reached over and gently pushed her hair behind her shoulder. She wondered if he could tell how badly she was shaking. If he couldn't now, he probably would in a minute. When he began touching her. *Really* touching her.

Her pulse went from throbbing to thrashing. She could feel it everywhere, especially between her legs.

"I hope you know there's no way we can do this back here," she told him as he moved closer, hearing a high note of anxiety in her voice. "We should—"

"We can. I'll make it work. Trust me."

He pressed light kisses to her neck, under her chin, around to the other side. She sighed, rolling her head around to give him access, loving the light burn of his stubble along her skin. "Trust has to be earned."

"Right," he murmured, and continued his task. "But you're here. You trust me a little already."

"I don't know why, but…yeah. I do."

Her top and bra weren't very substantial at all, so when his hand slid up her side to her breast, she felt it almost as acutely as if he'd touched her bare skin. Her hands flew to his shoulders; her nipple tightened under his palm. She couldn't stop the sound that escaped her throat when he circled the tight peak with his thumb, and his answering groan elicited a flood of heat that left her trembling for more.

He shifted toward her until she lay back as far as she could, splaying her legs to give him room. There wasn't much to give, but she managed. Her bare thighs gripped the rough denim covering his hips. She wanted to know what else it covered. He was so hard everywhere else, she could only imagine what he had in his pants right now.

And, for some reason, her unkissed mouth wouldn't stop babbling. "In just a few minutes we could be at my place—"

"Fuck, Macy, I don't think I can wait a few minutes."

Oh, God, she was with him there. A few minutes and a cool-down and she might come to her senses, and she didn't want to. If she didn't have him inside soon…it didn't bear thinking about. She couldn't remember the last time she'd been this turned on.

He grasped the hem of her shirt and wrenched it upward. She started to raise her arms so he could remove it, but he stopped as soon as her breasts were uncovered then dove to kiss the swells above her bra cups. Her breath hitched and his hips thrust between her legs, forcing them farther apart until her skirt rode up, baring her panties. The denim of his jeans abraded her clit through the thin cotton.

She wished it were his fingers. *Touch me, oh God, touch me...*

He kept her waiting, content to kiss her heating skin until she reached up and pulled her bra cups down, exposing her nipples. As soon as she did, he sucked one hard, the answering throb in her pussy causing her to grind against his erection. She could feel it now—*oh, God, yes*—rock hard and straining damn impressively against the denim separating him from her needy core.

She needed that. She'd been needing it for a long time, she just hadn't realized how much until this moment. And now that she was exceedingly aware of her need, she wanted it *now*. His breath caught when she reached for his fly, and she gave him a light squeeze through his jeans before she went to work on it. "Fuck," he breathed, and when he shifted above her, it took a moment for her to realize he was digging in his back pocket.

Wallet. Condom. Oh, hell yes. She was damn glad he had one on him; she'd had the foresight to put a couple in her purse, but it was somewhere up front and the thought of letting go of him even for a minute was intolerable.

A pull of his zipper, a sharp yank of his button, and his cock was in her hands...big, thick and hot. Devastatingly hard. Circling it with her hand, she gave it a swift stroke...and stopped when the edge of her thumb encountered something small, hard and round on the underside.

What the...

Holy shit. He had a piercing.

Any other time she might have recoiled or

freaked out or bailed out of the car at the thought of something like that coming anywhere *near* her vagina. But said vagina was so desperate for something to come near it that Macy couldn't be bothered to care...except to wonder with some concern how it was going to feel.

The only conclusion she could come to was that it was going to feel damn remarkable.

She had to reluctantly let go of him so he could sheath himself with the condom. Macy hooked her thumb in the side of her panties, only bothering to remove one leg. To hell with the other.

The breath whooshed out of him when he saw her. He put both hands high on her thighs, almost framing her with his fingers while she squirmed desperately, trying to get him to touch. She was hot, burning up, at odds with the cool air circulating over her now.

Gently, too damn gently, he trailed the tip of one index finger down her clit. Her hips nearly wrenched off the seat, but he held her down with his other hand, content to play with her with that maddening slowness, that teasing, almost timid exploration. She wouldn't freaking break, damn. She wanted him rough. Wanted him hard. Her muscles were clenching on emptiness; she wanted to be full. Full of him.

"Please," she whispered.

He slipped his finger inside her, and they both moaned in sync. As he thrust it slowly and added another, she could feel how wet she was. How greedily she gripped him. More, she needed more. She licked her lips, rolling her head, aware that he watched her but not caring. A third finger, and she almost came. Light spasms rocked her, shivers radiating out from her middle.

He must have felt that. He left her, and she muttered an incoherent protest, but then he was there again, both of them locked in a breathless moment as he poised his blunt head at her entrance. He stared into her eyes, his a maelstrom of need and heat and some emotion she couldn't identify. Whatever it was, it broke her heart.

But what was he waiting for? Her?

"Yes," she whispered, just in case he needed one last assent from her, one last word of permission. She caught his face in her hands, wishing she could kiss him, but for whatever reason he didn't want that.

He pushed. She opened, so slick and ready but aching and burning—it had been so long. He groaned and dropped his head to her neck, she sighed and sank her teeth into the firm muscle of his shoulder. Inch by inch she took him, that little ball on the underside of his cock slipping inside and stroking parts of her that made her tremble and clench around him. She found herself repeating that little word of assent, over and over and over.

When she thought she might lose her mind, Macy plunged her hands down the loosened back of his jeans and kneaded the firm muscles of his ass, praying he'd put them to good use soon. His hand shot out to the front seat, grasping it until the vinyl creaked. God, he used the leverage to get even deeper, so deep she expected to feel him in her throat. The pain of his intrusion fused with the ache of her arousal and created something that swamped her mind and inhibitions, leaving nothing but blind, devastating pleasure. She only wanted to sprawl wider for him, get him even deeper, never let him go.

"Put your foot on the driver's seat," he rasped. "Can't get enough of you." Yes…*yes,* that sounded wonderful…but when her leg wouldn't obey the impulses from her brain and could only tremble helplessly around his hip, he did it for her, his fingers denting her calf hard. Everything about him was hard. Rough. Raw, just like she'd wanted. He thrust forward and forced a cry from her.

"That's it," he breathed.

"More," she pleaded, pushing against the seat to get some movement, some friction to stoke the heat.

"Yeah?"

"Please."

Slowly he pulled out, groaning along with her as her slick heat gripped him rhythmically. Their breath mingled but still, he didn't kiss her. Her hands fisted his shirt then tore it upward, desperate for the feel of smooth, hard flesh, for *something* to cling to. He didn't disappoint. As her hands smoothed over the muscles of his back, she wondered at all the ink that must be under her questing fingers.

"You're shaking," he whispered. "Are you okay?"

She nodded quickly, feeling his piercing more intensely as it neared her entrance. When the head of his cock slipped free she gasped and inched her hips down to reclaim it, practically cramping from the emptiness he left. As unhurriedly as he'd withdrawn, he gave it back, long and deep and so damn thick. Macy sighed with pure bliss.

She couldn't believe she was doing this.

He breathed something against her neck, something that sounded like "So fucking perfect," but she couldn't be sure. Even the possibility made her heart turn over in her chest. She wanted to be, yes. She wanted to be perfect for him right now, because he damn sure felt perfect himself. Scarily so.

He withdrew. Pushed back in. Again. Each time faster, each time harder. Her head fell back as far as the panel behind her would allow; he arched his back so his mouth could explore the swell of her breasts, her nipples, everywhere. Tonguing, sucking in time with his increasingly heated thrusts. The car had to be rocking by now. If a cop came by—if… "Oh, God, yes, there…*there!*" she cried, wishing she knew his damn first name so she could call it out.

CHAPTER SIX

*H*oly shit. Holy fucking shit.

Maybe if he kept thinking it, and stopped looking at how beautiful she was, stopped feeling how tight and wet she was, he could stave off the orgasm threatening to erupt any second—he *couldn't* come yet. If he had to sing the damn "Star-Spangled Banner," he couldn't come yet, because she hadn't. When a girl like Macy gives you a shot, you step the fuck up. Make her not regret it. Make her dream about it for days, hell, years to come.

It was a glorious dichotomy—whenever he thrust into her, the absolute mind-numbing pleasure was offset by the bite of her fingernails in his back. Whenever he sucked her nipple hard, she raked them lower. He longed for more light so he could see, but it didn't matter; she was beautiful, too fucking beautiful to bang in his backseat. But he'd thrown down the challenge and she'd accepted.

He braced himself up on his arms as best he could and swung his hips into her, giving it to her hard and deep, all the way in, all the way out. Her whimpered cries and digging fingers and tightening pussy around his thrusting cock told him she was close.

"God, that's good…please don't stop," she whispered, her eyes clenched shut, breath panting gently in rhythm with his movements.

Stop? What in the fuck? She must've had a minute man in her past. "I got you, baby, don't worry," he said, and she opened up her pleasure-glazed eyes to stare up at him. "I got you."

Maybe it was knowing there was no race to the finish, knowing he wasn't stopping until he got her there, but she came almost before he finished his promise. Her thighs gripped his hips hard and she thrust erratically against him, her sweet pulls on his dick driving him to the edge. And she *bit* him again...fucking hard this time. On his shoulder, through his T-shirt, and he hoped it left a mark so he could have even temporary proof of this. His flesh clamped between her teeth muffled her cries, though he would've loved to hear them high and wild and all for him.

It was all he could do not to let her pull him down into her bliss, but he wasn't done yet, not with her, not with this moment. He gentled his movements to give her a respite, easing down when she released her grip on him, kissing her neck.

"Yeah," he whispered as she came back to earth with a series of drawn-out sighs. He still throbbed almost painfully inside her, but managed to keep control, keep breathing, keep from losing his fucking mind with lust for this girl. It was dark, but she was more beautiful right now than he'd ever seen her.

Getting his arms under her and gathering her up, he shifted to a sitting position so that she straddled him. He loved the way she draped weakly over him, as if he'd sapped her of all energy. "Don't zone out on me now," he murmured playfully in her ear.

A lazy chuckle greeted his words. He rolled his hips up, turning the sound into a moan. God, she still gripped him in little aftershocks. His movement spurred her to make her own. Apparently, Macy wasn't done yet, either. She gripped the seat on either side of his head and began to ride him in long, slow strokes. Base to head, oh, fuck, over and over until the back of his head met the seat and he was gritting his teeth trying not to come yet. Macy dropped her face to his and that vanilla-scented curtain of hair fell around him. Her lips trailed over his forehead, down his cheek, around to his ear. When she blew lightly into it, he almost lost it.

He wrapped his arms around her waist and pulled her off, growling at the loss of her warmth. His cock bobbed in the empty air and he growled with the agony of that, too. "Fuck. Don't move."

And what did she do? Make a feminine little sound of distress and grind her clit against his stretched-taut stomach muscles. "Shit! Macy, *don't move.*"

"I want you to come," she whispered in his ear. "Give it back to me."

But he didn't want to.

Because then it would be over.

Then she would be gone. It was inevitable.

His balls ached. His dick throbbed. Tension thrummed like a current under his skin. She blew into his ear again.

"Goddammit," he all but snarled, flinging her back into her former position and surging into her. She wanted it, she would get it. And God, did she want it—her arms and legs locked around him; her cries in his ear were delirious with pleasure. She clawed what felt like bloody strips from his back, a new series of them with every orgasm he gave her.

Three, by his count, before his strength gave out completely and he poured everything he had left into her, drowning in her.

Relief swooped through him like sunlight as he emptied. His mind remained a pleasant humming blank for one heavenly moment before all those turbulent thoughts came rushing back.

He heard her voice in his ear, sounding far away even though her lips were close enough to tickle. "Oh my God."

Moving seemed an impossibility, but as he came back to himself, he realized he must be crushing her into the seat. Crawling back, he slipped free of her body and missed her immediately.

Macy glanced down at herself and quickly set about fixing her bra and shirt—modesty seemed a little ridiculous at this point, but whatever. She sat up and reached for the panties that still dangled from one ankle. He wanted to snicker, but didn't think she'd appreciate it at this point.

But damn, she was beautiful. He doubted she would appreciate him watching her tidy up either, but there was little place else to look when her lovely skin was still pink with the remnants of desire and her eyes dreamy with the bliss they'd made.

He stripped off the well-used condom, stuffed it in a little trash bag he kept on the floor, and zipped up. She finished her own task, pushed her hair away from her face with both hands, and finally the two of them sat still, staring forward, just breathing.

"Wow?" he said at last, making it a question.

She laughed, and he relaxed. "Wow. Really. Wow."

Her left hand rested on the seat between them,

pale in the darkness. He inched his toward it and twined his fingers with hers. Her gaze shifted down to their joined hands, where her skin was clear and lovely and his was mottled with black ink. The question she asked then was the last thing he expected. "Do you ever give yourself tattoos?"

Chuckling, he nodded. "All the time. You know, if you want something done right..."

"Good point."

Silence descended again. He wasn't comfortable in silence, and usually it wasn't a problem for him to come up with stupid shit to talk about. But the intensity of what had just transpired here had him desperately racking his addled brain for something, anything. Something to keep her here. He wasn't ready to part ways yet; he wanted to spend the night with her, take her back to his place, or back to hers. He opened his mouth to ask the first thing that came out of it, whatever it might be, but she beat him to the punch.

"Um...could you do me a favor?"

"Yeah, okay. Absolutely."

"Don't tell anyone about this."

Okay. Sure. Nope, there was no blade sticking out of his chest. He knew, because he checked. And because goddammit, it felt like it.

She rushed on to try to soften the blow of her words, but he was deaf to all of it. Something about drama, and Candace, and whatever the fuck. He even managed to say all the right words back to make her feel better, apparently, because she finally sighed in seeming contentment, leaning her head against the seat.

"God, what time is it?"

And that sounded like a lead-in to goodbye. Shit.

"Close to two, I would think."

"I've really got to go."

But don't you wanna...can't you just...ugh, shut up, dumbass.

"I kept you out past your bedtime again."

"It's all right." She gave him a smile, just a slight curving of her lips, holding his gaze with her sleepy one. "I had a great time. Obviously."

Her shy little laugh then nearly undid him. He was fucking idiot for even thinking it, but yes, he wanted to see that sleepy smile in the morning. He wanted to hang on to her all night. Instead, she would go home, probably go to sleep, and he would be wired for the rest of the night. He wasn't the roll-over-and-crash kinda guy. Great sex was more likely to amp him up than wind him down.

But he doubted a girl like Macy was looking for the clingy dipshit he was trying to be. So he returned her smile, lifted her hand and kissed the back of it. Savored the feel of her skin under his lips for as long as he dared. Again racking his mind for something to say. In the end, he could only say what he meant. "You took my breath away."

You took my breath away.

It was probably the sweetest thing a man had ever said to her. Who would have thought?

Macy drew a shaking breath as she steered into her apartment complex. Ten hours ago she'd vowed to never let anyone hurt her again, never be where her best friend was ever again. *Ever*. And here she was, still trembling in the aftermath of the best sex she'd ever had and wishing the future promised more of it. But it couldn't.

Sex for the sake of sex had never really been her style, but it wasn't as if she'd never done it before. She'd handled it well, not getting attached, only getting caught up in the fun of it. As she'd expected, the spark had burnt out fast. She'd gone her way, he'd gone his, no harm, no foul. Only fond memories.

But damn.

Damn.

She'd have more than fond memories from this. She feared she'd compare all future encounters to that one. Hoping someone, somewhere, someday, could make her feel what he just had. A guy whose real name she didn't even know—who apparently didn't *want* her to know.

Why not? Was he hiding something? Ugh. What had she *done*?

Nothing. She'd done absolutely nothing except have a good time. That was all. No sense romanticizing this. She'd thrown caution to the wind for the first time since her accident. It was good for her. She'd gifted herself with a memory to savor for years to come. She'd taken a shot. She'd...

Hell. She'd had, like, four screaming orgasms. That *never* happened to her.

Now, for once, Macy wished she could go to her friends with this, talk it out and get some perspective. But it occurred to her that lately her and her friends' perspectives were worlds apart, and it wouldn't do any good to go to them because she wouldn't agree with them anyway.

Sam would tell her to go for it. Candace would too. Nope, that wasn't a conversation worth having. She'd asked Ghost to keep this to himself so she couldn't very well tell everyone. Hopefully that hadn't offended him. Macy simply didn't want Brian to know, because...well, because it was embarrassing. Then Candace would know once she and Brian inevitably reconciled. Then Macy would never hear the end of it.

So she would ride this out, and hope by morning it would all seem like a really hot dream.

No such luck.

Not the next morning, when she could practically still feel him inside her, and not for many mornings after the ache faded. Ghost was still at the front of her mind, and that was the most frightening thing of all. Whether at home, at work or hanging out at her parents' ranch, the little chime of an incoming text message could make her heart lurch. He only texted occasionally though, almost as if nothing had happened, as if they were still carrying on their flirting. He didn't call her. She had to sit on her hands sometimes to keep from calling him.

Then the totally expected call finally came: not Ghost, but Candace trilling and gushing over her reunion with Brian. Her parents had finally eased their stance and reined Jameson in, which made Macy want to collapse in relief. Not just because she was off the hook, either. Hearing Candace happy again was like the first sunny day after weeks of nothing but storm clouds.

"I'm so happy for you. Seriously," she told her friend, and did her best to infuse her voice with that enthusiasm as she flopped back on her bed and stared at the ceiling.

"Are you really? I mean, I know how you feel—"

"No. I'm truly happy. To hear you like this instead of all gloom-and-doom? Girl. I'm *thrilled*."

Candace laughed merrily. "You don't know how glad I am to hear that. What you think does matter to me, you know. Whether I take your advice or not."

"Oh, you shouldn't give much of a damn about what I think," Macy said, trying to keep the words lighthearted but hearing a pathetic tone of self-loathing she couldn't do a thing about. Who the hell was she to give advice anymore?

"Okay. Something is *wrong* with you. I haven't wanted to ask because I knew you wouldn't tell me anyway. I've been so wrapped up in me and my problems, and I'm sorry about that. What's going on?"

"Nothing."

"Now that you've gotten that out of the way, go ahead and give me the real answer."

"Nothing! Really. I've been worried about all this mess with Jameson and now it seems to be over, so... that's great. Things can get back to normal."

"Maybe we can start working on you now."

"What does that mean?"

"Well, you'd told me you and Ghost had been seeing each other."

"We're not *seeing* each other. We're friends." With one night of screaming, clawing, biting benefits.

"You can move beyond that, you know."

"Not if you have no inclination to do so."

"Come on! After the way you were carrying on when you admitted you were with him when you saw Jameson at Dermamania? You said there was something about him."

"There is. I'm not going to be with every guy I think there's 'something about.'" Now she was being dishonest with her friend again, and after the misery they'd all just gone through, she didn't want to go there. "Just forget about all that; he's cool but it's not gonna happen. What's the plan with Brian?"

"I can't even believe how this worked out. We've been making up for lost time." She gave a low chuckle.

"I bet."

"And I'm probably going to spend the weekend at his place. I might never go back home."

Macy opened her mouth to tell her friend not to move in with him so soon, then promptly closed it again. It was going to be hard to learn her new place—she was always the one doling out sensible advice, but Candace didn't need it, and Macy no longer felt like the sensible one anyway. She'd been judgmental, hypocritical, dishonest. Jesus. And the thing she'd done a few nights ago to help her feel better? It only made her feel worse now. Because she'd dragged someone else into her shame spiral, and he didn't even know it. Neither did he deserve it.

But if she kept seeing him, she was going to fall for him. And she couldn't.

"You guys need your alone time," she said instead

of lecturing her friend.

"I'm going to let him pierce my belly button."

"*Candace!*"

Okay, so it was going to be even harder to learn her new place than she thought.

CHAPTER SEVEN

He didn't know what he'd done or said wrong, but his last few text messages to Macy had gone unanswered. Okay. Whatever. She'd seemed a little sparse in her replies before now but he'd chalked it up to her being on-call for her grieving friend...but now Candace and Brian were back together and inspiring nausea and cavities all over the place. So she should be feeling a hell of a lot better...he knew he was, and so was the rest of the staff at Dermamania. Brian could be a drag when he was down, and until a few days ago the dude had been more down than Ghost had ever seen him.

No more, though. He had a spring in his step. Bastard.

But Ghost was tired of bullshitting around. He didn't go for games; he'd had an ex who'd thought herself a master at them and he'd shown her a thing or two. Once that relationship was over and done with, he'd vowed not to play anymore.

Macy. He liked the girl. He wanted to see her again. With one simple request—*don't tell anyone about this*—she'd taken all hope of that and dashed it on the fucking rocks, it seemed.

But he wanted to hear it from her. And not in a text message.

In a break between clients, he stepped out the back door—where Starla was taking her smoke break. She exhaled a stream and cocked an eyebrow at him. "The fuck are you doing back here?"

Glancing down, he kicked at the accumulation of old cigarette butts littering the ground. "Least you could do is clean this shit up. You're the only one who comes back here anymore."

She flipped him off with a black-and-white tipped finger and he moved around the corner of the building to his car.

He dialed Macy. Got her voicemail. Checking his watch, he decided to give her the benefit of the doubt. She had a job; maybe she didn't like to talk at work. Brian didn't necessarily like them to hang around up front yakking on cell phones either, even if they weren't busy.

Her cheerful voicemail greeting ended, twisting a knife in his gut. The beep sounded. "Hey. Ghost. Call me back." Short and sweet (of course, he'd probably sounded more sour than sweet, which hadn't been his intention), and he'd only left it on the off-chance she had turned her phone off and didn't see she'd missed a call from him. He hated leaving fucking voicemail unless he was jacking around with Brian or something. But in those cases, he only left a string of curses or obscene breathing or pretended to be calling about a subscription to a kinky magazine or some other shit he made up.

It was a cloudy, dreary day. He tilted his head back and stared up at the leaden, oppressive sky, hoping his phone would ring in the next few minutes and brighten his outlook on things. No such luck.

He thought of driving around for a few minutes, but unfortunately, he'd spoken the truth to Macy that night. He couldn't get in his car without thinking of her. It was probably only his imagination, but he thought he could still smell her. Sweet. Warm. Vanilla. Fleeting.

Damn.

He ambled back inside, passing Starla who was now obviously on the phone with her boyfriend. He only had to catch the "Listen, motherfucker!" before the door shut to know that much.

Not everyone was wrapped in a cocoon of love and sunshine and warm fuzzies like Brian. Far more people were trapped in a web of pain and anger and doubt and couldn't see a way of untangling themselves.

Maybe he'd rather stay with them. Far less to lose.

So when his phone didn't ring that day, he decided to count it as a fucking blessing.

M acy listened to his message over and over just to hear his voice. It was terse, strained... so different than the one that had whispered and groaned in her ear.

He was pissed at her, and she couldn't blame him. But he'd be okay. He was much better off without her...but now that Brian and Candace were back together, the huge glaring problem was that she would probably be bumping into him from time to time. Ugh. Awkward.

Folding her arms on her work desk, she dropped her forehead to them with a thud. There was no time for crap like this. Her parents' outdoor sports store wasn't going to run itself, and on top of everything else, her dad was here prowling around today. Usually he left her to her job. It always made her antsy when he showed up, like someone had taken complaints to him or something. He might be her dad, but he was still her boss. She didn't worry that he would fire her but listening to him lecture her for an hour wasn't on the top of her list of fun things either.

With that thought, she propelled herself upward. The least she could do was look alive. She checked her reflection in the mirror she kept in her desk drawer, noticing her eyes looked red and glassy, like she had the flu or she was about to burst into tears at any moment.

Not. An. Option.

Jaw clenched in frustration, she chucked the mirror back in its drawer and slammed it shut, then left her office for the floor to see if she could find out what her dad was poking through.

She had a life. She had a job to do. She had great friends to get her through whatever this funk was—at least she would if she could stop herself from pissing them off.

Ghost would be all right. He probably did this sort of thing all the time. To think she was the first one to ever be in his backseat—it had probably been a lie. And he hadn't even kissed her! Really. She was torturing herself over this?

Call you? Yeah, okay. Maybe when you decide to tell me what your damn name *is, for God's sake.*

Her dad took one look at her as she approached and unknowingly called her on all her acrobatic mental bullshit, his eyes keen with insight beneath the bill of his John Deere cap. "What's the matter, Macy girl?"

She contemplated running away from the question, bursting into tears and pitching herself into his arms, or grabbing and throwing the nearest thing she could reach. In the end, she did what she always did.

Smiled, said "Nothing," and carried on.

"Lizzy Hale."

"Maria Brink."

"Alissa White-Gluz, motherfuckers."

The nominees for the never-ending hottest-chick-in-metal debate flew fast and furious, all the guys of Dermamania shouting out their preference almost simultaneously as soon as the question was posed. It was kind of a running joke whenever a certain client of Brian's was under the needle. The guy needed constant conversation to get through the pain, and they all tried to accommodate.

"*I'm* the hottest chick in metal," Starla said, her usual response when she was present.

"Alissa could kick all our candy asses," Ghost said of his nominee. It was all in fun, because there'd been only one girl kicking his ass lately and he'd be forever grateful if he could only exorcise her from his fucking thoughts.

It had been a couple of weeks since he'd heard from her. He'd made some manner of peace with the fact that something had freaked her out. He didn't know what; she'd obviously had a good time.

Maybe that was all she'd been after. If so, hey, he couldn't judge. It wasn't as if he hadn't done the whole disappearing act before.

Karma was biting him in the ass, that was all. Hell, sometimes he thought his ex, Raina, was a source of rotten, stinking karma flowing ever toward him, never depleting, never tiring of watching him squirm. It seemed as long as that girl walked the earth, a little storm cloud was going to rain on his head. He wouldn't be surprised if she hadn't hexed him somehow.

Candace came in. Ghost watched her stroll over to where Brian sat on his stool and drop him a little kiss before heading toward the back to wait for him. Brian's dimples didn't smooth out for at least ten minutes after that. Ghost's need to rib him about it almost exceeded his capacity to resist, but somehow he managed.

Then his phone rang. His sister.

He caught Brian's eye and stepped toward the front, away from the ongoing conversation. The waiting area didn't offer any more privacy than the stations, though, so he moved on out the front door into the humid early summer air. Only then did he answer, lungs burning with the breath he hadn't realized he was holding.

"Hey, Steph."

She didn't respond right away. The pause was all he needed to know that she was calling with news about his grandmother, and the news wasn't good.

"Seth? I need you here."

Fucking karma. It could kick him when he was down all it wanted; it didn't have to go after the people he loved.

"I'm there."

Brian caught his expression and frowned as soon as he entered. Ghost tilted his chin up at him and walked past, not wanting to be under the scrutiny of anyone present any longer than he had to be. "Need you for a second, man."

Ordinarily a remark like that would be cause for any number of humorous innuendos. Brian only nodded solemnly. "Let me finish up."

"All right."

But Candace was waiting in Brian's office, and Ghost stopped short the second he saw her there tapping away at her phone. "Sorry, forgot you were here," he said, turning to go to the drawing room.

"It's all right," she said quickly, getting out of her seat. "I don't want to get in anyone's way."

"You're not."

She made a move to walk toward him where he stood in the door. "I'll just go wait—"

"No. Sit. Please. Damn if I'll be the source of his deprivation."

"He's not that bad off without me, is he?" she laughed, obviously flattered.

"You have no idea."

Maybe Macy's best friend could offer a bit of insight about her. But no, that was lame, not to mention too little too late. Candace had already rebuffed him once in an effort to keep him away from her. He couldn't recall her exact words, but maybe he should have heeded whatever warning she'd given him. He only had himself to blame, and that sucked.

But then Candace shocked him to his core. "Have you talked to Macy lately?"

What the hell? She *knew?*

"Huh?" he said stupidly.

"I know you hung out together. She won't talk. Anything...brewing there?" She grinned at him.

"Apparently not."

"Oh. Hmm. Well..." She gave a shrug and went back to her phone. "I'm texting with her now. I could tell her you said hi."

"No. Don't mention me."

Candace's gaze snapped back up to him, and he cursed himself for the bitter edge that had crept into his voice. "Okay then," she said.

Brian appeared behind him and clapped him on the shoulder. "What's up?"

Caught now between the two of them, Candace inside the office and Brian blocking the only escape route, Ghost rubbed his hand over his face and hoped he could hold it together. He could ask to talk to Brian alone, but fuck it. He'd never been one to care much about who knew his business. Unlike some people.

"I need some time off. Like...a lot of time."

"Your grandmother," Brian said. It wasn't a question. Brian knew what was going on; they'd even spoken once about this possibility and he had assured Ghost he would always have a job to come back to. "Sorry, man. You gotta do what you gotta do."

"Yeah."

"Is there anything we can do to help? Check on your house, water your plants and shit?"

Ghost scoffed. "I don't have any fuckin' plants. But yeah, you can check on things for me. You know where the spare key is."

Candace had remained pensively silent while they spoke. Macy would probably hear all about this. He didn't care. It wasn't like anything mattered now. Who knew how long he would be gone? By the time he came back she'll have moved on. It was almost a comfort to know he didn't have to agonize over it anymore. It was done and there were far more pressing matters to worry about.

Matters he didn't want to give any thought to right now. The dark months that lay ahead, his grandmother's failing health...the knowledge of their imminence had been pressing into the back of his mind for a long time now. He'd kept it out as best he could. Now that the reality of it all was upon him...God, he wasn't prepared. Not in the fucking least.

"I need to get out of here and make some phone calls," he told Brian. "Get packed, get on the road."

"Sure, man. Call and let us know how everything's going."

"I will."

"Are you sure you're okay?" Candace asked as he turned to go. He smiled as reassuringly as he could at her sincere concern.

"I'll make it. I always do."

He bumped fists with Brian and walked away, leaving them staring after him.

*G*host is leaving! Like, LEAVING.

Macy frowned at the text from Candace, sitting up straight in her desk chair. She'd been feeling okay the past few days, but this sudden, jolting exclamation among the dozen other mundane messages she and Candace had been sending back and forth undid *all* of it. Just like that.

What?

He told Brian he needs a lot of time off. His grandmother is sick. Brian said she lives in Oklahoma.

He'd mentioned something about that, hadn't he? Oh, no. How awful. When she sat for too long trying to conjure a reply, another message from Candace popped up.

Aren't you going to do anything?

Like what?

I don't know! Go see him or something. He's so sad.

How could she? She didn't know where he lived. Even if she got the information from Brian, if she showed up now after making herself scarce all this time...it wouldn't be right. *I'm sorry she isn't doing well,* she told Candace, *but I can't go see him.* She sent that one and then quickly typed, *Gotta go. ttyl,* and tossed her phone down.

She couldn't deal with this crap anymore.

It was for the best, right? Macy didn't know how many more times she was going to have to tell herself that, but this should be the clincher. Really, he had his grandmother to worry about. She could go on now, unburdened with this...guilt. Or whatever it was. Though she really didn't know what she had to feel guilty about. Neither of them had promised the other anything. Nothing was lost here. It wasn't.

The inventory on the computer screen blurred in front of her face and she swiped at her eyes with frustration. Anger welled up in her chest and erupted in a growl as she snatched several tissues from the holder on her desk. "God!"

The chatter right outside her open office door stalled and Bruce called, "You okay, Mace?" Great. That's just what she needed, their oldest and most trusted employee calling her dad and telling him she was having a breakdown on the job.

"Fine!" she called back as cheerily as she could. "Got a papercut." *On my heart.*

Bruce chuckled. "Those things are deadly."

Weren't they just.

Her eyes drifted to the pictures on her desk. The one of her parents, the one of Macy accepting her undergraduate diploma, and the one of her and Candace and Sam all crowding in with tans and glowing smiles a couple summers ago when they'd driven down to a Galveston beach house for a week. Candace had to assure her parents repeatedly she was only going with Macy. They loathed Sam. That trip was one of Macy's fondest memories, just the three of them, no man drama. They'd lain on the beach and shopped and drank a little and dodged come-ons right and left. A blast.

Sylvia Andrews had come back to Macy's office to visit once and Macy had been on the edge of her seat hoping the woman didn't spy that picture. She chuckled at the memory now and finished drying her ridiculous tears. Enough of that. She was at work.

And Ghost...well, it just wasn't meant to be. But she didn't have to be a rude bitch, either. So she picked up her phone and pulled up the messages again, typing one out to "1969."

> *I'm sorry. I hope everything works out. Be safe.*

He could take that apology however he wanted. She was sorry for his grandmother, sorry for ignoring him, sorry for everything.

For a while, she didn't think she would get a reply. She couldn't blame him, but she hoped he'd gotten the message at least. Hoped even more that he believed it. Because she so meant it.

It came two hours later as she was getting in her car to go home.

> *It's okay, killjoy. See you down the road.*

Smiling, she cranked the engine, then just sat for a moment enjoying the relief in knowing he didn't hate her. "See you down the road," she repeated out loud.

Maybe he would.

ACKNOWLEDGMENTS

Here's the thing about writing books: it never gets easier! Whether it's your first book or your fifteenth, the struggle might be different, but it's no less real. I'd like to take a moment to recognize everyone who helped make this story happen.

Thank you so much to my agent, Louise Fury. You always fight for me and give me a voice when I don't know how to use mine. You cheer me on, talk me through, and keep me writing. In this business I've always felt like a lone wolf, and I rather like it that way, but I'm so glad to have you in my corner!

Hats off to the team at Entangled who helped me whip this manuscript into shape: Liz Pelletier, Hannah Lindsey, Stacy Abrams, and Greta Gunselman. To the fantastic crew in publicity: Holly Bryant-Simpson, Jessica Turner, and Riki Cleveland, you guys are so on top of things and handle all the heavy lifting so I don't have to. Thank you all so much.

To my husband, Brandon, who's always worthy of a dedication in every single book: I don't know what I would do without you. Sometimes I think I'm an extra full-time job on top of your own, but you never complain. You take up my slack when I'm in the writing cave. You make sure things get done. And you're always there to support me and the kids in everything we do. I love you!

Kids, you two keep me laughing every day and, let's be honest, you're probably the main reason I ever leave my house. A, if I didn't have your epic knock-knock jokes and time away from the computer to cheer you on in softball and gymnastics, I don't know how I'd make it. D, I'm so proud of the person and writer you've become. I know you're destined for great things and I can't wait to see what you do!

And finally, to you reading this right now. I honestly think I have the best readers in the world. There aren't enough words for what you all have given me: the opportunity to live my dream. From the bottom of my heart, thank you, thank you, thank you! I'll see you next time.

Love,
Cherrie

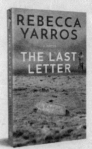

An emotional, touching story for fans of Nicholas Sparks...

"A stunning, emotional romance."

—Jill Shalvis, *NYT* bestselling author

"Yarros' novel is a deeply felt and emotionally nuanced contemporary romance…"

—*Kirkus* starred review

"*The Last Letter* is a haunting, heartbreaking and ultimately inspirational love story."

—*InTouch Weekly*

"I cannot imagine a world without this story."

—Hypable

From New York Times *bestselling author*
Victoria James comes a poignant
and heartfelt romance.

The *Trouble* with *Cowboys*

by Victoria James

Eight years ago, Tyler Donnelly left Wishing River, Montana, after a terrible fight with his father and swore he'd never return. But when his father has a stroke, guilt and duty drive him home, and nothing is as he remembers—from the run-down ranch to Lainey Sullivan, who is all grown up now. And darn if he can't seem to stay away.

Lainey's late grandma left her two things: the family diner and a deep-seated mistrust of cowboys. So when Tyler quietly rides back into town looking better than hot apple pie, she knows she's in trouble. But she owes his dad everything, and she's determined to show Ty what it means to be part of a small town...and part of a family.

Lainey's courage pushes Ty to want to make Wishing River into a home again—together. But one of them is harboring a secret that could change everything.

She's just one of the guys…until she's not in USA Today *bestselling author Cindi Madsen's unique take on weddings, small towns, and friends falling in love.*

Just One of the Groomsmen

by Cindi Madsen

Addison Murphy is the funny friend, the girl you grab a beer with, and the girl voted most likely to start her own sweatshirt line. She's perfectly fine answering to the nickname "Murph," given to her by the tight-knit circle of guy friends she's grown up with. Time has pulled them all in different directions, like Tucker Crawford, who left their small town to become some big-city lawyer, and Reid, who's now getting hitched.

Naturally the guys are all going to be groomsmen, and it wouldn't be the same without "Murph" in the mix. The fact that ever since Tucker's return to town, she can't stop looking at him and wondering when he got so hot is proof that she needs to mix things up. She'd never want to ruin a friendship she's barely gotten back, but the more Addie comes out of her tomboy shell, the more both she and Tucker wonder if there's something more there…

Northern Exposure meets *Two Weeks Notice* in this new romantic comedy series from *USA Today* bestselling author Amy Andrews.

nothing
but
trouble

by Amy Andrews

For five years, Cecilia Morgan's entire existence has revolved around playing personal assistant to self-centered former NFL quarterback Wade Carter. But just when she finally gives her notice, his father's health fails, and Wade whisks her back to his hometown. CC will stay for his dad—for now—even if that means ignoring how sexy her boss is starting to look in his Wranglers.

To say CC's notice is a bombshell is an insult to bombs. Wade can't imagine his life without his "left tackle." She's the only person who can tell him "no" and strangely, it's his favorite quality. He'll do anything to keep her from leaving, even if it means playing dirty and dragging her back to Credence, Colorado, with him.

But now they're living under the same roof, getting involved in small-town politics, and bickering like an old married couple. Suddenly, five years of fighting is starting to feel a whole lot like foreplay. What's a quarterback to do when he realizes he might be falling for his "left tackle"? Throw a Hail Mary she'll never see coming, of course.

AMARA
an imprint of Entangled Publishing LLC